LINDA KENNEDY

Copyright © 2025 **Linda Kennedy**

All rights reserved. No part of this publication may be reproduced, distributed, or transmitted in any form or by any means, including photocopying, recording, or other electronic or mechanical methods, without the prior written permission of the publisher, except in the case of brief quotations embodied in critical reviews and certain other noncommercial uses permitted by copyright law. For permission requests, email to the publisher, addressed "Attention: Book Rights and Permission," at admin@bookhavenliterary.com or visit www.bookhavenofficial.com.

Published in the United States of America

ISBN 978-1-970703-21-4 (Paperback)
ISBN 978-1-970703-22-1 (Hardback)
ISBN 978-1-970703-23-8 (Ebook)

For Book Rights Adaption and other Rights Permission.

Call us at toll-free **601-914-6178**.

DEDICATION

Well, here we are at book number three and I have someone special to thank for this journey. She thought I could do this when I didn't. In loving memory of Barbara Jeanine Oakley Harkins.

And to my daughter Cheri McMasters who takes care of the computer side of my books because she is smarter than I am about that.
THANK YOU, Darlin'

TABLE OF CONTENTS

Samantha was through milking the cow and had collected the eggs from the chickens and was walking past the garden. She was going to have to bring water to it this morning the plants were wilting already and it wasn't even ten a clock yet. The tomatoes and squash were looking good already it was going to be a good year if it started to rain. Please God let it rain this year. She was leaving a trail of dust in her wake from just walking it was so dry.

After Sam got the milk she strained it through the cheesecloth and got it in the cooler she would change and go to Mrs. Maxwell and see if she could trade for some of her honey or some of her homemade jelly. She was running low on anything with sugar in it and she was getting scared, she was going to be in trouble soon. It was too soon for any of the berries around here to be making. She didn't have much money for sugar if there was any to be found around here anyway. The war had made most things impossible to find right now. The deer were starving and eating anything they could find around here, even her roses. Some of the people around here had honey bees and she traded with them for honey.

Sam would have to wait for Wayne to get here she couldn't go anywhere alone anymore. Nathan had seen to that when he had caught her at the fishing hole two weeks ago. He had made it pretty clear he would take what he wanted even though she was married. He would have then except her hired hand Wayne showed up and told him to leave. Wayne was the only hired hand she could afford anymore and he had to be in his fifties but he could still handle a shotgun. He ran Nathan off so she could dress and get back to the ranch. No more swimming in the afternoon even in this heat, she was basically a prisoner in her own home.

Samantha couldn't understand why Nathan wouldn't leave her alone. There were plenty of other women falling all over themselves to get to him but he wanted her.

Her husband had been gone for over a year now and she hadn't heard from him in almost three months and his father was as worried as she was. He was a Confederate Captain and the war was going badly and was supposed to be almost over but there had been no word from anyone lately. Sam saw a horse coming up the road and she recognized Wayne so she went back inside the house. When he got close he got down off his horse and came inside. He looked at her funny and then he said.

"It's over Miss Sam it is finally done the South surrendered." She looked down at her hands and then at him.

"Do you think Eliot will come home or do you think he will stay with Claude somewhere back South?"

"One way or the other he will write and tell you what he is going to do so you can at least know what to do next."

"I don't think he will ever come back I don't think he can face his father. Maybe it is better if he stays away at least he and Claude can have a life somewhere." Wayne just looked at her and said.

"Don't you want a life as well you can't have one as long as you are married to him?" she looked at him and kind of smiled.

"It is all taken care of, the judge saw to it when he married us I have an out in the marriage contract, I can use it whenever I want. Eliot knew he might not be coming back all I have to do is tell the judge and he will annul the marriage with no questions asked. He understood all the time what was going on. Eliot was just trying to protect me from Nathan and that was the only way he could." Sam looked out over the little ranch there wasn't much left, her father had sold most of the land and the animals to just survive the war and when he died she had kept what was left for her and her brother Jeremy. There were only two horses a cow and calf and the house. She had a garden and that was keeping them fed with what she could trade for from the neighbors. Wayne occasionally shot one of the deer but they weren't much they were starving too.

She had some money hidden for buying extras but Jeremy didn't know that, or it would be gone. He gambled everything away when he was drunk and that was most of the time lately. Samantha and her brother owned equal shares of the ranch what there was of it. Jeremy wasn't here much anymore he stayed in town with their aunt. She was out here by herself or with her maid Tillie who stayed when she wasn't with her boyfriend in town. She didn't really mind she liked to be alone out here, it had been her and her father for so long before he died. It really wasn't that different until lately when Nathan started showing up unannounced.

"Samantha you going riding today?" Wayne looked at her as she gathered up the eggs.

"Yes I need to go over to Mrs. Maxwell's and see if she has any honey or jam I am getting low on anything sweet and there is no sugar to buy and it is too soon for berries."

"How low are you, are you all out do we need to start worrying?" as she loaded her saddle bags she looked at him.

"Not yet but I need to start find something sweet to put in this house and soon." He helped he load her bags and then he went and got her horse and brought him to her he was a big gold palomino stallion he was the only one around here and she was really proud of him. He was papered in her name only because she was afraid her brother would gamble him away and so was her father. She had been offered a lot of money for him and she had never sold him she would starve before she sold him.

"Wayne can you ride with me I don't feel comfortable going that far alone anymore. I feel eyes watching me maybe it is just my imagination." Wayne looked at her and then he said.

"It isn't, someone is camping up on the ridge at night and keeping watch on the house. He is making sure you don't have visitors. He is keeping Jeremy busy at the card tables as well and he is losing big and I don't know where he is getting the money to lose."

"All he had left to sell was his horse and daddy's pocket watch and ring and then he is broke and he doesn't know about the money I have stashed in the box in the library. I was hoping to buy a few cattle with that when this war was is finally over so we can start again."

"Sam what if he loses his half of the ranch too Nathan what then." She looked at him and was almost in tears.

"Then I am done maybe I can sell the other half for enough to start somewhere else but there is nothing else left. Surly he is smart enough not to lose it all?" but she knew she was talking to the wind her brother was a lost cause and she knew it.

They started down the road to the next ranch and she saw a man sitting on the hill above them, Wayne was right Nathan was having her watched. When they got to the next ranch about an hour later they were meet outside the house by an older lady she had known her whole life, she had been widowed the year before.

"Well good morning Samantha I was wondering if I was going to see you this week I was running low on eggs and company." Sam jumped down and hugged the older woman.

"Wayne says the war is over the South surrendered." She just watched the older woman's face.

"A little too late for me, my boys are already gone the war took them and grief took their father. I guess you could say the war took them all. I don't even have graves for my boys. Well how are you doing I have saved you some honey that is what you have come for isn't it, you must be getting low?"

"Yes ma'am I am, you are a god send when there is no sugar to be had. Honey works just as well or better." This woman was the only one besides Wayne and her maid who knew her secret besides her brother. She had to have some sugar ever day or she got sick there was something wrong with her and her father had taken her to a doctor in Spain to find out how to treat her. It had a long name but the gist of it was her body didn't make enough sugar and she had to have some extra sugar so she didn't get sick.

When she was a child she didn't wake up for hours at a time and almost died before they figured out what was wrong. Her father heard of a doctor in Europe and took her there but there was no cure just management so they came home and she kept it under control. Summertime was easy there were plenty of berries and they made jam for winter till the war now it was so hard to find sugar so she depended on Mrs. Maxwell for her honey. Her father had always made sure there were plenty of sweet things in the house when she was young and doted on her, sometimes to the exclusion of her brother. She sometimes thought that is why he avoided her and stayed away, she thought he hated her.

Her mother had died when she was 10 and he was 12 it had been just them and her father till he had passed away two years ago and then her brother couldn't stand to be around her any more. He spent more and more time in town with their aunt it was obvious he didn't want to be around her. Their father had been a lawyer and his partner had split the business proceeds with the two of them. It wasn't a whole lot but it was some. Samantha had put up her money aside but her brother had gambled his away.

What little she had left was hidden after he had come in one night and torn the house apart looking for it. She told him not to come back and she hid the money better. She had a lock box with the papers for her part of the house her horse and two hundred and fifty dollars in a small box. It contained her father's and her mother's wedding bands as well as a locket and silver chain her mother wore. That was all that was left of a lifetime of work for two people but she wasn't going to let her brother lose them at a poker table so she hid them. He had found his father's pocket watch and a gold ring from law school and took them from her and they were probably gone but there was nothing she could do about them now. There was a cabinet in the den with a shelf that moved, her father had showed it to her a long time ago, and it made an excellent hiding place.

"All I have for you right now is three bottles of honey they are just getting started making, will that get you taken care of for a while?"

"Yes that will do me for at least a month or more, we will be good and the berries should be making by then. If the war is really over maybe things will start getting back to normal soon and we can start getting some supplies in here again."

She invited them for lunch but they knew she was as low on supplies as everybody else was so they polity refused. Samantha had traded her more eggs than usual because her hens were laying eggs really good she could always pickle them. They headed back to the ranch and it was already getting hot. Wayne looked up on the hill and saw they were still being watched he was really worried about leaving her alone anymore he was thinking about moving his things to the barn and staying there since it was warm. He worried about her all alone out here. Nathan wasn't the kind of man that gave up that easy and rape wasn't out of the question. He had already told everybody in town if Eliot didn't come back Samantha was going to marry him. It didn't seem like she had a say in the matter.

"What are you going to do this afternoon?"

"I have to water the garden and refill the water tank for the cattle and the horses."

"I will help you do that and then I am going to town and I am moving my things back to the barn and I am going to make a place up in the hayloft to sleep." She just looked at him.

"What am I missing, something is going on and you are scared for me?"

"Nathan wants you real bad honey and he thinks he already owns you and he is telling the town that. He scares me especially after finding him at the pond, he would have raped you if I hadn't showed up and you know it." She didn't even argue with him she had been too scared to ask but she was glad he wanted to do just what he said he was going to do.

"Thank you I would appreciate it if you would move out here. I will pay you some extra for your trouble but I would feel better if you were here Nathan scares me to death I wish he would find another woman to fixate on and leave me alone. I don't know why he wants me so bad?"

"Because you are the only one who says NO and it infuriates him." "I don't want you in the barn loft the tack room is better we will clean it out tomorrow. You can move in there that will give you time to pack tonight and you can take the extra horse and wagon to load your things on to bring out here tomorrow." He shook his head and it was settled he would help her get the garden watered and then start getting the tack room cleaned up. He would move out here, at least until it got cold maybe they would have heard something from her husband Eliot by then. By the end of the day they had worked themselves hard Tillie had showed up and cleaned the house and cooked supper. After they ate Wayne was headed to town with the extra horse and wagon Sam went to her room to bath. Tillie told her good night and told her she was going back with Wayne to see her boyfriend and didn't know if she was coming back tonight or not. Samantha locked the house and went to bed.

She heard a noise downstairs and went to see what it was and there was a light in the parlor so she went downstairs. She figured it was Wayne he and Tillie were the only ones who had keys to the house. Jeremy had one but he hadn't been out here in months. When she got to the parlor there was a man pouring himself a drink and it wasn't Jeremy it was Nathan. She just stood there stunned. He turned and looked at her and then he smiled she was just dressed in her nightgown.

"God you always look good even in that ugly thing you will look even better when it is off."

"What are you doing in my house get out of here immediately?" He just grinned as he drank her father's whiskey.

"No my dear it is my house your dear brother lost it to me this evening I have the papers to prove it right here, want to see them? I own it now and everything in it including you." Samantha stood there stunned how could her own brother have done this to her?

"Wrong, Nathan only owned half of the house as for me I am married remember."

"No my dear you are not, I came to tell you the sad news you are a widow, your father- in- law got the news today Eliot is dead Claude sent a telegram. I told him I would tell you the news." He just stood there and waited for her reaction he was so pleased with himself. He had brought her world crashing down around her head in one blow and he was waiting to see how she reacted. Sam thought she was going to be sick Jeremy had lost it all; too Nathan no less. There would be no bargaining with him she might as well give it to him and leave, he had finally won.

"I will start packing, in the morning I will sign over the other half of the house to you and I will leave and you can have it all the house everything except my horse." She turned and started to walk away as he grabbed her and turned her around.

"You think I did all this for this house and this grubby piece of land?

I did this to get you and only you." She jerked away from him.

"I don't come with the furniture and the land, now I am a free woman I can do as I please and it won't be with you." She ran up the stairs and locked her bedroom door. She started to open drawers and take out clothes when Nathan kicked open her door and grabbed her and threw her down hard against the end of her bed. She landed wrong and she hit her ribs and all she felt was pain as they cracked but she got back up and tried to run. He grabbed her gown and she heard it rip down the back as he turned her around and punched her in the face. The next thing she knew she was on the bed and her gown was being torn off of her. She lay there barley conscious as he undressed and he was yelling at her.

"This didn't have to be this way Samantha I have asked your father for years to marry you and he refused but now I have you and you are going to be mine. I never could understand what you saw in that sissy Eliot." He was on top of her and he was trying to kiss her and she was having none of it, she was trying to fight back so he stopped trying to be gentle and he plunged inside her and she screamed and he stopped and her grabbed her face and made her look at him.

"You are a virgin he never made love to you why. The rumors are right aren't they?" she still wouldn't answer him so he continued his assault on her until she pleaded for him to stop.

"Tell me why you never consummated this marriage or I will make this more painful than it has to be." She was crying he was hurting her so badly she was going to have to tell him what nobody else knew.

"Eliot married me to protect me from you while he was gone but he and Claude were going away to be together Eliot never wanted me, it was all a shame he didn't like women." Nathan looked at her and smiled that evil little smile of his.

"Good that means I will be the only man that ever touches you now or ever do you understand me Samantha, promise me." When she didn't he continued his assault until he was finished but she wouldn't answer him.

"I guess we will have to have another lesson later until I get it through your thick head you are mine." She just rolled over and covered up and he went downstairs to get the whiskey bottle.

Tillie had come home and had heard what was going on upstairs and went to help Samantha and found her on the bed barely awake. She was trying to get up and dress. Tillie was helping when they heard him coming back up the stairs.

"Go now, Wayne will be here in the morning wait for him and we can do something then, just wait and hide he will hurt you too." Tillie ran outside and waited in the barn as she heard Samantha screaming from her bedroom all she could do was put her hands over her ears and wait until daylight.

Nathan had come back in and wanted her to promise again and she wouldn't, so he raped her again but she hurt so bad by then she didn't even care much. She finally passed out and he left her alone and went to sleep. When Wayne came ridding in Tillie met him in the barn and she was hysterical. He finally got the story out of her and he went into the house with his shotgun and went running up the stairs. Nathan woke up but not for long Wayne hit him in the head with the butt of the gun and pulled him off the bed and went to Samantha. She already had a black eye and her ribs were black but they didn't feel broken but when he felt them she moaned and looked up at him. He covered her up and tried to help her get up.

"Samantha I am going to kill him right now."

"No you can't they will have the law looking for us and we will never get out Texas and I have to get out of this country now, will you help me?"

"Yes little girl, where are we going to go?"

"Help me get to Mexico and then I will go further into South America into the jungle and he won't be able to find me there. Tie him up and Tillie will help me pack what I need and bind these ribs so I can ride. Can you get me the box from downstairs you know where it is. Saddle the horses and we will go to the train." He just nodded and dragged Nathan out and down the stairs where he tied him to a chair naked. Wayne got her box with her papers and went back upstairs. Tillie had her dressed in her chemise and pants and was trying to wrap a bandage around her ribs until Wayne finally told her.

"Let me it has got to be tight or you will never be able to stay on a horse till we get to the train." He put it on as tight as she could stand it and still breathe and she just smiled at him but when he looked at the bed and saw all the blood and her face he still wanted to kill the son of a bitch. The girls packed just what was needed except a dress and some shoes she wouldn't leave behind and then Wayne packed the horses, his things were still on the other horse and wagon and now hers. As they walked out the door Nathan was awake and he was yelling at her.

"I was your first man and I will be your last I will find you Samantha you belong to me you always have." She looked at him and took the papers for the house out of the box and went over to the table and signed them and said.

"It is all yours don't come looking for me you won't find me and I won't be back and you won't ever touch me again." Wayne helped her to the horses and helped her get into the saddle and then he told Tillie.

"We will be on the noon train give us that much time and then let him loose I am going to turn his horse loose so it will take him some time to find him. I am going to put your horse in the orchard so you can find him easy but you don't know that. Tillie stopped them before they got too far.

"In one of the saddle bags there is the honey you got yesterday wrapped in cloth so it won't break be careful if you ever get to a safe place send me a letter. No better not Nathan might be watching me."

"Tillie in the egg money jar there is ten dollars take it for helping me before he finds it and thank you." Wayne and Samantha started riding as fast as she could and he watched, she could barely stay in the saddle. He finally stopped and took her down and laid her in the wagon and took her the rest of the way to the station unconscious. She hurt so badly but they got to the train before it left at noon. He got them a railcar for the horses and they were going to ride with them he didn't want any more people than necessary seeing her. He left the wagon by the station with a man he knew and loaded the rest of their belongings but he had to carry her on to the train she was long past walking.

Wayne put their packs and her suitcases in with the horses and shut the front of the rail car so they couldn't be seen. Wayne laid out blankets and got Sam lay down and got her as comfortable was possible. There was still some time so he went and bought some food they could keep in with them mostly canned goods. They wanted to be seen by as few people as they could for as long as they could Sam and that horse of hers were too easy to be remembered and they knew Nathan would be looking for them. Finally the train started moving and they started to breathe again Wayne lay her head in his lap and she looked up at him.

"What is it you are wanting to know, ever since we left the house you keep looking at me funny?" he looked down at her and brushed her blond hair out of her face and he could feel she was shaking, she was hurting he was going to have to find a doctor for her and soon.

"Nathan said he was your first and there was blood on the bed, you and Eliot were never man and wife?"

"You always suspected and you were right about Eliot and Claude I never quite understood their arrangement but there was a clause in the marriage contract if I ever wanted out all I had to do was go to the Judge and say the marriage had never been consummated and it would be annulled. The judge set it up so Eliot never had to come back if he didn't want to, the judge was his uncle and I guess he has always known. When Nathan found out he was furious and he just hurt me more because he had to wait. Seems like either way I angered him, I just couldn't win, I have to get far away from him."

"You go to sleep I will get you to Mexico but what will you do then?"

"I have enough education to make a good governess to someone's children hopefully somewhere deeper in South America maybe I can get lost in the jungle." She slept and they rode all that day and most of the night. They stopped in a small town and she was hurting bad. They had a wait so Wayne left her and asked the conductor if there was a doctor in town and he was told yes. The train was to be there most of the night so he found the doctors house and went to it and got the doctor out of bed. He had to almost threaten him but Wayne got him to come and look at Sam. When he saw her he asked Wayne if he had done this to her and he said no they were running from the man who did. The doctor quickly examined her and then told Wayne to pick her up and follow him.

"We have to get her in a bed or she isn't going to make it she is bleeding inside. Come on I will bring your horses we will hide them at my ranch and she will be safe there. Quickly let's do this while it is dark." Wayne picked her up and carried her to the doctor's surrey and put her in and got the horses and they were gone before anyone saw them. The doctor took them out of town to his ranch and he put them up there. He lived in town above his office during the week and out here on the weekends so they would be safe. They got her to a bed and they undid the bindings around her ribs and sure enough she had a large bruise on her ribs and down her side they got her settled and the doctor started putting cold packs on her side.

"Is she going to be alright?"

"If we can get the bleeding to stop inside her she is hemorrhaging." He was looking at her face and the black eye. He was putting cold cloths on it as well. They were undressing her when he looked up at Wayne.

"He raped her as well?" Wayne just nodded his head. "Did you kill him?"

"No she wouldn't let me she said it would bring the law down on us and we couldn't get away and they would be after me for killing him."

"Too bad this man deserved killing." Wayne just looked at him as they covered her up he agreed with him.

"She needs sleep and to be still I will give her Laudanum for the pain and that is all we can do. It is a miracle he didn't break a rib or she would already be dead. Let's find you a bed she will sleep for a while and I will watch her." She woke up later in a strange room with a strange man sitting across from her and she panicked. He heard her before she could get out of the bed and went to her.

"It is alright I am Dr. Brian your man Wayne brought you here to my ranch to hide you till you were better, you have to be still. Your ribs are cracked and you are bleeding inside and you need a day or two before you can go on, I will get you some painkiller so you can sleep. Your man went back and collected your things from the train then I put him down the hall he was exhausted." He turned to get her something to drink and some painkiller and she grabbed his hand.

"Thank you we didn't have any place else to go." He just nodded his head. He went to the hallway and poured some laudanum into a cup of water and brought it back and held her up as she drank it. He laid he back down and she drifted back to sleep as he changed her cold compresses. Someone had taken out a lot of anger out on this young woman. He had seen it before and he would see it again but it always made him angry because he generally couldn't do anything about it. This woman seemed to have someone trying to help her get away and he was going to help them as well.

His wife was gone and his daughter was living in town with her husband and if she ever came to him like this her husband wouldn't live to see daylight but her husband seemed to be one of the good ones, thank god. He hadn't noticed before but she was wearing a wedding band he would have to ask in the morning if her husband did this to her. Things weren't adding up from the things he was seeing. When she was resting he finally went to bed himself and got up when the sun came up. Wayne was already in the kitchen cooking breakfast.

"Hope you don't mind I thought I could at least help with the cooking so you could sleep. I looked in on her she looks better this morning."

"I will check on her after breakfast and then go back to town so no one thinks it strange I am out here in the during the week." Wayne just nodded.

"We appreciate the help I don't think she could have gone much further."

"She has on a wedding band do I need to ask where is her husband in all this drama?" Wayne didn't say anything for a minute he just flipped the eggs he wasn't going to tell him everything then he changed his mind.

"The man who did this to her came to give her the news that the war was over and her husband was dead. He has wanted her for a long time so he just took what he wanted. He planned to keep her whether she agreed or not." The doctor just looked at him.

"Nice man, no wonder she ran, can she run far enough?"

"We are not sure but we are going to try even if it takes going to another country." Then he looked at the doctor and didn't say any more. The doctor understood what he didn't know he couldn't tell. After he ate he told Wayne to keep changing the compresses on her side and face and how much laudanum to give her. He told him to try and get her to eat and he would probably be back after dark unless somebody had come looking for them, if they did he wouldn't lead them out to the ranch. He told him to keep their horses in the barn so no one would see hers from the road. There was not supposed to be anyone on his land besides him during the week so they shouldn't be disturbed.

He didn't come back that night and Wayne was afraid he had run into trouble and sure enough he had. Men had come to his office that morning looking for an injured blond woman and an older man and started tearing his house in town apart until someone called the sheriff. They were escorted out of his house and they went to the hotel and stayed the night. They left the next morning and he finally went back to his ranch to check on the girl and her man. Wayne met him at the door.

"Is everything alright?"

"They were in town they came to my office I didn't dare come out here yesterday for fear they would follow me. You gave that man a pretty good thump on the head he is wearing a bandage around his head."

"To bad I didn't crack it open do you think it is safe you came out here now?"

"Yes I always come out here on the weekends and take care of my ranch this is where I am supposed to be, how is she doing?" Samantha came around the corner and answered him.

"She is doing much better thank you." Samantha was smiling at him she did look much better.

"I want to check you out and I think you should stay one more day and let them get a little further down the line looking for you. Then you can get back on the train and maybe you should be able to get where you are going." When he had her alone her wanted to talk to her.

"I don't exactly know how to say this to you but he damaged you badly inside. I don't know if he has taken your fertility from you or not. I was afraid I was going to have to operate to keep you from dying but you finally quit bleeding but he may have left you barren. She just looked at him and told him, Nathan never really wanted children he always said they ruined a woman's figure. I guess beating them to death didn't count. Is there anything you can do?"

"I did all I could Mother Nature and time will tell the rest he may have left you with nothing but your life. You will have to see what Mother Nature left you with. Children aren't the only thing that makes a woman."

"I think that is easier coming from a man's mouth than it is from mine. Thank you for saving my life Wayne says I was in pretty bad shape by the time I got here." She just looked at the floor she had always wanted children; maybe she should have let Wayne kill him.

They waited till Sunday and they started again but they rode as far as they could until she couldn't ride anymore and then they found the train again. They watched until nightfall and then went down and again paid for a railcar and put the horses inside along with their things and closed it up and started riding again. It took three days more before they crossed into Mexico and another day until they were in Mexico City. Wayne got her to a descent hotel and settled then put their horses into a good stable. He then went back to the hotel room beside hers.

"I ordered us some food and you a bath so you could soak for a while. I am going to go check and see if anybody is looking for you around here I will be back in a while. If the food gets here before I get back eat."

"Yes sir I will, don't be gone long I worry." He just smiled at her and nodded his head after what she had been through he just wanted her to be safe. She took a long bath and washed her hair and put on some clean clothes or as clean as she had. When the girl came in to bring her dinner she asked her in Spanish if there was someone who could wash her clothes and was told yes so she sent out her clothes to be washed. She didn't have much and they had been patched so many times they were barely holding together but until she could buy more they were all she had.

After she ate she was looking out the window and saw a shop where there were women going in and out buying clothes and other things that she needed but she couldn't go over there looking like this. She still had a black eye and she was going to need a corset if she was going to be riding anymore. She asked the girl who took her clothes if she would take a message to the owner of the store to come to her room after she closed tonight and she gave her a coin for the errand. She watched as the girl walked over and talked to the owner and she pointed to the window. Sam watched the woman as she left her shop. The woman knocked on her door a few minutes later and she told her to come in. Samantha didn't turn around immediately.

"What are you to good to come to my shop Senora?"

"Not exactly, what I need I would rather get after dark when I can't be seen so well." Then she turned around and the woman got a good look at the woman in front of her.

"I would like to get a job as a governess but I don't think most men would find this acceptable would you. I also need some under things and clothes. I was wondering if maybe you would open your shop after hours and show me how to cover these bruises up until they are gone?" The woman at the door sucked in her breath and then started talking.

"Is he still looking for you?" Samantha just shook her head yes. "How far are you willing to run?"

"I will run all the way to the bottom of South America if I have to." The lady just shook her head yes as Wayne came in the door.

"This is my friend Wayne he helped me get this far. I am sorry I don't even know your name?"

"Camille Rivas nice to meet you, while your friend eats would you like to go over to my shop and we will do a little shopping?" she looked at Wayne.

"Anybody looking for me down here yet?" he shook his head no. "Then you eat and I will go get some clothes and some makeup for

this eye I can't interview with a black eye it will cause too many questions.

There may be someone bringing my clothes back in a little while I had them washed there is money on the counter. You have a bath and some supper I will be back later you have a room next door and I will be at that shop across the street." Wayne watched as the two women walked across the street and into the shop and the lights came on inside the shop, then he sat down at the small table and started to eat. The women went to the back and Samantha started to look at the ladies camisoles and under things they were of high quality and just plain cotton as well.

"May I try some on I haven't bought anything in a long time and I have lost some weight. I am going to need a corset as well." Camille looked at her funny and then asked her.

"What in the world are you going to need with a corset if you are going to be riding into the jungle and I assume that is what you are proposing to do if you are running from this man?" about that time she unbuttoned the front of her shirt and pulled up her chemise and turned sideways until Camille could see her side and Camille just said.

"I will go get some and we will find one that fits there is a screen over there."

"It has to fit over some padding and binding as well." Camille just nodded her head and went to the back of the store and when she came back out she had several in her hands.

"Who is going to wrap you up before you put it on?" "Haven't figured that one out yet?"

"When you get that far down the road I will help you get ready to go." Samantha just nodded yes and they went on trying things on.

"Will he come this far to find you?" Samantha turned and shook her head yes.

"He has wanted me for a long time and he thinks I belong to him so he will probably still be looking for me. I would like to find a job as governesses, do you know of anyone looking for one around here or do I need to advertise. I am running short on time?"Camille thought for a second and then said.

"I have heard of a couple of men who are supposed to be looking for someone to take back with them to teach their children. Let me check it out and see if they are looking for teachers or a mistress."

"Thank you I would appreciate that, if I need to move further down into Central America I need to be going soon." They tried on several more things until she settled on what she needed then when they were leaving she saw a dress, a teal colored ball gown on a manikin.

"That dress is beautiful I envy the lady you are making it for."Camille looked at her strangely.

"I made it for a gentleman's mistress but when she wanted to marry him he refused her so she went back on a ship with Carlotta. She went back to raise more money for her husband's revolution to keep Mexico. She thought she would do better in France. Maximilian is running out of funds here but I don't think his wife will be back, she is slowly losing her mind. Now I have a ball gown and no one to wear it. The gentleman refused to pay for it and the jewelry she picked out as well. So I am going to lose a considerable amount on that little fiasco."

"To bad it is a beautiful gown it should be worn by someone not just left to hang in the back of your store." They went to the door and started to walk out and a carriage went past them. A man inside the carriage saw Samantha pass under the streetlight for just a brief second. He turned and looked back at the blond haired woman but she didn't look at him as she and Camille were walking across the street. He thought to himself it was much too late in the evening for Camille and her friend to be walking alone on these streets. He didn't see Wayne meet them and escort them to their destinations.

The next morning Camille meet them for breakfast in the patio of the hotel and she had news there were three men who were looking for governesses but she would only recommend she see two of them. When Sam asked why only two Camille told her the third mans last governess was in a house on his property awaiting the birth of a baby his, so she didn't recommend him as a potential boss. Sam agreed. She made arrangements to meet the other two at lunch time this afternoon in the patio with Camille watching.

The first interview went alright until the gentleman told her he and his family was going to Europe in six months and she would be required to travel with them and Samantha told him she wouldn't get on a ship ever again. She thanked him for his time and then waited for the other man as she sipped tea. The other man came a little after the first one from across the courtyard it seems he had been watching her all this time. He was the man who had seen her in the carriage last night.

"Hello I am Clayton Hayes and you are?" she looked him up and down he was a good looking man and a big ma he had to be at least six foot two and there was no fat on him.

"I am Samantha Rodgers what are you grinning for?"

"Why did you turn down a trip to Europe most women I know would kill for a chance to go abroad?"

"I have been to Spain and I don't want to ever have to get on a ship again it was not a pleasant experience. Does that answer your question?" he just looked at her and then he sat down and ordered a whiskey for himself.

"Would you like one as well?" "No thank you I don't drink."

"Oh lord are you one of those women who is going to tell me I am going to hell if I have a drink?"

"I don't care one way or the other what you do, I just don't drink." Then he looked at her she wasn't being condensing she really didn't care.

"Why is a well cared for and intelligent married woman looking for a job in this part of the country?"

"I am a widow now and my brother lost our ranch to someone in a card game recently. My options are becoming smaller by the day. I spent some time in Brazil and loved it there so I decided to come down here and start over again is there a problem with that?" he studied her for a minute and then said.

"That's not all is it?" she just looked at him and finally told him. "No I have some health problems and the weather down here is better for me. Satisfied, now how about you how many children do you have and do you have a wife?" she wasn't scared of him and that said a lot, most women were and went running at the first loud voice he used. He smiled at her his size could be intimating.

"I have two children a boy seven, Steven and a girl almost four her mother died after having her. Steven usually goes with me to learn how to run the plantation but the girl needs an education and someone to be with her when Steven and I aren't around. Do you think you can handle that?"

"I take it you want me to teach your son the basics as well reading, writing how to count or is he just going to be you made over?" He looked at her and kind of smirked and then he asked her.

"You have a smart mouth is that how you got that black eye or are you running from someone? I saw you coming out of Camille's shop last night; it is too hot for you to be in this sunlight if you want to keep that eye a secret." She scooted her chair back into the shadows and then decided if she wanted to answer him or not, so she looked over at Camille and she nodded her head yes, so she gave him and answer.

"I am running from the man who did this to me and there is more than just the eye. I am running just as hard and fast as I can. He has taken everything from me there is nothing left for me to go back to, so if you don't want my services you can leave and I will start looking for someone else to go to work for." He looked at her again and smiled.

"I guess I will have to buy you a horse in the morning and we will leave as soon as possible. Do you think he will come this far looking for you?" she shook her head yes.

"Alright there is something else you will have to do for me. Tonight we have to attend a party. If we are leaving in the morning, I have to sign some contracts before I leave and I can do it there. Do you have a party dress?" she looked at him like he was an idiot.

"You have to be kidding I was on the run and everything I own was on the back of a pack horse. By the way I have my own horse you won't have to supply me with one but I do not have a party dress or shoes so you will have to go to this party alone." He turned his head around and looked at Camille and then turned back.

"You and Camille have been sharing looks since I got here hasn't she got something suitable you can wear tonight and maybe a piece of jewelry that won't break me?" Samantha thought of that teal dress and grinned maybe she could do her new friend a favor if he was going to make her go to this thing.

"Alright let me and Camille see what we can come up with and I will put it on your bill, but are you sure you want to take me I am nobody?"

"You are somebody now before the hour is out this whole town will know I have hired you so I might as well show them who you are." before he left she asked him another question.

"You have told me your son's name but you have yet to tell me your daughter's name, why because your wife died giving birth to her."

"You just push and push don't you, are you trying to get fired." She stood up and came around the table and stood in front of him. He had to admit she was no shrinking violet what kind of man had made her run.

"Her mother had been told not to have another child her heart was not good she didn't tell me, but she got pregnant anyway and she died having Melanee. He said the girls name almost like a curse if she had any doubts about going they were gone now this little girl needed her.

"So you blame the girl for your wife dying is that it?"

"What does it matter it is done and if you are thinking I would make a good husband think again I don't plan to ever marry again." She raised her eyebrows.

"Don't look at me I don't want you or anybody else for that matter my experiences with men lately haven't been the best. Well are we done I have a dress to find and a party to get ready for and a black eye to cover up. So when will you be picking me up or do I just stand at the curb waiting breathlessly for your arrival?" he laughed out loud, this woman would drive a saint to drink.

"I will be here at seven and take you to dinner and then we will go to the party."

"Well if I am not here I am still at Camille's trying to get into a dress or making one out of the drapes. I will see you at seven." Then she turned and went over to Camille's table and they left and she never turned back to look at him and he was disappointed he hoped she would. He was smiling anyway tonight was certainly going to be interesting.

CHAPTER 2

When she got into Camille's shop she went to the teal colored dress first thing and they took it off the manikin and she tried it on. The fit wasn't bad the sleeves were too short as was the hem the dress wasn't finished and it needed a little letting out even with the corset it was tight the other woman was smaller and shorter than she was. They added lace to lengthen the sleeves and started fixing the hem. There were plenty of hem for the extra length they needed. The dress was only half finished so there were plenty of seams to let out to make it fit Samantha; it just took two dressmakers to do it.

Camille sent for her seamstress and they went to work. Sam told her she needed a piece of jewelry probably a choker that was large and not too costly. Camille told her to wear her hair up and she told her she couldn't then she took off the scarf she had been wearing all day, then Camille saw why she had to have something on her neck. There were finger marks on the front and back that Samantha couldn't hide with makeup or not all of them anyway. Camille didn't say anything she just went to the back, when she came back out she had a necklace in her hand it was white turquoise with teal streaks through the pieces. It was a choker about two inches tall and then it came down into a rounded U in front it was perfect, it covered everything and it looked good with the dress and it wasn't too expensive. It came with a matching bracelet and earrings. Camille already knew nobody was going to be looking at the jewelry this woman was going to be wearing tonight anyway.

"This looks like it was made for this dress."

"It was, the gentleman wouldn't pay for it either, and you are bailing me out of debt by taking this off my hands. The gentleman will probably be at the ball tonight he will have a fit I wish I could see his reaction. He told me I shouldn't have made the dress without his permission so it was going to be my loss. Then he told every man in town how he left me in a bind and he thought he was so cute." they worked all afternoon and into the evening getting the dress done. Camille brought out some cheese and bread for her to nibble on while she stood for the fitting and gave her juice and pieces of mango. She was in heaven with all this fresh fruit. They didn't realize how late it was getting until Clayton walked into the salon and said.

"You look absolutely stunning in that dress." She thought he was making fun of her till she turned around and looked at him and the look on his face was one of a man who wants the woman he is looking at.

"Thank you it was the best we could do on such short notice." Camille went to put the necklace on her and he said.

"I thought you would have put your hair up but it looks good down. There aren't many blonds around here and you will stand out in the crowd. Here let me put the necklace on." And both women said at once.

"No." he looked at them strangely and then he walked over to Sam and said.

"Let me have the necklace I am paying for it." She turned around reluctantly and pulled up her hair and then he knew why she wasn't wearing her hair up. Then he also understood why they didn't want him to put the necklace on her, there were finger marks on the back of her neck. He stopped right there and turned her around and looked at the front of her neck and there were some there too. She couldn't cover them all with makeup. He turned her back around and clasped the necklace and pulled her hair out and laid her hair down on the back of the dress and didn't say a word. She had warned him there was more.

He sat down in a chair across the room and crossed his legs leaned back and watched, while they finished dressing her. She wouldn't look at him and wouldn't say a word. When they were finished a few minutes later he escorted her out the door and put her in a waiting carriage then sat across from her, he wanted to be able to talk to her and look at her.

"This man you are running from he did that to you as well?" she just breathed deeply then she nodded her head yes.

"Should I fear for my family?"

"I don't think so, it has always been me he wanted he tells me he has loved me for years. I don't think he would hurt anybody else but me."

"That is how he showed his love for you, why do I think there is much more you won't tell me?" She just looked at him with her gloved hands crossed in her lap she guessed it was now or never.

"If you think I am putting your family in danger I will resign the position and I will pay you for the gown and jewelry. This is not your problem it is mine it always has been." He couldn't get over the feeling if he let her go when he came back to Mexico City he would find out this man had found her and killed her and he couldn't stand the thought of that.

"You don't trust me but you will go into the jungle with me are you sure about that?"

"Right now I trust one man and that is the man I came down here with me but I will have to learn to trust you just give it some time I have no other options. So do we still have a deal?"

"We still have a deal, we will leave tomorrow but if this man shows up on my land I will shoot him." She said under her breath 'NOT IF I SEE HIM FIRST.'

They stopped at a small outdoor café had a quiet supper and just talked but they were on a short time schedule so she ate quickly. When she was through they again got in the waiting carriage and headed to the party.

"You shouldn't have any trouble here I am going to introduce you as my new governess then sign the papers I need to sign after that we will go. If anyone bothers you I will be in plain sight just come and get me you should be fine."

"I think I can handle myself at a dance I have been to one or two in my life I probably will just disappear and watch." He doubted she could just disappear someone would certainly notice her why did that bother him so much. He knew keeping her close to him would draw even more attention to her and he didn't want that either.

They continued on to the ball. He kept riding on the other side of the coach so he just watched her she didn't say anymore to him. When they got to their destination it was a brightly lit house and she was afraid it was too bright. He lifted her down from the carriage and took her inside and up some stairs and the lights weren't so bright inside.

After introducing her to several people he led her inside and she was asked if she wanted a drink. She took a glass of champagne and he looked at her strangely because she said she didn't drink. He escorted her around and she didn't say much and then he went to talk to some men and she went to an outer balcony and stood alone in the shadows. All the time she was with him he noticed she carried the glass in her hand but she never took a drink out of the glass. He went upstairs to a lot of questions as to who she was so he didn't notice the man slip on to the balcony to talk to her.

"I saw you take a glass of champagne but I have yet to see you take a drink of it Madame."

"I don't drink but it easier to just take a glass and carry it around than explain about why I don't want any?" he laughed and then came closer to her.

"The man with you is your husband I presume?" she smiled at him. "No he is my employer I am a widow." He came a little closer.

"He is a very lucky man. I am curious what are you employed as?"

"I am going to be governess to his two children." He shook his head and smiled at her.

"He has very lucky children. Oh they are playing a waltz do you dance Madame, so many of the people in this country still think the waltz is to risquй?"

"As a matter of fact I do waltz I learned in Spain several years ago in Andalusia, from a couple there, who taught a dance school." he looked at her strangely.

"I know of only one couple who teach there and they are Gabriel and Lena Baca and they teach Flamenco."

"Yes that is them they taught me a how to dance when I was in Spain seeing a doctor. My father and I got to go to another Ball with them. Gabriel and I did a performance at the palace for the Queen." She thought he was going to fall down. She had him sit at the small table on the balcony and gave him a drink out of her glass as she fanned his face. He just stared at her in disbelief.

"Are you all right it really wasn't that special they went there all the time performing, my father and I just got to tag along this time. Lena was ill so I danced with Gabriel. The queen helps support the school so they give a performance every so often." He just looked at her and smiled this woman had got to go to a Ball at the palace.

"Please would you come with me and let's dance. I don't even know your name, mine is Duke Alexis Duarte."

"I am Samantha Rodgers but you can call me Sam." He pulled her out on the floor and he went to the orchestra and asked them to play a piece of music and Sam recognized it. It was a waltz by Bach and then the Duke pulled her into his arms and they danced and he guided her around the room like she was floating. She did know how to dance even though it had been a long time since Spain. Most of the others moved and let them have the floor and the men talking to Clayton stopped talking and said.

"Well finally looks like the Duke found someone he could dance with. She is good and pretty where did she come from?" Clayton turned around and he couldn't see her face but there was no mistaking that teal dress and long blond hair. She was floating around the floor with the Duke. The music stopped and everyone was clapping. The duke asked for another piece of music and it was the Paso Doable and she smiled at him as he bowed to her.

"Do you know this one as well Madame?" she nodded her head yes and they were off and the crowd was roaring it was a fast passed dance and she was good all the people watched as did Clayton. It was a gypsy dance about bullfighting and she did it well she was outpacing even the Duke and he was good. When the dance was over the room erupted in applause then he bowed again as she curtsied to the Duke. Then he took her back to her balcony where she could disappear again.

"Who is she?"

"My new governess, we leave tomorrow." One of the men asked him.

"That is the woman that was looking for employment? Now I wish I had some children." When he got through with his business he went down to the balcony and she was still there talking to the Duke in the shadows. She had told him she was leaving tomorrow when he had asked her to come with him she had refused. Clayton listened for a bit before interrupting them and then he walked out on the balcony. Clayton introduced himself to the Duke, shook his hand and then they left.

Clayton collected Samantha and got her downstairs after saying his goodbyes to the hostess. He got her in the coach and he sat beside her this time and put his arm around her back but didn't say a word. She didn't say anything either. He got her out of the coach walked her upstairs to the door of her room and she turned to say goodnight.

"You might as well let me in unless you have a maid in there, someone is going to have help with all those buttons you and Camille did up this afternoon." She had forgotten all those buttons and there had to be twenty of them.

"I will figure out something."

"Not unless you grow another set of arms in the next five minutes you won't. Calm down I am just going to unbutton that dress I think you have had enough of everything else lately and I don't rape women I don't need too. I can generally find an accommodating woman if I want one." She almost laughed, from what she heard this evening he had his pick of the women around here at least for a night or two. He only seemed to take a woman for a short time and then he left. She let him in the room and lit the light and then she turned around and she pulled her hair back and Clayton undid the necklace. Those finger marks still made him mad when he saw them.

"Camille said I could return the necklace and bracelet and she wouldn't charge you for them."

"No keep them we will probably have to entertain occasionally at the plantation and they look good with the dress and I think I can afford them. You looked good on the dance floor tonight someone taught you well, I didn't expect a small town Texas girl to know how to dance that well."

"Neither did the Duke he was impressed that I had danced at the palace in Madrid and met Queen Isabella a few years ago." He had stopped unbuttoning her gown and turned her around.

"You met the Queen of Spain and danced at her palace in Madrid?" "Yes, I danced with some royalty what is so special. I told you I went to Spain to see a doctor and I met some people who taught me to dance and we went to the palace one night and I met the Queen she is very nice." He just kept staring at her. And then he reached down took her in his arms and kissed her and she just stood there.

"Why did you do that?"

"Just making sure you are real, sometimes you make me wonder. Why didn't you kiss back?" she turned around and he continued undoing her dress she didn't know how to tell him she didn't know how to kiss a man because she never really had. He finished with the dress and then he left just like he said he would he didn't ask any more questions, she still might just get away with this. She took off the dress and hung it up then took off the corset and it was already rubbing, it was so good to get that thing off, she didn't know how she was going to ride for several more days in it. She had taken to calling it the torture chamber because that is what it felt like when she had it on. The bruises were getting better but they were never going to heal until she stopped riding and rested but she couldn't do that until she was safe. She could still feel the hair standing up on the back of her neck. He was still after her she couldn't wait to leave and put some more miles between them.

After she got undressed she put on a gown and robe to go to the balcony and walked outside then just breathed in the moist fragrant air it was like nothing else she had ever smelled. There were so many different trees in bloom everywhere. She didn't know it but Clayton was down at the corner watching her room he wanted to make sure the Frenchman didn't come to see her after he left. He knew he shouldn't be but he was furious at the man for just dancing with this beautiful blond woman tonight. All his big talk about not needing a woman in his life seemed to be dissolving rapidly.

She was smart and the more he found out about her the more she surprised him. She didn't realize the effect she had on people especially men. He watched her in the moonlight and a hummingbird settled on a trumpet vine growing on a wall near her. She just stayed perfectly still while it fed then the little bird just looked at her for a second then flew away. What had he gotten himself into she was something he wanted, he just smiled as she went back inside and he watched until her light went out.

"Well Clayton this little bird is yours now, can you catch her?" When her room was dark and he was sure she was alone he went back to his own hotel room and went to sleep and waited for what tomorrow would bring.

Camille was there early to help her dress and Clayton came up the stairs and was at the door and it was cracked and he overheard a conversation he wasn't supposed to hear.

"We'll tell me everything how did it go at the dance last night; you are the talk of the town this morning. I have already had the man come in who wouldn't pay for the dress screaming at me saying I embarrassed him by selling it to someone else. He wanted to know who you were and then he told me you were at Queens Isabella's palace and dancing with a prince. Now he is ruined for cheating me. It made my whole morning. So tell me everything." Samantha was shaking her head.

"The Prince was fourteen and I was fifteen and his mother had plans for him and they didn't include a rather tall Texas girl. A

French Duke did ask me to marry me last night and sail away with him to France, not bad for one evening but Frenchmen are always in a hurry. I did get a kiss from Clayton though and then he asked me why I didn't kiss him back?"

"What did you say to him? You didn't say anything did you, Samantha why didn't you tell him?"

"No, what did you want me to say I had a sham marriage to a man who liked other men and Nathan was too busy beating me to death. So by the way I don't have the foggiest idea how to kiss a man. I just turned around, besides he says he doesn't want another woman or he can get one any time he needs one and apparently I am not on the list. I guess he doesn't like blonds or maybe it is just me, I don't know." Clayton was outside the door and he turned and walked quietly away, talk about putting your foot in your mouth. He went quickly down the stairs he would come back in a little while. Camille went on talking to Samantha.

"I don't care what he has said I saw his face when he saw those marks on your neck and that was a man that was mad. Then when you were getting ready to go and you were in the dress he was a man that was looking at a woman he wanted so he may be lying to himself but he wants you."

"Great another one I don't know what to do with." Camille laughed. "We should all be so lucky."

"If I had time you could teach a class and I would your first student lord knows I need some lessons."

"Oh, honey I think he is going to teach you all you need to know but if he hurts you come back here you always have a place here with me."

"Lord I am quickly running out of country's to hide in." Bind me up and help me get in this corset on he will be waiting on me."

"I don't know how you are going to wear this thing for several more days you may have to tell him what is going on I don't think you are going to be able to stand this thing that long." The men came up and gathered up her bags and carried them down to the waiting horses and she went to the market and bought some candy and two more bottles of honey and then she found a small horse auction going on at the back of a barn and she saw a small palomino mare on sale.

The man didn't have her up for bid yet and when she asked how much he wanted for her he quite rudely told her.

"I will get at least 75 dollars for the stubborn little monster because she won't be broke so I will sell her for meat." Samantha looked at the whip in his hand and the marks on the little mares back and she told him.

"I will be right back." She went looking for Clayton and she found him rounding up horses and pack animals and she grabbed his arm.

"I need some money can I borrow some from you please I will pay you back."

"How are you going to pay me back?"

"Whatever you want I will work in the fields scrub floors, muck stalls, whatever you want?" when he raised his eyebrows she started sidestepping. "Almost anything you want and I thought you didn't want that." As he looked at her his resolve was crumbling fast.

"What do you want to buy?"

"A horse and they are fixing to sell her and if I don't buy her they are going to sell her for meat." She was talking so fast he had to slow her down.

"Here take me there and let me see this animal." She pulled him along explaining about this mare she wanted and how she had almost all the money she was just short some and she wanted to borrow some from him, it was the first time she had ever asked him for anything. When they got back behind the barn she showed him the little blond mare she was almost the color of her hair and she was half starved but Sam wanted her and the man selling her was giving Samantha grief about her.

"I have already told this Punta that this mare can't be broken and I will sell her for meat and she won't listen to me." Clayton didn't know if Samantha knew what the man had just called but he did and now he didn't care how much he wanted for the mare if Sam wanted it she was going to have it.

The man knew he had made a mistake when he looked at Clayton's face and when asked how much for the horse again the price went down and Samantha had enough money to pay for the mare herself. She went in the corral and put a halter on the mares head and then turned to the man and spoke to him in Spanish so she did know exactly what he had called her, a whore. Then she went over to the edge of the corral and took off a small saddle and put it on the mare and said something to the man. Apparently that was part of the deal as well or it was after he called her a whore. He picked up a whip and he was going to use it on Samantha but Clayton had already pulled out his pistol and told him.

"One mark on either of them and I will put a hole in you and don't ever call my woman a whore again." Sam heard what he had said to the man and thought he had just misspoken so she just kept going. He opened the gate and Samantha walked out with the mare and Clayton asked her.

"Who is the little saddle for?"

"Your daughter, you seem to forget she is alive so I think it is time someone remembered don't you?" he just let that remark go by he wasn't going to fight with her.

"He says the horse can't be broken what about that?"

Most things people use a whip on fight back wouldn't you? Don't worry about Melanee I won't put your daughter in danger, besides I broke my horse and he was a wild stallion caught off the range." When they got to the stables there was her horse a very large stallion the same color as the little mare and the same color as Samantha's hair except for a white mane and tail. The men were having some difficulty with him so Sam went over and took his reins and just led him over to Clayton and he followed her like he was a tame dog.

"We have been together for five years this is Sundance." He was a beautiful blonde color and a good sixteen hands tall, she looked small beside him and the mare was smaller than him too.

"I am thinking with some good feed she will get a little bigger she is still young and her coat will look better we could use her for another pack animal if you want.

"That is fine I have already bought one she can just travel with us and you can work on breaking her I think I am going to enjoy watching that. Are you about ready we have everything packed?" he went to help her up but she was already in the saddle. As they started to leave Wayne was walking up carrying a saddle and she got back down and she was smiling at him. Wayne took off the saddle on the big horse then she stood back as he put the most beautiful saddle any of the men had ever seen on a horse. It was exquisitely tooled with silver Conchos' and studs on it and the top of the saddle horn was silver as well as the bottoms of the stirrups. It was a very costly saddle and Clayton had never seen a saddle anywhere like it before.

"You had it I thought my brother lost it gambling but you had it all along."

"I hid it in town so he couldn't find it, there was nowhere on the ranch that he couldn't find it and he would have hurt you to get it. I had it in the wagon but you have been too preoccupied and hurt to notice." She just reached over and put her arms around his neck and hugged him.

"I left everything with Camille you send anything to her she will be able to find me. You know I love you take of yourself. Are you going back to Dallas?"

"Don't know yet might just stay here Camille is a pretty woman and there are several jobs at ranchos around here as well. Just send anything to Camille she will find me."

"You take care little girl you know where I am and that I love you like my own. If you need me I will come a running." He tipped his hat to Clayton and then he said.

"Watch out for her Mr. Hayes, Nathan is still looking for her." Clayton looked back and he saw Samantha shiver like it was cold. She climbed back up on her horse and they started down a road and he rode up next to her and looked at the saddle and he finally asked her.

"That thing has got to have cost as much as several horses I take you didn't buy it for yourself?"

"No it was a gift from friends in Spain a few years ago, I helped them out of a situation and that was a gift for my help." He just watched her for a few minutes and didn't ask any more questions and then went back up front. He was actually kind of afraid of the answers he might get.

They were on the trail for several hours until they stopped for lunch and she was glad to get off the horse she didn't know how she was going to be able to stand that corset for several days it was already cutting and she was already hurting. She reached into her saddlebag and took out the second bottle of Laudanum and it was almost gone so she put it back up and figured she would wait until tonight and use it so she could sleep. She couldn't find any more in Mexico City without going to a doctor and then everybody would have known her secret. Lunch was just tortillas and beans but she had bought some mangos at the market and she split them with the men before they left. She was getting ready to mount back up when Clayton came up behind her and asked her.

"Is that enough sugar for you for right now or do you require more?" she turned around and looked at him.

"I am good for now. When it gets really hot I may need more but I have my honey and I generally know the signals and I know when to start paying attention to take care of things."

"Maybe you should tell me what to look for just in case?" she looked at him she didn't really like other people knowing what was going on but he had a right to know and out here she might need some help.

"I get shaky and goofy like I am drunk and then I will fight you and tell you I don't need anything, don't ask me why I just do. And don't let me have a drink of alcohol it makes it worse much faster, just get me to eat something sweet, candy, honey, sugar water or fruit just do it before I pass out, then I am in real trouble."

"What happens if you pass out?"

"My parents finally figured out that if they used an eyedropper filled with sugar water a little at a time I wouldn't choke and I finally woke up."

"After how long Sam?"

"The longest was half a day, that was when daddy took me to Spain it was getting worse and they were looking for answers before I just didn't wake up." Clayton looked at her and put his hand in her hair.

"They didn't get it fixed did they, so you just maintain what you have going, no better no worse?"

"That is about it. But you don't understand down here is like heaven there are fresh fruits and citrus where I came from I had to pray there was honey. You don't know how wonderful this is to me. The market this morning had more fresh fruit than I have seen in years and some I have never seen before this is wonderful." He smiled and commented.

"I am glad you are so pleased." Before she could think about it he reached down pulled her hair back and softly kissed her and she gently kissed back.

"Better and you taste sweet." He stood back and looked at her again.

"That is another signal my skin gets a sweet taste not that you will taste my skin." And she smiled. He was thinking want to bet but she kissed back a little anyway she was learning.

"Want some help up in your saddle?" she was already half way up and she looked down.

"No thanks already done."

"I figured you would need a sidesaddle most of the women in Mexico City ride one of those?"

"Have you ever sat in one of those things?"

"No I have never been in a sidesaddle." He was mounting his horse and she was grinning at him.

"You ride in one for a day and then see if you don't want to find the man that invented them and shoot him I dare you. You think several days travel is bad in a regular saddle try in of those torture devices and see what is worse."

"I thought regular saddles were supposed to be bad for women's parts." "Really, no worse than for a man's I would assume, except for falling off the stupid thing and that could be damaging." he started laughing. He could see himself on the ground in a heap with her watching and a sidesaddle taunting him to get back up on it. It made for a ludicrous picture.

"You are being called up front by one of the men." He left her with her mare and stallion and one of the other men TY but he didn't care for him much he had hired him in Mexico City and he didn't like leaving him back there with Samantha alone he didn't trust him. They walked alone for awhile and then he began to talk to her. He wanted to know where she had come from and who her people were. Sam realized she was being pumped for information and she didn't like it.

"I can ride alone why don't you go up front and ride with the other men?"

"What I am not good enough for you or not rich enough that saddle must have cost someone a pretty penny. You leave him behind is that who you are running from?" she was beginning to hurt real bad and she didn't want to have to keep sidestepping this man she was going to lose her temper and say something she didn't want to. About that time Clayton came back and told the man to head up front they were making camp for the night. They rode in quiet for a few minutes and then he asked her.

"You are tired aren't you?"

"Yes, too many days on the trail and I am just worn out it will be good to get some rest." She tried to smile but she was to tired and hurting to bad to even do that. They stopped a little ways ahead and when she dismounted this time he was there to help her, the only problem was when he grabbed her to help her down he grabbed those bruised ribs and she almost groaned it hurt so bad. She couldn't say anything he was trying to help but it hurt.

"Why in the world are you wearing a corset get out of that thing and don't wear it tomorrow understand me?" She just nodded yes. She walked over to a small clearing and took off her shirt and then the corset and that did feel better. She left the bindings she would never get them back on by herself. Now she got out the Laudanum and took what was left in the second vile, that left one vile she was going to have to ration it for the remaining trip left.

She sat down for a little bit until she felt better and then went to supper. Again they had tortilla and beans with rice they had eaten the fruit at lunch and then someone brought out her honey. They were dumping it in the tortillas before she could say anything Clayton grabbed the jar and took it away.

"Who has been going through her saddlebags?" No one would answer so he went over and checked her saddle bag. There was only one jar left and it was almost gone. Sam looked into the other saddle bag with the candy in it and it was all gone. Samantha looked at him and said.

"I may be in trouble is there any place to by some fruit or sugar cane around here."

Not for at least another day and that will be pushing it." She looked at the honey and figured she could make it that long.

"I will take my chances with the honey that is left if you are willing but that is going to take you out of the way isn't it."

"It makes the ride a little harder and we come closer to some of the Indian camps but I think we will be alright there is a monastery near here and we can make it in one more day. The priest raises Honey."

"We are going to have to go to the monastery to the east tomorrow it is a bit out of the way but the lady needs some more honey and since you men seemed fit to steal hers we will have to get her some more." TY put his two cents in about now.

"Why do we need to put ourselves in danger for this lady we don't know her she is your piece anyway. She had the candy and the honey and we wanted it so we took it is no big deal."

"It is now you are fired so you won't need to go with us you can go back to Mexico City I don't need a thief on this trip and anymore of you that would like leave start packing. No one else stood up so TY got his animal ready and was going to leave in the morning. Clayton came back to Sam and she was in a corner with her horses looking to see what else was missing but she found only the candy and honey gone until she looked and the bag she hid her money in and her little box with the jewelry was gone as well. She looked up at him and said to him.

"I don't know if he has got it or not but the box with what little money and my parents jewelry is gone as well, it wasn't much but it was all I has left of them." He helped her check again in every saddlebag and both saddles the old one and the new one and it wasn't there.

"Where was it the last time you saw it Samantha?"

"It was in the bag with the Honey because I had them double wrapped so they wouldn't get broken so that was the safest place I didn't expect anyone to touch my honey."

"No one should have been messing with any of your things or anyone else's for that matter your saddlebags are yours no one else's." He started back out to the campsite and she followed him but he didn't see her pull her pistol out of her saddle bag this might get ugly and she wasn't letting him get hurt just because of her.

"Ty where is her parents jewelry and don't tell me you don't have it because it was in the bag with the honey and you have already said you took the honey. I won't ask but once and then I start taking you apart looking for it, now where is it she wants it back." TY looked at him for a minute and then at her and walked over to a dead tree stump by the water and dug around a little and took it out and then threw it at her. The little box opened in her hands and out fell the money and the jewelry it wasn't much but it was hers.

"Thank you it is all I have left of them." Then she turned and walked away.

"In the morning after you eat you are out of here and I don't ever want to see your face again."

"Kind of dangerous for a man alone out here don't you think I could ride to the next stop with you?"

"No I don't want you anywhere close to me or my people."

"Your women you mean none of the rest of us mean anything." Clayton turned around and went back to Sam he was going to keep her close tonight this man might try something else.

After supper he tied hammocks up in the trees and she knew she was not going to be able to sleep in one of them she could barely sleep flat she wasn't going to make it bent in half. After everyone was asleep she got out of the hammock and found a tree that was relatively flat and made a bed on that and got some sleep. Just before morning light she heard something rustling in the undergrowth and she saw a snake. She had heard about the big snakes down here and that they didn't generally hurt people so she just watched. He was huge and he just kept coming and coming she figured he had to be at least eight or ten feet long and he had beautiful markings. About that time someone put his hands on her and leaned down next to her and she asked Clayton.

"What kind of snake is it and is it poisonous?" he smiled at her, most women he knew would have already been running back to the city and she was just sitting here watching it and asking questions he had a feeling she wanted to touch it.

"It is called boa constrictor and it is not poisonous but it has a mouth full of teeth and they are nasty and the longest one we have killed was ten feet but we think they get longer in the wild. There are some in the deeper jungle called Anacondas that get much bigger some as big as twenty feet maybe more. They are not around here they live by water we see them sometimes when we are on the river in boats." She looked at him like a kid.

"Can I touch it?" He knew she was going to ask.

"Carefully and then get away from it." She put her hand down on the big snake and stroked it and it just kept going like nothing had happened so she continued finally Clay said.

"Alright you are pushing your luck lets go before he realizes you aren't a branch and comes looking to see what you are." she turned around and started to get up and he grabbed her arm and pulled and she almost screamed she wasn't prepared this time and he caught her off guard. She yanked her arm away and grabbed her side as he looked at her and when she started to breathe again he sat her back down a little further from the snake. He had her look in his eyes and asked her.

"The corset wasn't just vanity was it? What else and if you lie to me I will take you back." When she could breathe again she looked at him.

"I have at least three cracked ribs Camille wrapped me up and helped me put on the corset so I could ride and I have been taking Laudanum for the pain off and on but I couldn't sleep in the hammock so I sat up by the tree." He just looked at her.

"Take off that shirt and let me look at those ribs I want to see how much damage that corset is doing to you." She unbuttoned the shirt and he could see blood spots in different places already from the whale bone stays of the corset where they were digging in. The chemise was clean except for the blood but in this humidity she was at risk for an infection or all kinds of insects breeding in those wounds.

"I have some salve for those open wounds and I am going to have to clean them. Can you ride without the corset?" she shook her head no.

"How many days have you worn that thing?"

"I have worn bandages since I left my home and all through Texas but the corset only since Mexico City we tried to put extra linen at the top so it wouldn't rub. We traveled a lot of the way here on trains in boxcars with the horses."

"Well we are going to have to start using extra padding or you are not going to make it this way. I am cutting those whale bone stays out or shorting them so they don't cut you."

"You mean you are still taking me to your plantation?" he just shook his head yes at her.

"Anybody that would go through this much pain to get away from somebody I intend to help." Stay here and don't go looking for the snake we don't need any more problems." She pulled the shirt the rest of the way off and when he came back he sucked in his breath at how pretty she really was.

She had her back to him and she pulled her hair around to the front of her and he could see her back. He came up behind her and told her to be still as he lifted the chemise and undid the ends of the linen Camille had tied and he started to undo it. When he got it undone Clayton could see the bruise on her side, it was healing but it was still green and yellow. There were other bruises on her neck and back and he could see one on her hip this man who told her he loved her had a funny way of showing it. He had also brought a bowl of clean water and a rag to wash the bleeding spots and some salve his housekeeper sent with him to be used on sores and burns.

"Talk to me and tell me about this man and your husband, how did this get so out of control." She told him the story of her marriage and her brother and Nathan she made it sound so boring but he was enthralled. How could so many men betray one woman and leave her so helpless in a country that wasn't even hers.

"The back is done you are going to have to let me do the front now." "I can do the front myself."

"No you can't, you can't even see the wounds under your breasts. Hold up your chemise and I won't even be able to see your breast if that is what you are worried about." She did just that and then turned around. It didn't make much difference, what he was looking at was her ribs anyway, she had been hurt from the front and if he didn't know better he would have thought the man was trying to kill her. The bruise on her hip was worse from the front and he didn't even ask as he undid her jeans and pulled one side down and back there was a bruise there too. She put one hand down to stop him and one breast almost fell completely out of her chemise. She didn't notice but he was almost in tears he had never seen a women beaten so badly. He gently moved her hand aside and touched the bruise as if he could heal it and then he went up to the one on her ribs then he went higher and rubbed the backside of his fingers against her soft breast. She didn't say anything as she looked down at Clayton.

"This is not how a man makes love to a woman I'll show you how it is done one day." He didn't even realize what he had said to her. She shivered all over as she looked down at him. He went back to cleaning up the wounds and then rewrapped her.

"We will wait till the last minute to put on the corset. Let me have it I am taking out those stays at least those things won't dig into you anymore." She handed it to him and went to the horses till it was time to leave. He brought the corset back and helped her get it on and it did feel better with the stays gone. They went at a slower pace and he kept her within sight now. Ty had made a fuss about leaving and Clayton had finally told him.

"We are not that far from Mexico City and we are on a well travelled trail I could have left you in the jungle and I would have if you would have pulled this further down the line. I won't tolerate a thief in my employ so go back now and anybody else who doesn't agree with me can leave as well." One other man went with him and it wasn't long before they were out of sight as the jungle swallowed them up. Clayton turned and they headed to the village he told Sam about. She felt guilty about being such a problem and Clayton kept looking at her strangely. It was hours later and they stopped for lunch and she started to dismount and he was there to help her, then he walked her out of the others view and said.

"Let me see if you are bleeding through the bandage." She opened her shirt and sure enough she still was in several places.

"Sit here and I will bring you some lunch, just rest." She didn't know how to react to someone helping her besides Wayne. She almost asked him what he wanted from her. He brought her some lunch he had her take off her shirt and he applied some more salve and then he asked her.

"Do you need more laudanum or do you think you can make it till we get to the village you will have a bed tonight if I have to build one?" she looked at him strangely and then asked him a question.

"Why are you doing all this, you have already told me you don't want me and you can have any woman you want so why?" he couldn't look her in the face and then when he did all he could say was.

"The Aztecs and Mayans think fair haired people are gods did you know that? When I first meet you I thought you were just a wounded bird looking for a place to hide; now I don't know what to think of you. As for not wanting you every time I get close to you all I can think about is touching you. I didn't think I would ever want another woman like I wanted my wife but you are quickly proving me wrong. We will be at the village soon and you can rest." Then he turned and left, he was angry and she was discovering he couldn't put his conscience to rest over her. He didn't know how to make sense of his feeling for her.

She tried to stay out of his way at lunch and when they were ready to leave she was already on her horse when he came back to check on her. She made sure she stayed as far back as she could the rest of the day. When they got close to the village it was getting dark and she had gone just about as far as she was going to be able to go. She was hurting and she really needed something sweet to eat. As soon as they got off their horses she was digging in her saddle bags and that is when he came up behind her.

"What is wrong you can barely stand?" she didn't answer she just kept digging until he moved her aside and turned her around.

"What is it Samantha what do you need out of the saddle bags." "Some honey and I need it now." He picked her up and sat her over on a log while he got out the honey. There wasn't much left so he grabbed a spoon and gave it to her then she got some out of the jar and ate it and then another spoonful. He had his man go and get her some water from the well and bring it back and as he watched she was getting better. Her color changed she stopped shaking and within about ten minutes she was better.

"Why was today so bad so quickly and not yesterday?" as he watched she took another bite of the honey.

"Depends on what I eat, bread seems to last longer and if I am in pain it speeds it up, like I said a game you have to learn how to play." He didn't like this game it could kill her and he didn't know all the rules.

"Come on let's get you feed and you can get a bath and get a good night's sleep the owner keeps a house here for when he comes through to check on his properties. He is a friend and I have got permission to use it. She followed him to the small house it wasn't large but it was very nice the man liked his luxury when he was here. Supper was good she found out later it was iguana she didn't care it tasted good anyway.

There were papaya and oranges and she ate several of them nobody realized how lucky they were to just be able to reach out and pick them. Clayton took her to a large bedroom where there was a bath waiting and he told her they were going to stay for another day so she could rest, so bath and go to bed. A dark haired girl came in and helped her with a bath and to wash her hair and then left. Sam was drying her hair and then she sat down at a little table to brush her hair when she saw him walk in the door. He was wearing only white pants and barefoot like the natives and he came up behind her. She turned and he took her breath away he had a tattoo on his chest and arm and it was beautiful. She stood up and touched his chest and hand and just looked at him. Then he took the brush from her hand and starting brushing her hair.

He didn't say anything he just held her hair and brushed it and pulled it back from her face. He leaned down and kissed her neck, all she had on was the bath sheet she had tied around her when she got out of the tub. He turned her around put his arms around her and kissed her.

"Do you want me?" she shook her head yes.

"Put your arms around me and kiss me back and I will teach you what it is like to have a man make love to you that wants you and won't hurt you." She looked up at him and put her hands on both sides of his face and asked him.

"You told me this is exactly what you didn't want to happen between us." "I lied even to myself." Then he stopped.

"Do you know if your man in Texas may have left you pregnant?" She kind of laughed to herself and looked up at him.

"No, he beat me and raped me so badly there was no chance of that. From what the doctor told me maybe never a chance of that ever, but it wouldn't hurt to be careful anyway if that is what you are asking." His wounded bird was more than wounded she was broken.

"Nathan took everything from me except my life and almost that." Maybe if he had her he wouldn't want her anymore. As she watched him he was somewhere else so she asked him.

"You sure you still want to do this you can still leave I am a bundle of problems." He reached down and untied the sheet around her and led her to the bed and stood her in front of him. He looked at her ribs and hip and then he saw her knee it was healing green and yellow too. He looked at her with a question in his eyes.

"He threw me against the end of my brass bed and I hit it hard and then I landed on the floor unconscious."

"I am sure I want you and I will be careful so we can figure out the rest later." He pulled off his pants and then they lay down next to each other. She was so soft and he pulled her next to him so he could just touch her. Her breasts were against his side and she was running her hand down his chest, he had his hand in her hair and he was kissing her neck and the side of her face. She had put her leg in between his legs and she was just looking at him until he asked.

"What are you looking at?"

"You, I have had a husband and you know the rest but I have never just been able to look at a man and you sir are quite good looking, are all men this good looking? The tattoo was it for your wife?" he didn't know how to answer the question but he had just decided he didn't want her looking at anybody else's body but his ever.

"Well tonight my body is the only one you need to concentrate on and I will love looking at yours. The tattoo I got long before I married while I was on the ships my father owned." He pulled her mouth to his and kissed her until she was kissing back and he was holding her hair in his hands like it was spun gold. The first thing that came to him was they would make beautiful children together. His mouth went to her breast and he suckled it until she was squirming in his arms and he went lower to her stomach. Nathan had never been gentle with her and he ran his hands down her leg it was soft as velvet. He rolled her over and entered her and she looked up at him in surprise and then she joined him when she got the rhythm. She was clawing the sheets and he told her.

"Hold me and look into my eyes I want to watch you when you climax I want to be the first man who brings you over the top." She clung to him as he stroked and stroked and she looked at him and she finally came as she arched back to meet him. Then she began to breathe again normally and he retreated before he came just in case. He had left his seed on her stomach and he went to get a cloth and clean himself up and her and when he came back and cleaned her up he was almost sorry he had done that. He couldn't help thinking he wanted this woman and getting her pregnant would be the best way no matter what that doctor in Texas had said. He lay down next to her and she rolled over and looked at him.

"So that is how it is supposed to be." He looked in eyes that should be his now and he was already regretting his earlier actions.

"Yes a man shouldn't have to beat a woman to keep her. Would you mind if I spent the night in this bed with you Samantha?"

"I think I would like that if it isn't going to be a problem." Oh it already was a problem and he had started something he didn't know how to finish. He pulled her to his side and she drifted off to sleep and he just listened to her breath. How terrifying it must have been to her parents to not have been able to awaken her and not know why. Now he was just watching her and wondering why he couldn't sleep. After a while it began to rain and he slept as well.

She awoke to a sound and she wasn't quite sure what it was but it was something. She listened and then she got out of bed and lit the candle by her side of the bed. She picked up the bath sheet shook it then tied it around her again. Then she pulled the machete out of the scabbard on the table and started looking around the room. Clayton was awake by now and said.

"What are you looking for?" he started to get off the bed he was concerned about her having the machete in her hand.

"There is something in here and it is moving and I can hear it. Can you light the lamp beside you without getting out of the bed?" she was coming around the bed as she asked him that question. He did as she asked and then she found what she was looking for.

"Don't move there is a large snake beside the bed and if you get out of bed you are going to step on it."

"It is probably just another constrictor nothing serious." She looked at him and said.

"This one looks different it looks like the rattlers we have in Texas it has a large triangle head and it has distinctive blotched markings but I don't think it is a friendly snake." As he looked down at the snake on the floor he scooted over on the bed.

"You my dear are absolutely right. That one is called a Fer-de-lance and it is deadly and you probably just saved my life. What are you going to do now?" she looked up at him and smiled.

"I think the best idea would be to kill it don't you." Then she grabbed a broom from the corner and pulled him out a little further and with one swipe cut off his head. Then there were men knocking at the door and she was standing in the middle of the room. She was putting the snakes head on the end of the machete and she was taking it over to the table and she put it in an empty bowl.

"Be careful with that thing." Clayton was getting out of the bed and going to the door as the men entered.

"Oh I will he is not dead enough yet but I want to look at him later." He told the man at the door everything was alright as he handed them the dead snake. They just looked at her, machete in hand; half dressed looking at the dead snakes head with her blond hair falling down her back.

"Ask them if I can have the skin?" she didn't even look back at their startled faces. Clayton hustled them out of the room. He took the knife out of her hand and led her back to bed. He got her covered back up and she snuggled down beside him and went back to sleep. He just lay there smiling like an idiot he didn't think anyone would ever take the place of his dead wife until tonight and now she was laying in his arms. She said she might never have children after what had been done to her but he already had two children would that be enough for her. Could his children fill the hole in her life? One step at a time she was still learning to trust him, don't rush things or your wounded bird might fly away from you.

He awoke before the first light and was kissing her neck and started fondling her breast again. He couldn't seem to get enough of just touching her skin he couldn't understand how a man could have done so much damage to her in the name of love. What was his plan after he beat her half to death? Did he really expect her to stay around and love him forever or marry him what an idiot? She awoke to his kisses and put her arms around his neck and pulled him to her she was beginning to enjoy his body on hers. Now she wanted to touch and feel as well so she pushed him back and in the gentle darkness and she began to learn what a man likes as well. He took her hand and he led her where she had never been and then she started to wander on her own and before they knew what was happening they were making love again and this time she had started it.

She ran her hands over his back and down his buttocks and then rested in his hair and then she watched him again as he took her over the top. Her world exploded and she went flying it was wonderful better than she could ever have believed. If this was the only man she ever got she would have this to remember. He had retreated again even though he really didn't want to this time but he did. He again cleaned her and himself up and then he promised himself the next time this happened she would be all his or it wouldn't happen again. The smile on his face told him it was going to happen again.

"Go back to sleep we are staying here tomorrow so you can rest."

"I thought I was delaying everything and you were in a hurry?" as he pulled her closer he smiled into the dark.

"Things have changed somewhat since Mexico City we will talk some more in the morning." She just put her arm over his chest and went back to sleep whatever he wanted was alright for now, tomorrow was another day. Since his wife died he almost never kept a woman more than a night and then he generally sent them away. If they stayed the night he never wanted them to sleep close to him but he couldn't get her close enough he was almost laying on her. He wouldn't let go of her hair and he had her leg in between his like she was going to go somewhere. He could feel her breath on his chest in gentle puffs and then he laid his head on top of hers and went to sleep. When she awoke in the morning he was gone and she got up to dress when he came in the door.

"Stop what you are doing and get back in bed you are going to rest today we aren't going anywhere for a while at least." He had a tray with fruit and water and a glass of juice on it and tortillas and there was enough for two. He pushed the door shut with his foot and he put the tray down on the small table and she just looked at him. She did grab her gown and pulled it on and sat down.

"Oh I liked it much better with no clothes at all." She looked at him sideways and smirked.

"I am sure you did but I feel better with something on." she sat on the bed beside him and looked at all the food and then he took her face in his hands and kissed her.

"Are you all right this morning?" she just smiled back and kissed him gently on the mouth and didn't say anymore. Then she started to eat as he watched her. He had noticed she always drank the juice first then she ate, it was like she knew that was what she needed first, so he put that away in his memory. He was learning the rules fast. He planned on learning them all because he had decided last night he was never letting his little bird go.

She took tortillas and wrapped meat and tomatoes in them and ate them and then quite a bit of fresh fruit. She even had some hot tortillas with butter mixed with honey. When she had had enough Clayton told her he was going to go check on the men and animals and would be back later for her to go back to bed. Then he turned and asked her.

"I am going to the monastery this afternoon to get you some more honey and they are excavating and old Mayan ruin would you like to come with me? We will walk the horses so you don't have to put on that torture chamber of a corset on to go that small of a distance?"

"I would love to come especially to see the Mayan temple."

"I will come back in a while and we will have lunch and then we will go." She just lay back down in the bed and went back to sleep it was the first time she had felt safe in a long time. She slept hard because it was several hours later when Clayton came back for them to have lunch. They ate in the small dining room and were waited on by several of the staff that kept the house for the owner when he was gone. More hot tortillas and butter with what was left of the honey, fresh squeezed orange juice and some sort of meat. She had stopped asking she just ate it if it tasted good she kept her mouth shut. During the war they had eaten a lot of different things and she had stopped asking what it was, she did the same here.

"That was delicious and the meat was wonderful." He looked at her funny and then said.

"You aren't even going to ask what it was." "Not unless it is going to kill me?"

"Actually you killed it. It was the Fer-de-lance it has been marinating in milk and it was served to you because you killed it. That snake was responsible for the deaths of two of the village children in the past couple of months and if not for you it probably would have got me last night. The village thinks you are a snake spirit because someone told them you petted the python and took the head of the Fer-de-lance.

"Did you tell them I was just curious about the python?"

"I did and that confused them even more they don't understand why a woman would even wonder about a snake let alone touch it. Then I told them you thought it was pretty and now they are sure you are a snake spirit."

"Do I even want to know if that is that a bad thing, or a good thing about the snake?" Clayton was smiling at her.

"A good thing a very good thing the Mayans revered the snake it is part of the folklore and now so are you."

"All right then now can we go see the ruins?" As she got up there were several people standing around and she asked Clayton what was the problem.

"They just want you to tell them you were pleased with the meal especially that woman over in the corner it was one of her children that were killed by the snake. Samantha went over to the lady and leaned down to her ear and said something in Spanish and the woman started to cry and Sam hugged her and then she thanked the rest of the room and she walked out the door with Clayton. When they got outside their horses were saddled and she went to get on Sundance and Clayton stopped her.

"What did you say to her?"

"I asked her if she had other children and she said yes. I told her, her child could rest now, so she could take care of the others the danger was gone."

"Is it gone how can you be sure?"

"Most snakes have a territory unless they are breeding and that was a big snake so this was probably his territory so they ought to be all right for a while till another snake takes it over. Shall we go?" he helped her up on her horse and off they went as he looked back the woman was going into the room they had stayed in last night and he bet it was spotless when they came back.

"Did you ask if I can have the skin it would make a beautiful belt or a hatband?" Clayton just looked at her and smiled.

"I did ask. I am sure they would love for you to have it. I will check on it when we get back."

CHAPTER 3

They rode and just talked and it was most pleasant the road was wide enough for both of them to ride side by side and she didn't have to wear her corset. When she saw the church she began to get cold chills it didn't belong out here it was something that belonged in Spain. It was one of those tall brick buildings she had seen there but this one couldn't have been more than fifty years old stained glass and all. It sat a distance from a Mayan ruin and there were priests working on the ruin trying to restore, from what Clayton said. They stopped as a priest came towards them and Clayton got down and helped her down and introduced him.

"Sam this is my old friend Father Michel he is the head man around here and he is the head beekeeper." She just nodded and stood her ground. Clayton had never seen her act this way towards anybody.

We were wondering if you had some extra honey we could buy from you my lady needs some and I will donate to the church of course." They both laughed Sam didn't she still stood back away from him and said nothing.

"May I go and see the ruins that they are working on?" Clayton looked at her she was being rude and she was never rude. She remounted Sundance and rode towards the ruins. It wasn't far so it didn't take long. When she got there she got off her horse and started up the stairs. She could see they had been making progress putting back the broken stones to see the outside walls again. A priest was coming down to meet her when a man about her age started screaming above her. She and the priest started running and she could see Clayton coming as well. When they got to where the boy was, his arm was caught under a piece of stone they had been trying to put in place on the wall.

As she got there one of the priests had a machete and was going to cut the young man's arm off so she stopped him. He turned and looked at her and he was furious. She got in front of him and was trying to push the stone off the boys arm or trying to pull it up. Clayton saw what she was doing and told her to quit he was coming. He was afraid she was going to damage those ribs some more. The priest started talking.

"Move woman after I cut off his arm we can move the stone without damaging it, the boy is of no consequence. Sam turned around and backhanded the man and he landed on his butt. He came up mad and he had that machete in his hand ready to use it on her. A shot rang out and the machete fell out of the priests hand and as he was shaking feeling back into it Samantha went back to the boy. Clayton was coming and she grabbed the machete and put it under the rock and pried the stone up and off the boy until he got there. Two other young Mayan men were there by now helping her take the weight off of the boys hand and when Clayton got there they got him out from under the stone.

Father Michel was there by now asking what was going on. Father John started to explain.

"We were trying to set this stone so we could see what the symbol is when the Indian dropped it on his arm. I was simply going to chop off his arm and then take my time resetting the stone when this woman interrupted me."

"You would have chopped off his arm just so you wouldn't mess up your stone what kind of man are you."

"He is just a heathen whose people sacrificed people on alters they are nothing, they are expendable." She looked at him and shook her head and then she let him have it.

"What about the French revolution where they beheaded men, women, children and babies just because they were aristocrats. Or your own Spanish inquisition that was sacrificing on a grand scale but as long as you do it in the name of your lord it is all right. How much blood has been spilt in this world in the name of someone's god? I was in Spain when they burnt a woman. She confessed to being a witch in front of her husband and child so they would strangle her before they burned her. Her husband swore she was innocent. I stayed and watched in the shadows as the Bishop who accused her watched her burn." she was furious as she tried to help the boy in front of her.

"The Queen herself hid me that night. The next morning I was escorted to a boat by her personal guard and the Bishop was waiting at the pier for me as I got on board. As we sailed away he was furious I knew too much and I got away. I saw all your pretty clean churches while the people starved outside and this priest would have cut off this boy's arm for a stone so who here is the heathen. They only try to hold on to land that has been theirs for thousands of years, I would fight too." She was furious and screaming at the priest.

"Now I am taking this boy down and try and take care of him so get out of my way. By the way the symbol on the stone is a bird and it looks like it was painted at some time different colors maybe it is one of those birds that live in the rain forests a Quetzal." She started leading the young man away and the priest reached for him.

"He isn't hurt that bad he can continue working and then he will be tended too I will see to it." And then he kind of leered at her. She could see the whip marks on his back and she already knew what kind of treatment he was going to receive so she smiled back and said.

"He is coming with me now his arm is broken and if you don't like it come on we can go at this again." He had picked up the machete again and had it in his hands and was coming at her when the elder priest called him off.

"Father I don't know exactly what you have in mind but I think you owe this woman an apology and she will take this young man down and help him and you and I will talk later after supper. I wasn't aware of what was going on up here and I think we need to talk about your treatment of the men under your control." He walked up beside Samantha and helped her with the young man to get him down the stairs. They got the young man down the stairs and Clayton put him up on his horse and got up behind him. Samantha went ahead and was going to get things ready. When she went into the bedroom there was a man lying on the bed with his arms crossed behind his head.

"Well, well who are you?" she just looked at him.

"I could ask you the same question but I don't have the time right now, move I need some things and you are in my way." She went to rummaging through her saddle bags and got her laudanum and set it aside and then got some linen for bandages. The man was standing at the doorway just watching as they brought the boy into the room. The girl that had helped her bath was at the door as well and she was looking at the boy like she knew him and she was scared for him. Samantha saw the look that passed between the two of them but she didn't say anything instead she asked the girl to help her. Clayton was helping the boy into the room when he saw the other man.

"Hello Russell what are you doing here?" the man stood there with his arms crossed and then answered him.

"Well I planned on using the room tonight but it looks like it is taken, is she?" both men looked at Samantha. She looked up and said.

"Put him over there against the wall I am going to have to set that arm and he will have to be straight when I do it. What is your name honey?" she was looking at the girl and was speaking Spanish she was ignoring the man at the door and he knew it.

Te'a mistress how can I help?" her English wasn't wonderful but she could at least understand her, the boy only spoke Mayan Clayton was going to have to talk to him. She looked at the girl and told her.

"I will need some straight sticks and a glass of water for him to drink and a bowl of water to clean him up with can you get that for me and bring it back here?" the girl almost ran out of the room as the priest from the ruins came into the room. He reached down to grab the boys arm and she brushed it away. Then he grabbed her hair and started to pull her up. That didn't last long he was promptly thrown out by two very large and angry men. Clayton handed him off to Russell and said.

"Deal with him before I do something stupid." Russell was holding the man by his collar and his feet were almost off the ground.

"Why me you are the catholic? I think it is time for you to go Padre if you know what is good for you." He took him outside and rather forcefully pushed him out on the porch.

"I really think you should stay there Padre." Then he went back inside he wanted to watch. He wanted to see if that woman could get that Mayan boy to let her set his broken arm without both Clayton and him sitting on him. When he got back she was starting to get things together and she took a glass of water and put a couple of drops of laudanum in it and had Clayton tell him to drink it. He shook his head no, she just looked at him and smiled and then she took a sip. He again said no. She handed it to Te'a and whispered in her ear and then she backed up a little and left them alone. Te'a sat down beside him and laid her head on his shoulder and he put his head on hers then she spoke into his ear and he looked at Samantha. He reached out and took the water from Te'a and drank it all and laid his arm in Samantha's hands.

"Samantha what are you going to do now it looks like he trusts you." "Not me he trusts her. She is something to him maybe you can find out while the painkiller goes to work. Who is the man over there?" Clayton looked back over his shoulder and told her.

"His name is Russell Henderson he lives on the next plantation to me which is to say he lives about twenty miles away from me, but he is my closest neighbor. Russell this is Samantha Rodgers she is my new governess." He was looking her up and down like she was a piece of beef. So she finally asked him.

"You through yet or do you want to look some more." He just grinned at her.

"Oh I could look all day but that is not what I really want to be doing.

How in the world did he find you?"

"I advertised for a job and I picked him for an employer it is as simple as that." He kept staring at her; nothing was as simple as that. Clayton walked back over to her and she turned around.

"You are the one from the dance they are all talking about that governess?" she just nodded her head.

"You were right they were to be married and she was captured by some raiders and brought here and he came looking for her he was captured as well and that priest bought him and the other two boys and he has been using them ever since. They keep it secret about the two of them because they were afraid of what the priest might do with the information. I will talk to Father Michel tomorrow about the situation and see if I can do anything." The look in Sam's eyes told Russell this woman wasn't going to wait until tomorrow to do something so he was just going to wait and see what she did, this was getting good.

Samantha sat down beside the boy whose name she still didn't know and took his arm. She told Te'a she needed to pull it to straighten it out and align the bone and she would have to hold the end of the arm by the elbow if she thought she was strong enough. The men started to object and she just looked at them.

"A man can put up with a lot more pain than you think when the woman he wants is watching so back off and leave us alone if we can't do it then you can help." She looked at Te'a and then felt his arm and she could feel the bone where it was broken and she looked at the boy and then she put her hand over the break and said.

"Are you ready? I am going to pull until it is in place and then I will stop if I can't get it in place I will stop and one of the men will take your place." She shook her head and held his arm and the Sam started to pull and gently turn till she felt the bone slide back in place and it was smooth again then she stopped. He had never made a sound but the men behind her were cringing. There was a reason men didn't have children the race would have died off civilizations ago. She smiled at the boy and patted his face and looked at Te'a she was going to get them out of here somehow.

"I am going down and see if I can get some food for him to eat I am sure that priest won't let the girls bring any up unless I go personally. I will be back in a little while and wrap it just have him rest. You two figure out the sleeping arrangements." As she went to the kitchen she found on her plate at the table a carved figurine made of what looked like green jade, a small one you would wear on a necklace. She was pretty sure it was a Mayan figure of the snake she had seen at the ruins. She picked it up and held it in her hands for a second when Father John came in.

"You kill a snake and now they give you a pagan emblem to wear what are you going to do with it you should smash it."

Samantha just looked at the priest he was angry about the boy but there was more to the story.

"Why are you restoring that ruin you obviously don't like these people or their beliefs so why?"

"I was ordered here to do it, I would much rather be deciphering scrolls at the Vatican but they felt I was more valuable here." Right he had pissed somebody off and got sent here for punishment. He would never be sent back to Spain. She looked up and saw the woman from this morning and smiled and took the figurine and put it in her pocket and winked at her she would put it on a chain in a while. She would be proud to wear it. She went to the kitchen and got plenty of food and went back upstairs there was more than enough but she had something in mind and Clayton probably wasn't going to like it. When she got back Clayton and Russell were arguing outside the door and they didn't see her put most of the food under the bed and she put her finger to her mouth when she turned around so Te'a wouldn't say anything. She went to the boy and started to feed him with some stew she had brought with her and then gave it to Te'a to feed him. Clayton came back in the room and started talking to her.

"Russell is taking the room next door to us tonight and then he is leaving with us tomorrow. You can treat your patient until tonight and then he going to have to go back with the priests that is the best I can do Father Michel said he would watch out for him." Russell was watching her face he could see this woman wasn't going to let that other priest let him anywhere near that boy again but she just hadn't figured out how to get them out of here yet.

"Sam, are you listening to me that is the best I can do about it right now?" She looked behind him to Russell and he was smiling at her and she realized he already knew she was going to do something; maybe he would help her if she asked him. Clayton walked out of the room to the porch to talk to the priest and ask them if they wanted to have supper when they came back tonight. When they left she walked over to this man she didn't know and just looked at his smiling face and said.

"Well any ideas or are you just going to stand there and smile at me all day?"

"You need a distraction of some kind and I don't know what but you have to keep all eyes on you for a few minutes so they can escape can you do that somehow?" he was still thinking when she turned and grabbed a small box off the dresser and took out a silver chain and then the carved pendant from her pocket. She threaded the chain through the little snake pendant and turned around and asked Russell to hook it for her. When he saw what it was she hooked on it and then asked her.

"You are the woman who killed the Fer-de-lance last night?" she just nodded her head and started waking outside. They had put the snakes head in a glass jar in the dining room filled with alcohol. They said she wanted to look at it later the whole village was talking about her. This blond beauty took off that snakes head half dressed at night, he just smiled and followed her outside.

Father John was still arguing, he wanted the boy now and they were trying to talk him out of it.

"He needs rest and you can't take him now I forbid it. You will have to go through me to do it, so shut the hell up. You can have him after supper or not at all." The men had all shut up by then and were just watching the two of them.

"The bishop should have killed you when you were in Spain."

"He tried. The woman he had strangled wasn't dead and by the time she awoke he had sent all his guards and her husband and child away so he was alone with her. He didn't see me in the shadows and I just watched and listened. When she awoke he told her she shouldn't have refused him. This was a good lesson to any woman who ever thought about refusing him ever again and then he lit the fire. She saw me and then he saw I was hiding in the shadows. He looked at me and he had an evil grin on his face."

"Now you know what happens to any woman who refuses me. You are the girl from the castle last night aren't you?"

"Then the other woman said 'RUN'. I turned and ran. He chased me all the way to the castle but his men were too far away to catch me and one of her majesties ladies in waiting hide me until the next morning. I wrote down everything I heard and saw that night and gave it to her majesty. The Queen was afraid of the bishop and now she had some leverage against him. The next morning my father and I left with a royal escort and the bishop watched me from the harbor he couldn't stop me. I stood on the side of that ship until I couldn't see him anymore." Father John said.

"You lie you were never at court and you never danced for the Queen I don't believe you." Samantha looked at Russell and smiled and said.

"I could prove it to you if I had a guitar player that knew the flamenco I would dance it tonight at supper, and you leave that boy alone until then." Russell smiled and said.

"If I have to go back to Mexico City I will find a guitar player but I think I have a man good enough to play what you need or he has been bragging about how good he is. I guess we will find out tonight at supper."

"Good tonight at supper then." She turned and walked back inside she had things to do and not a lot of time to do them in. When she got back inside the first thing she did was check the boys arm and make sure it wasn't swelling to bad just as two men were looking at her from the back door. Father John had posted them there to make sure she didn't let the boy go. Well if everything went well tonight she would have to get their attention as well. While Clayton was still busy she took the empty laudanum bottle and the full one and put half of the bottle in the empty one and put the cork in it. She showed it to Te'a and then hid it with the food she had hidden under the bed. She then talked to Te'a before Clayton came back in the room. Russell had already come back and was watching at the door for anyone else.

"Te'a I am going to dance tonight and try to attract everybody's attention for a few minutes when I do you have to get both of ya'll out of here and into the jungle do you understand me?" Russell translated to the boy and he nodded.

"I put some laudanum in the pack under the bed now only give him one or two drops no more and wait as long as you can it will make him sleepy." That was all she could say, Clayton was coming back and she had to shut up. Before he came back in she took off her machete and slid it under the bed beside the pack so no one could see. She rigged up a sling for the boy to take the pressure off his arm as Clayton watched and then she took out a bag she had been carrying since they had left Mexico City and pulled out a beautiful black ruffled dress and a tortoise shell comb and a pair of dancing shoes.

"May I use the room next door to dress in so they can have some time alone?" Russell just nodded and left to go talk to the man who was going to play for her tonight and Clayton followed her into the other room. She sat down at a table and brushed her hair then pulled it up to put in an intricate carved tortoise shell comb. Then she had him help her into the corset. Samantha had Clayton help her put on the most beautiful dress he had ever seen. It was yards and yards of black ruffles low on her shoulders and cut up the front to show her legs and feet while she danced. The only thing it didn't cover were the finger marks on her neck they still showed.

"Do you want your necklace to cover them?" she shook her head no when she moved tonight they would be in the way. She would try to cover what she could with makeup and that would have to do.

"Whose dress is that and where did you get such a beautiful comb?" she smiled in the mirror at a blond flamenco dancer.

"The lady that taught me to dance Lena Baca, she sent it with me; I didn't find it until after we sailed she died shortly after. She knew she didn't have long and she wanted me to have the dress. The comb came from The Queen to hold up my hair." He took her hands and stood her up and looked at her, he didn't believe her of course it had to be a lie.

"Are you as good at this as the dances at the ball?" "You are going to have to wait and see."

"I am sorry things didn't work out like you wanted them to about the boy I will try again before we leave." She didn't say anything and that worried him.

"Time to go the light is fading give me a kiss for luck." He leaned down and kissed her as Russell watched. They walked into the dining room and even Father John knew a flamenco dress when he saw one. They had set up the porch out back so everyone could watch and most of the village was behind the porch as well. The rest of the men were inside and she saw the guards at the door were watching as well.

Russell was watching the guards and would signal when Te'a and the boy were gone. So she began they had set out candles for more light and she had her castanets in her hands. She began to clack them and the guitar began to play slowly and then faster as she began to move her feet to the music. Then she started to turn and tap her feet and brush her dress against the men closest to her and she was getting all the attention she wanted. She even brushed up to the guards and got there undivided attention. She went around the room twice and Russell had nodded to her on the first time they were gone so she gave them a little more head start.

By the second time she was exhausted and she had to stop so she made a grand flourish and swirled on the flour to a standing ovation. She could barely breath Clayton had to help her up she was so tired. The guards were back in place and she could barely stand she really needed to eat she hadn't had lunch; she had sent all of her lunch with Te'a and the young man. With all this exercise she needed some sugar and some food. She was going to eat so she sat down at the end of the table she hadn't even got a plate before that priest figured out what she had done. She was barley seated when the guards found out their captives were gone and Father John came after her.

She just sat there while he railed at her and Clayton was mad as well he knew she had helped them escape he was furious. Russell just sat at the end of the table and grinned at her. She rolled her eyes and got up and went back out to the porch and looked at the jungle.

"Do you think they will get away?"

"I think so from what I hear out there Father Michel is saying he is not going to send anybody after them. He is also yelling at Clayton something about honey, what is that conversation all about?"

"I needed some honey to get to the plantation. I need the sugar but now he may not give any to Clayton after this little stunt I pulled." She was leaning against the porch railing with her hands on the rail and he was leaning over her and he reached down and kissed her shoulder.

"Do I make you that nervous you are shaking like a leaf and you taste sweet what is going on?" Clayton was listening and then he yelled from the dining room.

"Catch her before she falls." Russell grabbed her around the waist before she fell over backwards off the porch and then he picked her up and carried her to Clayton who grabbed her wrist. He put his head on her chest and listened and then turned around and looked at the table and her place was empty and he couldn't remember when she ate last.

"Damn, bring her in here and put her on the bed she is barely breathing." Russell laid her down.

"What is going on she was just fine a few minutes ago?" the woman who gave her the pendant was at the door and Clayton rattled off some instructions and Father Michel was standing at the doorway.

"Is this what you were talking about Clayton? Can you wake her?" Clayton shook his head no.

"I will be back soon you do whatever you can until then my friend." Russell just looked at her and Clayton was taking things from the woman walking back into the room.

"How can I help?"

"We have to try and get some sugar into her a little at a time and not choke her. Her body doesn't make enough and she was so intent on helping them escape she didn't pay attention to herself." The woman had brought a small spoon for a child and scooted the men aside so she could get to her and she was spooning orange juice slowly down her throat. She motioned to Clayton to help her get the dress off of her so she could breathe easier. The men held her up while the woman took it off and then the corset and while they were doing that Russell saw the bruise on her rib. He looked at Clayton and asked him.

"You better not have done that to her."

"I didn't she is running from the man who did, that is why she is working for me." They just kept spooning juice down her throat.

"I take it this has happened before?" Clayton looked up at him and then answered him.

"Several days ago on the trail but it wasn't this bad. She said when she was little it happened and it took them longer to bring her around I should have been paying more attention. She says it is a game you have to learn how to play." About then Father Michel walked back in with a jar of honey in his hand. Clayton took the small spoon and put a little of it in her mouth and just let it dissolve and she began to come around. They had covered her with a sheet but she didn't know for a second who all these people were and she panicked. Clayton grabbed her hands pulled her to his chest and talked softly into her ear.

"Samantha its Clayton you passed out, you didn't eat and we are trying to get some honey down you so stop fighting me and eat some more honey." When Clayton leaned her up and was talking to her Russell could see more bruising on her back and a large one on her hip he would talk to Clayton later. The woman in the room she seemed to trust the most so Clayton told everybody else to leave and he left as well. Samantha talked to the woman in Spanish and she told her what had happened until she could remember and then Sam touched the pendant on her chest. The woman touched it and smiled and told her to lie down she would bring her some more food she would be back in a few minutes. Clayton stood at the door and Sam finally looked at him and said.

"How bad was it this time? Did they get away? I don't remember?" Clayton walked back into the room and sat on the side of the bed and pulled her back up to his chest. He held her head next to him but she still wasn't quite sure about who he was yet.

"You passed out this time for about an hour after you did the flamenco. You got them out of here I don't know why you didn't trust me to do it, I might have taken longer but I would have gotten it done."

"They needed to be gone from here before someone hurt her she can still give him a family I couldn't risk leaving her here and not letting her have that chance. Nathan took that away from me. I could at least give that to them."

"We are not sure about that Samantha, the doctor in Texas could be wrong." She just looked at him as the woman came back in the room with some warm tortillas and tamales so he left so she would eat. He went to the porch and Russell was there waiting for him and he wanted some answers. He had a cigar in his mouth and they could hear drums in the distance in the jungle. Russell offered him a cigar and he took and lit it and they stood there for a minute before Clayton pointed to the jungle and asked.

"When did those start I didn't hear them until now." Russell looked out over the jungle and pointed into Samantha's room and commented.

"Not until she finished and the boy and girl were well into the jungle. They have been getting louder ever since, I think they are looking for him, I think they have been for some time. Who is she and who did that to her and what about a Texas doctor?"

"How much did you see?" Russell looked at him and then told him. "Enough to kill the man who did it so it better not have been you." "It wasn't I didn't find about it till we were already several days into this journey and she was hurting so bad she couldn't hide it anymore.

I found her through Camille Rivas in Mexico City she wanted to be a governess. She is a widow but a man in her hometown wanted her and beat her almost to death to prove his love." Russell just looked at him.

"Don't ask me it doesn't make sense to me either but she is still running from him and I am taking her to my plantation."

"She sleeping with you what are you planning on doing with her, marrying her or is she going to be a conquest like some of the other plantation owners around here."

"Why are you asking Russell? I saw how you looked at her you always have a woman on your arm what would you do with her.""She is different than most of the women I meet she goes out of her way to help a Mayan boy get away and wants to go into the jungle to live. She could be a woman to marry and keep on a plantation out here, what was that talk about the doctor in Texas that she is so worried about?"

"The man in Texas beat her so badly he may have taken away her chances of having children and I already have two so she thinks that maybe somehow makes it alright. I am not sure she would even marry me. Right now she doesn't have the highest regard of men."

"Good to know, I could always buy her some children. What do you mean two children I thought you only had a son."

"I have a daughter too." Russell just looked at him he thought his daughter had died with his wife.

"What is this man's name if he happens to show up at my place he won't show up at yours he will be food for the crocs? Was she using laudanum for pain?"

"Yes how did you know that? She takes it so she can ride you saw just a little of the damage he did to her."

"She gave the boy half of what she had when he left for his arm." Clayton looked at him.

"Of course she did and she wouldn't have told me she would have just dealt with the pain." Russell was standing there puffing on his cigar and smiling at him.

"Just say the word and I will wait here with her till she is better and then take her to my plantation no questions asked if she will come with me. I like a challenge." About that time Sam came out dressed in a gown and a robe and came to stand by them both she put her hand on the post holding up the roof overhead and just looked out at the jungle.

"What is with the drums?" about that time Father John came into the dining room yelling at her and she just sighed.

"Here we go again." About that time an arrow hit the post she was holding on to just below her hand and the drumming stopped. She froze where she stood. She went to move away and another arrow hit just above her hand so she just stood her ground. Two men were pushed out of the jungle with their hands tied in front of them and a stick behind them between their elbows and back. They were being pushed by two other men into a small clearing and then they stopped. They were saying something she couldn't understand but Clayton could so he was translating.

"They want to know if you are the woman who helped the boy escape today the snake lady?" she just nodded yes and out walked a large man with a large horseshoe headdress on. He pushed the other two men forward and then said something else. Russell turned to Father John and asked him.

"You sent those men after the boy and the girl didn't you even after Father Michel told you not to."

"They were mine and I wanted them back." Father Michel was in the room by now and he was furious and he was asking Father John the same question? "Do you ever follow any of my instructions or do you do exactly as you wish?" the man below was talking again so Clayton was listening and then he turned and told them what had been said.

"It seems you captured a Mayan Chieftains son and now he has him back and he wants the other two boys as well in exchange for these two men. I suggest you get them and give them to him if you don't want all the people in this village dead." Sam was still standing on the porch it seemed the Chieftain wanted her in his sight so she just stood there.

"Who is this man and why are you so scared of him?"

"He is like a chief of an Indian tribe only Mayan and right now he is mad and it seems you are the only one he likes." It didn't take Father John long to get the other boys back to the house and they were on the porch and standing beside her. After he had pushed them out he hid behind the door. She could see why he wouldn't come out he had beaten them and their backs were a mess. She turned and looked daggers at him.

"Clayton please get me a jar of that salve out of the saddlebags in the bedroom please." When he brought it to her she took down her hand and took one of the boys hands and put the bottle in it and had Russell tell them how to use it and then she pointed down to the other two men and sent them on their way. She didn't even realize she had let go of the pole till she looked down at the man in the clearing and he was smiling at her as she quickly put her hand back up on the pole and kind of nodded her head sideways and smiled. When the boys got to him he was not a happy man and he was going to kill the other men and she yelled down to him.

"We had a deal." They all held their breath, she was yelling at a Mayan Chieftain, he turned and told one of his men something and then there was another arrow shot at her, this time there was something tied to it. It hit right under one of the other ones and tied to the arrow was a small green bottle, her laudanum, their deal was done and the other two men were almost to the porch and the drums had stopped again. The man below nodded to her and she bowed to him and he smiled and she took the arrow and stepped back inside with it. When she looked back everybody was gone and the clearing was empty. Both men just looked at her as she walked past them but she stopped when she got to father John and slapped his face.

"You almost got all of us killed. You shouldn't be left in charge of servants or workers you don't take care of them."

"You have no right to talk to me that way woman or give me orders." He turned to walk away but Father Michel stood in his way.

"She may not but I do from now on you will work in the church and not on the ruins unless someone else is overlooking the dig. She is right you care nothing for anyone but yourself and that ends now. We will be leaving I will see you and your party off in the morning." He stopped in front of Sam and took her hand and kissed it.

"I hope you are not afraid of all of the priests of the church we are not all alike." Then they left. Clayton took her arm and they went back to their room for the night. Russell just watched. He was really hoping Clayton would screw this up she was a woman worth waiting for. Clayton got her into the bedroom and sat her down on the bed and asked her.

"Have you had enough to eat or do you need more honey before we go to bed?" it was almost funny his concern but it was always like this after she had a blackout everybody panicked, sometimes she thought that was why her brother disliked her so much was because of the attention everyone gave her. Maybe that was why he went to drinking so much just to get someone's attention because he sure wasn't getting it any other way. She wondered if he was alright she had the strangest feeling he wasn't but she couldn't help him from here.

"I am fine now. I just gave all my lunch and everything else to the children and didn't have time to eat and after the dance I had just used up all my energy and crashed. It was stupid on my part and I won't let it happen again. Shall we go to bed? I heard you talking to Russell out there a while ago and I have been thinking maybe this should be the last night we sleep together until we figure out what we are going to do at your plantation." He turned around and looked at her.

"Are you afraid I would use you like some of the other plantation owners and then throw you away is that what Russell has put in your mind?" she turned around as he came over and put his arms around her and pulled her into him. She didn't struggle she just looked up and stroked his face and then said.

"No but your son has always been your priority and until today Russell didn't even know you had a daughter I think we should take this one day at a time until I figure out where my place is in your life at the plantation. You have got two children and I need to see how they are going to react to me joining their world, so tonight is our last night together at least for a while." He didn't like what she was telling him but he would accept it for now he could always talk her out of it later. He took her hand and led her to the bed and then he dropped the gown off her shoulders and lay her down if tonight was all he was going to get for a while he was going to make the best of it and he wasn't going to retreat he was going to have all of her. He didn't know if that doctor was right or not he didn't care all he cared about was her and he was keeping her, Russell better keep his distance.

He laid her down and held her to him she wanted to be in charge tonight so she ran her hands through the hair on his chest. She leaned over him and looked down at him and then she asked him a question.

"Why did you change your mind about me you were so intent on not having me take your wife's place and yet that seems to be just what has happened?" he had his hand in her hair as he looked at her face in the moonlight and he didn't know how to answer her. His wife had always been the center of his world and now she seemed to have taken that place and in so little time it scared him. He pulled her face to him and kissed her. He pulled her up on his chest and just looked at her and her blond hair and she leaned down to him and it didn't matter to either of them why anymore it just was. She sat up on his chest as he put his hands up her ribs carefully to her breast and turned her over under him and then he was inside her.

"Somewhere along the way I have fallen in love with you and you are mine and only mine." That feeling he always made her feel was starting and she felt like she was on fire. She lifted her head back as he kissed her neck and then suckled her breast. He was never going to let anyone hurt her again as he brought her to the top. She looked at him and said.

"Don't leave this time please." He looked down into her face as he was coming and smiled.

"I wasn't going to; never again no matter what that doctor said it makes no difference to me we will try." After he was through he just held her, she still had no illusions about her fertility but she wanted that doctor to be wrong. She wanted children of her own she always had. He just held her for a while till she fell asleep while Russell stood on the porch and smoked his cigar he had heard most of it and he still had hopes he could win her even though he was pretty sure he had already lost. He put out his cigar and went to bed.

CHAPTER 4

Samantha woke to someone watching her and she almost jumped out of the bed. She turned to find Clayton and Russell on the other side of the bed on their knees with men holding knives at their throats. When she looked up she saw the Mayan man from this afternoon in front of her Te'a and the boy were in the room as well and something was wrong. She started to get up from the bed and she wasn't exactly dressed for company.

"Te'a what is wrong?" Te'a brought the boy closer to her and his arm was terribly swollen and his hand was purple and his father was mad, there was a man behind him screaming at the chief. She could see the problem someone had wrapped the arm so tightly it was getting no circulation and the boy had to be in terrible pain. She grabbed the sheet and wrapped it around her and lit a lamp and sat the boy down and reached for the knife in the sheath on the boy's father's leg and started to cut the bandages off. The other man was still screaming at her.

"Te'a tell that man to shut up." Te'a shook her head no so Sam looked at the boy's father.

"What is your name?" Te'a translated his name was Balik.

"Balik get him out of here so I can take care of your son." the other man was escorted rather forcibly out of the room.

"Stop threatening those men or I won't help him." She had stopped what she was doing to his son's arm while he decided. Balik looked at her for a few seconds while he decided and then had the two men released and she hurriedly went back to work.

She was taking off the bandage as fast as she could and carefully rubbing the boys' hand trying to get the circulation going again. She went to the table and grabbed the laudanum and poured him some, she knew he was hurting. His father tried to stop her and she just looked at him until he let her go then she propped the boy up with her pillows and gave him the glass and sat beside him while she worked on his arm. He smiled at her and drank the laudanum he knew what it was and he trusted her.

His father just watched as the color came back into the boys hand and he began to hurt less.

"Clayton where are those whale bone stays you took out of that corset?" he was still naked they had yanked him out of bed and they weren't polite about it.

"They are under the bed in your saddle bag." She pulled it out and got several of them and after his arm was back to almost a normal size she used them to stabilize the arm and rewrap it and she again told Te'a what to do.

"What happened why did that other man do this?"

"The shaman thought he knew better than a white woman so he redid it and when the pain got so bad Balik finally brought him back to you." Sam continued to work on the boys arm until the circulation was good again then she went to rewrapping it. She took the whale bone stays and made a splint out of them and then she showed Te'a how to do it. When she was finally pleased with the new bandage she stood up and looked at the Balik.

"What is the boys' name?" she was answered by the boy's father as he led her out to the porch. She still had the sheet wrapped around her and Clayton and Russell were inside. It seemed like he wanted to talk to her alone. He said the boys name was Telic and then he pulled her out into the moonlight so he could look at her. He lifted her hair and just let it fall through his fingers and ran his hand down her arm and felt her skin. He looked at the pendant around her neck and then he said something and Te'a came to him.

"He wants to tell you that the pendant is usually only worn by a priest." She started to take it off her neck and he stopped her.

This man was taller than most Mayan men he was at least six feet two inches tall. It seemed he wanted something from her.

"He says you should wear it you are the snake spirit you have earned it. If you ever need help have someone get on the drums or send that pendant and he will come for you." She looked up at him and he was watching her as she looked at him and Te'a translated. Samantha started to talk to him.

"Listen to Te'a she knows what to do, don't let that Shaman near your son again or he will lose his arm promise me." He smiled and ran his hand down her arm again and shook his head yes. He was saying something to Te'a and then she told Samantha what he said.

"Some of Balik's men will accompany you to your destination and see you are safe and so he will know where you are. He will make sure you are safe from now on. No one is ever going to hurt you."He turned around and gathered up his son and Te'a but before he left he took a purple orchid that Te'a had in her hair and put it behind Sam's ear. Balik then took his people and left, and then Sam went back inside. Clayton and Russell were waiting for her. Clayton looked at her and asked.

"Are you alright did he hurt you?"

"No he just said I am a snake spirit and if I ever need help to send for him." Both men just looked at each other and were glad they were still alive. This woman now had a Mayan chieftain for a friend.

"Can we go back to bed I am tired and morning is not far away." She crawled back into the bed as the men heard the rain start to fall again. "Well we can't leave till it stops raining and dries some so just go back to bed we will start as soon as possible, personally I will be glad to get home." Clayton was looking at the woman already asleep in the bed so was Russell.

"Like I said I will stay till she is better if you want?" Clayton just looked at him, no way was he leaving her behind if he had to go at a snail's pace home especially not with Russell.

"I think the sooner we get out of here the better I am not so sure he won't come back for her. Father John is already on his list and not in a good way the good father hurt his son and I don't think that man forgives such things." When Russell left he got back in bed with Samantha and pulled her closer to him and just worried, there were too many men around here wanting her, it was time to leave he just wished he could leave Russell behind. He also noticed the orchid Balik had left behind her ear.

The next morning the rain dried quickly and they left before noon. The trail was narrow so Sam was in the middle of the group but as the trail widened Russell kept creeping up to be close to her and it was really bothering Clayton. They stopped early evening for the night and they were ready to kill each other. She finally told them to knock it off or she would ride at the back and not talk to either one of them. She ate her supper and then went to find her a suitable flat tree while they set up the hammocks. Clayton came looking for her.

"We are going to have to figure a way for you to sleep in a hammock it is too dangerous for you to sleep on the ground around here. I think I have come up with an Idea for tonight and tomorrow we will have a better place for you to sleep. We will be home the next day." she followed him and he had a hammock set up with several blankets in the bottom of it. It made it almost flat but she was going to have to be still or fall out.

"Just lean over and settle in I will help you." Sam did and it wasn't too bad. Clayton had hung his hammock next to hers and when he lay down in his he was up against her.

"Maybe this will give you a little more stability and you won't fall out. Tomorrow night there is a small hut where we stay with stables. I haven't come this way in years so I hope it is still in decent shape. It isn't much but it has a flat floor and doors and then we are home the next night." She was quiet for a while just listening to the jungle. Then she said something he didn't expect.

"If I forget to tell you thank you for all your trouble on my behalf to get me to your home Thank You. Most men wouldn't have bothered for a woman they didn't know. Goodnight Clayton." She closed her eyes and went to sleep. He lay there for a long time and listened to her breath. He reached over and put his hand on her side just so he could feel her body close and then he whispered.

"I love you little bird you are mine now and I am never letting you fly away." Then he went to sleep.

When he got up the next morning she was gone and he panicked until he saw Russell watching something and he went to see what. He looked up and she had the little mare doing circles in a little clearing while the men cooked breakfast.

"She is good with the mare I have been watching her. She is patient and she just talks to her and they walk. Where did she come up with her?" Clayton sat down on the log and starting watching he had been watching her do the same thing several time since they left Mexico City. She had been right you don't have to use a whip to break a horse. Melanee was going to love this little mare.

"She bought her at an Auction for my daughter to ride that is who the little saddle is for Melanee." Russell looked at him.

"You know until the other day I really didn't know you had two children you never talk about a little girl." Clayton didn't say anything that was all Russell had to hear, nobody knew about that little girl and now Samantha was going to fix that. He smiled to himself that might be the crack in this relationship that little girl; Clayton could screw this up yet. Samantha was bringing the mare into the camp and tying her up. She pulled off her gloves as the men called them to breakfast. She walked up and Clayton pulled her to him and kissed her so she kissed back.

"How did you sleep last night? Was the hammock alright?" she looked at him funny the bulls were already fighting for territory this morning.

"Yes it worked out fine I was most comfortable we should have tried that before." As he wrapped his arms around her waist and interlaced his fingers behind her back and kissed her again with a good deal more passion.

"I thought we had decided to be a bit less open about this or have things changed?"

"I love you and we will go for appearances at the hacienda for a while, but we aren't there yet and it was just a kiss. You just look to good this morning."

"Did you just say you love me?" She started to pull his arms away. "Don't do that Samantha I am not Nathan I won't hurt you. I can say I love you and still be gentle not all men are like him." "You are just saying that because Russell is here and you are jealous and you think you have something to prove."

"Is that all you think of me is that why you asked me to try and get you pregnant were you going to raise a child of mine by yourself did you think I would let you?" she was beginning to panic and she didn't know why but something was wrong. He finally pulled her to his chest and held her to him she was shaking and he held her until he asked her.

"Now tell me what is really wrong?" she was close to tears and she just wanted to be alone. She walked away from both of the men and found a tree and sat down. Juan had just brought her some oranges. He spoke Mayan and Spanish and they had been trading words and she was getting to where she could understand him and he her. He put and orange in his hand and rolled it on the log and then cut a small chunk out of the end.

Then he put it up to his mouth and started sucking out the juice. Then he did the same for her orange, now she had juice on the run she could drink it all afternoon with no glass. She was finally smiling. Both men left her alone and went back and ate she was something and she adapted quickly. They had to ride single file down the trail the rest of the morning and she stayed in between them she seemed to be thinking about something and she didn't want to talk. When the trail widened out Clayton got next to her and told her.

"There is a jaguar stature up ahead I thought we would stop at for lunch because there is a spring behind it. You would probably like to see the statue if it isn't covered with vines." She smiled and shook her head yes and didn't say anything she was bothered about something and she wouldn't talk to him so he left her alone. When they got to the statue it was indeed mostly covered with vines. She got up next to it and started pulling them off so she could see the head.

"Samantha let me get things settled and I will help you don't hurt yourself." Before he could get to her two of the men that had come with them from the village were helping her including Juan. He was giving orders to the other men. Clayton looked at Russell and asked him.

"Did you hire any of those men to come with us?"

"No I thought you did. The way they speak Mayan I think they are escorting Samantha so Balik knows where she is going to live so he can find her." They just looked at each other.

"I am not sure how I feel about him knowing where she is.

"Well Clayton I am not sure there is anything you can do about it now and think about it, our plantations will be safe from attack if the Mayans get stirred up again at least not by Balik." They just looked at each other as the three men uncovered a beautiful limestone statue of a jaguar.

"Are ya'll about ready to eat? Samantha come up to the front of the Jaguar and I will lift you up and you can see the face and mouth a little better." The men had pulled the cut vines away so she wouldn't trip and she came to the front she had examined almost every other part of it. He just watched as she put her hands all over the statue like she was petting it. Clayton lifted her up on his shoulder so she was level with the head and she could see the teeth and tongue. She put her hand in and felt the inside of the statue then she asked him a question.

"How long do you think this has stood here?" Clayton slowly slid her down and held her just off the ground with her face level with his.

"I have not a clue, but a lot longer than any of us have been around. Maybe if you ever see that Balik again you should ask him, they have a working calendar that goes back at least a thousand years." She shook her head at him.

"You lie. Put me down."

"I do not ask your helpers. By the way we didn't hire them where did they come from?" she looked around at the men and then asked them. Then she laughed it was the first time she had laughed all day.

"Balik sent them to watch over me till we get to your plantation he doesn't trust the priest yet." Then she asked them another question and she stopped laughing. She turned to Clayton. "Can you get word back to your Father Michel and warn him to keep a watch on Father John I think he is danger. These men say Balik plans on taking revenge on him for what he did to his son and his friends." Clayton looked at her and said.

"I can't send one man back and if I send more it is too dangerous for us to be that shorthanded out here. One man could get lost and die alone. I warned Father Michel before I left they had angered that chief and to keep his men close I hope he listened to me. Come eat we need to be leaving if we are going to get to our next stop."

"The statue is so lovely."

"There is a bigger one close to the house on the plantation and it is a snake deity you should feel right at home. What is wrong you haven't acted right all day long and don't tell me it is that kiss this morning."

"I have got this bad felling and I can't shake it but I don't know who yet. We will talk about it later." Then she walked away. After that they were again on their way this time she rode beside Clayton but she didn't say a half a dozen words all afternoon. They got to the little way station and it wasn't much it was almost gone. There was a small adobe house with a bay window a door and nothing else. At least the roof was still there if it decided to rain. They tied the horses and ate and then went to bed she was worn out. They made her bed in the bay window and tied their hammocks up. Clayton tied his next to hers to make sure she didn't fall down during the night. He awoke several hours later and she was sitting up staring out the open window holding her arms around her legs and crying.

What is wrong are you hurting?" She looked at him strangely and the answered him.

"My brother Jeremy is dead and I think Nathan killed him trying to find me. When we get to your hacienda I think I should go on from there, further south he is still after me and now I think I have put your family in danger too." He just stared at her she wasn't joking that is why she had been so quiet all day.

"How do you know all this?"

"I have always known when someone close to me was sick or dying and I have felt all day something was wrong with Jeremy but a while ago I felt him drowning. He is terrified of water he would never willingly get in a large pond and I felt him drowning then dying. Nathan killed him. I think he knows I came south I always talked about coming to South America since I came back from Spain. We stopped in Rio in Brazil I have always said how much I loved it there. He is coming I know it."Clayton took her in his arms and held her like he would a child and then looked at Russell." We have already talked about this and we are pretty much the law on our own land. Tell us this man's name and what he looks like and if he comes on our land, either of our lands he won't ever leave them alive."

"This isn't either of your fight why would you get in the middle of this?" "No man should be able to get away with this with any woman. Tell us."

"His name is Nathan Miller and he is a couple of inches taller than both of you an about twenty pounds heavier with dark black hair. This isn't the first time he has beaten a woman they say he killed one of the saloon women but her body was never found so he wasn't prosecuted. The first thing people notice about him, his hands are very large he has broken at least two men's jaws that I know of. That's about it." Both men just looked at each other if he broke men's jaws she was lucky he hadn't killed her or broke her jaw.

"I really think I should go further south and get away from you he will be coming after me and your children are in the way if he finds me at your home." Clayton just held her and looked at Russell and then told her.

"If he comes we will deal with him and he won't hurt you ever again. Lie down and go back to sleep you can't do anything from here. I am sorry about your brother if you are right about him." Clayton got her covered up and back to sleep then he and Russell went outside to talk.

"What do you think could she be right about her brother?"

"She has been right about everything else why not about that. This man could be coming after her lord knows why; he only wants to hurt as far as I can tell but men like that never did make sense to me anyway. Tomorrow we will be at my hacienda and we will go from there maybe he will get tired of looking for her." Russell looked at him and then looked back at her.

"I wouldn't give up would you?" neither man said any more they both knew he was coming.

CHAPTER 5

The next morning they got an early start Clayton wanted to get home today. Samantha was so tired she could barely stand to let him tie up that corset. He was trying to joke with her about this being the last day she would have to wear the torture chamber but he couldn't even get a smile out of her. The nightmare of last night had left her grieving and he couldn't help her. They left the little house and were riding but the men didn't notice she was falling further and further back. Her Mayan guards didn't leave her side because they could see how weak she really was and she was getting worse by the hour. When they were getting close to the snake statue he went to looking for her and noticed how far back she was and went back to check on her. When he got back to her one of the Mayan men were on either side holding her in the saddle and she was ghost white. He jumped out of the saddle and started to pull her down and she told him.

"No don't touch me I am not getting down out of this saddle again until we get to your hacienda. I left my home twelve days ago and I will sleep in a bed that is mine tonight." she kicked her horse to start moving again and he grabbed the reins to stop him.

"How much laudanum have you got left Sam because you aren't going to make it like this?" she just pointed to her saddle bags. He reached in and found the bottle and there wasn't but a few drops left she had been hoarding them. Russell was back there by then and asking.

"What is going on she looks like hell."

"She won't come out of that saddle till we are home and I am going to get her there. Juan squeeze me some juice and bring it here. Samantha I am putting the last of the laudanum in the juice and you drink it. I am going to get up behind you and we are going to run home we aren't that far. The men can follow with the rest of the horses and the pack mules." She took the juice and drank it all and Clayton climbed up behind her and took the reins from her.

"Russell stay beside me and when we get closer to the house you get there and tell them what we need. Samantha I know you are tired I gave you three drops of laudanum just lean back and let me hold on to you and I will get you to my house honey." He wasn't even sure she heard him her head leaned off to the side and she went limp in his arms so he kicked Sundance and they started running. His hacienda was about an hour and a half away from the statue but the way the horses were running he figured they made in about forty minutes. Russell had already gone ahead and his men were waiting for him when he got there. He handed Samantha to Russell while he got down and started yelling instructions. His housekeeper Juanita was turning around and grabbing things when he saw his daughter, she was hiding from him. Sam had been right all along she was afraid of him. He carried Samantha upstairs and took her to his wife's room he would have taken her to his room but she would have had a fit. He smiled at that.

"What are you smiling about and this better not be your room."

"It isn't it is my wife's old room. I figured I would catch hell if I took you to my room." She smiled or the best imitation of a smile she had at the moment.

"Please help me get out of this corset and wrappings for one last time so I can breath and then let me sleep." He helped her undress and get into a gown when his housekeeper walked in to see what was left of the bruises and then Clayton sat her down on the bed.

"This is Juanita and she has got a glass of juice for you if you drink it all I will let you sleep for a while but you have to eat later, deal?" she shook her head drank all the juice and lay down. Clayton covered her up and left the room she was asleep before he got to the door. Russell was waiting at the bottom of the stairs and asked Clayton.

"Well is she better?"

"She is better, I hadn't realized she had been on the run for so long she just finally ran out of steam. She has been with me since Mexico City but she said it has been twelve days since she left home and her man carried her unconscious out of her house on the first day. Come with me we will get some supper and you can meet my children." he walked into the dining room to catch his son Steven pulling his daughter out of a chair on to the floor.

You don't belong at the table you can eat in the kitchen with the servants as usual. Get out of here now." He reached down and grabbed his son by the scruff of the neck and lifted him up and turned him around.

"What makes you think you can talk to your sister like that. She is my daughter and she can sit at the table and you will treat her better than a servant." His son was furious he had never been reprimanded for going after his sister, truth is known nobody had ever even noticed except Juanita and he didn't have to listen to her.

"Why are you going after me now she has always been seen and not heard? What is your new piece making the rules now do we have to abide by her till you tire of her and throw her away." Clayton couldn't believe what was coming out of his child's mouth but some of the words he had heard before from Ty, before he fired him on the trail now he wondered where his son had heard words like that.

"Where did you hear such language, and it wasn't from around here so where did you hear it?" He still had the boy by the collar and he finally started talking.

"Russell's new foreman hired some new men and they are out in the barn waiting to go back to his hacienda with him. They were talking to me before you got here and I heard them say it about her. She is just your new mistress isn't she and we are supposed to think she is a governess." Russell wasn't aware of any new men but he had already headed to the barn to find out. Clayton reached down and picked up his daughter funny he couldn't ever remember doing that except the first day she was born. He had handed her to his wife just before she died and he never touched her again. She would have hated him for that. He looked into his little girls face and all he saw was his wife how he could have missed that. He had ignored her for so long he hadn't even noticed how much she looked like her mother. She wasn't even dressed like a little girl she was wearing her brothers hand me downs Samantha was going to have his head.

He had both the children sit down and Juanita brought supper into them and then Russell came and sat down. He sat at the end of the table and told Russell they could talk later after supper. It was the first time except Christmas or a birthday he could remember sitting next to his daughter at a dinner table and he didn't remember many of those. She was so very quiet but her brother had a steady supply of insults he threw at her until his father told him to shut his mouth. Russell just sat there and listened this could still be his way in if Clayton didn't get his son under control Samantha would leave. When the children were taken to bed Russell wanted to talk to Clayton alone in the parlor.

"Did you fire a man named Ty from your party early on and send him back?"

"Yes I did he stole all Samantha's honey, her money and jewelry so I fired him and then he used those words my son used tonight, so I kicked him out and sent him back." Clayton shook his head and said.

"I thought it might be something like that, he tells it a little differently that your woman got him fired because she was too friendly with him."

"You know Sam; believe what you want and that was before we were sleeping together before I found out about the corset. Camille had wrapped her tightly with linen then put a corset on her so she could ride and it wasn't until almost three days later that I found out about it. By then that corset was eating her alive. I told her she was going to have to let me see or I would take her back. I don't know how she stood it. I cut out the whale bones and that helped but we wrapped her every morning and put that damn corset back on. Then we gave her some laudanum for pain and just kept riding. We could have stayed in Mexico City for longer but she was so afraid he would find her we just kept running but she can't run anymore."

"You have a beautiful daughter and I think that is going to be a problem between you and Samantha. If it becomes too much of one send her to me and I will make a safe home for her and even your daughter if you can't stand for her to be around." Clayton looked at him for a long time and then said to him.

"You take care of your world and I will take care of mine and that includes my daughter. I haven't done right by her but I am going to learn and Samantha is going to teach me how to put my family back together."

"Or kill you trying." Both men smiled and Clayton poured out some good Brandy in snifters and they sit back and waited for Sam to wake up.

"My housekeeper is making up a bed for you for tonight and you might as well go to bed because I am going to let her sleep until I absolutely have to wake her to eat." Russell drank his Brandy and then got up and the housekeeper led him to the room that was set aside for him but he stopped at the room that he had seen Clayton put Sam in and just wondered if she was lost to him and had the strangest feeling she was. He also had the feeling she was part of his future somehow as well and that brought a smile to his face.

Clayton just watched as Russell went to the guest bedroom and then he went upstairs and went to his room and changed. He put on the white pants he slept in and went barefoot down the balcony outside his room to hers. There were shuttered doors on the outside so the rooms were well ventilated and so many citrus trees blooming around the house it looked like it was snowing. His father had brought them here from other islands when he was traveling and they had flourished. The banister was wrought iron and it went around the whole side of the house so he walked to his wife's old room and opened the door and sat down in one of the chairs in her room. He was just watching Samantha sleep she looked peaceful and her color was better. He just listened to her breath. She had been asleep almost five hours and he knew she had to eat or she would be in trouble so he went over to her and sat on the side of the bed. He gently shook her till she awoke and the he told her.

"I am sorry but you have to eat something or you are going to be in trouble so you have to wake up." She looked at him and then tried to move as every bone in her body complained.

"Really can't you just let me stay here and become part of this bed it is the most comfortable thing I have felt in days? I think my bones have all been broken." He looked down at her and grinned. He pulled back the covers and reached under her and picked her up and started down the balcony to his room. She started to complain but the sight of all the trees just stunned her and all she did was look at him and smile.

"It takes my breath away it is so beautiful, you sure know how to show a girl a beautiful evening or am I just dreaming?" she just put her arm around his neck and looked at the trees and reached out to brush her hand in the blooms the fragrance was intoxicating. He took her into his room and sat her down at a table in his room. Juanita had already brought the food in here so she could eat. He had explained her problem as best as he could they would go over it better tomorrow but tonight he wanted to just get her settled.

"My arrival caused quite a stir didn't it?"

"Some but most of it is taken care of and the rest we will take care of tomorrow. I can have your food warmed if you want me too?" She just looked at him and then started to eat. He watched her there was something on her mind but she wasn't talking to him and that worried him. She asked him about certain foods she was eating and explained them as she was eating but she wouldn't look at him. He finally asked her.

"Do you plan on leaving when you feel better so Nathan won't find you here because if you do I already have men posted watching for him to come and watching for you to leave. Russell has men doing the same thing you won't get far, between the two of us you aren't safe out there he will find you and he will kill you next time."

"I don't want to put your family in danger and I think I am, you should let me go." He looked at her and then he took her hand.

"Tell me you don't love me like I love you and I will send you anywhere you want to go. I want you to know I haven't felt like this for anyone since my wife died and it will kill me if you leave me. I will fight to the death to protect you from this man so please stay." She sat back in the chair and just looked at him and then she took his hand and stood up and walked over to the bed, she lay down and pulled him in beside her.

"I will stay at least for a while." He pulled her over to his side and she drifted off to sleep again. Well it was better than nothing he would take it for now he hoped she would come to love his children. With any luck she would become pregnant with his child and he intended to make this permanent. He soon fell asleep and they slept until almost dawn when she awoke and quietly left his bed to go back to hers she still wanted this to be a secret. She went to the end of the balcony and was looking at the sunrise when she felt someone watching her so she turned around.

A little girl was watching her from the doorway so she just motioned for her to come over to her. She hardly looked like a little girl her long black hair needed combing and she was wearing tattered gown and she was tiny. She had the prettiest blue eyes she had ever seen.

"Are you my Mama?" Samantha was stunned she didn't know how to answer her.

"No honey I am the new governess, why do you think I am your mother?" the little girl just looked at her. She didn't realize she had white petals in her hair and her blond was almost glowing in the early morning sun.

"They all tell me Mama left when I was born and it was my fault so when you came I thought she came back and she wasn't mad at me anymore, my brother tells me it is my fault she left." She realized no one had told this child the truth about her mother's death they just blamed her for it. She looked like she was some beggar's child Clayton better enjoy his sleep because she was going to strangle him when he got up. She picked the little girl up and she was freezing.

"You are cold where do you sleep?" she pointed down the hall. Samantha decided to look later and put the little girl in her bed and then she lay beside her and she snuggled up to her.

"Your warm can I stay here a while?" Sam just covered them both up and tucked her in.

"Yes baby go back to sleep we will sort this out later with your daddy." She was still tired so she went back to sleep, she had just decided to stay and Clayton was going to get his priorities straight today. The little girl looked up at her.

"What is your name?" Sam looked down into those pretty blue eyes and answered her.

"My name is Samantha but you can call me Sam everything is going to be alright now so you go to sleep." She put her hand on the side of the little girls head.

"It is going to be better today Melanee I promise." then she went to sleep as well. Clayton had dressed and walked down the hall looking for Sam when he awoke and didn't find her in his bed. She was determined to make sure that no one thought they were sleeping together. He opened her door and saw she was still in bed and he leaned down to kiss her when a pair of blue eyes looked up at him in fear. Melanee was beside Sam in her bed. Melanee started to scramble away from Sam and she grabbed her as she looked around to see what was scaring her.

"Melanee stay put you aren't going anywhere." She pulled the covers aside and stepped out of the bed and stood up.

"She is afraid of you and that is going to change or I am leaving and I will take her with me." Clayton looked down at her and then he asked her.

"What makes you think you have the right to give me orders about my own daughter?" she looked at him and then turned and picked up his daughter.

"LOOK AT HER Clayton LOOK AT HER, until right now did you even know the color of her eyes? She is wearing hand me down clothes and she came in here last night asking me if I was her mother come back from the dead because she doesn't even know what her mother looked like. This is shameful, you would help a woman you didn't even know but not your own daughter you ought to be ashamed of yourself. Here take her she weighs nothing, does anybody feed her or does she just get scraps like a dog."

She handed him his daughter and Melanee didn't want to go to him but she did and Sam was right she weighed nothing. Melanee reached for Sam and she took her back from Clayton and he just looked at her.

"You think I would have a child with a man that would do this to one of his own." then she walked away. They started down the hall going room by room until she stopped at one and she walked into it. Clayton followed them and walked into the room as well. It was dingy and dark and cold. There was a small bed against the wall and no window it wasn't much more than a large closet.

"What is this place why are you in here?" Samantha turned around and she was furious.

"You really don't know? This is Melanee's bedroom your son makes her sleep here as punishment for killing his mother and since you aren't around and don't pay any attention to what is going on with her he has been getting away with it for years. It seems when she angers him he locks her in here to remind her to behave and she can't come to you because you won't listen to her." Clayton was still stunned by the room it wasn't a room he would even put a servant in. His son Steven came in about that time and didn't see his father in the corner just his sister and Sam.

"What do you think of her room? Fitting don't you think she killed my mother I wanted her someplace nice. I plan on you being out of my mother's room soon." Sam just looked at this boy who already hated her with a vengeance and asked him.

"What are your plans to get rid of me I would like to hear them?" He looked at her and started talking.

"I am going to tell father you are helping the brat and that you are messing around with one of the hands and then he will get rid of you and maybe her as well and then it will just be me and him again. We don't need anybody else."

Sam just raised her eyes to Clayton and Steven turned around to see his father standing there. He didn't know what to do he had run of his sister for so long, as well as most of the ranch, his father had been lost in grieving for so many years he had gotten away with everything. Now he had brought this woman home and suddenly his father's eyes were open and he was caught.

"Samantha please take care of my daughter for a while, we will talk later and please find her a better room. My son and I need to have a talk we will be back in a while." Sam just nodded her head.

"Let's go get some breakfast and then we are going to dress you in something besides this and find you a better room."

When she came out of the room Russell was waiting at the stairs and smiling."

"My offer still stands and that pretty little girl is invited as well."

"Shut up and come eat breakfast while I decide, you still have a long ride home either way." He laughed all the way to the dining room. After breakfast she had decided and she bid Russell goodbye. He was getting ready to get on his horse when he turned around and grabbed her and kissed her soundly on the lips. She was holding Melanee and Sam pushed him away.

"What was that for I already told you I am not going with you." "I know I just had to see what it was like one time."

"Happy now?" he smiled and got on his horse and looked back at her.

"Anytime you need a place besides here come to my place just follow the road it will lead you right to me." She turned around and saw Clayton and walked towards him and the hacienda with Melanee still on her hip. She walked upstairs and she had a bath waiting for the little girl. She brushed her hair and trimmed it and tried to make it as even as possible when she was done the little girls hair was lovely. She bathed her and put her in some girls clothing that she had Juanita borrow from the women around the hacienda until she could get to the town and buy some. Seems Juanita had been waiting for somebody to come and help this child for a long time and now she was here.

When they went back downstairs she wasn't the same little girl she had pulled her hair back with a ribbon and she had on a skirt and a peasant blouse and she was adorable. They sat down for lunch and Clayton was at the head of the table and she was at the other end and Steven was on the side but Melanee wouldn't leave Samantha's side.

"Well are we going to talk or are we going to eat in silence?" Clayton couldn't stop looking at Melanee she looked just like his wife how had he not noticed that before and she was terrified of him. Samantha had enough of the silence so she started talking.

"Steven I hear you ride which one is your horse I saw most of them in the corral today." He finally looked at her and started talking he figured she wasn't going away so he was going to have to talk to her.

"Mine is the bay with the blaze face and white mane and tail."

"We will have to go riding maybe you can show me the way to the village I need to buy your sister some clothes and some material to make some new clothes for us both."Clayton looked at her and smiled.

"Have you ever seen a Singer hand cranked sewing machine?"

"As a matter of fact I have and I have used one. There was one in town I came from and several of the women learned how to use them and we started to make shirts for the solders at the last of the war why."

"There is one upstairs my wife wanted one and she was just starting to learn how to use it before she passed away, it probably needs oiling and some maintenance but it should work."

"Don't worry about that I learned how to work on them from one of the soldiers who came back home after he lost his leg he taught me how to maintain it and I am pretty good."

"You and Melanee don't go to town without an escort and that means me and some men and I will pay for anything either of you need. I mean it Samantha you could disappear in this jungle. There is a festival in a few days so we will go you should be able to find what you need then. We will all go and make a day of it."

"Sounds like fun." She reached over and brushed Melanee's face and got a smile from her and pointed at her plate for her to eat some more. Clayton just watched, his daughter wouldn't even look at him she only had eyes for Sam. When supper was over she took Melanee's hand and they headed upstairs into her new bedroom it was one of the guest bedrooms and they had worked all day to make it hers. She got her in a clean gown and got her in bed and then she asked her.

"Well is this better are you warm enough in here?" the little girl shook her head yes and then looked over Sam's head as her father came in the door carrying something in his hand. He sat down on his daughter's bed and then he handed her a small picture.

"This is your mother several months before you were born she wanted you so badly and she only got to see you for a few hours before she died. I think maybe she should be in here watching over you at night since I haven't been for so long and maybe you can forgive me someday." Then he got up and walked out of the room. Melanee looked at Samantha and said.

"Does he like me now?"

"He is getting their baby but he has got to forgive himself for how he treated you for so long first but he is getting there. You go to sleep now I will see you in the morning." She kissed her cheek and got a hug and she left the room with the door cracked. She went down the hall and checked on Steven and went inside his room and started to pull up his covers and he said.

"Don't touch me I don't want you here just leave me alone." She pulled the covers up anyway and then left the room.

When she got to her room she walked out onto the balcony and just let the hummingbirds fly around her, she liked to hear them fly. He slid his arms around her from behind and held her. They just stood there in silence and listened to the birds.

"Well my little bird how do I fix this? She is terrified of me and my son has treated her like dirt for years and I didn't even see. Bringing you here was the best thing I could have ever done can you fix my family?" she turned around in his arms and looked at him.

"It took time to get this way it is going to take time to make it right but we will make it right." He kissed her and almost lifted her off the ground in the process. He picked her up and started down the balcony to his room.

"Maybe this isn't such a good idea tonight."

"Please don't leave me alone tonight I feel like this is the only thing I have done right in a long time bringing you here and loving you." He stood her on the floor and then he sat on the bed and laid his head on her stomach. She put her hands in his hair and just held his head next to her and didn't say anything she thought it was him who had something to say.

"You know I watched you the first night after the dance I was so jealous of that Duke who danced with you and I didn't even know why. I thought I was saving a broken bird that I was going to be your savior why is it now I think you are going to be mine." He looked up at her and then pulled her back on to the bed with him.

"I know you won't stay the night so just stay a while." She rolled over to the side of him and he pulled up the sheet and she curled into his shoulder and just listened to him breath. Her mind was working on a plan to get this family back to a family again and it wasn't going to be easy. She started to pull away it was dark and his breathing was slow but his grip tightened on her and then he was kissing her in the dark he hadn't been asleep he had just been watching her. He didn't say a word he pulled up her gown over her head and dropped it to the floor and she pulled him on top of her. She could see his eyes even in the dark and she was smiling at least this was right they would figure the rest out later. He went slowly tonight there was no hurry this was his world and he wanted her to feel like she was a part of it. He kissed her neck and suckled her breasts and went lower to her belly with sweet kisses and further down her legs till she was pulling him back to her and saying.

"Enough already you made your point, you want me and I want you, make love to me already before I explode." He was smiling a delicious little smile as he entered her and she arched up to meet him with her nails in his back.

"Alright big man make this a night to remember." as she pushed him over and looked down on him and they were soaring towards something she hadn't found yet. He watched as she leaned back and he pulled her back under him as she reached new heights and the look on her face was one he was never going to forget. He took a little longer and he was still looking at her as she watched him climax and he just kept coming it had never been like this before even with her.

"Marry me, tomorrow." She smiled rubbed the side of his head and said.

"NO. It is way too soon we have to wait and get things in order around here before we throw that at the children don't you think. Your son hates me and your daughter is terrified of you one thing at a time. Ask me again later." He rolled off of her and just lay beside her he hadn't ever felt this good with anyone he turned and leaned on his arm and looked down at her.

"I will ask again you know?"

"I know and the timing will be better next time and I will say yes. Now go to sleep. Tomorrow will be better." He pulled her close to him and they went to sleep this time. She got up later and put on her gown and started down the balcony when she stubbed her toe on one of the chairs. She was hopping around like an idiot when Melanee came sneaking out to the balcony.

"Damn it." She grabbed her little toe. Sam went to move the chair further back and she saw the moon up above and she moved the chair so she could see it better and not trip over it tomorrow night. She was still moving the furniture when somebody from behind her said.

"You cussed you aren't supposed to do that. Why are you out here anyway?" caught by Melanee she was going to have to start locking her door or this child was going to catch her in her father's bed. Now what was she going to say.

"I was going to close my door and I was looking at the moon and tripped over a chair in the dark. Then I decided to rearrange them so I could try something tomorrow night with the hummingbirds and I was making too much noise." Melanee just looked at her like she was crazy and the asked her.

"What were you going to do with the hummingbirds?"

"I was going to put out a red cup full of sugar water and if they will come we can listen to them and watch them feed." She sat down and the little girl came to her and sat in her lap.

"They don't make noise do they?" Samantha just looked down at her. "Of course they do their wings beat so fast they hum that's why they are called humming birds, but if you listen they make a chirping sound as well. Did you know the real pretty ones are the males and the plain brown ones are the females?" Melanee just shook her head no.

"There are all different colors of males and sizes too. We will see if we can get them to come and feed and we can watch them."

"How do you know all this?"

"A man in my town had a book about hummingbirds and he let me have it to read. When he went to war he had me keep in case he didn't come back."

"What if he comes back won't he want it back?"

"He was my husband and he isn't coming back, he died in the war but I brought the book with me we will dig it out and you can look at it tomorrow. Maybe we can see some of the birds in at the feeder." Melanee looked up at her and asked.

"Do you miss your husband like my daddy misses my mother?"

"No I don't. I didn't love my husband like you daddy loved your mother." She looked at Samantha funny.

"I don't understand."

"Neither do I baby and I don't think I ever will it was different between him and me. Come on it is getting cool let's get to bed. It is still a long time till daylight."

"Can I sleep with you again it is warm in your bed?"

"Alright just this one more night now scoot." Melanee went and jumped into bed as Sam looked down the balcony to see Clayton watching and listening to them. She just looked at him as the sadness washed over her.

Eliot had tried to protect her, it just hadn't worked. Melanee told her as she shut the louvered doors.

"You still have petals in your hair from the trees. When I came in here I thought you were an angel your hair glows in the moonlight and the white petals were falling on it, you look almost like an angel in the paintings." She crawled in beside her after she had shaken the petals out of her hair. She covered them up and pulled her close.

"Well I am no angel just a woman from Texas with blonde hair. We are going to start working with your horse tomorrow and getting her broken for you to ride."

"She is really going to be mine; I don't have a saddle for a horse?"

"I bought you one when I bought her. So go to sleep it is going to be a long day." She didn't know how right she was.

She got her up in the morning and the first thing they did now was fix Melanee's hair and find something descent for her to wear until they could get to town. She was going to work on the sewing machine in the afternoons but she needed some machine oil and she assumed she was going to have to wait until she could get to the village for some. She had found the book she was looking for when Clayton came into the courtyard with Steven and he was yelling for her. When she came down the stairs he had a lovely pot with purple orchids in them, and she felt a chill go down her spine. They were potted with part of the tree they were living off of. It was a beautiful pot with a snake painted on it so it was meant for her. She looked up at Clay and he said to her.

"There is more, you need to come with me Balik sent a message and it is for you."

"Let me get my boots and I will be right back." Steven was saying he was coming too and his father was telling him this was something he didn't want to see to stay here. When she got downstairs again they mounted and they were off but Steven wouldn't leave it alone and he got on his horse and followed his father. When they got to the snake statue she could see what the message was. Father John or what was left of him was hanging on the statue and there wasn't much left. He had been used as a sacrifice and his heart was in a bowl at his feet but he had been whipped for a long time before he died. Balik wanted people to know not to touch his people or Samantha and now he had made that quite clear to anybody who was watching or listening. This would be all over the jungle soon the drums were already talking.

She heard an intake of breath and turned to see Steven ride up and the boy was white as a sheet and fixing to fall out of the saddle of his horse. She got to him before his father could and got him to the ground and shielded his face from the carnage in front of him. Clayton told the men to cut him down and wrap the body up he would see that it was returned to the monastery. Sam called for some water and washed the boys face. She held him in her lap until he realized where he was and then he began to cry, and all he could say was.

"Why did they do that to him?" she looked at Clayton and he nodded his head so she told him.

"He had some Mayan boys as slaves and he was beating them and he would have done worse in fact he wanted to chop off one of the boys arms until I came along and stopped him. I helped the boys escape and he hated me for it but the Mayan chieftain would have killed the whole village including your father and Russell. I helped to get his people back; one of the boys was his son."

"Samantha forged a peace even after Father John tried it break it and the chieftain likes her. Sam will you take him back and we will clean this up."Steven could hardly walk so Sam had Clayton put him in front of her on Sundance and they went back to the hacienda. He didn't say anything for a while and then he started talking to her.

"You must think that makes me a baby to cry in front of you." She just kept going.

"Why would you think that, the first time I saw and injured man hurt that bad I went and threw up but I came back to help dress his wound." "And then you saved his life right. You were the nurse who took care of everything." "No, actually we had to cut off his leg because of gangrene and we didn't get to it in time and he was dying in agony. He was a soldier and he had come home for help but he didn't get home in time for us to save him. We were out of medicine and couldn't help him it was too late. I finally gave him enough laudanum to just let him die in peace. Satisfied?" he turned around and looked up at her.

"You let him die why."

"Because I couldn't help him live anymore and he was suffering. What would you have done if the positions were reversed?" He thought for a minute and then he said.

"I hope I don't ever have to make that decision for anybody how do you live with that."

"You just do." He put his arms around the arm that was holding him to her in the saddle and it seemed like they had a truce of some kind at least for the moment. When they got back to the hacienda the drums were still going in the jungle they weren't very loud but enough to make her skin crawl. She handed Steven to one of the men and when she got down she had the men take her horse away and she told the children.

"I want you two in the house until we know what it going on and stay with Juanita your father will be back soon and I have a feeling the Mayan chieftain is going to be here soon so stay inside until I tell you to come out. Steven watch over your sister she is under your protection now do not hurt her." Before she could leave he asked her.

"Please come upstairs with us you can watch from the balcony." He had never asked her for anything so she went with them. She took them both out on the balcony and they all sat in the big chair and she wrapped a blanket around them. Steven was still shaking and Melanee didn't know what was going on. They just sat there and watched the little birds and Samantha watched the courtyard. She didn't think Steven realized but he was clinging to her arm like she was going to disappear. She just put her arm around him and pulled the blanket up over them all and watched the courtyard as those drums talked to each other. Clayton rode up later with a body slung across the back of one of the horses and a couple of Mayan men with him. He looked at her on the balcony and motioned her downstairs and then he told the children.

"Ya'll start getting ready we will leave for the fiesta as soon as you get dressed." Sam thought that was kind of strange but she would ask him when she got downstairs. She walked down the staircase and he asked about Steven. She told him he was better now. Then Samantha wanted to know.

"Stop stalling what is going on with the drums and why display the priest's body to me instead of leave him at the monastery?"

"He wanted to prove to you and anybody else that had any ideas of hurting you or anyone at this hacienda to back off. I think he got the message across don't you. Now he is broadcasting what he did to the rest of the tribes that you have just become off limits to everyone."

"If it wasn't so terrifying it would almost be an honor, I think. What now?" we take the children to the fiesta and I send Father John's body home to Father Michel with a warning don't take Mayan prisoners because next time Balik won't be so forgiving."

"That is forgiving?"

"He could have killed every man woman and child in that village and I think that was the original plan. You are the only reason he didn't, you took care of his son, and no other white woman would have done that."

"Do you think he will come here himself?"

"I don't think so and neither do his men he has done what he set out to do and that was to protect you." She didn't say anymore the children were coming down the stairs. Steven had his own horse as did his father so Melanee rode with Samantha. Melanee was elated she was high up on that beautiful horse with the shiny saddle and she looked pretty today they wouldn't laugh at her.

They rode into the fiesta and there were several stalls selling fabric and some with already made clothes. Sam found some little girls shirts and small skirts that would fit Melanee. She planned on making her some split skirts for riding so she just needed material for that. She wanted to try some pieces on her so she asked where she could fit her and a woman pointed to the back of the courtyard but she was a little suspicious of this lady walking off with her wares. Samantha told her who she was and anything was to be billed to Clayton so even if she stole it bill him for it. The lady agreed and let her take anything she wanted after that. They went back to a small building that was empty and tried on the clothes and some of them fit so she gathered up the rest and went back outside.

As she started back to the sale tables she watched a young man teaching a young woman how to dance and he was doing it badly. When she would misstep he would swat her with a switch on her bare leg. She would scream and then he would say that is the only way you are going to learn.

"This is how the great Lena Baca taught her students how to dance and you can learn as well."

Well Samantha wasn't going to let him get away with that, no way her beloved Lena ever taught someone how to dance by hitting them with a stick. She walked up to the man took the stick away from him and started to break it in half and then in half again and again.

"How dare you interrupt a dancing lesson you have no right Punta." They always wanted to call her a whore and around her that would get him killed.

"Who ever made you think you could teach dance, you don't use a switch to teach and I should know I was taught by the best."

"Really I'll bet you can't do the simplest steps, most of the peasants around here don't know anything except how to stomp their feet." She just looked at him and grinned and then she told Melanee.

"Sit down by the guitar player for a minute baby while I teach this man a lesson in manners. Would that be alright with you Senor?" The man looked up from under his hat and smiled at her and she got the biggest grin on her face and just winked at him. Then he nodded back as she felt two arms go around her waist and a head lean down on her shoulder and kiss it gently.

"I have been looking for you Nica but I wasn't looking here till I walked past that horse with that silver saddle on it and I knew you were here. I have been sending letters to Texas and they have been coming back with no answer what is going on?"

"I will tell you later, now will you just dance with this Punta."
"Who dared to call you such a foul name?"

"Your man over there called me that after I took a switch away from him. He was hitting the girl with it when she made mistakes and then he told her that was how Lena taught dance and I called him a liar." Gabriel looked over at the man standing in the courtyard and told him.

"Watch someone dance who my Lena taught and who is still one of the best around." Clayton and Steven had showed up some time ago and had listened. The dancers were attracting a crowd and by now, the plaza was filling with people. Clayton told his son.

"Just watch her it is really beautiful when she dances." He walked over by Melanee and sat down and tipped his hat to the man playing the guitar. The music started and the older man stayed behind her and they danced across the plaza and then he reached his hand up and took her hand and twirled her around and they danced, it was like they were one person she knew when he was going to move and he knew when she was. They were one fluid being and it was so graceful but Clayton saw something else, even though this man had to be twenty years older than Samantha he was in love with her and not like a father. Maybe now she just might look at him differently because the woman he was looking at loved this man as well. They went from one dance to another as easily as walking together. They finished the dance and he leaned down and laid her across his knee and she leaned back with her hair and one hand touching the ground behind her it was wonderful. He lifted her back up and the crown went mad clapping.

He hugged her a little too long for Claytons taste but he couldn't do anything about it. They were walking this way with his arm around her waist. Then he walked in front of the man who had insulted her he told him.

"Now you can apologize to this woman and my wife who taught her. This lady is one of the best left in the world and you sir are not." The man apologized to Sam and then she turned and hugged the man behind her.

"Where did you come from it is so good to see you and where is Antonio?"The man standing beside her just locked his hands behind her and started talking as if they had never been apart. Clayton started walking towards her this man was getting to close to the woman he wanted and even she didn't realize that the older man wanted her. Clayton walked up to introduce himself and Sam was taking this man's hands off of her and walking towards him. Both men looked at each other and they knew what the other was thinking they were rivals over this woman.

"Clayton this is Gabriel Baca and he and his wife taught me to dance while I was in Spain. His son Antonio helped as well." The older man just looked at her and then asked her.

"That is the entire story you told him? What about the Bishop or sneaking Natasha and Patricia out of the palace onto the boat right out from under their father's nose." Clayton was looking at her again like she was a strange creature.

"Why don't we sit down and have lunch it is a long story and I hadn't got that far yet." As they were being brought lunch she ordered more and she introduced the guitar player to Clayton. She knew Gabriel was here when she saw who was playing, Gabriel was here somewhere.

"Clayton this is Lucas Garza and he has played for Gabriel for as long as I have known him." Lucas shook his hand and then said to him.

"I have been with him for almost thirty years and we are still going. I decided to come with him when he finally left Spain.

When Samantha got Antonio's bride out of the castle, it seemed like a good idea to leave the country. The Bishop was looking for anyone connected to Samantha and Antonio's bride's father was tearing up the countryside looking for her and her sister." Clayton looked at her and then said.

"Well you better start talking." She kind of smiled and the she just sighed.

"I told you the Bishop was trying to find me; well he stood outside the palace all night and just watched. He couldn't get at me I was with one of the Queens lady's in waiting. Her name was Natasha Castillo and she was in Love with Antonio that is Gabriel's son. He had come with us that night to see her. He was my dance partner some of the night and Gabriel was my partner the rest so they could be together. Her father had already made arrangements for her to marry a much older man with a nice title who would make her father a rich man. Natasha didn't want that so we found a very large chest and put her in it and had her carried out as my luggage the next morning and loaded on the boat."

Clayton just looked around the table at the men and they were smiling the Mayan boy wasn't even the first time she had pulled such a stunt. And she kept getting away with it.

"When we got down the coast Antonio was waiting for us as well as some other people who needed to get out from under the Bishops eye. Gabriel followed after his wife Lena died she didn't want to leave Spain. She knew she didn't have much time left so they hid until she died and then he and Lucas came to Brazil. The weather was bad and we had to land at Rio in Brazil for supplies and I loved it down here and I always told myself I would come back to South America someday. Antonio and Natasha stayed in Rio and started a dance school and Gabriel joined them later."

"What about the saddle where did that come from." Gabriel answered this time.

"That was a gift from me and the Queen. She found out about the chest and what she had done and the papers she had signed. The papers had given her some leverage over the Bishop so she helped me get it made and we had it sent on the next boat after it was finished to Texas as a Thank you for all your help to her and to me. Have you enjoyed it?"

"It is beautiful but I am afraid to even ask what it is worth."

"Don't even ask, I was scared at the price, just enjoy it and the Queen said don't ever come back he still looks for you and he will kill you if he ever finds you."

"Good to know, good thing he is still in Spain."

"I need to leave you gentlemen and collect my parcels from the venders they are shutting down we will be back soon. Will you have supper with us tonight or better yet will you stay the night?" she looked at Clayton and hoped she hadn't overstepped her bounds but she wanted to talk to Gabriel. He just smiled and said that was a wonderful idea. Lucas went with her to help with the packages he could see the men needed to set some ground rules. Finally Gabriel turned around and asked Clayton.

"She is terrified and she wasn't that scared of the Bishop and she should have been. This man following her what really happened to her." Clayton just shook his head no and then he said.

"She won't tell me, it was days before she told me she was hurting and I don't know what was keeping her in that saddle besides laudanum and just plain fear. The beating she took should have killed her and very nearly did. I know you think more of her than a daughter I see it in your eyes but she needs someone like a father to talk to, this is eating her up inside and she won't talk to me." He looked at this man and realized he was going to have to give up the idea of ever being more than a father figure to Sam, well that was all right he would be what she needed whatever that was.

"She wants you at the hacienda tonight so maybe she will talk to you, she has been talking about leaving and going further south and if she does he will find her and I think he will kill her next time."

"Do you love her really love her?"

"I lost my wife and I didn't ever think I would replace her but she walked into my life like she was always meant to be here and

I will kill this man if he shows up on my land. I just need to convince her she will be safe here and she isn't putting my children at risk."

"Is she putting them at risk?"

"It is a possibility and there is nothing to do about that except keep guards out watching for him. My neighbor is on guard to, we were at a way station and he saw some of the damage he did to her. He has said he would help protect her as well as a Mayan Chieftain."

"How did you manage that one?"Clayton just pointed to Sam she was walking back their way and he said.

"I will tell you about that tonight she helped his son escape from an abusive priest." Gabriel just raised an eyebrow and then looked at Samantha.

"This seems to be becoming a habit with her, irritating priests."

"It gets better she is a snake goddess to the Mayan now, she even wears a pendant reserved for a Mayan priest."

"Oh this just gets better and better." As Samantha walked up she could see they were talking about her but she didn't want to know about what. She wanted to go home even now she considered it home but she was afraid she needed to leave to keep everybody safe. She put Melanee up in front of her and Steven rode beside her now, things had changed between them, he was hers now even if he didn't want to admit it. Clayton and Gabriel rode in front and Lucas and the other men rode behind her and the children with the pack animals. She knew it was to protect her and the children, around here children were great hostages if somebody wanted a ransom. Melanee fell asleep on her and Steven kept looking at her funny until she asked him.

"What is wrong did I do something today to upset you?" he pulled his horse closer to her and asked.

"Where did you learn to dance like that you are so graceful and it looks like you are floating." She was so stunned she almost thought he was kidding then she realized he was serious. She never realized what she looked like when she danced she just danced.

"Well that man up there and his wife taught me years ago and they were very good teachers. But when I get on a dance floor I feel like I am another person one who can fly like those little birds for just a little while." Gabriel and Clayton rode a little further ahead not quite out of hearing range and Clayton asked him.

"She is better than most isn't she?"

"Oh yes, I have never taught better and she doesn't even realize it, she just dances. The first day she walked into our patio she was watching our son Antonio do some flamenco steps and when we saw her she was imitating him and she had them down perfectly. She remembers after seeing them one time and she is light on her feet, it didn't take any time and she was dancing with our son and giving him a run for his money. We didn't learn until one day she was sick when her father came and told us. She was tired and she collapsed then we started learning what to look for to take care of her. I guess you are learning how to look for the signs to keep her well?" Clayton nodded.

"I will talk to her tonight and see if she will talk to me. You have to promise you will keep her safe if she stays here or I will convince her to come with me." Clayton looked at the older man and figured he probably could talk her into going with him and that scared him.

"I will make sure she is safe she will have a good life here." The older man just nodded they were riding into the courtyard of the hacienda and Sam was wondering what that conversation had been about.

She got everybody settled into a room and then they ate supper the children were too tired to even watch the birds tonight. After everybody was settled it was just the three of them on the terrace and she asked Gabriel if he would like to go for a walk she wanted to show him the snake statue down the road. He said he would love to, so they started off with her taking a machete with her for snakes. The moon was full and high so there was plenty of light so they just walked and talked at first.

"What really happened after we left that day the Bishop was to petty to just let it go did he come after you and Lena?"

"Yes they rode up about two hours later and came rushing in and he was screaming he was going to tear the place apart only to find Queen Isabella's guards sitting at my table having drinks with me and Lena. The Captain asked what the problem was and if he could be of any assistance and the Bishop turned around and left. After he left the guards helped us pack and got us somewhere safe. You knew the Queen helped finance the school for years as did her mother. We stayed at one of her friends rancho's outside the city and Lena had the best care until she died. I buried her next to her family then it was time to leave Spain." He looked into the night remembering his lost wife because he too could never go back to Spain.

"What happened to you Samantha I don't think I have ever seen you so scared and Clayton says he is afraid you are going to run and the man chasing you will find you and kill you next time? If you want to run come with me I will protect you."

"No one can protect me and that is the problem I should have killed him when I had the chance but I didn't. We needed time to get away and get down here and I thought he would leave me alone but I was wrong."

"Tell me what he did to you Clayton says he knows some of it but nobody knows it all." She sat down on the short wall surrounding the hacienda and just started talking into the air like nobody else was there as she stared out into the night. She told about her marriage and about her brother and him losing the ranch and the night Nathan came and then everything that came after. She never looked at him and she never cried as she told the story like she was talking about someone else. She told him everything including the ride on the train and the doctor in Texas and what he told her. Getting to Mexico City finding Camille then Clayton that was when she stopped. She turned and looked at him and just said.

"Now you know he should have killed me he left me with nothing, no home, no family, no honor." He just looked at her she felt like she was the one who had done something wrong, she was right someone should have killed that man that morning.

"You shouldn't blame yourself for this it isn't your fault it is his." She looked at him like she was in a trance and said.

"Then why do I feel like everything I do brings trouble down on top of the people I love, even you and Lena. You had to run because I saw too much."

"We ran because you helped Antonio get the girl he loved out of that castle and now I have a grandson to love because of it."

"Nathan killed my brother trying to find me and now he is coming and I am just too tired to keep running."

"Then don't run anymore, Clayton will protect you and he says there are others who will as well. It is time to stop running and stand up to this man and fight. You are going to have to make a stand somewhere and this is as good a place as any. A man like him won't stop till he finds someone else to fixate on or he gets killed. We are coming back at the Christmas festival and I was hoping you would dance with this old man. If you still want to leave I will take you with me and we can make other arrangements then, it is only a couple of months from now." She nodded her head yes but he figured by then she would have already be a part of this world and lost to him but that was alright he just wanted her happy and safe.

"Shall we go back now?" she took his arm and was walking back down the road to the house.

"No I want you to see something else. Look up at the statue it is a Mayan Snake statue. Appropriate don't you think for the snake spirit maybe she will protect me from Nathan." He looked down at her.

"She, why is it a she?"

"I think anything as deadly as the snakes around here ought to be a she don't you?" he looked down at her this blond haired woman with the moonlight on her, she was almost glowing no wonder the Mayans thought she was some sort of snake spirit.

"Only you would think that way about a snake. Use it against Nathan and if he comes after you again you be the deadliest snake you can think of and kill him this time. Don't think about it just do it." She didn't say anything they just kept walking down the road to the hacienda. When they got there Clayton was waiting under the trees at the table with a cigar in his mouth a brandy in his hand and a decanter on the table. She walked up with Gabriel and looked at both men and could see they wanted to talk so she just told them goodnight. Clayton reached up and grabbed her hand first and she leaned down and kissed him on the lips and then told him.

"Good night I will see both of you at breakfast." They both watched her walk away and then Clayton turned and asked Gabriel.

"Well did she talk to you?" the older man looked at him and shook his head yes.

"It is worse than you can even imagine and I am not sure she will ever tell you all of it but she blames herself for it. She is sure her brother's death is her fault and that she has no honor because of what Nathan did to her."

"I thought as much this man is something, I wish her man had taken care of him and ended this in Texas but now she still fears he will come for her. I would think she was foolish but she has been right about too many things and I am afraid she is right about this too." They sat there and drank Brandy and just talked about Gabriel coming back at Christmas and her dancing. Clayton got the feeling there was something else going on with her but he didn't say anything, he just left it alone.

When she got to her room and went inside she saw the children on the balcony sitting in the chairs covered in blankets. She walked out to them and asked.

"What are you two still doing up it is so late?" Steven answered her he was almost in a panic.

"We were waiting to talk to you. You aren't going to leave with that man are you?" she smiled as Melanee climbed up in her lap.

"I thought that is what you wanted was me gone and you and your father all to yourself again?" he couldn't look at her and she was ashamed of teasing him.

"I am sorry that was mean. No I am staying at least for now as long as I am not putting you two children in danger, but if I think I am I will leave. That man comes around I won't let him hurt you two to get to me."

"Daddy will protect all of us so you will stay promise." She just nodded her head that was the best she could do for now.

"Let's get ya'll to bed it is late and your sister is falling asleep in my lap." She walked them down the hall and got both of them to bed and covered up and then went back to her room she changed clothes and was starting to climb into bed when Clayton walked into her room. She shook her head no and said.

"Not tonight I need to think." He walked over to the door and locked it and then turned around and picked her up and walked her down the balcony to his room. He sat her down on the bed and looked at her. "You sleep here it is where you belong, if you need to think you do it lying beside me. You would have gone with him and something changed your mind and I am not going to let you change it back again tonight if I can help it. I love you the children love you and you are staying here. I know he loves you too but you are ours now and he can't have you and neither can Nathan." Sam smiled up at him and pulled him down to her and kissed him and then she climbed into the bed and he got into the other side and pulled her up close to him and he just held her as they went to sleep. He was right this was her world now.

It was very dark and quiet but there was something and she could hear it. She easily climbed out of the bed and went to the balcony then looked down, the moon was high and the trees had a weird glow. She looked down at her feet and she saw an orchid a purple one. There was another one several feet further and another, she followed them down the stairs to the patio. In the trees across the road she saw movement so she went across and she went into the jungle, she didn't have to go far. Balik and Te'a were waiting for her. Te'a started the conversation.

"He wants to talk to you he heard what you said tonight to the other man." Sam just looked at them she hadn't seen anyone while she talked to Gabriel she didn't know Balik was keeping that close a watch on her. She should have known he was close after the priest was left at the altar today. Balik was saying something but she still didn't know enough Mayan to catch all the conversation. Te'a translated.

"He heard what was said and he will protect you from this man as well. He will have men watching you in this house and if you need him send for him or ask any Mayan just tell them who you are and he will come for you. This man will die at his hands if he tries to hurt you again. He wants you to know he saw you dance again today and you were lovely." Samantha didn't know what to say, how you thank someone like him for protection. She reached over and hugged him she didn't know if this was right thing to do or not but it had been a long day then she stepped back and looked at him and smiled.

"Thank you Balik I am staying here I hope I am not making a mistake?" he nodded to her and then they turned and melted back into the jungle. She walked out of the jungle and across the road and back to Clayton's room and started to get in the bed when Clayton asked.

"What did Balik say to you?" she looked up to see he was awake. "How did you know it was Balik?"

I saw the purple orchid's strewn on the balcony and watched you go across the road. He wanted to talk to you tonight as well?"

"He heard my conversation with Gabriel and he told me he saw me dance today now he is watching out for me too. If I need help ask any Mayan and he would come running."

"So what are you going to do Samantha?"

"This seems to be the safest place for me to be. Nathan would be a fool to come here now wouldn't he?" then she snuggled down next to Clayton and went back to sleep. Clayton had watched her meeting with Balik from the balcony he was always afraid Balik would just take her. He almost wished Nathan would make an appearance so he could kill him then Sam would be free, then maybe she would marry him and he could stop worrying about these other men.

The next morning they got Gabriel and his group off and headed back to their next destination. She promised to dance with him when he came at Christmas and she said she was going to invite a friend to come to Christmas to meet him. She wouldn't tell him who, it was going to be a surprise but it was a woman and she thought he would like her.

The children wouldn't leave her side for fear she would go with him. It would have been comical if they weren't so scared. Everybody was finally gone and they were getting back to some kind of a routine. Steven and Clayton went to check on the crops and Samantha and Melanee went up to the sewing room to look at the new materials and see if she could get the sewing machine running. When they got upstairs they opened up the room so the air could circulate and she was working on the sewing machine as Melanee wondered around looking at the material she had bought. She was acting like she wanted to ask her something but she just didn't have the courage to ask her. Samantha finally started a conversation with her.

"Is there something on your mind that you would like to talk about or are you just going to pace the floor all day." She asked without even looking up as she worked on the machine. Melanee came over to her and was looking at the machine even thought she didn't have the foggiest idea what she was looking at.

"You dance so well do you think I could ever dance like that?" Sam just kept working on the machine as she answered her.

"I don't see why not someone taught me I think I could teach you but it would be a lot of work I would love to try if you really want to."

"Do you think we could try without telling daddy or Steven until we see if I can do it or not?" Sam looked at her then she understood, she was afraid she would fail and they would laugh at her.

"It will be our secret. We will have to get you some shoes made and if you want we will practice when they are gone in the afternoons in the back patio on the stone steps alright, only Juanita will know our secret?" Melanee lit up like a Christmas tree Samantha didn't know if she would be any good but they would try. It was the first thing this little girl would ever do on her own to please her father. They worked on the machine till it was running perfectly now she could make Melanee some respectable clothes and if the dancing worked out she already had an idea for a special dress.

"Let's go out for a while and work with your horse I am anxious to get you riding so we can go to town when the men are gone."

"I like riding in front of you it makes me feel special in that pretty saddle on your golden horse."

"Well pretty soon you will have your own golden horse and I think you are special all the time." The little girl grabbed her hand and as they walked down the stairs she asked her.

"Why does that Mayan man want to talk to you all the time and bring you flowers?" Sam looked down at Melanee; she didn't realize how much the little girl had seen. Melanee had been ignored for so long she disappeared into the woodwork and people didn't notice that she saw and heard everything.

"How did you know about the Mayan man Melanee?" she stopped and sat in one of the chairs on the patio so she could talk to her face to face.

"I watched you last night go and talk to him and then you left and went back to daddy's room. Then I started to go back to the house and the man and the woman came out of the trees and she talked to me. She asked me my name and if I liked you. I told them yes I loved you and I wanted you to stay and be my mother. He just nodded and then she told me to go back to the house and go to sleep we would be safe from the bad man." Samantha thought about it for a minute and then told Melanee.

"Don't tell your daddy about last night's conversation that is our secret." Melanee looked at her and asked.

"Why is he a bad man will I be in trouble?'

"No honey I just think your daddy has all he can handle right now and you and Balik being on first name terms might spook him." Melanee just shook her head yes and they just kept heading to the corrals. Nathan didn't know it but he better stay away he would be messing with the wrong people down here. Now Balik was even guarding Melanee she couldn't help but smile. The little girl who wasn't wanted by anyone such a little time ago was being watched over by a Mayan Chief, how about that. Then she realized she said back to daddy's room she knew where she was sleeping.

Sam had the mare brought out to the corral and she was bridled and had a saddle on her. Sam was going to put a sack of grain on her today and see if she bucked or if she did well with it on her back, she was beginning to think this horse had been someone's before and maybe had been sold when things got bad. When the grain was strapped on the little horse was doing so well, she didn't buck and she had a beautiful stride. Melanee was sitting on the corral top rail and started asking her.

"Please let me try to ride her just once." Sam was thinking about it when Clayton and Steven rode back in and Steven told her.

"Let me, I know how to ride and if she starts acting up I can jump off." Melanee was almost in tears Steven was going to take her horse. Steven saw her and said.

"No Melanee just let me see what she does and if it is alright we can put you on I promise." Melanee looked up at her brother and it was probably the first time he had actually gone out of his way to be nice to her. She nodded her head and Steven got down off his horse and went in the corral and started to mount and the little mare went crazy and Sam backed her up and away from him. He started to try again and again she went nuts.

"What is it what did I do I didn't even touch her?" Samantha backed her up and over to where Melanee was sitting and Melanee was petting and stroking her and the horse was calm and nuzzling her.

"Clayton you come over here and get near her." He did and everything was fine then he acted like he was going to mount her and again she went crazy. Samantha pulled her to the center of the corral and calmed her down and then she put her foot in the stirrup and got in the saddle and rode the mare around the corral with not a single objection from the mare.

"Its men, she is afraid of men, she has been a woman's horse and then she was sold to that man in Mexico City and I don't know what else but there was something else and she is afraid of men. Melanee come over here and you try riding her." Clayton was coming undone.

"No you are not putting my daughter at risk she could get hurt." Not only Sam but Melanee and Juanita standing at the kitchen door all had their mouths open this man who couldn't stand to even be around his daughter only days ago was incensed that Samantha would try to put her on that horse.

"I won't let her get hurt Clayton I will be right by her side if anything out of the ordinary happens I will pull her off. Melanee do you want to try, if not we won't?" Melanee walked over and again petted the mare's nose and then Samantha lifted her up and put her in the saddle and they walked around the corral slowly. The mare acted perfectly fine then Sam let Melanee hold the reins herself but she still kept hold of the halter rope just in case. Melanee had a smile that glowed; this was her horse and no one else's. Samantha looked up at her and asked.

"Have you picked out a name for her yet she is yours now you get to name her." Melanee smiled.

"I picked a name but I was waiting until I got to ride her and knew she was mine before I told anyone her name it is Moon. She looks like that first night I saw you with the white petals in your gold hair and the moon was shining down on you. Remember I said you kind of glowed so her name is Moon." Samantha looked up at her and then at Clayton.

"I think that is an excellent name. I think that should be enough for today. We will do some more tomorrow maybe in a few days we can all go and do a picnic by that statue down the road and you can ride your Moon and Steven can ride his horse." They all agreed that would be a wonderful way to spend an afternoon. Clayton just watched Samantha she was pulling his world back together one piece at a time.

She started practicing with Melanee in the afternoons and it was taking time the child had never been taught to even walk straight much less dance but she was trying so hard. Sam would watch her practice when no one was watching while she was sewing at night. They rode around the ranch house so if Moon got out of hand they weren't too far away but she never did after that first day. Someone had mistreated the little mare and Sam didn't know if it was just the auctioneer or someone else but there had been someone.

If Melanee was going to dance with her at Christmas and that was the plan, she needed special shoes and she didn't have any shoes except sandals. Melanee really needed the right shoes if she was going to learn the steps she had to be able to make some noise with her feet. She was also making her a dress like her Flamenco dress with yards and yards of white ruffles she would love it. Samantha needed to go to town and she needed an escort so she asked Juanita what to do because she didn't want Clayton to know what she was doing. Juanita told her she had to go to town for supplies and Samantha could go with her. Samantha was trying to think of something for Christmas gifts but she didn't have a lot of money and there weren't a lot of shops around. She could always make dresses for Melanee she loved dressing up. Several of the women on the ranch or in the village embroidered so she could have hummingbirds or butterflies put on the dresses. She had no idea what to get for Steven or for Clayton.

Several days later after the Clayton and Steven left for the fields she and Juanita started to the village. Sam had Melanee in front of her on Sundance she still wasn't sure enough of Melanee's skill as a rider to let her ride Moon alone. They rode with three of the vaqueros as guards she wasn't stupid enough to ride alone. When she got to town she found a man who made shoes and she told him what she needed and then what she wanted added to the heels and toes. He looked at her and then at her dance shoes and he finally realized what it was she wanted but he had never seen any made for so small a dancer.

"She will dance with you like in the plaza that day?" she nodded her head and smiled.

"That is the plan but is a secret the patron mustn't know." He smiled at her.

"It will be our secret but I will have front row seats I want to see the little one dance like you." She winked at him.

"You and everyone else I think. I am looking for a present for the patron and his son can you think of anything he buys every year that I might surprise him with?" the man thought a minute and the pointed to a stall further down the side of the village.

"I know he always buys a new white straw hat for him and his son each year that might be something to think about. Maybe a silver hatband would be something to add to the hat." She smiled she had something else in mind for the hatband and nobody else would have anything like it. Melanee and Samantha walked down the stall at the end and they talked to the man there and before they left he was laughing and she had her present for the men taken care of, she would bring back what he needed the next time she came back to town. The man watched her walk away she was right nobody would have a hatband like it.

She ordered some food before they started back and some fruit and they sat under the trees in the plaza and ate then she gave Melanee a dance lesson while they had a smooth surface to practice on. She was getting better and better every day. She got up and showed her some steps and they began to draw a crowd. She began to notice how much of a crowd so she told Melanee they should go and a man stopped her.

"Don't leave now just one dance I haven't seen a descent Flamenco since I left Spain and I have a feeling you can do one can't you even though you don't look like a Flamenco dancer with that blonde hair. Though I saw one blond dancer several years ago in Spain for just a minute one night, was it you?" she walked up to him and quietly said.

"Please don't say anymore not here." He just looked at her she was the same woman a little older but the same woman.

"Dance for me one time."

"I need some music and there isn't any?" then he smiled at her and he motioned behind him at a man that had been playing guitar in the courtyard for him and his friends. Samantha nodded to him then she sat down and changed her boots for her dancing shoes and stood up again and went further out on the plaza and the guitarists began to play. She began to tap her feet and it got faster and faster till you couldn't see her feet move anymore. She glided and turned and went around the patio and returned did a final flourish and then quit in front of the man.

"Satisfied because I am done now? Melanee it is time to go home darlin'." The crowd was clapping and the man that was making Melanee's shoes was smiling at her and she smiled back as he told her again.

"I will have a front row seat." Samantha winked at him.

"I will save you one of the best ones my friend." Then she gathered everyone up to leave. The man who had accosted her before stopped her.

"You are the same woman that was at the palace aren't you?" she backed him up so nobody could hear them talk and said to him.

"Please be quiet I danced for you now keep your mouth shut. I am the woman that was in Spain but I would just as soon not everyone knew that here. I remember seeing you as well I think the party was for you was it not? You were the bull fighter who had won all those bullfights the champion Renaldo Sanchez. The people here just think I am a governess to that little girl and her brother and that I dance and I want to keep it that way." He just looked at her.

"Why, who are you hiding from?" well he hit the nail on the head with the first strike.

"A man that tried to kill me and probably will if he finds me again, satisfied." The man in front of her stared at her then stroked her cheek with his hand.

"He is a fool but I will never tell of your whereabouts I wish you good fortune I am sorry I don't even know your name?"

"Samantha Rodgers, I need to leave now my little lady is getting tired." She walked towards her horse mounted and then the man following handed her Melanee as he looked at the saddle she was riding on. He put his hand underneath the front flap and lifted it up and saw the brand of the Queens Saddle maker and then looked up again at the woman riding the palomino horse.

"I have never seen one of Her Majesty's Saddles out of Spain before, do I even want to know what you did to get one, she doesn't give them out to just anyone?"

"I guess you will have to ask her the next time you see her and then you can tell her Thank You from me, good day sir." Sam turned her horse around and her group started home one guard in front and two behind. The man she left behind asked the man she had talked to in the crowd.

"Who does she work for?" The man was reluctant to tell him.

"Clayton Hayes a plantation owner outside of the village why do you want to know?"

"I was wondering about her. She said she was going to dance at Christmas what is that about?"

"A friend of hers a man named Gabriel Baca is coming at Christmas and they are performing for the village." Gabriel Baca was coming he knew who he was, he too had fled from Spain after some Dons daughter and her sister had been spirited out of the castle by someone and they had escaped to a boat and disappeared. They suspected Gabriel and his son of helping them with some American girl. It was also said the American girl helped the Queen with the Bishop somehow, nobody knew how but she did. He was smiling to himself it was all beginning to fall into place he figured he had just met the American girl and Gabriel was coming to dance with her at Christmas he was going to have to make a trip back here then.

He was down here promoting bullfighting in South America. She had caught his eye that night but her father and Gabriel had made sure no one got to close to her she was off limits. He was otherwise occupied with a Counts daughter he should have paid more attention to the blond Texas dancer. He would see to it he was back for the Christmas celebration. They were calling him so he turned to leave but not without taking one last look at the blond woman on the horse in front of him disappearing into the jungle.

Clayton was waiting for Samantha when she got home in the courtyard and he was to say the least bit anxious.

"What is wrong you look like a thundercloud what has happened?" he took Melanee down from the saddle and was holding her as Sam got down he wasn't even aware the little girl was looking at him like he was a total stranger. She was walking the horse to the corral as they talked and he was still holding her and she didn't know exactly what to do. Samantha finally stopped and said to him.

"Will you tell your daughter it is all right that you are holding her that she is not in trouble she is scared to death?" he looked at his little girl and she was indeed scared and he just hugged her.

"You are never going to have to be scared of me again little girl I promise alright?" Melanee looked at her father and then at Samantha and then she reluctantly put her arm around his neck and they continued to the corrals. Well it was something.

"Where have you two been the men said you went to town but you were gone so long I was about to come looking for you. Why didn't you wait and I would have come with you."

"I took three men and it was not that far and we needed some more material and you weren't going till next week what is the problem? She gave the horse over to one of the hands as they walked back to the hacienda and he wasn't telling her something.

"What is it what is going on you are afraid of something what is it?" "We have something killing livestock and we don't know what, Russell sent over a man today and he is losing animals too but he is as mystified as we are. We think it may be a big cat but we aren't sure, usually Jaguars don't kill livestock and not this many. I want you to stay close to the hacienda for a few days until we know what it is, alright?" they walked into the house Steven met them at the door.

"Juanita says let's eat." Russell carried his daughter all the way inside to the table as Sam watched then she turned and listened as she heard a scream in the jungle and it was close. Why would it be this close? After supper she headed upstairs and she went to her bedroom and changed her clothes then Clayton came down the balcony and stood at her door and just looked at her.

"Do you think we are keeping this a secret from anyone? I am pretty sure Juanita knows she gives me this stupid grin in the morning every morning." He walked into her room and locked his hands behind her back and pulled her to him and then kissed her.

"Well your daughter knows." He stood back a little and looked at her. "Really how much does she know?"

"That I go to daddy's room at night, you all forget she has been ignored for so long but she sees everything and hears everything and you just don't notice her but she doesn't miss a thing." He stood there soaking in what she had said and then he grinned and asked her.

"Well, what does she think of us together?" she smacked him on the arm.

"Really you are a cad. She thinks it is great she loves me and wants me for a mother." He smiled again.

"Good marry me and we won't have to keep this a secret anymore." "Have you not noticed your daughter just barely tolerates you and that will be better before I marry you, today was a start but you still have work to do a lot of it." He leaned down and kissed her and took her hand and they went down the balcony to his room but they stopped as they again heard the cat screaming in the jungle and it was closer this time.

"Clayton would that cat come into the courtyard it sure is getting close?" he looked down at her and then at the yard.

"I don't think so but I don't know about this cat, there is something wrong with it, the tracks are disfigured like it has been mauled by something that is why we think it is attacking farm animals they are easy prey. It tore up a pig at Russell's place and barely ate anything. Just killed it that is not something a big jaguar would do."

"What are you going to do about it?"

"Russell's men shot at it today they don't know if they hit it or not but tomorrow some of the men and me are going to try and hunt it down and kill it. Something is wrong with it and it is dangerous and it needs to be put down and soon we have to find it."

"Let's go to bed it sounds like tomorrows going to be a long day." they lay down in the bed and left the louvered doors open so the breeze could come in and went to sleep. Later that night Samantha awoke to Clayton whispering in her ear.

"Quiet do you hear him, he is on the roof?" she didn't at first so she listened then she heard soft padded footsteps crunching on the tilled roof and she shivered. The cat was walking towards the balcony and the doors were open. She felt Claytons hand on her shoulder and then he slid quietly out of the bed and went to the doors and closed them and slid the bolt home. He came back to the bed quietly and leaned down to her and asked her.

"Did you close the doors in your bedroom before we left tonight?" she panicked did she close them; yes she did so Melanee wouldn't come in unexpectedly. She nodded yes.

Put on your robe and get the children and meet me downstairs in the den and close all the main doors so he can't get in anywhere. Wake Juanita and get everyone to the library I will meet you there I will close everything up here stay as quiet as you can so he won't hear you." Sam didn't say anything she just pulled on her robe and started down the hall to the children's room. She opened Melanee's door and went to her open louvered doors and shut them first then turned and Melanee was awake and looking at her. She stared to say something and Sam put her finger to her mouth to tell her to be quiet and just picked her up and they left the room and went to Steven's room. She sat her on Steven's bed while she woke him and got him out of bed they didn't understand what was going on. Sam shut the windows in this room as well and then started down the stairs with the children to the library. When they got there she had the children sit on the table where she could see them from anywhere in the room.

"You sit right there where I can see you while I light a lantern alright?" they were terrified but they were listening to her. After she got two lanterns lit she sat one on the table and told the children.

"You are safe here I am going to go get Juanita stay right here I will be right back for you promise me." Steven asked her.

"What is going on where is daddy?"

"He is shutting doors to the house that jaguar is on the roof and he was afraid he would get on the balcony. He will be here soon now you watch after your sister I will be right back do not leave." Sam took the lantern and went down the hall shutting the back door and the side door. They were half doors to keep snakes out of the house but that cat wouldn't have a problem jumping over that short door. They needed to have a better ventilation system with fewer open doors. Sam got to the kitchen and quietly shut that door as well and went into Juanita's room. Sam almost scared her to death; she had to put her hand over her mouth to stop her from screaming.

"Quiet you have to be quiet we have a problem come with me now." Juanita grabbed her robe and followed Sam into the library where the children were and they were meet by Clayton he was loading a Winchester rifle.

"Do you know where he is?" Clayton kept loading the rifle as he talked to them.

"I heard him jump onto the balcony but I can't see him from the house I am going to have to go outside to see where he is hiding."

"Give me a pistol then I am going with you."

No you are not I am going alone." She just looked at him and said. "It is dark and you are alone out there with a dark spotted cat and you think I am going to let the man I love go out there alone you are out of your cotton picking mind now give me a pistol." Melanee and Juanita were giggling and Steven was stunned, well it wasn't a secret anymore.

"Well alright then I will get you a pistol."

"Maybe the men in the bunkhouse have noticed that things aren't alright up here maybe we could get some help from them or at least not get shot by one of them."

"Juanita keep the children in here away from the windows and we are going to the kitchen stay quiet. Let's go honey we will see if anybody is awake in the bunkhouse." They walked to the back door and they could hear the cat off and on growling low but not too loud they didn't know if the men in the bunkhouse would hear that or not. The horses were rustling around in the corrals. When they got to the kitchen they could see a light in the bunkhouse there was someone awake so Clayton took a cloth and put it over the lantern for just a moment and then took it off and then someone did the same in the bunkhouse. Clayton looked at Sam and said.

"I am going to step out and try to get a better angle and maybe one of the men down there will to, then we can see him better I don't know what else to do at least the moon is full we will have a little light." He walked out and around the tables on the patio and was just under the tree when she looked up but it was already too late the cat was sitting it the crook of the orange tree.

"Clayton look out it is in the tree." He only had time to hold his rifle up and keep the jaguar from ripping his throat out and it was on top of him he couldn't get away from it and those claws. The men at the bunkhouse were coming but they weren't going to get here fast enough so Sam started running. She got there in seconds but it seemed longer it was so dark she couldn't tell Clayton from the jaguar so she got as close to Clayton as she could and then she put that pistol in that cats belly and fired and then fired again and again until it didn't move any more. The cat was laying on both of them and it wasn't moving but neither was Clayton and he wasn't talking to her either then she panicked. The men from the bunkhouse were there by then and she was screaming.

"Get it off now he is hurt." She was almost screaming Clayton wasn't saying anything and it terrified her. The men from the bunkhouse started to pull the big cat off of him when he started yelling.

"Wait he has his claws sunk into the upper part of my leg you are going to have to get them out first." Sam wiggled out from under the cat as Clayton tried to get him off as well.

"Be careful you are on the business end of this rifle just get back and let them pull it off of me." She grabbed a lantern and held it up for the men to see. As they pulled the cat off of him Clayton started to complain.

"Can you get the claws out of my leg they really hurt and then you can get it off of me." Sam leaned down and saw the claws in his leg and she carefully pulled them out but she had to do it one by one. When she was through he was bleeding badly and she wanted to get him to the house. Clayton stopped her and then he asked his men.

"Turn him over I want to look at him." The men pulled the cat several feet away and then turned it over. When Clayton reached down to look at one of the front paws Sam could see what the problem with the cat was. One of his paws was deformed and it was turned to the inside and the claws had grown into the pad of the cat's paw. It must have been in terrible pain, now they knew why he was just killing at random and not eating his kills.

"Alright it is time to take care of you the men can deal with the cat." Clayton tried to walk but he was bleeding badly and two of his men had to hold him up and help him in the house. When they got him upstairs Samantha was appalled by the damage caused by the cat in such a little time. He had four deep gashes as well as deep puncture wounds on his leg as well as teeth marks on his neck. If not for his rifle the cat would have ripped out his throat. She got him undressed and then got him to the tub and washed off all the blood they could but she couldn't get the leg to stop bleeding.

Juanita had brought some herbs that she used for wounds around here and they applied them to the wound and they seemed to be working. They had wrapped the wounds and he was sleeping when he awoke hours later and he was calling his dead wife's name.

"Clayton wake up its Samantha look at me." He looked at her with unseeing eyes. He was burning up with fever.

"Who are you where is my wife, go and get her now I need her. Juanita where are you, get this woman out of here." Samantha just left the room it was no use making him more agitated than he already was. Juanita came out and met her outside the door and she asked her.

"What are we going to do now he is burning up and I don't know what to use down here maybe if I was at home I would know but not here." Juanita was drying her hands off and then she looked at Sam.

"I have some herbs I use around here but they aren't like the ones the medicine men use they are the best. You would have to ask a Mayan shaman for them and they want something in return and you have to know someone to even ask. Do you know someone?" She knew someone alright but she had made him mad the last time she had seen him would he even help her or would he kill Clayton just for spite?

"Let's see what the next few hours bring and if he is no better I will ask for help."

"He is falling asleep when he is asleep you can go back in and we will see how he does." It wasn't long before he was asleep and she went back in and was bathing him with cold compresses to keep down the fever but his leg was swelling at the injured site and his fever was increasing. The teeth marks at his throat were swelling to and it was causing him to have trouble breathing so she decided it was time to go. The wound was now angry red and swollen past the bandages so they took them off it was then she left the room and told Juanita she would be back. She went downstairs and started towards the corrals when one of the men walked out.

"How is the patron doing?"

"Not well at all can you saddle my horse I am going for some help as soon as it is light." She went to the barn and got a rope and then went to the jaguar and tied it around the head of the cat and then to her horse. Sundance was not happy to be standing that close to that cat. She got up in the saddle and wrapped the rope around the saddle horn a couple of times and off she went dragging that cat behind her. She went down the road to statue of the jaguar and then she took the rope and looped over the head of the jaguar statue and then pulled the cat up. She got off the horse and tied the jaguar off at the bottom of the statue and then she started screaming into the jungle.

"Balik I need help. Please send me your shaman Clayton has been hurt help me." Then she got down on her knees in front of the statue and waited ever so often she screamed Balik's name into the jungle. One of the men from the plantation had followed her to make sure she was safe and now he was just watching her. He watched and he saw her kneeling and calling out for someone. He stood there for hours and as the rain started to fall he just kept watching until he decided he was going to get her and take her home and then some men came out of the jungle. Three Mayan men and a woman and they went to her and helped her stand.

"Balik, I wasn't sure if you heard me or if you would come." Balik just looked at her and started talking through Te'a.

"I told you I would come if you needed me and here I am. I brought my shaman but you will have to make amends to him before he will help you."

"What does he want I will pay whatever he requires?" Balik smiled at her.

"Who killed the jaguar?" "I killed it. Why."

"He wants the hide and the claws it will make a fine robe and powerful medicine but you have to present it to him as a gift."

"Whatever he wants I will have it bathed and skinned if that is what he wants just let's get back to Clayton he is very sick." Balik smiled at her then said.

"No all you have to do is formally present it to him and he will be satisfied." Samantha went over to the now very stiff jaguar and lowered it down to the ground and then she went over to the shaman and said. "Please accept this jaguar as a gift from me to you." Then she did a bow and stepped back. He said something to Balik and pointed to his neck and she assumed he also wanted the necklace she was wearing so she started to take it off as well but that was when Balik told Te'a.

"Samantha, Balik says no you are to keep the necklace it is yours and if you ever need help send someone with it and he will know it is you so you keep that." Sam figured the medicine man was just trying to take to many liberties and Balik stopped him at that one. She didn't care she wanted to be gone from here. About that time the man that had been watching her walked out and he had another horse so they loaded up the medicine man and Te'a on one and Balik and Sam on her horse. The ranch hand and the one remaining Mayan would stay with the jaguar and skin it. They hurried as much as they could caring two to a horse and got there in about an hour. Juanita was waiting for her at the kitchen door and Sam led them upstairs to the bedroom. The shaman looked over Claytons leg then told Te'a what he would need and Sam and Juanita stared gathering pots and bowls with boiling water and cloths to use for bandages.

"Juanita you understand them better than I do try and remember what he uses so we will know next time what to find in the jungle." The women watched as the medicine man went to work as he took off the bandages. Sam thought she was going to be sick. The wounds were already very infected and his leg was almost twice the size as when she had left hours ago. Clayton was fighting with him and screaming for his wife and it took all the men to hold him down. The shaman pulled out some powder from a bag and blew it into Claytons face and after a few minutes he calmed down it seemed like he went into a trance he didn't care what they were doing to him anymore. Samantha turned around and looked at Balik and asked him.

"What is that powder?" Balik smiled but he wouldn't tell her she guessed that was something she wasn't supposed to know about. She just watched as the medicine man worked and then he started to take a knife and open the claw marks and she went to object when Balik stopped her.

"They have to be opened and drained or they won't heal it has to be done and I don't think he even knows what he is doing." She stood back and watched as he cleaned the wounds and she didn't even realize she was crying or that she was clenching her hands so tight she was drawing blood until Balik took one of her hands and opened it and then led her away. He took her down to her bedroom and led her inside then he sat her down on the chair and just stood there. Te'a came in and Balik started to talk.

"He is calling for his wife he is not calling for you does that not bother you?" she looked up at him and she knew what he wanted to hear but she wasn't going to say it.

"Of course it does but he is sick and he can't be held accountable for what he says when he is like this. When he is better things will go back to the way they were." Balik looked at her and just nodded he wasn't as sure as she was, he already knew that she had killed the cat and he wasn't sure a man like Clayton could ever forgive a woman for saving him. Clayton was going to have to recover from this attack and he was afraid he was going to take his hurts out on Samantha.

"You rest, the medicine man will take care of him and I will come get you if he calls." She nodded and then lay down and she fell asleep, she was exhausted. Balik stood outside the door and just watched her for hours it was all he could do right now. Samantha woke a little while later and got up she was light headed and she wondered when the last time she had eaten was. There was a glass of juice on the table but it had been sitting there for a while and she didn't think it was a good idea to drink it. She walked out to the balcony and down to Clayton's room to check on him and when she went in he saw her and he asked her.

"Why did you bring these people into my house I was perfectly fine without them here. You have no right to do this without my permission. Who do you think you are?"

"Clayton you were sick and we didn't know what to do we were afraid you were dying."

"My wife Alice would have known what to do without bringing them in here they could have killed me."

"If they don't I may." She started to escort the men out of the room and get Te'a out before she could translate what had been said because Balik would have killed him right there. About that time something smashed against the wall it was a bowl full of water and he had sprayed her with it now Balik was furious. She just kept pushing them down the balcony and she heard Juanita talking to him behind her. Balik turned around and took her arms in his and had Te'a tell her.

"Come with me my wife is dying you can take her place I will keep you safe." Samantha felt like she had been slapped that was all she needed and she was crashing and she desperately needed some sugar. She walked over to the chair and just landed in it. Te'a knew what was going on so she grabbed an orange off the tree above her and leaned down to help her. Balik was on his knees as Te'a explained what was going on as she pealed the orange. Sam looked at him and smiled as she ate the orange and began to feel better. She put her hand on his face as she told him.

"Don't you understand I love him and I haven't given up yet, not yet? Can you tell me what I need to do to get him well and if this isn't better, well then I will have other options won't I." he took her hand and held it and then stood up and walked away she knew he was there and hers if she wanted him. The shaman stayed for a few minutes longer and gave her instructions through Te'a on what to do and then they left as well. She just sat there for a while and then went back to Clayton's room and started over again.

CHAPTER 7

Russell showed up two days later and Sam couldn't have been more pleased to see anyone. When he got down off of his horse he was appalled by the way she looked. She was worn out and disheveled he had never seen her look like this even on the trail. She came up to him and hugged him and she was almost in tears.

"What the Hell is going on here we heard someone killed the jaguar and that Clayton was hurt but when we didn't hear anymore I decided to come over and find out what was going on. My men say you had a medicine man helping you that wouldn't have been the one you pissed off at the village would it? Samantha just nodded and smiled.

"That means Balik was here too that must have made Clayton mad?"

"It did but everything I do lately seems to make him mad so it really doesn't matter a great deal. Would you like to go inside we were about to sit down to lunch?" he looked at her funny and then took her arm in his and walked her inside and then turned and asked her.

"Where is the jaguar I wanted to see it my men say there was something wrong with its foot that is why it went crazy."

"It is gone that was the price for the medicine man to help Clayton, that and me apologizing to him. Its front paw was deformed and the claws turned inside so its foot was mangled." Russell had stopped and was staring at her.

"You had to apologize to him, that blowhard? You killed the jaguar didn't you I'll bet that is killing Clayton."

"There are a lot of things bothering Clayton and that is the least of them right now."

"What does that mean Samantha?" she didn't say anything she just kept walking and as Russell followed her he was about to see exactly what was going on and he wasn't going to like it. As they got inside Juanita was setting the table and the children were sitting down for lunch and Clayton started yelling from upstairs.

"Juanita you take care of him and I will take care of the children. Russell you can go up and see him if you want I will stay down here it will be better that way." Russell looked at her funny she was acting strangely and Juanita was too. He would just go upstairs and see for himself what was going on. When he got upstairs and he got to Claytons room he saw a man that was lucky to be alive. His neck had been slashed and his leg was a mess, that medicine man was good or he would have been attending his funeral.

"Well did you come to see if she is ready to leave the invalid? Did she tell you she had to kill that jaguar to keep it from killing me, well she was wrong I had everything under control. She had no right to bring Balik and his medicine man into my house, what did she trade for his help because he doesn't do anything for free." He was being mean and Russell had had enough so he was going to have his say now.

"What part did you have under control his ripping out your throat or his shredding your leg, have you looked in the mirror lately I think you owe that lady your life. I know a man like you wouldn't want to owe anyone a debt like that though, you would rather be dead right? You really think she would betray you; if you do you are a fool."

Russell turned around and started back down stairs he had heard enough for one day. He had lunch with the family and then Samantha went upstairs to clean up and rest and Russell went to the patio. He had been there for about an hour when he saw Clayton limp into Samantha's room across the balcony and he could hear every word; Clayton wasn't even trying to be quiet.

"Well has Russell come to take you away from all this drama, you have so many options now don't you? You wanted to take over my wife's position in this house but you weren't quite up to the task were you? Well are you just going to stand there or are you going to answer me?" Russell had headed up the back stairs and was watching as well as listening he couldn't believe this was the same man that had brought her here just months ago he was brutal to her.

"I don't know anymore how to answer you I don't seem to say the right thing no matter what I say so I just stay out of your way, I thought that is what you wanted. Is this how you treated your wife when you found out she was pregnant is this the tender care you provided her or did you think she betrayed you as well?"

"When I found out about the baby I wanted her to get rid of the child. She wouldn't so I ignored her in the hopes she would see her mistake. She didn't and she had the child anyway and it killed her."

"That mistake is your daughter and Alice gave up her life to give her to you and you have all but shunned her all of her life. Now I understand why she finally just gave up and died it was easier than dealing with you. Maybe it would be better if I left too I don't seem to be what you want anymore either."

"Maybe it would, you are not the woman I thought you were. I guess it is a good thing you can't have children at least we don't have to worry about that now do we."

He regretted the words the second they came out of his mouth and he couldn't have hurt her more if he had slapped her. He backed up and started to think about what he had just said and how he could take it back but she wasn't going to let him get away with anymore.

"If that is what you want I can take care if that right now and leave. I can go to town until Gabriel gets here and then go back with him to Rio and you won't have to be bothered with me again I am done. I thought Nathan was bad I was wrong."

"You don't have any money how do you think you will live in town?" Russell was behind him and still listening.

"She won't have to worry about money I will see to it she is taken care of, start packing Sam and I will get you out of here. There is no reason for you to stay and put up with this anymore." Damn he had forgotten Russell was still here, of course he would take care of her he had just put his foot in his mouth and sent her running right into Russell's arms what a fool he was today.

""That won't be necessary. Juanita please come up here." They were waiting for Juanita to come up the stairs and Sam had already begun to gather her things on the bed when she came in. Clayton leaned over and said something in her ear and she went back down. She returned several minutes later with a small bag with coins in it and handed it to Clayton. Juanita kept looking at Samantha as if she wanted her to say something but she wouldn't.

"You won't have to rely on anybody here is wages for your service here." he handed her the bag she took and lifted it up and it seemed heavy she guessed he was buying her off so she would go away. He was really making sure she wouldn't do anything stupid until he could make this right. Juanita kept looking at her funny but she didn't say anything as she gathered her clothes. It didn't take her long she still didn't have much she had some new skirts upstairs but they weren't finished so she would leave them behind. The last thing she loaded was the black dancing dress and her dancing shoes and he finally realized she was going, OH LORD what had he done.

"Samantha maybe I...." he didn't get any further Russell stopped him he could tell what he was going to say and he wasn't going to let him. He wanted her out of here and he was going to do just that.

"Come on Samantha lets go let me take your bags my men are already waiting downstairs." He took her arm and led her outside and down the balcony to the waiting horses and when they were mounted Sam called Juanita over to her and said something to her. Then they left and she didn't turn back to look at him and for the first time he knew he was in trouble.

They were going down the road to town and she wouldn't say a word or even look at Russell until he finally said.

"Talk to me why did you put up with this you knew you could call on me or go to town and I would come get you? Did you just stay for the children tell me what makes a woman like you put up with that?" she still didn't say anything for a bit and then she stopped and let the men get a little further down the road until they were alone and she could talk to him. She turned in the saddle and looked at him and simply said.

"That Texas doctor was wrong Russell." She said it calmly more calmly than she felt and he thought he was going to be sick she was lost to him he could see it in her eyes.

"He has no idea?" she shook her head no.

"After what he just said to me you are the only one who knows and the only who can know. When Gabriel comes I will go with him and then I will disappear into Brazil and he will never know." Then she kept riding back to town as the tears streamed down her face. Russell just rode beside her and left her alone and they rode into town and he had never wanted to kill any man so badly in his life. Even then there were eyes watching her leave the hacienda.

He got into town and there was a small place that was used as a hotel it only had five rooms but it was clean and it would have to do. Russell got her upstairs and then he got a room for himself and his men. He would send his men back to his place tomorrow with instructions for his plantation and he would stay here for a while at least. He ordered some supper and then went back upstairs to see if Samantha was alright. She was standing at the balcony just looking out into the growing darkness.

"You really don't have to go you know we could go back to Mexico City and get married then you could have the baby and he would never know whose child it was." She turned around and looked at him and smiled and said.

"You would and some day we would be arguing and you would let it slip, a secret like that can't stay secret and you know it. Russell you are a good man just not for me. I have Gabriel bringing someone with him to the festival I want you to meet I think you will like her. Her name is Patricia and she is redheaded spitfire and I think you two will be perfect for each other."

"Are you fixing me up now? Where did she come from anyway is she one of your strays?" Samantha leaned her head to the side and smiled.

"Her sister is the one we sneaked out of the castle that night in Spain. Her father wanted Patricia to marry an older gentleman who had already buried two wives it was said he beat one to death. Her father didn't care it seemed the man was paying a high price for the Patricia. She didn't want to marry him so he was threatening to put her in a convent until she relented and did what he said, nice man right. While we were putting holes in a large chest to hide her sister in we stole a guard's uniform for her. There had been some actors there the night before and they helped us with a wig and a fake mustache for her it was wonderful. She walked out with five other guards the next morning right past her father. No one noticed that six guards went on the boat and only five came off except the queen who was watching from the dock and she was smiling and waving." Russell was just staring at her, she was like an onion the more you peeled the more you found it was a little scary.

"So she will be coming with Gabriel?"

"Yes she likes a little adventure and this is a good place for that, I thought you might want to show her around your place, Gabriel says she loves it here in South America." Russell was smiling at her.

"What is she really like?"

"Her sister was always trying to please their father but Patricia was the one who was running the ranch and taking care of everything else. Then her father was going to remarry and everything changed his new wife wanted the girls gone and her new husband wealthy. Patricia's sister was easy until she met Anthony and then things changed and Pat was always going to be a problem. He decided he would put her in a convent where they would cut off all her hair and she would have to pray and be quiet for oh say a year or so and then she would do whatever he said. So we decided to sneak them both out of the country. I'll bet he is still cussing me he was a man who liked getting his own way. I wonder if that woman married him or not?" Samantha just sat there and smiled.

"Oh you are something else and now I can't wait to meet this woman she sounds a lot like you. What happened on the ship coming back to the Americas?"

"We ran into rough seas and I ran out of sugar and I got very sick it was miserable that is why I said I would never get on a ship again. The captain of the ship was wonderful. We stopped at every little island we could and took on fruit until we got to Brazil and loaded enough to get home to Texas. We had to stay a week in Brazil because I was so sick I just couldn't go on. Pat took care of me and then we swam in the bay by the boat and we loved it there and they stayed and waited for Gabriel to meet them there. They started another dance school and Antonio married Natasha and they have a son but Gabriel says Patricia is still single and is still looking for someone, she still hasn't found what she is looking for."

"And what is she looking for Samantha?" Sam smiled at him.

"We talked a lot on that long voyage to get here and all she could talk about was having a home and a man who she could build something with and have children and a life. Someone who would love her like a partner not a servant, can you understand that? She is a smart lady and she knows how to run a ranch and her father hated that she could do it better than him. I hope he lost it after we left."

"You like her very much don't you?"

"She is a very special lady I think you will like her to. I am getting tired Russell let's call it a day." She got up and went inside to her room and he went down to his with the thoughts of a redheaded woman in his mind. She went to hers and sat down in the chair by the door and leaned back and just let the tears fall.

Melanee had heard them yelling at each other and she had seen Sam leave with that other man. She had waited for everything to settle down and then she went to Stevens' room and stood by his bed. She wasn't making a sound but he woke up anyway and saw her standing by his bed crying.

"What is wrong are you hurt do we need to go get Sam?" she came over to him and put her arms around him and cried so quietly and he wondered how many times he had made her do the same thing and he hadn't know about it or cared but he did this time. He pulled her up on to the bed with him and wrapped the blanket around her and then he asked her again quietly.

"What is wrong Melanee?" she had her head tucked into his chest as she started to talk.

"Sam and daddy had a fight and she left with that other man, daddy was screaming at her that she wasn't as good as mama so she needed to go. He said he wanted mama to do something about me and she wouldn't so he was mean to her till she died what was he talking about Steven?" she could feel Steven tense up and she didn't understand that he knew what had been going on even as a little boy and he knew more now how his father had acted towards his mother.

"I has nothing to do with you we will take care of this tomorrow if she is gone we will get her back or we will go to her she can't have gone far she promised. Here just lay down in the bed and go to sleep we will figure this out in the morning." This was the first time in his life he had ever gone to bed hating his father. He knew exactly what Melanee was talking about; he could remember how his father talked to his mother when she was pregnant with her. Now he understood what he had been saying to her. When he remembered back he could see his mother's sad face and now he needed to get Melanee out of here and back to Sam well maybe there was a way.

The next morning he woke Melanee and they started down the hall and he saw Juanita coming out of his father's room and she was in a hurry.

"What's wrong Juanita?" she just kept walking down the hall then she turned and said.

"Your fathers fever is back and I need to get the women and take care of it now. One of the other women will take of you today so go downstairs and have breakfast." Melanee looked at her brother and said.

"Now what do we do?" Steven looked at her and he had been planning to try to go to town and find Samantha.

"I wanted to try and go to the village but we can't go alone so I don't know what to do."

"Why can't we go alone it is not that far and we know the way. We could have the men saddle our horses and tell them we are just going to ride around the house and with daddy sick no one is really going to be watching us today. If we wait they will stop us and she might be gone when we get there."

"Let's go eat breakfast and packs some extra food and then we will get the horses saddled and leave while everyone is busy with taking care of daddy. Get your hat and a jacket and put them on the patio so no one notices. Are you sure you want to do this?" Melanee looked at him and then looked upstairs and remembered what her daddy had said last night.

"I want to find Sam he doesn't want me and never has if you want to stay just help me get out of here and I will be alright getting to town." He wasn't going to let her go alone besides he missed Sam already. One of the other maids fed them and then she left them alone so they packed up what was left in towels and took it with them to the patio. While Steven took care of the horses Melanee took care to get the jackets and their hats, she almost got caught by Juanita going down the stairs. She heard her coming so she dropped the hats and jackets over the railing before she saw them.

"What are you doing Melanee and where is Steven?"

"I am right here we were going to go outside and sit on the patio it is cool and then we thought we might brush the horses when the men had time to catch them for us is that alright?" she just looked at Steven he had changed since Sam had come and now she was gone, well she didn't have time to worry about it now she had to take care of her patron he had a high fever again.

"That will be fine just stay close so the men can see you and I will have the women take care of you at supper time." They just smiled at her and watched her go back upstairs and then they started outside.

"It is not too late to call this off we can just play in the courtyard or walk the horses around the coral we don't have to try to get to town Melanee." He was beginning to have a bad feeling about this and he was a little afraid that jungle was a big place and they would be unguarded. Melanee just grabbed her jacket and hat and kept on walking she was going with or without him where had she gotten all of this courage all of the sudden or had she always had it and he just hadn't noticed it before. They got to the stables and the men had the horses saddled and one of the men asked then where they going? Steven answered.

"We are just going to ride around the hacienda for a while everybody is taking care of daddy and we are in the way. We will be back later we won't go far. We will go down to the snake statue we have some food for lunch and there is water there we will be fine." The men didn't know anything about this but they weren't always told what was going on and most of them didn't know that Samantha was gone. If they had known those children were riding off alone they would have never let them go. But nobody knew what the children had in mind so they rode off in the direction of town with nobody the wiser.

They had been riding for about two hours and Steven was getting increasing nervous he had expected Melanee to get scared and turn back by now and she hadn't. The jungle was so quiet and he finally said.

"Melanee it is time we went back I don't think we are going to make the village before night and I don't want to be out here after dark." She turned around on her horse and just looked at him.

"I am not going back I will call for one of Balik's men and I will keep going you can go back if you want to." He looked at her.

"There is nobody out here that is going to help you maybe kidnap you but not help you."

"Really watch this. Por favor, Balik's man I need your help come out please. Now we wait." Then she sat in her saddle and started to wait.

"I don't know what you think you are waiting for who is this man Balik?"

"He watches over Samantha he is the one who killed the priest and hung him up on the statue that you saw that day and he guards her and now me at the hacienda now his man will come."Steven was now terrified that was the man they were counting on to protect them he was a murderer they had to get out of here now so he reached for his sisters reins just as a man came out of the jungle. The man started towards them and it was a Mayan Indian, Melanee had been right he couldn't have been very far away. He walked up to Melanee and she pulled a necklace from inside her shirt and showed it to the man and he nodded to her and then took hold of her reins and started walking her towards town or what he hoped was town. Steven walked up beside her and asked her.

"What is the necklace you showed him?" Melanee picked it up again and let her brother look at it. He had never seen it before it was a shiny black claw put on a leather string.

"A couple of days ago Balik's daughter or I think it is his daughter Te'a brought it to me and told me about the man watching the house. She said if I needed help to call and show him the necklace and they would help me and that is what I did. It is from the Jaguar Samantha killed and it is big medicine to the Maya."

"Aren't you afraid of these people after all they killed that priest you didn't see what they did to him?"

"You didn't hear what Sam told me that man did to Balik's son while he had him captive maybe he shouldn't have killed him but he was going to cut off the boys arm." They didn't have time to talk much more they began to hear voices in the distance they were almost to the village.

Russell was trying to talk Samantha into letting him take a small house on the edge of town so she would be more comfortable and she was having none of it. She told him she was just fine where she was. The house had belonged to a man that had owned a small parcel of land around here but his wife absolutely refused to live in the jungle so she stayed in the small village which she hated as well. It hadn't taken long for the man to take a local woman and he divorced the unhappy wife and sent her back to Mexico City where she found a much better match. The man married the local woman and they had moved onto his land. The house was available but Russell couldn't talk her into it.

"I am just fine where I am Russell I have plenty of room and when Gabriel comes I will be leaving." Lord he hated this he didn't want her to go even if she was here with Clayton. Then he looked up at the road and started to smile and he patted Samantha's hand.

"NO Russell I don't need a bigger house."

"You may. Turn around Sam and look behind you that room is going to be too small." She turned around and there were Melanee and Steven being led into town by one of Balik's men, she just started running. She got close to Moon Melanee's horse and she jumped off into Sam's arms and she was babbling.

"What in the world are you two doing coming to town alone do you know what could have happened to you?" she looked up at Steven and he was almost in tears he was so scared but he was looking at their escort, he was terrified of the man that had brought them into town. Well one thing at a time. She had Russell thank the Mayan man so he could disappear before the townspeople got to inquisitive she would get the rest of that story later. Russell had been talking to the their guide. He gave him some money and he disappeared back into the jungle.

Russell took Steven's horse and Sam took Moon and they walked to the table where she told a man to take the horses to the stable. She ordered some food for the children and got them seated and then started to listen to their story. Melanee was talking so fast she had to slow her down.

"You left us all alone and daddy didn't want me so we started coming to town and then I called to the man in the jungle and he came and got us."

"Slow down you are not making sense Steven start from the beginning." Steven looked uncomfortable so Sam asked Russell to take Melanee and take care of supper she would know what they would like to eat so she could talk to Steven. When they were gone Steven started to talk to her.

"She came to my room crying she heard your argument with daddy and she didn't understand what he was talking about. You know when my mother was pregnant with her but I did. All she knew is that you had left us and you promised you wouldn't. She heard enough to know he didn't want her before she was born so she wanted to come find you and she was going to do it whether I helped her or not. Someone brought her a necklace and told her if she needed help just call into the jungle and there would be help there. Sure enough there was a man and he brought us here. She wants to go with you and so do I, so here we are now what do we do?" Sam didn't have the foggiest what to do now she was surprised there weren't men hot on their trails looking for them already.

"How did you get out of the house without anyone noticing?" "Daddy's fever is bad again and everyone is taking care of him and we just left." Her stomach rolled over, he was sick again and she wasn't there to help, well he sent her away. She had to send word to Juanita that the children were with her she would be out of her mind as soon as she realized they were gone. Russell was coming back and she had things to do.

"Russell it looks like I am going to need that house after all so get started on procuring it for me Please." He just grinned he had already rented the house and it was ready for her when he talked her into moving into it.

"I need to write a letter to Juanita and send it back to the hacienda with one of your men as they go back to your place if that is all right with you. I will get the letter ready."

"You get whatever you need done and I will take care of the rest of it. We will be waiting down here while I feed the children. I take it they are not going back?"

"NO they are not." And she went upstairs to write a note to Juanita it wasn't going to be long and she wasn't going to like it but too bad."

JUANITA

The children are with me in town and they are safe. They came by themselves to find me after hearing Clayton's little speech last night, they are safe here but I didn't want you to worry. I hope he is doing better.

SAMANTHA

When she got back downstairs the children had been fed and were falling asleep in their chairs. She and Russell started walking to the little house he had been talking about and it wasn't so little. The people down here had no idea what little was it was a modest ranch house for a family. She walked inside and several women were already there cleaning and getting beds ready. The inside of the house was clean and ready for occupancy. She turned around and started to scold him about taking too many things for granted but he was right about this one and she appreciated it. She found bedrooms off to the side and both children down for the night and then turned around to Russell and said.

"This is perfect for right now you were right."

"You know he wouldn't let you take his children with you don't you not both of them anyway?"

"I wouldn't think a descent father would let me take even one of his children would you?" She was right a father would fight for his children no matter what.

"I am leaving now I will see you in the morning and we will see what happens then." She just nodded and followed him to the door and locked it and then went to find out where she would be sleeping in this house. Her world was falling apart and she just wished Gabriel would get here.

The next morning men arrived at her house while she was feeding the children and handed her a note and she sat down and read it. The man on the horse was anxious and kept saying he needed to be going get the kids ready. She looked up at him and said.

"Wait here a minute I have a message to send back with you." The man waiting was mad and started to get down out of the saddle until another man came out of the house and told him.

"Just stay where you are she will be back in a minute and then you can leave." Samantha came out of the house and she had a letter in her hand and she handed it to the man on the horse and then she told him.

"Give this to Juanita it will explain everything and no the children are not leaving with you they are staying right here with me. If you have a problem with that the Patron can handle it himself." he snatched the letter from her hands and wheeled around and started back to the hacienda. Well this was a wasted morning and he had better things to do than hunt down two lost kids. He headed back to the hacienda and when he got there Juanita was waiting for him at the kitchen door so he got off the horse and handed her the letter the woman had given him.

"Where are the children?" the man just pointed to the letter and walked away to the corrals to put up his horse. Juanita sat down at the table under the tree to read the letter Samantha had sent her.

JUANITA

The children took a chance coming to find me after Melanee heard that little rant of Claytons' the other night and then she went to her brother to ask him what it meant. He didn't tell her but he knew what she was talking about so they decided to find me. I promised them I would not leave I broke my promise, I won't again. I can't send them back and risk them trying this again so if Clayton wants his children he is going to have to come get them himself and explain to his daughter and son just what he was talking about I am not sure either one will forgive him. I guess we will see.

SAMANTHA

Juanita read the letter twice then folded it and put it in her pocket she knew this day was coming and now it was here.

Clayton had always treated his daughter like she wasn't his well now Melanee had someone who wanted her and she also suspected Samantha was pregnant by Clayton as well. It wasn't going to matter if she couldn't keep him alive and right now that was the question. Clayton was calling again the fever seemed to be breaking and his leg seemed to be getting better too if they could get through today and tonight they might be on the downhill side of this. If Sam hadn't gone for that medicine man he would have been dead by now. She got up slowly from the table and started upstairs she was glad Sam had kept the kids it was one less thing she had to worry about around here.

When she got upstairs Clayton was sitting up in the bed and he was looking a little better. He was going to get up and Juanita stopped him. "Where do you think you are going?" she grabbed him just before he fell on the floor.

"I need to go and apologize to Sam I think I said some things the other night to her, can you have her come in here? Come to think of it why isn't she in here I figured she would be helping you take care of me." Juanita couldn't look him in the face as she got him back in the bed but when she had him settled down she backed away.

"You told her to leave among other things and Russell took her to town a couple of nights ago." He just looked at her.

"How bad was it?"

"Bad you told her she couldn't compare to your first wife Alice and it was a good thing she wasn't pregnant so you didn't have to worry about that." He didn't say a thing he just sat there.

"Is she still in town or did he move her to his hacienda?"

"No she is in town waiting for her friend Gabriel to arrive for the Christmas dance she won't leave till after that."

"I still have some time then to win her back?"

""You have to be well enough to get to town to win her back so let's try and get you better."

"The children are certainly quiet tonight where are they?" she couldn't tell him anymore not tonight.

"They are playing elsewhere so they wouldn't disturb you." Well she wasn't lying really now was she.

"I could really eat something and then you can change this dressing and I will go back to sleep and we will start again in the morning." Juanita cleaned the wounds and rebadged them as he ate some chicken soup and then she asked him if he needed some pain medicine. He was still having a lot of trouble talking that cat had barely missed cutting his throat she was surprised he could talk at all. After she had him cleaned up and he was resting again he asked her.

"What have I been taking for pain I don't seem to remember anything or I have vivid nightmares of horrible creatures."

"I don't know exactly what it is Balik's medicine man left it. You don't seem to have any pain after I use it on you. I think it has another use but I was afraid to ask." She started to have him drink the laudanum she had poured out but he wouldn't take it.

"Not yet I need to be lucid for a few minutes and you can go downstairs I will be alright I will drink that later." He waited till she was gone until everybody was downstairs and then he started to walk or hobble down to Samantha's room. He was holding on to the balcony for dear life but he got there and then he collapsed into the wing back chair in her room. He thought his leg was better than it was. He half expected to find Melanee in Sam's bed that is usually where she was. The room was so empty the bed was made the cabinets were empty her table was clean except that red cup she feed the hummingbirds with.

He had expected the children to beret him for letting her go and they should have been in here by now and he was getting a bad feeling about this, so he stood up with his leg screaming at him and started down the hall to Melanee's room. He could hardly stand when he got there so he was leaning against the wall for support. When he walked into her room all he saw was a made bed and a tidy room she wasn't there he didn't even stop he turned around and went down another door into Stevens room and found another empty room. By now he could barely walk so he sat down on the bed and lit a lantern and there was a maid passed by carrying laundry.

"Go and get Juanita and tell her I want to see her NOW!" the girl dropped what she was holding and started running downstairs as Clayton tried to get back to his room. Juanita found him half way to his bedroom and helped get the rest of the way to his bed. They didn't say anything until she had given him the laudanum to drink and he was covered up in the bed and then he asked her.

"Where are my children?" she just reached into her pocket and handed him the letter Samantha had sent her and then stepped back and let him read it.

"Did she come and get them?"

"No they talked the men into saddling their horses and they rode into the jungle alone and about halfway to the village one of Balik's men came out and escorted them the rest of the way to Sam. Apparently Melanee is wearing a necklace with a jaguar claw so she can summon help from the men in the jungle if she needed it and she needed it." Clayton just kept staring at the letter and then he looked at Juanita.

"What am I going to do she could disappear with my children and they would go with her willingly?" Juanita looked at him and then left the room and was gone a few minutes and then came back with a couple of skirts in her hands and she put them on the bed.

"What is this, should I hold her skirts for ransom I don't think that will work do you?" Juanita reached down and held up one of the skirts by the waist band and made him look closer.

"Look it has extra hooks so the waist band can expand." Clayton just looked up at her and then the light finally dawned on him.

"You think she is pregnant and the skirts are made to be let out. Oh lord and I said that awful thing to her she will never forgive me for that."

"You have a lot of fence mending to do if you want your family back and I mean all your family because she could walk away with everything. Steven is ready to go with her as well, he has figured out what was going on in this house when his mother was pregnant and he doesn't like it. Now he is Melanee protector and he is furious with you and how you treated Alice. I think you need some sleep now and tomorrow maybe you will think better."

"What if she leaves before I talk to her?"

"She won't leave before Gabriel gets here for the Christmas dance she has promised too many people so you have some time. She took a small house in town so the children would be comfortable. You are going to have to convince a lot of people beside her that you won't hurt her again or she won't come back and Melanee is one of them."

"Why didn't you leave me when I treated Alice so badly?"

"Because Alice asked me to take care of Melanee until someone came into her life to love her and now someone has. If you can't love that child like Alice wanted I will let Samantha have her because that is what your wife wanted." He just nodded his head and they didn't say anymore.

Even though he tried it took two more days before he could walk without the help of two men helping him. Every time he did Juanita had to redo the bandages because he started bleeding but he just kept on trying and he kept get getting better. He could finally talk, the swelling was going down in his throat and he could even swallow better. Juanita had rounded up a walking stick for him and he was using it to get around and that helped so he had decided they were going to town tomorrow. She didn't tell him she had been in contact with Samantha every day they had been sending messages back and forth so she could check on the children and tell her how Clayton was doing. Juanita went looking for him when she was shutting down the house and couldn't find him so she went to Samantha's room and sure enough there he was sitting in the dark.

"You know I never noticed how dark and quiet this house was until the last few days. Alice always told me that children were the life of a house and should be the life of my world and I never listened I should have. Samantha came into this house and made it live again and I ran her off I seem to do that to the women in my life don't I?"

"Well you have a chance to fix it this time don't mess it." she noticed he had Sam's skirts in his lap and she wondered at that and she pointed to them.

He looked down and then he looked at her as if he was just realizing he had them.

"I thought I would take them with me tomorrow and see that she got them back she might need them even if she doesn't need me." And then he gave a sad little smile. Juanita looked at him and she had never seen him look so broken.

"Tomorrow you will make this right so don't give up she was meant to be here from the start, now you just have to convince her of that again." He looked up at her and smiled a better smile this time and then he got up and she helped him walk to his room and he went to bed. Juanita went back downstairs and thought to herself this house did feel like a tomb without the children in it. Who was she kidding without Sam in it she had brought this place to life when she came.

Tomorrow she hoped he could fix this and the world would be right again. She had hardly got downstairs when she heard him fall. Back up those stairs she went.

Gabriel had arrived the day before and he was settled into the small hotel but when Camille showed up she went straight to

Sam's house and didn't leave. Sam had wanted her to come for the festival but more that that she wanted her to meet Gabriel there was something about Camille, ever since she had meet her she reminded her of Gabriel's wife Lena. Not in looks but just something about her had always made her think of Lena since she met her in her shop. Sam couldn't wait to introduce them.

"Camille it is so good to see you I didn't think you would ever get here." she embraced her friend and then looked into her face and something was not right. Camille pushed her back.

"He is here and he knows where you are or he knows the general area."

"Who?"

"We both know who, Nathan. He paid me a visit before I came down here; he had been talking to people who were at the party he even beat a man pretty badly when he didn't get the answers he wanted. He finally wound up in my shop and thought he would hurt me to get the answers he wanted but several of my customers got some soldiers to come to my aid before he could hurt me. I made sure no one knew where I was going when I left town but he knows where you were going and who you were with. Why are you not at the hacienda with Clayton instead of here he can get to you here?" About that time another letter came from the hacienda and she led Camille inside and they sat down so she could read the letter and they could talk out of the heat. She read the letter and then sort of let it fall down in her lap so Camille took it out of her hand and read it. She looked at Sam and asked her.

"What is going on around here? If he needs you why aren't you there? Why are his children here instead of with him?" she looked at her and shook her head.

"It is complicated."

"Alright so explain it for me, do you love him and are you pregnant with his child?" Samantha shook her head yes.

"Then fix this and do it right now you never know when you won't have the chance to make this right."

"You didn't hear what he said to me how do I forgive that?"

"Figure it out and fast you have a man hunting you and you are running out of time. Clayton is sick and he needs you, get your world together before you lose it all."

"You can't understand you have never had to deal with a situation like this."

"No you are right my husband is dead at the hands of his backstabbing commanding officer so don't tell me I don't know about this. You are a fool don't waste chances in this life you may not get another one. You may wind up like me alone in a shop just watching your life pass by. You can have it all Clayton and the children if you will just fix this." Samantha was just staring at her she hadn't heard much after she had said she had a husband and that he was dead.

All of the sudden the pieced began to fall into place this beautiful woman alone in a town full of men and yet still alone.

"I am sorry about your husband. Nathan didn't hurt you did he?" Camille just smiled at her and shook her head no.

I generally have some protectors nearby and I had some on that day as well. If I had known he was coming I would have had the men shoot him but I realized to late who he was."

"Who watches over you Camille?" Camille looked at her and smiled. "Some of my husband's solders are always around and have been since my husband's death. His commanding officer was betraying his men to the French and my husband found out, he killed him for it. Victor was a good man and his men respected him and this man had the nerve to come to his funeral and flirt with his widow. When he left his men wanted him dead but we came up with a plan that wouldn't get them lined up against a wall for killing an officer. I was to be the bait with them watching. He charmed me for several weeks and took me to dinner as my husband's men watched and we waited for him to make a mistake and he finally did. He had too much to drink on night and told me he was meeting someone the next day and he would be fixed for life. After that we could leave the country and live like royalty, would I marry him. I was stunned I was never going anywhere with this man I could hardly bear for him to touch me so I told him.

"I will give you my answer in the morning I have to think tonight it is so sudden." As soon as he left one of my husband's solders came to the door and I told him what was going on and he went to get the other men. They met at my house and a plan was made. By the morning he and the French he had been trading secrets with had been caught and they were brought to the jail and as he walked past my shop I didn't come out. That night I was allowed to see him in the jail for a little while with a guard. I had brought him some food and a bottle of wine. He was so happy to see me.

"Camille you came I knew you would you have to see if you can convince them I am innocent of these charges. They want to execute me in the morning there is got to be something we can do." I just handed him the food and the wine and leaned back against the wall and sighed.

"Why would I want to help you when it was me that put you in here? You killed my Victor and then you come after me all the while betraying your own country not a chance in HELL that I will help you. I just brought you your last meal so I could tell you it was me that betrayed you. Goodbye, maybe some of your other women will morn you." Then I turned and walked away. He never stood before the firing squad though, he took that wine bottle and broke it and slit his wrists he was too much of a coward to even die well.

"I didn't' know it then but some of the people in town thoughtless of me because of the man I had been keeping company with. It made it hard for a while until I found a stash of cash hidden in my shop I guess he had left it. I really don't know where it came from but I used until I got back on my feet. Then it got out what really had happened and things were better. I didn't care one way or the other it was done." Sam just looked at her she was a spy wrapped up in this beautiful package. Neither had noticed Gabriel had come to the house and had been listening to their conversation and was spellbound. This was the woman that Sam wanted him to meet the woman that she said reminded her of Lena and she didn't know why, he did quiet determination and fire. She was ten years younger than him but she had already lived a lifetime he hated to interrupt but he wanted to meet this woman.

"Am I allowed to interrupt this conversation because I think this pretty lady is right, life if fleeting, take what you can and don't waste a minute?" Sam looked at both of them and then read the letter again and then got up and asked them.

"I may be gone for a couple of days can you two take care of the children until I have you bring them to the hacienda for me?"

"Of course we can, you go get dressed." He turned towards Camille and smiled.

"I am Gabriel." She smiled and he thought to himself my world just started turning again.

"I kind of figured that, I am Camille I am pleased to meet you Samantha has talked a lot about you." Oh please let it be good.

"Shall we go get some breakfast and wait for the children and maybe you can tell me some more about yourself." She smiled again and he felt ten years younger already this day was getting better and better by the minute.

Samantha didn't take that long to dress and she didn't pack much by the time she was ready the horses were waiting outside and two men were waiting for her the same two men that had brought the note. They had stayed to eat breakfast and they were to take a note back instead they were taking her. Once they were in the saddle they were gone it still took them a while to get to the hacienda. The note had said she couldn't get him to rest anymore all he could talk about was coming to town and seeing her and the children and he intended to do it anyway he could, in the wagon or on a horse. Juanita said he had already fallen once and had torn a couple of stitches but if he kept this up he was going to be back the way he was.

It was barley morning when they got to the hacienda and she got off her horse and handed Sundance to one of the men and went into the kitchen. Both of the maids were fighting over who was going to pluck the chicken for tonight's diner. She guessed because Juanita was taking care of Clayton the house was having to run itself, well it was time to stop this.

"What is for dinner ladies?" they turned around so quick they almost fell they hadn't expected Samantha back."

"Gordita's and squash if the patron is here for supper?" both women figured she wouldn't scold them after all she wasn't mistress here.

"The patron is going to be here for supper and he is going to be here for breakfast so you better get busy."

"We don't take orders from you." Juanita walked in behind her. "You do now. Please tell me you are staying." She shook her head yes and headed up the stairs. She dropped her bag off on her bed in her room before she went to his room and then she stopped at his door before she went in. She stopped and looked at him he was pale as a ghost as he tried to stand with a cane. He just had on white cotton pants and they weren't much whiter than he was.

"Come on Clayton a few steps more today and we can go to town and see them." He was talking to himself as he tried walking forwards and he was going to fall but she caught him before he did. He had closed his eyes against the pain and he didn't realize until he opened them and saw her golden hair that she was holding him up and then he wouldn't let her go.

"You came back to me, please tell me this isn't one of Balik's dreams or if it is just let me stay for a while longer." She started to set him back down and he still wouldn't let her go until she said.

"I am not going anywhere Clayton lay down and let me look at your leg." He lay back but he wouldn't let go of her arm he was afraid she would go away again so she sat down on the side of the bed and pulled back the bandage. Juanita was right he had pulled some stitches but it was better if he would stay still he would get well.

"Let me see your neck. The leg is getting better but you are going to have to stay off of it Clayton. Juanita is sending up breakfast and you need to eat .Maybe later you can sit in the sun on the balcony."

"You are going to stay?" "If that is what you want?"

"That is what I want. Where are Melanee and Steven?"

"I left them in town with Camille and Gabriel until I knew how you were feeling."

"Are you really pregnant?"

"That's what a doctor tells me." She couldn't look at him.

"You really would have left and never told me." She didn't even answer him. She didn't want to have this conversation so he reached out and pulled her to him and laid her across his chest. She wouldn't look at him this was harder than she thought.

"I am sorry for what I said I don't even remember most of it but Juanita filled in the blanks. Can you try and forgive me?" About that time they brought his breakfast to him and he let her go so they could put it on the bed and she scooted out of the room to go to her room. When she got to her room Juanita met her there and she had some questions of her own.

"Are you going to stay?" Sam looked at her and pulled out the little red cup and sat it on the side table and then another voice ask her the same question.

"Well are you?" she turned and Clayton was standing or doing the best imitation of standing he could right now at the door to the balcony. Both women looked at him and they both wondered how he got there he was all but falling down.

"If you are this determined to have me here I will stay if you will please stay in bed until you are healed, will you at least agree to that?" He nodded and then started to her bed and both women helped him get there.

"When will you bring the children home?"

"I will have them brought home tomorrow but you are going to have to deal with their resentment towards you yourself. I am not going to try to do that it is your problem." He nodded he still had some problems but he was too tired to deal with any more today.

"Back to bed and you stay there and you eat or I won't bring the children home alright."

"You have to sit in my room and talk to me and eat something I bet you haven't eaten yet either." They got back down to his bed and settled and she sat in the chair across from him while he ate and they talked like old times. She told him Gabriel was in town as was Camille and they were taking care of the children.

"What is wrong Sam I can see it on your face something is going on and you won't tell me." She didn't say anything for a minute she got up and went to the balcony and just stood there and then she decided she better tell him or he would worry about it until she did.

"Nathan hunted me down in Mexico City he even accosted Camille and he knows who I came down here with. He has a pretty good idea where I am Clayton and I don't know what to do about it." He was quiet for a minute.

"Does Russell know about this?"

"No I didn't have time to tell him before I left this morning. Oh god I should have shouldn't I. I am going back and getting the children right now he could get to them what a fool I was for leaving them."

"You aren't going anywhere. JUANITA get up here now and bring one of the men. You sit right there. You say Gabriel and Camille are in town well we bring them out here with the children and they will be safe here." Juanita was running into the room by now with one of the hands behind her.

"Juanita Nathan has found her. We will have guests soon I am sending men to town and retrieving my children and Samantha's friends and they are coming out here where they will be safe from this man. The men will take a wagon and gather everyone up and bring them back here before nightfall no argument Samantha they will be safer here."

I will send a note to Camille and tell her what is going on and they will come." She just smiled at him he was already looking better he was in control again, she looked at Juanita and she could see it to. He was getting better but she thought it was Sam coming back he needed her.

"Well people let's get busy we have a long day ahead of us." He was starting to get out of that bed and Sam stopped him.

"We had a deal remember, you keep your butt in that bed or I will leave, we will take care of this."

"You promise me you don't leave this house and you don't go anywhere alone Juanita you make her behave." She nodded she would watch out for her now, especially since that man knew where she was. She walked out the door when Clayton motioned he wanted a moment alone with Sam.

"You have to very careful Sam until I am up an on my feet again he could sneak into the compound and get to you. Sit down I want to ask you something, are you just staying because I am hurt or do you still care for me?" she leaned over and kissed him and then he wrapped his arms around her and kissed her again more deeply this time until she finally pulled away.

"Does that answer your question I never would have left except you told me to go and if you ever tell me to go again I won't come back." She got up and went across the room and when she got to the door he said.

"I won't ever say those words again." She just kept walking she had things to do.

CHAPTER 9

Both women had things to do to get ready for the people coming. Sam didn't know just how many were coming but she suspected Gabriel would accompany Camille now that he had met her and she wanted to make sure everything was good here. Sam made sure the rooms were ready and Juanita started cooking she could smell beans and chicken already. The windows were opened and beds made and she looked in on Clayton to see if he was alright. When his lunch was brought up he started yelling for her and she was going to ignore him but that wasn't happening.

"Samantha I am not eating alone. You either join me or I will come to you." She stopped what she was doing and went down the hall and met a smiling Juanita.

"I will bring another plate you need to eat anyway."

"Bring it out on the balcony we will take him out there in the shade he needs some fresh air and the girls can change his bedding while he is gone." She nodded and went back downstairs while Sam went into Clayton's room.

"So I am finally going to get you to myself for a little while." And there was that wicked grin well it was worth it to see him smile again.

"Come on do you think you can lean on me and we can get you out to the chair on the balcony or should I call one of the men to help us." He reached up and stood and put his arm around her shoulder and they started to the door.

"I don't need anyone but you ever again." He said it with such feeling she thought he meant something else but she didn't want it to mean something else so she didn't even look up at him. They walked to the door and down the side of the house and to the table where she sat him in one of the big chairs and then she put a light blanket over his legs. She rearranged the chairs so they could talk and then Juanita came upstairs with the food. She sat it down and then she was gone and they were alone and Sam felt very self conscious. She poured water in the glasses while he just stared at her and they ate in silence and then she started to get up and leave.

"What do want a boy or a girl?" she just looked at him, what a stupid question. She hadn't even stopped long enough to ask herself that question.

"I doesn't matter a healthy baby, my child." she finally realized she was going to have a baby and she smiled.

"Would you really have left without telling me, I thought you loved me more than that?"

"It was supposed to be your Christmas present. I had a note all thought out to put inside the present I was giving you but things didn't go the way I planned." He reached out and took her hand and squeezed it and they just sat there looking at each other.

"Do the children know about the baby yet?" She shook her head no. "Will you marry me now; you always said you would know the right time is it that time yet?"

"After Christmas if everything is all right with the children and Nathan hasn't showed up Yes I will marry you and we will settle down and await this baby birth is that satisfactory?" he was smiling and Juanita was at the door crying. Clayton nodded towards Juanita and she took off down the hall. Juanita returned with rings obviously a set, a wide gold band which was the wedding band and an emerald engagement ring one large stone and two small stones on each side.

"My father started in this country as a geologist he helped find some of the biggest gold and emerald deposits around. Then he let other people dig he said you got killed mining for the stuff too many bandits. He pulled out what he wanted from the mines before he sold out and had some rings made for my mother. Now Samantha will you marry me?" and he started to put the ring on her finger. She pulled her hand away.

"NO it is too soon. Things are still to raw between us and the children and when I put that ring on I promise you I won't ever take it off unless I have no other choice." He took back the rings and put them in his pocket and then he smiled.

"All right until later." he leaned back in the chair and finished his lunch as he watched Sam. There were horses coming into the courtyard and he could see the children and Sam started down to meet them, he grabbed her hand and pulled her down and gave her a kiss.

"Let them see that things are better with us and maybe it will make things better with them as well."

She meet the children at the wagon and Melanee jumped into her arms she was so excited. Steven had been watching her and his father as they rode up and he asked her.

"Is everything alright now between you and daddy?" she looked at him and shook her head no.

"It is better, do you want to go up and talk to him he wants to talk to you." Clayton didn't understand everything wasn't going to fall into place just because he said he was sorry he had hurt her and she wasn't going to forget that so easily.

"Maybe later I want to get settled right now, is that alright?" she just shook her head yes she wasn't going to push this just let them go at their own pace. Melanee was still on her hip and all she wanted to do was hold on to Sam. When she looked over at Camille all she could say was.

"She was been upset since she got up this morning she thought you left her behind again. I was so glad when the men came to collect us, I was afraid she was going to make another run to find you. You can't leave without that child again she is yours now whether you like it or not." Melanee was almost choking her she was holding on so tight.

"Honey you are home now and I won't leave without you again I promise, unless someone drags me away." She said it half kidding.

"Then I will still follow you." This little girl said those words without a single bit of humor she wasn't kidding she would follow her anywhere. Somehow that scared the hell out of Samantha. She just grabbed her and held her to her chest and looked over her head up to the balcony and thought to herself.

'I better make this right because this little girl needs me.' They walked inside and started to get everyone settled and Samantha could swear she felt eyes on her back; she even turned and looked back. There were eyes watching alright and not all of them were Batiks' men. Juanita had rooms for everyone so they started upstairs and Camille went into Clayton's room to say hello. When she got into his room she could see some of the damage the jaguar had done to him and she was surprised he had lived, his quick thinking with that rifle was all that had saved his life.

"Well Clayton like it or not you got all of us in this deal. We wouldn't let her or the children come back alone until we could see that you were going to act like a gentleman again. I told her once before she could come back and live with me if she didn't like it here so now you know she has other options."

"Camille she has always had other options that is the problem or it is my problem. I know, I know I am a jealous man wouldn't you be if you were me? She is the only thing I have really wanted in a long time and she is always just out of my reach. Then I act like a damn fool and send her away now even my children can't tolerate me." Camille was smiling at him as she shook her head.

"My my, don't we have the poor me attitude today. That won't work on me and it won't work on her either she will see right through it so you better straighten up before she gets up here." Sam was calling to Camille from down the hall and she stood up to leave but before she left she leaned down and said to Clayton.

"Looks like she saved your hide from that cat you should have been a lot more grateful." He didn't even answer they were right and he knew it so he just watched from his bed as she got everyone settled. As the afternoon went on things were going smoothly and it was time for supper. Sam got everyone seated and then down the stairs came Clayton with the help of Gabriel.

"Don't even start Samantha I can at least have supper down here and then I will go back upstairs to bed." He was looking better and he ate better than he had in days Steven even talked to him, Melanee said a few words at least it was a start. The women cleared the table and the men were going to have some Port Wine on the patio but Sam said that was enough for tonight maybe in a day or so but not tonight. Gabriel and Samantha helped Clayton back upstairs and to bed then Gabriel left.

"Stay with me tonight I have missed you." Sam finished getting him in the bed and put his medicine next to the bed if he needed it and then she told him.

"We were short on beds so Melanee is sleeping with me so I can't stay in here and you can't come to my room. I told you this was still a problem for her and you didn't believe me well now you know that is the only reason she would stay."

"She hates me that much?" Sam walked to the balcony doors and turned back and answered him.

"She really doesn't know what to think about you she just knows she loves me and I won't betray her and I intend to honor that. Go to sleep we will start again tomorrow." She walked down the side of the house and noticed a storm was brewing but sometimes they built up and didn't do anything. If it decided to get to bad she would come down later and see to shutting the doors but it was too hot right now. When she looked around the corner she saw Melanee waiting for her at her bedroom door she hadn't come looking for her, she had just waited. She didn't know what it was going to take to make her trust her father. That little girl had spent too many years wanting his love and she had finally given up and given it to Samantha now he was going to have to earn it.

"Come on baby let's go to bed I may have to get up later and shut the doors if this storm decides to get bad so if you wake up and I am not here I am just taking care of the doors." The little girl just nodded and looked outside as the lighting cracked across the sky. Sam awoke a few hours later and she could hear the thunder rattling the windows she got out of the bed and put on her robe and went to the edge of the balcony and looked down. Juanita was below in the kitchen she was already shutting the doors downstairs. Sam just waved at her and she went about taking care of the upstairs windows and doors. She was almost finished when the rain started and she was running to get back to her room when an arm reached out and pulled her into Clayton's room and pushed her against the wall. He kissed her and then he gave her a towel to dry her hair.

"It is dangerous on that balcony in this lighting are you done out there yet?" she was drying her hair and she stood away from him in the doorway and when the lighting flashed, Melanee was right her hair did glow.

"All the doors are shut so it can rain all it wants to now. I need to get back to my room but I may have to go down the hall instead of down the balcony it is raining to hard now." He was smiling at that he wanted her to stay all night if he could talk her into it but he wasn't going to be able to do that. He pulled her to him again and she went willing she wasn't going to fight him there wasn't any reason. For a few minutes it was like it was just the two of them no complications and then the real world came back as she heard Melanee call her name. Sam looked up at him and caressed his face and then she broke the embrace.

"I have to go now your child is calling she doesn't like waking up alone." He looked at her and then she walked out the door. She went back to her room got back in bed with Melanee and went back to sleep, Clayton didn't.

The next few days went the same just staying around the house but in the afternoons Melanee and Sam would disappear for a while with Lucas and his guitar. Camille and Patricia kept Clayton busy while they went off to practice. He still didn't know that Melanee was going to dance in the Christmas pageant and they wanted to keep it that way.

They were practicing at the back of the barn it was flat and smooth back there and they could dance and there was a breeze to keep them cool. They had been practicing and the little girl was tired so they decided to quit as they started to go back to the house they could hear the horses having a fit. The closer to the front of the barn they got the more they heard and then Melanee started running.

"That is Moon screaming." Sam tried to stop her but she was too far ahead of her but she and Lucas were right on her heals. When they got to the corral they found Melanee climbing under the rails to get to her horse. There was a man holding the little horse's reins and a whip and he was hitting her. Nobody was supposed to touch that little girl's horse except Sam or Melanee and Jesse who ran the ranch and the fields. When Melanee ran up to the man she was hitting him and yelling and he turned around and knocked her down in the dirt. Sam didn't even have time to react or get to her before Clayton did, he was just there and he had the man by the collar and he was beating him with his fists. Sam got to Melanee and was holding her as they watched Clayton go after that man. Finally Gabriel and Lucas pulled him off of the man before he killed him Samantha had never seen him in such a rage before. She didn't know how as badly hurt as he still was.

"You dare to touch my daughter and I will kill you, pack you're belonging and get off my land now. Don't bother looking for work within a hundred miles of here you won't be welcome anywhere close I will see to that." He walked over to Melanee and asked her.

"You alright baby did he hurt you?" she shook her head no.

"I am alright daddy your hand is bleeding." He just looked down at his hand and his knuckles were bleeding he didn't even care that was the first time she had even spoken to him and she had called him daddy.

"That's alright why don't you come with me and maybe Sam can fix them?" she just shook her head and followed him inside. Well it was a start. Sam stayed outside for a minute more she wanted to find out what that man was doing. Seems he wanted to ride the little mare even after he had been told not to, he had been a problem lately about everything. Somebody was offering money a lot of it for information about Samantha and he figured if he messed with the horse he might get her attention. He wasn't stupid enough to mess with her stallion Sundance he would have killed him but he thought he could handle the mare he didn't know how spooky she was about men touching her.

"Who is offering money for information about me?" he looked up at her and smiled with what was left of his face.

"Some guy in town wants to know where you are from and who you are living with. Some skinny dude with an accent wants to know." Well it wasn't Nathan but he could be working for him.

"Well I hope he paid you well enough to lose this job now get off this land." Then she turned and walked towards the patio to Clayton and Melanee. When she got there Juanita had brought out a bowl of water and some towels and Melanee was gently washing her father's hand with the towel.

"Now tell me if I am hurting you I will try to be careful." Then she looked up at him and asked him.

"Why do you hate me?" it seemed like the whole jungle around them went quiet Samantha was even holding her breath she looked at Clayton and thought this is the moment you convince her one way or the other she is loved by you. He was sitting there and he took a deep breath and she started to get up and leave and he put his other hand over her little one and stopped her.

"I never hated you. I was just so afraid of losing your mother I couldn't see what a gift she was leaving me when you were born. I couldn't see that until Samantha showed me how lucky I was to have you and how badly I had treated your mother and I am ashamed of that. There is no fixing that or going back so maybe you will let me make the rest of your life and Stevens one that you will know you are loved by me?" she looked at him and went back to washing his hand and then she said.

"We will see." Samantha was smiling as she watches the two of them at least it was a start. They put some salve on the cuts and Sam had Melanee take the bowl back to the kitchen while Sam helped Clayton back upstairs neither one of them wanted Melanee to see the blood on his pants.

"You got a little ambitious and tore those stitches again well not torn just pulled. Where were you when we came around the corner?"He sat down on the bed and they looked at the leg and it wasn't too bad and then they covered it up with a towel when Melanee came in to say goodnight. After she left Sam looked at it again and took care of it.

"The better question is where are ya'll are going in the afternoon while I am being sidetracked and if you don't tell me I am going to follow you tomorrow." She looked at him and then sat down on the bed.

"Your daughter is dancing with me at Christmas and we practice in the afternoon and you are not supposed to know so keep your mouth shut." He sat there grinning and then he asked her.

"Is she any good I don't want her to be embarrassed?"

"You really think I would take her out there to embarrass her, what kind of woman do you think I am. Yes she is getting really good. You are going to be so surprised when you see her but you can't let her know that you know she wants to surprise you so badly."

"If Nathan is close I don't want you to stray far from the house have Gabriel go with you to and I will not interfere he could carry a gun as well." She just nodded it was not a bad idea and she would feel safer.

Melanee and Sam practiced every day and then in the heat of the day they went to sewing room where she was making a dress for Melanee. It was like her dress except white, yards and yards of gathered white lace on that tiny body she was going to look like a living doll. She had the shoes which were costing her a front row seat and a hand carved tortoise shell comb for Melanee's hair another front row seat, it was well worth the cost. The hats with the hatbands she had ordered for Clayton's and Steven's Christmas was ready and they were to be delivered at the dance. The day of the celebration the family was coming back that night to have their Christmas at the hacienda then. Everything seemed to be going so well they hadn't heard anymore about Nathan and they thought maybe he had lost track of her.

It was two days before the festival and the house was decorated in the way the people down here celebrated it was different from where she came from but the last few years there hadn't been much celebrating at all. Melanee dress was finished and everything was ready but she kept getting the feeling there was something she was forgetting. Clayton was walking almost normal and they figured he could ride to town when they went in but she just kept feeling something was wrong. She looked out into the jungle and she could swear someone was watching her and she figured it was still some of Balik's men so she just wrote it off to nerves.

There was someone watching her and it wasn't one of Balik's men but he was being watched by them. He had been watching for a week now. As soon as that man that had worked for the ranch had told him what she looked like he had come out here and started to watch her and he had been here ever since. He was sure this was the blond Texas woman he was looking for. He was going to go back to a nearby town tonight and tell that other man she was here. He broke camp and was ready to leave when he turned around and there were two Mayan men standing in front of him, he hadn't even heard them coming.

"What do you want? Get out of my way I am leaving." Well they probably didn't speak any English. He started to mount his horse and one of the men stopped him.

"Why are you watching her?" well I guess they do speak English. "None of your business get out of my way." They knocked him down.

Over the next couple of hours they would make it their business and the man would tell them everything he knew about Nathan unfortunately they didn't get the chance to tell Samantha. The man would never be seen again and Nathan just thought he quit. One man disposed of the body while one man stayed and kept watch, the jungle does a nice job of disposing of bodies.

One more night and then the festival and everyone was excited the supper table was loaded down with food turkey, squash, mango, cornbread and tortilla everyone was stuffed. Clayton kept watching her he was making her uncomfortable. The house was settled and everybody was ready to go to town in the morning.

"Now this is going to be the best Christmas in a long time." When everyone was in bed he was standing at her door she started to protest but he had made arrangements with Camille so they could have tonight alone. They walked down the balcony to his room and she walked inside and the room was filled with orchids all colors. Since she had come down here they had become her favorites even though they didn't have a smell. He turned her around and shut the door and pulled her into his arms and kissed her.

"It has been to long I feel like you have been gone forever." Then he reached behind her and locked the doors he didn't want his daughter poking her nose in here tonight. Samantha smiled up at him and said.

"Are you afraid of intruders Clayton?" then as he was pulling her gown over her head and leading her to the bed.

"Damn right I am as you said once before Melanee sees and hears everything but maybe if we are married she will approve." Her hands were busy taking off his shirt and then she pushed him down on the bed and she walked up to him. Lord every time he took off his shirt he took her breath away. He put his hands on her growing tummy and then lay his head on it.

"Still so flat are you sure you are pregnant?" he looked up at her with all that long light blond hair in the candlelight as she stroked his head.

"The doctor in town verified it, more than three months this is the time I have it be careful." He pulled her closer.

"What do you mean?" She breathed deeply.

"After all that happened the first few months are when something could go wrong."

Should you dance is that too much?" he laid her down in the bed and he took off his pants and he put out the lights while they continued to talk. He climbed in beside her as she replied.

"The doctor didn't seem to think that would make a difference it is not that much of a strain." He pulled her to him lord how he loved the feel of her next to him. He nuzzled her neck and down to her breast but he wanted more.

"Is it alright if we make love?"

"I hope so that is what I have been waiting for, is your leg up to the task?" he pulled back from her.

"My leg that's what you are worried about I was worried about you." With that settled he rolled her under him and he was inside her and they were one again.

"Look at me Samantha and tell me I am the only man you will ever love." She took his head in her hands and kissed him until they were both spent and then he looked at her.

"Why didn't you say it?"

"I can't promise forever to anybody not right now not even you. You don't have to have a declaration of undying love every minute we are together. Go to sleep tomorrows is a long day." Well that was going to have to be enough for right now he was pushing again and she wasn't going to commit to anything else.

The morning came early and they headed to town she wanted to get to the house and get ready before the festival and have time to rest before it started. Patricia had stayed in town at the house and from what she had been hearing she had been having Russell as a regular visitor of late. She wanted to hear all the details. As they rode up to the house Russell was sitting out front having breakfast with Patricia on the porch just like he belonged there she had never seen Pat so happy. It looked like her friend liked the jungle around here as well. Clayton helped her off of Sundance and she asked him.

"Good morning are you ready for the festivals today?" they both stepped down and helped get the children and packages unloaded and into the house.

"We have been waiting for ya'll to get here the whole town is buzzing with anticipation there is even a bullfighter that has come to the house looking for you. I need to talk to you alone when you have a moment." She shook her head and they finished what they needed to do and then they went inside. Patricia pulled her aside and they went to the patio. There were several packages out there.

"I didn't know what to do with them and didn't know if Clayton was to know about them so I put them out here till I talked to you." Sam was looking through the boxes and she found the shoes for Melanee and then she found the comb and the lace mantia but she didn't see the hats she had ordered.

"Did a man come by about some hats?"

"Yes he said they were ready and he would bring them to you personally today at the festival so that Clayton didn't see them." She just nodded her head she needed to get some money to pay all these people and she didn't have any. She was going to have to ask Clayton for some, well she was owed some salary. She gathered up the packages and went to try on the shoes and then to talk to Clay she needed to get things done and get to the main courtyard so they could start getting dressed.

"Clayton I need some money." He looked at her funny.

"Why are you going somewhere, I can pay for anything you need?" "I have some salary coming don't I? There are things I have to pay for it is Christmas after all and I have obligations of my own." He looked at her and realized she had bought presents and she needed to pay for them and she had used every dime she had getting here and he was being an ass.

"Give me a few minutes and I will have some money for you darlin'." He went to the next room and got Russell and asked him if he has some money on him and he kind of looked at him strange.

"You coming up short now Clayton should I tell Samantha you can't take care of her." There were times when this man was so dense.

"The money is for her you idiot she needs to pay for something and I don't have any cash on me right now I will repay you in a little while." He handed him the cash he had on him and he went back to Sam and gave it to her and the women started out the door.

"I know I am not supposed to know about certain things but you and Melanee are not going anywhere without a guard today, either me or Gabriel will be with you understood." She did understand and was glad for the company and the extra guards. As she walked past Russell he pulled aside and asked her.

"What happened to the bag of money he gave you the night you left?" she just looked at him and suddenly realized she didn't remember where it was or that she even had it.

"I think maybe it is in my room I had forgotten all about it, I need to pay you for all you have done forgive me my mind has been elsewhere. By the way how are things between you and Pat going?" the smile on his face said it all.

"That good huh, has she seen your hacienda yet I hear it is something special." Russell looked at her and he was almost blushing.

"She is something special you sure can pick them she is just what I need in my life. I think I can make her happy and her father be dammed he will never have a chance to hurt her again." She turned and went back in the bedroom and after a little digging found the bag of money and when she came out they were ready to go. She got on her horse and Clayton handed Melanee to her and then get everybody else loaded and they started to town. The crowd was already bustling but she stayed close to Clayton or one of the men as she went about paying the people for the presents and picking up a few more for tonight. They had planned to open presents later after all of today's festivities and they were back at home. Juanita had a pig roasting and the smell of it this morning was wonderful. Clayton held her arm as he walked beside her and he held Melanee on his hip and Steven walked in front of them just like a family. Gabriel pulled her aside and told her they needed to head down to the plaza and start getting dressed so she left Clayton and Steven behind.

"I have to make one more stop before we leave and I have been waiting until we were without the men." She walked over to one of the stalls and it was obviously a hat maker and he saw her and he reached for two hatboxes.

"They are ready for you senora and the hatbands turned out just like you said they would. I have had several people offer to buy them I had to box them up because I couldn't make anymore with those hatbands." she looked at the hats and was very pleased.

There were laced together at the ends they were quite handsome. She reached in the bag for the money and took out extra because he had done such a good job with the skins.

"I told you there would be none like them and you did a good job on the skin I wasn't sure if there would be enough for both hats."

"It was a big one there was enough, you come back anytime. I can bring them to you if I need to?" She shook her head no and they left holding her packages until they got to the plaza and there were rooms in back for them to dress. Camille was waiting for them with the dresses and Sam had the other items they needed. As they got into the room Gabriel was almost fit to be tied.

"Well are you going to tell me what is in the box or am I going to have to pry it out of you."

"Melanee open one of the boxes and show him what is inside." She pulled out her father's hat and showed it to Gabriel. He took it in his hands and looked at it.

"What is it Samantha I know it is some kind of skin but what?" "Remember that snake I killed the Fer-De-Lance I had the hat maker make hatbands out of it I thought it would be unique." He just looked at the hat and smiled.

"Well it is that, no one else will have one like it, is that what he was talking about, people wanted to buy it." She just nodded as the women started to dress.

"I will be outside while you get dressed and there will be a man at the back door as well just call if you need anything." Camille started brushing Melanee hair so it could be put in a bun just like Samantha's. While Camille worked on Melanee Sam was dressing and putting up her hair and Patricia showed up.

"I thought ya'll might need some help, besides you left something at the house and I thought you might need it." It was the package with Melanee's tights in it.

"Where were they I had them in my hands I must have set them down somewhere?" Patricia was pulling out tights and Samantha was almost dressed and had her hair done.

"Where did you find those tights Patricia?" they were busy putting on her dress of white ruffles she was going to look like an angle."

"They were beside your bed I saw them when we were locking up the house. Russell posted a couple of men there to so no surprises if you go back there tonight."

"So he told you what is going on."

"Hard to keep that a secret, I wonder if we are going to spend our whole life running from someone."

"Not if I can help it I am stopping here. Russell seems to think you are too."

"He sure paints a pretty picture big house lots of land a family and far away from my father I just hope far enough."

"What do you think of Russell he thinks a lot of you."

"Don't go there Pat there is nothing between us never has been he just helped me when I needed some help when Clayton was being an ass." Pat just looked at her and nodded and they were done. Then Clayton decided to make an entrance.

"How are my girls doing?" he said as he sticks his head in the door." Pat reached the door first and was shutting it as Sam was yelling.

"OUT Clayton go sit down and you have to wait to see just like all the rest." Well he stood back from the door but he did see Sam in the black dress lord she looked good but he wanted a peek at Melanee he hoped this day went well for her. He went back outside and sat down he had a front row table with several men he knew were venders that was strange. That Mexican bullfighter was here too as was his guitar player. Lucas, Gabriel's guitar player was here as well and the two of them were on the other side of the plaza talking. Then they took places one on each side across from each other. They began to play softly until they were in unison and they kept signaling to each other.

The women were almost ready Samantha was finished and pulled out her tortoise shell comb and put it in her hair. Pat smiled.

"I remember the night at the castle when you danced and the Queen gave you that comb. The ribbons wouldn't hold your hair and you were having trouble with it flying everywhere. We were all so impressed that the Queen would take it out of her hair and give it to you. Then she said it would look so pretty in that blond hair and you curled it back up in a bun and put it in your hair. You turned around and showed her and then you curtsied and said.

"Thank you your grace I will treasure it always." Camille and Melanee both were just listening to the story when Melanee said.

"You saw a real Queen and she gave you that comb?" Sam smiled nodded and pulled out a small package then unwrapped it and went over to her. Inside was a smaller version of the comb she was wearing carved out of tortoise shell as well. Sam had hired a man in the village to make it for her.

"This one is not from a queen but I think it will do and it will look so good in your hair. Turn around and let me put it in. Alright are we ready to do this?" they walked out the door. Camille turned and looked at Patricia.

"She really did all that stuff they have been telling me about it is not just stories?"

"I don't know what they have been telling you but I doubt it was stories. She danced for a Queen saved me and my sister's life and made a bishop mad enough to kill her that is the short version if you want to know more we will talk later. I want to see her dance it has been a long time since Spain." Camille just stood there with her mouth open.

Everybody was waiting when she and Gabriel walked out they were met in the center of the plaza by that bullfighter. Clayton could see her but not Melanee she was still inside out of sight with Pat and Camille they were watching through a side window. Gabriel handed Samantha off to the bullfighter and the music began to play it was the Pasa Doble Clayton didn't know where this guy had come from and why Sam was dancing with him but they were good together. He took her around the plaza to where Gabriel was standing and then the music changed and it was a waltz at least he knew what this one was. This one he had seen her dance at that ball in Mexico City he thought the other one as well. He still liked the flamenco the best.

The dancing stopped for a bit and she was resting as the men brought a table out and put it next to the fountain and stood next to it and then Samantha went to the opening of the building and brought out Melanee dressed in white ruffles just like her dress only not cut so high up the front. He could hear her shoes tapping on the flagstones and then he noticed her comb it was just like Samantha's where in the world had she found that. She walked her over to the table and one of the men picked her up and put her on the top of the table. Then she took out her castanets and put them on her fingers. The crowd at this point had been silent until Sam said.

"Ladies and gentlemen my newest flamenco partner Miss Melanee." And at that she took a bow and the crowd came to its feet. When the crowd calmed down the guitarists started to play and Gabriel started to dance then Sam would follow his steps and then Melanee and she got them all right then Gabriel on and on then just the girls were dancing when Melanee got too close to the edge one of the men next to the table put out a hand so she didn't step off the side. Gabriel and Sam did a dance in the middle of the plaza that brought the crowd to its feet and when it was over Sam went back to Melanee and they were to do the finish. Finally Sam could see she was getting tired so they were finishing up and she Melanee would have the last dance so she could swirl down on the table in a flourish it was perfect.

When it was all done and the crowd was all around then Clayton came up behind her and put his arm around her waist. A man came up to her with a bouquet of flowers and presented them to Sam. She stopped and took several orchids out and then they expected she would give those to Melanee but instead she gave the whole bouquet to her and kept the orchids. Then she did a kind of half bow.

"To the next grand dame of the dance on her coming out party." That little girl looked like her world was finally round.

"You stay out here with your daughter and I will start getting ready to go home, when she is done send her back and I will get her dressed to leave." "Thank you for this she is over the moon."

"Ever little girl should have one special day I hope this is one of many for her. I told you she was good." Sam walked back to the building to change she was tired she hoped this day was almost over. The bullfighter grabbed her.

"You aren't leaving so soon are you."

"No I am going to change into something more comfortable and put on some sandals. These shoes aren't exactly good for walking around in I will be back shortly." Then she continued back to the dressing room. She sat down for a minute and just rested then she grabbed a piece of mango, Juanita had put a plate of them in the room for her and covered them with a towel. Then she got up and started to take off her dress and put on her split skirt and then her camisole and shirt. She hadn't buttoned it yet because it was hot in here she was going to put on her shoes and then finish until she had the odd felling she was being watched. Suddenly she wanted out of this room.

"Lord you are a good looking woman Samantha sometimes I wondered if you were worth all the time I spent chasing after you but it was worth it. People had told me you could dance but I didn't realize you could dance like that we will have to find a place that you can dance just for me because there will be no more public performances for you. I don't like other men looking at my woman like that." She started towards the door but he was already blocking it, she was caught. She was shaking so bad she could hardly stand and she thought her heart was going to stop beating. She backed up as far as she could and then she finally said.

"What do you want from me Nathan I thought running down here would be far enough that you would leave me alone. I don't want you I never have and I will never be your woman." He was up in her face in an instant and he had his hand on her shoulders and his face in hers.

"You were always mine I was the first and I will be the last honey whether you like it or not you are mine."

"All I have to do is scream and the whole town will be in here what will you do then?" he was just looking at her when Melanee came in and Sam started to yell for her to run but Nathan put his hand over her mouth.

"You say anything and I will kill her. Come on in honey Sam was waiting for you. Get her dressed she is coming with us now and hurry it up. You know what I am capable of Samantha don't provoke me." He pulled Melanee into the room and shoved her towards Samantha. She wanted to say something smart but she was too busy trying to think of a way to get out of this mess. She took Melanee over to the corner and started to take off her dress and Melanee asked her quietly.

"Is that the bad man you are scared off?" Samantha nodded her head yes and continued to get her dressed but as she was putting the white dress aside she saw the hats and the hat boxes. Maybe if she left something in the hatboxes Clayton would realize what was going on. Melanee was watching what she was doing and she didn't say a word to her she just kept dressing so Sam just winked at her. She was going to get this little girl away from him as soon as she could somehow.

"Hurry up stop stalling; if anybody else comes in here I will just cut their throats." Sam got her dressed and they started out the door but Nathan went over to the hat boxes and she held her breath. He reached into each box and grabbed a hat and put one on each of them.

"It would look funny if you weren't wearing hats everybody wears hats in this hot jungle did you think I would let that slip by me did you. The horses are waiting be quiet and no one will get hurt." They walked outside and there was Sundance and several men waiting so she just followed him. As she got closer the hat maker stopped grabbed her arm and looked at her funny then asked her.

"I thought those were for the patron and his son?" she just smiled and got in front of Nathan before he could hurt the man and started bluffing the best she could.

"We are going to walk out wearing the hats and see how long it takes them to notice them. Then we are going to tell them it is their presents so don't give it away we will be out in a few minutes alright?" The man just smiled at her and turned away and went back to the festival with a smile on his face not realizing she had just saved his life. Nathan put his knife back up and they went to the horses. Samantha got up on Sundance and then Nathan handed Melanee to her to ride in front of her and then they were off. No one noticed one of the men at the back was being drug off of his horse and killed and another Mayan man was taking his place. He caught up with them quickly and worked his way up beside Sam so she could see him. She wasn't paying attention but Melanee was and she quickly realized who he was. Quietly she asked Sam.

"Get us back a little and look at the man beside us." Sam didn't understand until she looked at the man more carefully it was the same man who had brought the children to her from the hacienda he was one of Balik's men. She nodded her head a little and he did the same he was here to help now she had to figure out a plan. She could hear the men talking about what they were going to do with her horse and the little girl when they came to the river and they weren't needed anymore. She was going to have to do something soon. It looked like he had hired a couple of white men and three Mayan men to guide him through the jungle, he hadn't figured out he had one too many Mayan men yet. Balik's man had wondered over to talk to one of the other Mayan men and now he was looking at her. He soon came back and said quietly.

"Soon Sam it is almost dark." She nodded her head. She was falling further back until Nathan noticed and came back and was yelling at her.

"What is the problem we need to be moving hurry up?" She held her head in her hand and told him.

"I have got to have some sugar and something to drink I am crashing." "I thought you grew out of that problem you mean you still get sick?" she had pulled her horse up and the other Mayan man was close and waiting to see what she had planned.

"Yes that is why I always have honey or sugar around, what's wrong you don't want a sick woman you could just let me go." He was aggravated but he turned his horse.

"I will have the men get you something sweet to eat and at the next doctor we find we will get this fixed." She looked at the man next to her and signaled him to help her down then she turned Sundance sideways and started to get down.

"Melanee we don't have much time so listen to me, I am going to have this man get up behind you and you two are going to run back to your daddy. Don't argue with me, Nathan will hurt you to get to me you have to go now I love you and I will come back if I can, tell this man to find Balik and he will find me. Do you understand me?" Melanee just looked at her.

"I promised I wouldn't leave but I will if you say so. Please come back to us." She kissed her on the top of her head and got down off her horse the other man had heard part of what she was saying so she told him what she wanted him to do. He swung up in the saddle and Sundance turned and started running back the way they came from. The men were startled for a second because she was still there and then they went into motion. One of them pulled a rifle out of a scabbard and pointed it at them. Sam wasn't having any of that so she pushed the rifle stock up so he wouldn't hit them. By the time he was through fighting with her they were out of sight. Nathan came over and grabbed her by the hair and pulled her back into the trees with him.

"So being sick was all a ploy to get the girl away and that damn horse of yours." She looked at him and didn't say a word she didn't care what he thought and if she crashed it was her problem now and Melanee was safe. She just regretted she was going to have to sacrifice her child because Nathan would probable beat her to death. When they were out of earshot of the others he grabbed her and kissed her. She didn't fight back she knew that was useless.

"We are going to find a place that is ours and we are going to be happy there just the two of us like it was supposed to be." The he hugged her to him and she just let him there wasn't anywhere to run or hide not now anyway so she would go along till she could think of a way out.

When they started to mount up Nathan finally realized the Mayan man wasn't one he had hired. He talked to the other men and they didn't know where he had come from. Sam noticed the man he had talked to before kept watching her and now he was riding beside her. He spoke English and when they were away from the others he started talking to her.

Are you really Balik's snake woman?" she didn't exactly know how to answer that question Mayan men were very literal. At this point what did she have to lose? She nodded her head yes and they kept on riding. She wondered what was going on back at the festival and if Melanee was safe yet.

Clayton had started to wonder where the girls were so he made his way through the crowds and went back to the dressing rooms to find them. When he got to the rooms they weren't there but their dresses were, he went inside and picked up Samantha's dress and held it he didn't know why and then he lay it down. Then he picked up Melanee dress he smiled at how good his little girl looked in it today. All of the sudden it dawned on him neither one of them was here but there dresses were. He dropped the dress and started to run. He didn't even have to guess Nathan had her and Melanee too. He came running out of the dressing rooms or as good as he could, he still wasn't walking very well. When Gabriel saw his face he knew something was wrong.

"What is it?"

"They are gone both of them." Russell was there by now and they just looked at each other and started running to the back of the building. They found the dead man pretty quickly and Clayton said.

"That has got to be the work of one of Balik's men maybe he went after them. We need horses and we will follow too."

"What will we follow Clayton it will be pitch black in a few minutes and we won't be able to see in front of our faces. Besides if it is one of Balik's men won't he bring them back here or to your hacienda?" Clayton thought for a minute and figured probably yes.

"Let's get everybody gathered up and back home and wait until morning if we haven't heard anything we will start hunting." Camille and Clayton went back to gather up the dresses and everything else and when he found the boxes he asked her what they had in them.

"She got you and Steven new hats for Christmas and had them brought here to surprise you tonight. They had a special hatband on them a snake skin she said you would appreciate it. The hat maker said several people wanted to buy the hats for the hat band. I guess you know what it was?"

"I do it was a Fer-De-Lance she killed when we first met and the natives skinned it for her and she wanted the skin she said it would make a good hatband or a belt. Were the hats handsome?" Camille looked at him and just wondered as he held the box in his hands.

"Yes you would have liked them or you will like them when she wears it back tomorrow." When they were through he had packed the boxes too he just couldn't leave them behind they were the last things she had touched. When they got to the hacienda no one was sleeping everyone was keeping watch. Juanita was getting food ready for them to leave tomorrow. Finally close to dawn the men just sat down on the patio and they were having drinks when they heard the horses in the corral begin to get agitated. They heard a whiney from the road and soon they saw Sundance coming he was being led by a Mayan man and Melanee was in the saddle.

The man came into the courtyard and stopped as the men came out and Clayton grabbed Melanee before she fell off the big horse she was exhausted but she was holding on to that hat with a death grip. The Mayan man was turning to leave when Clayton put his hand on his arm.

Russell you talk to him and get him some food, find out what happened and where Sam is I will take care of Melanee and be right back." He carried his daughter up the stairs with Juanita not far behind and he put her on her bed and she awoke crying.

"Daddy she made me go she said he would hurt me to get to her so I should go, did I do the wrong thing she is with the bad man?" he just picked her up off the bed and held her to him Sam had sent her away because she was afraid Nathan would use her and now his little girl felt guilty. She handed him the hat in her hand.

"It is for Steven it is his Christmas present." Steven was standing in the doorway and he came in and took the hat from her and hung it on the end of the bed and just hugged her as she cried.

"I hope Balik finds him first." then he just looked at Melanee and his father he wanted Balik to kill him and he wanted Nathan to suffer. Clayton didn't know what to say after that to either of them he personally hoped the same thing.

"You did what she wanted you to do; now we will go after them and we will find her and bring her back don't you worry. You eat and rest now I am going down and talk to the man who brought you back so I know where to start hunting." He practically ran down the stairs and out on the patio where the man was eating and the Russell began to tell him what had happened.

"Seems Nathan hired some white trackers and some Mayan ones but this is the good part this man talked to the Mayan men they didn't know who they were kidnapping and now they do. At least one and now maybe more will protect her until Balik can get to her. Nathan had no money or very little they were supposed to be paid with her horse. Apparently he found a bag of money when he took her in the dressing room. I am guessing the money you gave her the night she left. This man is anxious to leave and find Balik because he says if she was ever taken he would personally kill the man." About that time another Mayan man came out of the jungle and the two men spoke and then the first man turned and spoke to Russell. After they were through the two men were going to leave but Juanita stopped them and handed them a bag and then they left. Russell turned and came back to Clay.

"Balik already knows she is gone and he is looking but we may have another problem they told me it has started raining upstream and the river will be flooded soon, if the men who have her don't get off the river they are in trouble. One of these Mayan men is going to Balik and the other is going after Nathan to keep track of him." The clouds overhead were rumbling and it was starting to sprinkle. Russell and Clayton both looked skyward and thought. 'NOT NOW.' But there was something else they could hear drums in the distance. Balik was already on the HUNT.

They had finally stopped and Sam was sure that Melanee was back at home by now they were at a boat landing. She got off the horse she riding, it was the one the Mayan man had brought with him. Nathan pulled out a bag of money and she recognized it as her money bag. He paid off the white trackers and now there were only the three Mayan men and man guiding the boat and Nathan, he was yelling orders and he took her aside and told her.

"You better behave around these men they won't hesitate to rape or kill you and it won't be nice so stay close to me and you will be safe. Now get on the boat." He practically shoved her down on the boat she caught herself as she hit the other side and none of this was lost on the men loading the boat. The Mayan man who was being nice to her was talking to the other men and she could see he wasn't making much headway but she was too tired to care. Once everything was loaded they started down the river and the same man handed her a mango to eat. When she leaned over to get it the little jade snake pendant she wore came out of her shirt. The man saw it and took it in his hand and looked at her strangely.

"Only priests wear."

"Balik told me to wear it and if I ever needed help send this with a messenger and he would come for me." The man continued to stare at her as Nathan was having a fit about something up front.

"Would you look at the size of that thing and it just keeps coming." When she turned around she could see a very large yellow spotted snake entering the water at the bank and Nathan pulling out a gun so she headed up front.

"I would leave it alone Nathan the snakes run big down here and I don't think you want that snake in the boat with us do you?"

"What do you know about it Samantha?"

"I have seen a 10 foot python and I think that is what is called a yellow anaconda and they can get to 20 feet or more from what I am told. You do whatever you want to do." Then she turned around and went back to her seat in the middle of the canoe. She sat down and watched as he put up his gun and was just watching the snake. When she looked in the water the snake was right under the boat and there was that urge again to touch it. She reached down into the water and spread out her hand, it didn't even go from one side to the other of the big snake. She was touching the big snake as it slid past. The snake didn't seem to notice as it swam underneath the boat. She kept her hand on the snake till it was up on the bank and then Sam brought her hand back up into the boat and dried it off and ate her mango. She didn't notice but all the men behind her were watching and if they didn't think she was a snake spirit before they did now.

In the distance they could hear the drums and they looked at her again, Balik was coming. They weren't even the same tribe as Balik but they knew better than to cross a chieftain as powerful as Balik. Samantha finished her mango and grabbed a blanket and lies on the side of the boat and fell asleep. One of the men covered her and then they were all talking, now she had three guardians.

Sometime later Nathan awakens her by grabbing her arm and yanking her up. She realized it was raining and they were trying to get the boat to the shore. It looked like a dock of some kind a small one as they drew up to it and he was pulling her to the side of the boat. Nathan shoved her ashore as the men pulled the boat out of the water and then got the supplies and started to follow.

"They said there is a house or something up here so we can get out of the rain so come on woman hurry up." She was trying to hurry but he was dragging her until she stopped and told him.

"Quit dragging me I can walk by myself and you are hurting me let go." He turned around and he was going to slap her but two of the Mayan men pulled out their machetes and he backed down he hadn't expected them to protect her. He just looked at them and then he let her go and they continued on but he was furious. Samantha looked back at which two men were protecting her and was stunned to find out it was the ones that didn't like her before she went to sleep. When they came to the house it wasn't much it was a Mayan long house one door, no window, a fireplace and a roof but it was reasonably dry and that was what counted right now. They got inside and there was firewood and she started to make a fire as the men got out some food and pans.

Nathan was looking daggers at her she wasn't doing what he wanted her to do and they weren't alone so he couldn't make her behave. He wanted her and this wasn't the place or the time he was going to have to get rid of these Mayan men though he didn't know why they were protecting her. The men put food out and they were eating Nathan didn't know what it was Samantha didn't even ask.

"How do you eat this stuff you don't even know what it is they could be poisoning you?" Samantha looked at him like he was a fool.

"During the war I ate a lot of things that I wasn't too sure of just to survive I guess you had it better than the rest of us common people."

"You didn't have to I would have taken care of you. Why did you marry Eliot he wasn't even a man?"

"Because he was protecting me from you, little good it did me. He thought a wedding ring would keep you away. Did you drown my brother Jeremy to find me?" he looked like she had slapped him.

"How did you know about that, no one was there except him and me?" and then he realized what he was saying but it was too late.

"He wouldn't tell me where you were and I was sure he knew but he didn't? I didn't know he couldn't swim I pulled him out to late and the towns people wanted to hang me for drowning him but it was an accident." He was trying to make excuses for killing her brother and she wasn't having it.

"You are a liar you kept pushing him under over and over until he didn't come up anymore but this is not your first murder what about the salon girl they say you killed where is that woman buried." He was just looking at her how did she know.

"Not far from your place but she was nothing she didn't want me either so I taught her a lesson she wouldn't ever forget and then I had to bury her. There is more than one woman out there in the plains but what is one more whore more or less. Your husband's friend Claude came back to town and brought Eliot's body to be buried. He told everybody you owned half of the ranch so I didn't have any right to it or what I did to you and Tillie backed him up. She was causing me more trouble in town so after it was said and done the ranch was put back in your name. Eliot's uncle made sure the town was on your side and I needed to leave. You won't need it we won't be going back."

"There is a price on your head isn't there, you can't go back? I will write to someone and give the ranch to Wayne he helped me to get here, I am not going back to Texas I am going back to Clayton." She looked him right in the face and she thought he was going to explode.

"I chased you across thousands of miles and you think I will let you go are you that stupid Samantha?"

"What makes you think I will stay with you after the loving way you treat me?" she wasn't upset she was calm he wasn't.

"I didn't treat you that badly it was just your first time." you would have thought they were alone they weren't paying attention to anyone else in the room even though the other men were listening to every word spoken.

"You have got to be kidding me I almost had to crawl out of that house with 3 cracked ribs my eye swollen shut. I was bleeding and I know you know this; you jumped that Texas doctor and asked him about me. If we hadn't stopped when we did I would have died. That doctor saved me from bleeding to death that is what you lovemaking did to me. You say you love me well I don't love you, never have never will so I don't know where we go from here but I won't let you hurt me any more either kill me or let me go." He turned around and looked into the fire and didn't say anything so she went back to eating but the men behind her had their weapons drawn and hidden beside them they expected trouble and so did she. She laid out a pallet and lay down on it and soon she felt Nathan against her then he was whispering in her ear.

"It is your game for right now you have too much protection but soon we will be alone and I will have the winning hand. I don't care if you love me are not you are mine and I am keeping you. If you're Clayton shows up I will just kill him. I should have tried harder to keep the girl she would have been good to keep you in line. You already knew that didn't you?" Sam kept her mouth shut and listened to the drums they were getting closer and Nathan wasn't counting on Balik. She just smiled and looked at the men around the room they were listening too. Nathan really was regretting buying these men metal machetes.

The next morning the rain was stopped and they began to move again and she wanted to know where they were going. She walked up to Nathan and she asked him.

"Do you have any Idea where you are going or are we just going to keep moving through this jungle until we find a spot that suits you?" she had reached down to pick up a sack and when she stood up again he hit her across the face, hard enough to knock her back down on the ground. She didn't say a word she put her hand to her face she could already feel her eye swelling. All of the sudden the jungle got deadly quiet and there were men all around them and off to her right she saw Balik. Sam just smiled at him. Nathan started babbling.

"Samantha be still they will kill us maybe I can talk us out of this or buy our way out." One of her men helped her up and Nathan was furious as he told her.

"Be still and maybe I can get us out of here if I use you as a shield that hair of yours might come in handy for once. Maybe I should see if they will take you in trade and let me go you are almost more trouble than you are worth. How would you like that, for me to trade you off like you were nothing now you better be nice to me?" The man that had been translating for her was talking to Balik now and if he could get madder he just did. Balik motioned for her to come to him but Nathan grabbed her hair and pulled her to him and then he did something really stupid he put a knife to her neck.

"Just be still and I will see if I can get us out of this keep moving back."

"Nathan they came for me and you are making this worse let me go. Those drums you have been hearing were that Mayan Chieftain and his men hunting for me ever since you took me. If you hurt me he will take his time killing you and I won't be able to stop him now let me go."

"Why would he protect you a white woman and how did they know you were with me?" Balik was talking and he was mad and he had a spear in his hand.

"He had guards watching me and Melanee at the ranch and the festival didn't you wonder where that man came from that took Melanee it was one of his men and he killed one of your men and took his place. I helped his son a while back and they think I am a snake spirit and if you hurt me they will kill you." Her man that was translating said.

"Balik says let the snake spirit go now." Nathan lowered the knife slowly and Samantha walked away from him towards Balik and as soon as she was several feet away Balik lifted a spear and threw it at Nathan and pinned him to a tree. Then he went to Sam and put his arms around her and held her and then took her face in his hands and looked at the black eye that was already forming. He called the men over that had been guarding her and said something to them she didn't know what. Then Balik led her over to Nathan, he wasn't dead he was squirming around on that spear like a bug on a pin. Balik took out a knife and handed it to Samantha to finish him but she refused. She walked up to the tree.

"I told you not to come after me, now I will never look over my shoulder again."

"You have to help me I will go away and never come back I promise. You can't leave me with these savages I have always been there for you."

"You really believe that don't you, my brother is dead those girls you killed and you don't think you are guilty of anything just because they got in your way. Well it is time for you to pay and he is going to be the one who collects the toll. I am not going to stop him. I told you to stay away from me and you didn't listen so now you are his. I could tell him to kill you quickly but I won't. You let my brother drown and that was the one thing that terrified him the most in this world so Balik can do whatever he wants with you. GOODBY NATHAN."Then she started to walk away but before she did Balik held out her hair and cut off a long piece of it and then motioned for her to go with the men.

Sam walked away and she didn't look back she didn't want to see anymore she let Balik finish it. She walked to the edge of the trees after she grabbed a bag of supplies and her men were beside her. Balik and his men joined her hours later. She never asked what he did to him she didn't want to know she just knew he was dead. They went back to the river it wasn't much better and she assumed he was taking her back home. They tried to go up river for an hour or so but it was futile the river was just too strong so her man told her.

"Balik says we are going to have to go inland until the river goes down it is too high to cross now so you will have to come with him he will keep you safe." She just nodded she could see they were fighting a losing battle and she didn't want to get anybody killed trying to get across the river. She knew Balik would take care of her. They were going to find a safe place to disembark and head inland they were watching the bank as it was falling away. They thought they had found a safe place so they pulled to the edge and were getting out. When it was Samantha's turn Balik reached for her and she stepped out but when she put her foot on the ground it dissolved underneath her. She was slipping and Balik couldn't hold her as she fell into the water. She was struggling for a hold on anything and she finally found a log rushing by and she held on for dear life. It drags her to the middle of the river into a jumble of branches where she got caught. She was hung up in the tangle literally she was hung on something it was wrapped around her foot and leg she couldn't get away from it.

The men on the other side could see her but they couldn't figure out how they were going to get to her. Some of the men started getting some vines and tying them together and then they were going to tie them to each other and try to stretch out to get her. Meanwhile Samantha had another problem she wasn't alone on that tangle there were a couple of caiman on the other bank and the tangle was getting closer to the bank all the time. All she needed now was a couple of those little crocodiles to make her day. She kept trying to make the tangle move away from them but she didn't want it to break loose entirely she could go down the river and drown because she couldn't get loose. The men on the bank had gotten the vines tied and were ready to come across but so were the caiman. She kept looking back and forth to see which one was going to get there first. She didn't think the caiman could kill her but they could take some nasty chunks out of her.

The men got down in the water Balik first and started across and the first caiman swam across and was on the tangle and started walking towards her. She grabbed a stick and was ready to hit it like that was going to do any good, when the tree that was holding this whole mess together started moving.

'Great she thought now this whole thing is going to give way and we are all going down the river.' Instead a snake head slowly came down and just hung there. The caiman was getting closer and the snake just stayed put until the croc was right under it then she caught the small Crocodile by the head and started curling around it and she could hear that caiman's bones breaking as she watched that big snake curl around and kill that caiman. The anaconda dropped onto the tangle and the weight of it broke it apart. Sam was free and when she turned around Balik's face was there and he had his arms around her. He and the men pulled her back to the shore and then they all watched as that big snake swallowed that caiman and then they just looked at her. She didn't know what they were thinking but they were looking at her sideways. Well whatever she didn't have anything to do with it but it was kind of weird. She touched the pendant around her neck put it to her lips and then they left.

They headed to Balik's village and it was still a long way to get there. The night was coming and so was the rain these people didn't mind the rain she was the one out of place and lord was she was out of place. She was hungry and tired and ready to just fall down. Balik and her men could see this so they got to a place not far away it was an old abandoned house. It wasn't the best but one side of the house still had a roof and a fireplace so they could cook and she could rest and that was all that mattered. Te'a had told Balik about how she got sick so he wanted to get somewhere he could make sure he could take care of her. He was glad the river didn't let him take her home he wanted her for a while. He wanted to show her his world even for a little while or that is what he kept telling himself.

When they got inside the house the men looked for snakes and other critters and then gathered firewood and got back inside before it started to rain again. Sam sat down this time and let the men take care of things she even asked her man if there was a mango she could eat. He found one it was a little smashed but at this point she didn't care. He sat down beside her and cut it and laid it open so she could get to it and then she lay down and went to sleep despite all the things going on around her. Balik didn't' even notice until later that she was curled up asleep with her man watching over her. He nodded towards the man asking if she was all right. He shook his head no.

Balik came over to her and took one of her boots in his hand and pulled it off it was the one she was tangled up in the roots. It was scraped and bruised so he had one of his men bring some water and a rag over and he washed the dirt off to see how badly she was hurt. She hadn't even acknowledged they were there until he started to wash off the dirt and then she woke up and then he could see why, she had a pretty deep cut higher up on her leg and it was still bleeding no wonder those Caiman had been so interested. She was pushing his hand away but he stayed right there. He cleaned up the cut and then took off the other boot and did the same to the other foot.

Supper was done and they were having turtle soup it seemed they had found a tortoise on the way here and now it was supper she hated to see one of the beautiful creatures die but pickings were slim right now. She did notice her translator wouldn't even touch the soup at all. She thought it strange but left it alone she would ask him about it later. They had seen a lot things float by them but not all of them you wanted in the boat with you or wanted to drag through the jungle all day. She ate all she could and then someone found another mango and she ate it as well. Balik had made a pallet in the back corner where it was dry and he led her there and she lay down and he lay beside her. He said something to her she didn't understand covered them up and she went to sleep. Her man had heard what Balik said to her and he wasn't sure he was going to tell her or not because he wasn't sure Balik would want her to know. Balik had told her 'YOU ARE UNDER MY CARE NOW.' Balik pulled her close and buried his head in her golden hair and was so glad he was in time to save her and smiled at the thought of the man he left hanging on that tree. Balik was the man who had dealt out vengeance for her and Nathan would never hurt her again.

She slept for several hours and then she awoke to something she didn't know what and then Balik awoke. Several men were coming into the house and they were agitated about something and then she heard a scream in the jungle. She said under her breath to herself. 'Jaguar.' But the men in the room looked at her, how did she know what that sound was.

Several of the men started spacing themselves around the room where there were no walls as guards. The sounds kept getting closer and then they stopped. Balik just looked at Sam and she said.

"She got whatever she was after." Then she lay back down and started to go back to sleep and sure enough they didn't hear that cat anymore that night. Balik was staring at her until she said.

"I heard one up close remember and you don't forget what they sound like ever, they have a very distinctive scream. Are we done now?" he was grinning again but he looked at his men and had them keep a watch anyway he didn't want one of those cats in here unannounced. The next morning she felt better but she could barely walk on that foot she didn't know what she was going to do. Then in walks a couple of men one of them is holding a bag. They walk over to her it is the man that took Melanee from her and was supposed to take her back to the hacienda. She tries to stand and greet him but Balik had her stay down as the man tells her what happened with the little girl.

"I take child back to father and she is alright. Woman at hacienda sent bag for you clean clothes and sandals. We got over river through trees but can't get across now it to high. We will wait here and start back in a couple of days to lead your man here when the river goes down." Sam just looked at him and then nodded her head at least Melanee was safe that was all she could have hoped for at this point. Sam looked into the bag and there was a pair of sandals and a change of clothes well she knew what she was going to need and she didn't expect her to get back home anytime soon. Well maybe she could at least walk in the sandals she couldn't get those boots back on. Her translator came over and she at least knew his name by now he was called Two Turtles and sat down beside her. His name, maybe that was why he wouldn't eat the soup but she thought there was more.

"Balik wants to know if you can swim?" she looked over at Balik kind of funny the water wasn't that high yet. After the river yesterday it was a little late to worry about that but she nodded yes anyway she wondered where this was going.

"He wants you come with him a short distance from here and I will help you walk there. He says you don't have to be afraid he will take care of you."

"Tell him I have never been afraid when I was with him and I won't be now." Balik nodded his head but he could hardly look at her. The men helped her up after getting her shoes on and with both of them on either side of her they started out the door. Two men followed them as they went down a fairly well traveled path. Both men were helping her walk her leg and foot was still pretty badly swollen.

"Balik wants to know if we need to stop or are you alright, we are almost there?"

"I am fine let's keep going if I can't go on I will tell you." They kept walking until they came through the jungle and stopped at a hole. Sam was unimpressed.

"This is it you wanted me to see, a great big hole." They walked a little closer and the hole was filled with water and now the hole was a different story. There were vines growing down the sides and flowers everywhere. And the water looked like glass and she thought to herself 'OH I would love to dive into that undisturbed water.' But that would be foolish she didn't know if there were rocks or how deep it was but OH it was speaking to her.

"What is this place it is like nothing I have ever seen?" she inched closer to the edge but the men wouldn't let her get to close. Balik was talking and two turtles starting telling her.

"It is called a Cenote and there is a cave at the back of it he wants to show you. You can't walk down all the way just part of the way and then you will have to be lowered down by vine and they will have to pull you back up when he is through showing you the cave. Will you go with him?"

"How deep is the Cenote and are you coming with us?" he turned and asked the questions and replied.

"He says the pool is very deep and the water is crystal clear the men like to swim to the bottom when they come here. He wants just the two of you to go to the cave there is something he just wants you to see." She nodded and they headed down the little path but when they got to the bottom and the men wanted to tie her to the vines to lower her to the water she turned around and asked Balik.

"Which way is the cave?" Balik pointed to the other side of the Cenote and Samantha put her arms above her head turned around and jumped from the edge of the Cenote the men just stood there stunned. She was underwater for a bit but they could see her and that blond hair streaming out behind her. When she came up she turned over and just looked at them and shouted.

"Well come on if you are coming or I will beat you there Balik." He wasn't quite as brave as her he went down the vine but he caught up with her quickly and led her to the cave. The men up above just watched her swim and kept guard. When they got to the cave entrance Balik climbed in and then he helped Sam up inside. There was moss on the floor and it was a carpet of green she expected it to be soft and squishy but it was pretty firm. She started to look around inside and there were little mineral deposits on the wall and some hanging from the ceiling she used to know what those were called but she couldn't remember she would have to ask Clayton.

Balik took her hand and pulled her further into the cave and she wondered where they were going. He stopped and pushed her ahead and she looked through a hole at another smaller cavern to the side with not so much water in it and there was a smaller opening at the top. She looked up and it was a long way to the top but she figured this side flooded as well when the rains were at their worst but she couldn't figure out why Balik was so dead set on showing her this part of the cave. The smaller cave was beginning to fill now. Sam started to back up and Balik wouldn't let her and then he pointed to the cave again so she looked back. This time she looked at the water and under the water and she finally saw what it was he was trying to show her. There were skeletons in the bottom of that Cenote several of them. She started backing away and Balik touched her and she pushed his hand away.

"This is what you wanted me to see bodies. Why Balik am I supposed to join them?" he grabbed her arm again to shake her and pointed to one of the skeletons and made her look again and sure enough it had blond hair.

""Is that what you are trying to tell me my hair puts me in danger here?" she was holding her hair as she talked to him and he was nodding and shaking his head yes.

"Did you know that woman?" and she pointed to the skeleton in the water and he shook his head yes. Why did she get the feeling she was in a story that was replaying itself and she and Balik were central players.

"All I can do is get home as soon as I can and get away from here and whoever did this." She took his hand and they started out of the cave when then he stopped her and ran his hand down her back and she jumped. He walked up behind her and pulled up her chemise and underneath was something black and nasty. Balik sat her down on the floor closer to the front of the cave and had her undo her chemise so she could pull it up over her arm. She was thinking she had done this once before. He went to scrape something off the wall and then he came back with it on his knife. He sprinkled whatever was on the wall on the creature and it shriveled up and he pulled it off. He showed her the nasty thing it was a leach. He laid it on a rock and smashed it and it must have been there for some time because it sent blood everywhere.

"Well I guess I picked that little beauty up in the river I didn't even feel the little monster." She might as well have been talking to herself because he wasn't listening to her. He was running his finger over the spot where that leach had been trying to get the blood to stop and then he just kept caressing her back. The next thing she knew he kissed her shoulder and he pushed her on her back. He caressed her breast and would have gone further but he was acting like a man that wanted her but something was wrong and then he said something. He wasn't really looking at her he seemed to be somewhere else. Then he laid his head on her shoulder and spoke again.

"Ella." Samantha just pushed him back gently as she sat up and cradled his head in her hands. He wasn't trying to hurt her or make love to her he just wanted some comfort.

"I am not your Ella, Balik and I don't think I would make a good substitute." Then she just held his head to her breast while he cried, something was wrong and this was the only place he could just let that out so his men couldn't see. He wasn't the Chieftain in here he was just a man. They both rested for a while with Sam soaking her foot in the water and then they returned to the Cenote. After they swam across they were lifted up and she pulled on a dress more suited for a Mayan woman, they were trying to make her blend in, hard to do with her hair. She searched around in the bag that Juanita sent and sure enough she found a scarf. She pulled her hair up pulled it into a bun and wrapped the scarf around all her hair and tied it around her head so you couldn't see what her hair color was. All the men were pleased with that it seemed she was making them all very nervous.

She found out his wife's name is Ella and she is very ill, now Sam wanted to meet this woman that made this man's world round. Balik had the men take turns holding a pole between them so she could sit on it and they could carry her with her arms around their shoulders they could move much faster.

She couldn't walk as fast as they could at the best of times. He wanted to get to his home and she had a feeling there was more to it than just the weather and that wasn't helping. It rained most nights or it poured but the days were better, the trees gave them some protection. Balik had been gone with his men hunting when she was taken that was why he and his men were so close but he had been gone from home longer than he wanted to be and was anxious to get home.

Two turtles told her when they stopped that night that they were close to Balik's home it should only take one more day and they would be there. Her foot was getting better but she was still limping. The men had made a sort of lean to with branches. She didn't understand if they went to this much trouble when they were out by themselves or if it was just because she was there. Balik had been staying clear of her, she didn't know if he was embarrassed or what? She waited for him to make the first move. Two turtles came over and sat down and asked her.

"Balik wants to know if you mind sleeping next to him or if you would rather sleep elsewhere?" she kind of smiled to herself now he was really embarrassed and she wasn't sure how to fix this.

"Please tell him everything is just fine and he makes me feel very safe always did and he still does and use those exact words have you got that?" two turtles smiled at her and then went over to Balik and told him what she had said and Balik looked over at her and smiled it was the first time he had smiled since they had come back from the Cenote. When they went to sleep that night Balik was at her side and had his arm over her like before and things were back to normal and she did feel safe again. She wondered what the woman was like that this man loved she must be something special.

The next day around noon they were getting close to the village and the men were scooting off to meet there families and there were children coming out to meet them. They walked into sort of a valley with sloped sides on it and round circles at the top she looked at the men beside her and was told this was where they played a ball games. When she asked if she might see one she was told they hoped not because the losers were generally killed. "Tough game." she said to men around her and they all nodded. It is generally only played by losing warriors. Then out off the jungle there is a pyramid it is just there it is not huge but it is a pyramid. Sam just stood there like an idiot and stared and the men beside her laughed at the look on her face. She had seen a smaller one in Mexico City. Sam turned and looked at Balik and he had such pride on his face, he was home. There were huge trees around the houses at the base of the pyramid and Balik led her into one. It was dark inside the room but there was a woman older than her sitting in a chair, it was obvious she was ill but at one time she had been a beauty, with blond hair.

"Hello I am Graciella Montoya, I am Balik's wife and you must be Samantha he has done nothing but talk about you since the first time he saw you. Come over here so I can see you." Te'a was coming into the building as was Telic as Samantha walked over to the woman then Sam grabbed the scarf around her head and undid her hair and let it fall.

"He was right you are as beautiful as Sofia that is why he has been so scared for you since the first time he saw you, when you helped our son."

"Maybe you can tell me why he is so worried for me?"

"Oh yes but Te'a will take you so you can bath and then we will have a meal and we can talk, I so miss talking in English I will probably talk your ear off. Go rest I am not going anywhere then I will tell you all the stories of my life till you are bored." Te'a took Sam away and Balik came in and sat down beside his wife and took her hand and kissed it as she stroked his hair. Samantha looked back at the woman she wasn't Mexican she was highborn Spanish if she was guessing, how in the world had she wound up here.

CHAPTER 11

"She is so beautiful my love if I didn't know you better I would be jealous that you spent so much time with her to get here.

She is everything I am not anymore and I should hate her for that but I fear she is someone I am going to like. What am I going to do my love I am not quite dead but not alive either?" about that time the medicine man came in and ordered Balik out of the cabin so he could check over his wife. Balik went but he didn't go far and Samantha was back by then and she was listening to what was going on. The medicine man was talking to Ella and telling her she had to do as he told her or she wasn't going to get any better. He left the building and stopped and talked to Balik and then two turtles told Sam that he had told Balik his wife was dying and he couldn't help her. He told Balik it was because of his trying to protect the white woman and not paying attention to his own people and now the gods were taking it out on his wife. So now it was Sam's fault. Sam just stood back until the medicine man left and Balik went into his wife and she stood at the door and watched them together. A younger woman came in with what she assumed was Ella's diner and sat it down on a table and then just stood there. She was a very pretty woman and she was obviously trying to get Balik's attention.

"She needs to eat and then she needs her rest so you must go now." She just stood there until Balik left and then Sam could see Ella didn't want him to leave but this woman ran him out of the room. Sam just stood there and watched she wanted to see what else was going on she didn't like the feel of this at all. The woman sat on the floor in front of Ella and started to spoon whatever was in cup out of the cup in her hand and it was obvious Ella didn't really want it. Samantha walked into the room and Ella saw her and looked at her with pleading eyes.

"What are you feeding Balik's wife?" the girl was startled like she had been caught and now Samantha was more cautious.

"It is a special coco with healing properties it will make her better." "If it is so healing maybe I should try it I am very tired from the trip here it might help me as well?" Sam reached down for the cup and the girl almost dumped it trying to keep it away from her. Samantha looked at Ella and they both knew right then something was wrong.

"I only made enough for the Chieftain's wife there isn't enough for you as well and she needs it." They both knew she was lying.

"I told Graciella we were going to talk tonight so I will see she eats all her coco and you can go." The girl looked caught she had made a mistake and she couldn't get out of it so she just tried to make the best of it.

"Good you see she drinks it all and I will leave the two of you alone I will see you tomorrow mistress." The look she gave them was one of a panicked monkey in a tree caught by a dog, fight or flight. When she left Sam stirred the coco and she didn't see much but it had a funny smell but she threw it in the corner anyway. It didn't smell like the coco Juanita made for her at the hacienda and that made her wonder what was in it. Ella was watching all this and then Samantha asked her.

"When did you first get sick?"

"Just after Balik found Telic, I had started to be sick then it was getting worse. When you made the medicine man mad it got really bad. Every time Balik goes to help you I got worse and the medicine man says it is your fault. Balik almost didn't come to you because he was afraid he would bring more harm to you from his own people." Sam sat there a minute just thinking and then she stood up and said.

"I will be back in a minute." She went outside and talked to Te'a and then she came back inside the hut and in a few minutes

Te'a came in with a bag. They spread out what was inside mangos and those green things some berries and she had got some turkey.

"Alright we are feeding you and I am sure what you are eating is fresh and good for you." Ella looked at her.

"You think something is not right with what she has been feeding me?"

"I can't prove it so until I can you don't eat or drink anything from her. You eat only what Te'a or I bring to you and one of us will always be close so she can't force you to do anything anymore. Tomorrow Te'a and I will start watching where she goes and what she does and see if we can prove that she is poisoning you but until then you have to act like you are still sick."

"Act like, I am sick, I am still sick." They heard a funny noise over at the side of the hut a kind of high pitched squeak and Sam went over to the wall of the hut where she had thrown the coco and there was a small mouse twitching it was dying. It was right in the middle of the puddle of that coco and it was making a high pitch squeaking noise. Samantha stepped on it and put it out of its misery and turned to the women watching her.

"Any questions, she is poisoning you slowly. I want to know if she has any help from the Shaman or if she is doing this alone?" Ella looked at her.

"Do we tell Balik?"

"Not yet I want proof and then we will tell him I have seen what he does when he gets angry so I want to be sure before I tell him. Besides if he knows you are better he won't be able to keep his hands off of you." Then she winked and smiled and so did Ella.

"Now I told her you would eat and you are going to, we are going to flush that stuff out of your system. What do you want mango or the green thing for supper?"

"It is called an avocado and both and some of that turkey as well I think my appetite is coming back."

"Now you must tell me how you wound up married to a Mayan Chieftain and I don't think you are Mexican I am thinking Spanish from Isabella's court maybe." She smiled at her.

"Now what would you know of Isabella's court? Don't tell me you are the one he told me about in the black dress that was dancing? He didn't know what you were dancing but when he described it, now I know you were doing the Flamenco. When he told me about the little clackers it made no sense now it does. He was so furious about them hurting our son he was ready to kill someone or all of them. You know don't you that you saved that village he was going to kill all of them for what was done to Telic?"

"I thought that might have been the plan I was glad to have convinced him not to." She just smiled.

"There are not many people that can convince him to change his mind. Back to my story my father got a land grant from the king and we were on a ship going to the Americas it was in California. We hit bad weather and had to find a port to nestle in, the seas were too bad. When we got to land there was a big rancho and the owner invited us to stay there until the weather was better, we had no other choice. We had been told the Maya were raiding ranches so we stayed close but word of our blond hair had got out and now we had men watching us and we should have been more careful. They hit the ranch one night late looking for supplies. We saw our father shot I don't know if he is alive or dead but we were captured by Balik and taken into the jungle and never saw the coast again. We met up with the Shaman and his men days later and it was a fight from the beginning he wanted both of us to sacrifice to the gods he said it would be for the best. Balik disagreed. As we got closer to here the Shaman got crazier and Balik more protective of me especially, he wanted me for a wife and he made sure his men knew that. There is a Cenote a couple of days from here and when we got close to it the Shaman made his move."

"I know where you are talking about he took me to it and showed me the little hole he wanted me to know I was in trouble and the Shaman was somebody to be feared."

"When we were close to the Cenote the Shaman took some of his men and my sister and they left in the night, when Balik found them missing he went after them but when he got there he was too late. The Shaman had her high on the edge he blew some power in her face and was saying the prayers then he pushed her into the water below and she never came up. He used that powder on her they use on sacrifices and she probably didn't know what was happening. I hope not she couldn't swim. Balik came back and took me to another village and had another Shaman marry us and then we came here I always assumed it was because he loved me I hope it was. Now he protects you the same way. He never took anyone to the Cenote before." Samantha just looked at her what was she supposed to say.

"He made sure I saw her body or what was left of it so I would be properly scared of the man as if I wasn't already. She still rests there."Ella just nodded her head.

"I wish that Shaman was laying beside her for your sake."

"Maybe we can see to that and I think he married you because he loves you."

The next morning Ella was much better and both women noticed but they couldn't let Balik see how well she was doing so they sent him hunting. The woman who was bringing her food came in with her food and she was insistent on feeding her but Samantha said she was going to feed her today and it infuriated the woman. She finally left after the women put her to work sweeping out the hut and she thought she was beneath that.

"D'ha wants your position and she wants it now Graciella. It wouldn't surprise me if your food isn't more heavily poisoned, you need to be gone." The women just looked at each other.

"Do you think she is doing this on her own or do you think she has help?"

"The coco is generally reserved for royalty and the shamans so the recipe is closely guarded and now she brings it to me regularly where did she get the recipe and the coco beans. You need to be careful where you dump that concoction so the animals around here don't get in it or it will kill them."Balik was gone for two days and Ella was getting better by the day and she was even starting to walk a little. They weren't paying attention to what she was doing when he came back several days later and he walked into the hut. She was walking across the room and he came in and he dropped the birds he was carrying and just stood there.

"Graciella." Everybody froze and turned around and there he was what was worse D'ha wasn't twenty feet behind him and coming fast. Balik was headed to Graciella and nothing was stopping him so Sam just got out of his way but she saw two turtles and called to him. She got his attention and waved at him and motioned for him to sidetrack D'ha away from the hut. He wasn't having any luck and she still kept coming. Sam turned and spoke to Ella.

"Graciella, D'ha is coming you need to be fragile tell him to play along please or we have lost this game." Ella leaned into Balik's neck and whispered something to him and he picked her up in his arms and Sam could have sworn he was shaking. He turned around and carried her slowly to her bed and gently put her down and just held her. Then he turned to Sam and just looked at her. He didn't say anything and he didn't do anything but she knew, he knew. D'ha was a dead woman and she didn't even know it yet. D'ha came running in to greet him and he stood there and played the part as he walked her outside the hut. Then he sent her away but when she was gone you could almost hear the tension cracking in the air. Two turtles came inside the hut and watched the door while everyone went to the other end where they couldn't be seen from the outside so they could talk. Balik sat down beside his wife and just looked at her and smiled and then looked at Sam and started talking. Graciella was translating.

"He wants to know how you figured it out when no one else could."

"I don't like the medicine man and I could see D'ha was in love with you and she wished to harm you wife. Maybe nobody else had the nerve to stand up to him and say what they were thinking. She is still not safe she is too easy to get to. We still haven't proved he was poisoning her or that the shaman was helping her and until then she isn't safe. Can we put her in the pyramid and then we can keep a closer eye on her?"

"You are not safe either he wants me to hand you over to him to sacrifice like he did her sister so he can save my wife he says that is the price that the gods demand. The only thing keeping you safe now is my men think you are some kind of special snake spirit so they are still protecting you from him. If they see that my wife is getting better since you got here they will think you did it and it will make him even madder." Sam looked at him and wondered now what to do should she take credit for helping her or was there some better way to handle this. Te'a came up with a plan.

"Why don't we take her to the part of the pyramid under the snake totem with Samantha and claim that it was the two of them that healed her that way it won't all be her and they will let her go home when the water goes down." They all agreed to that because she did want to leave she didn't want to become something they wouldn't let go home. They would have time to prove the Shaman was involved with poisoning her that it wasn't just D'ha. That was enough for tonight, they could all see that Balik just wanted to be alone with his wife so they left but they told them they would make sure no one interrupted them for a while.

D'ha showed up later with her death mug of coco and insisted to be let in and Samantha stopped her and D'ha was furious. Sam told her to take the drink and drink it herself that Balik was with his dying wife and they wanted to be left alone so go away. D'ha smiled at that and Sam wanted to slap that smile off her face but she went away. Two Turtles and Sam and Te'a were sitting in front of the hut when she came back with the Shaman and Sam didn't even bother to stand. That really made him mad and she didn't care he was such a blustering coward. He started to yell at her and Two Turtles was translating but she was beginning to understand some of the words and she knew Two Turtles wasn't telling her everything he was saying, he was threatening her. She didn't have to listen to it for it long because Balik came out and then she did stand up and the Shaman did notice that. She had no respect for the Shaman and she was showing it and the village people were watching.

"I am moving my wife to the pyramid in the morning where I can be with her and Samantha is going to take care of her.

Graciella fells better when Samantha is around so I want her near her and not you or D'ha." The Shaman was livid and the look he gave Sam was pure evil and he started screaming at Balik and Balik started to scream back at him. When they parted ways he looked down at Sam and gave instructions to several men and then pulled her inside and Two Turtle followed.

"Balik says you go nowhere without a guard the Shaman has sworn to kill you and he means it so you stay close. I will have some of my men that I trust always close by until I can get you back home to Clayton." He shook his head yes to her and she nodded back to him. She was standing outside the lodge and the moon was rising and she walked a few feet away as Balik was carrying his wife out.

Samantha wasn't paying much attention to what was going on but her hair was lighting up in the moonlight. She reached up to get some things tied to edge of the lodge and the scarf hiding the rest of her hair fell off and her hair went tumbling down and now it was really glowing in the moonlight. The people around her were just staring and then the Shaman started yelling again. She stopped and turned and just looked at him. Balik turned around said something to his wife then put her on her feet and she walked towards Samantha. While Graciella walked towards Samantha she was saying something and now the Shaman was livid and then the people around her were trying to touch her and she didn't know why.

"We need to get in the pyramid now, Balik told them it was you that made me better and the Shaman has figured out we know about the poison. You are in even more danger come we must go now, this couldn't be avoided." The Shaman ran up to her and grabbed Sam by the hair and pulled her to him and he was screaming at Balik. Samantha didn't understand what he was saying except she heard her name and something about the Cenote as he dragged her across the courtyard. Several of his men were by his side protecting him from Balik. This was turning into a battle in the courtyard as the people watched. Sam started to hit him in the side but he just kept pulling her until Balik stopped him pulled her away and hit him. The Shaman stumbled away from her and then the two men were screaming at each other again. Two turtles got her hand and pulled her back to where Graciella was standing. He then moved them both further back to the pyramid as the men kept yelling at each other. Several of Balik's men were surrounding them now so no one could grab her again.

"Two Turtles what are they saying I only understand a little of it?" he looked at Graciella and then at her.

"I will tell you when I can get you both safe inside. Balik has more men coming to protect both of you and the rest of his family so we need to get inside." Both women and Te'a and the family help were escorted inside the pyramid as the two men kept screaming at each other. Once inside Samantha stopped and turned around and just watched she would go no further until Balik was inside and safe. Balik came stomping in and grabbed her arm as he passed by her and they caught up with Graciella and they continued up inside the pyramid to chambers higher up. They finally stopped Graciella was tired she wasn't at her full strength yet. Balik picked her up and carried her rest of the way as Samantha followed. It was dark and eerily quiet inside the pyramid so she stayed close to Balik.

The maids were making places for them to sleep and setting out food so Samantha assumed this was where they were going to be staying. She walked over to a flat platform that led out to a ledge and looked down a flight of steps and wished she hadn't. This was a place of sacrifice and she had a feeling it wasn't always animals. She backed up and backed right into Balik he put his hands on her arms and turned her around and motioned her back inside. Balik started to tell Graciella something and she was crying and she asked Two Turtles what he said and he didn't want to tell her.

"You tell me right now and don't you lie because I will know."

"It seems the Shaman has been watching you since the first time he saw you that is why Balik had men watching you as well. The Shaman wanted to sacrifice you to the Cenote like he did Graciella sister you would have been big medicine but he couldn't get to you at the hacienda there were too many men protecting you."

"Why does he hate me so bad I gave him the skin of the jaguar he wanted wasn't that enough what else does he want?"

"He told people he killed the jaguar but some of the people suspect that is a lie. He has hated you from the minute he first met you when you took care of Balik's sons arm he will kill you if he can."

"Why is Graciella crying she is upset about something besides the Shaman and that damn cat what is going on that I do not understand?"

"He says he needs to keep you here and protect you that Clayton can't protect you that he can do a better job." That was as far as he got Samantha was across the room and had Balik turned around and was pushing him up against the wall as she was yelling at him. She figured someone would translate but he didn't need much translation because she was mad.

"Now you get this straight I am going back to Clayton with or without your help. You may be the big man here but I can protect myself even if I have to kill that crazy SHAMAN. So that is what I will do but I am going home so that is the way it is going to be. I will not shame your wife by staying here, you are her protector and husband not mine.

" Balik was backed up against the wall and several guards were wondering what exactly what they were supposed to do or who they were supposed to protect. Graciella started to laugh and everybody calmed down when she asked.

"Well that took care of that; shall we eat supper now I am getting hungry?" Sam turned around and went over to help Te'a with supper. Balik just stood there for a minute he didn't usually have people yelling at him it was a new sensation and now she was cooking supper like nothing happened. His men were looking at him like what do we do now so he just told them to place guards at the entrances and get ready for the night then he went over to have supper but he was smiling. After supper and everybody were fed they settled down for they night and it seemed that everybody had a partner but Sam. She felt very out of place because she could hear everything that was going on in those little rooms. It didn't seem to bother anyone but her but it did bother her so she picked up the brush that Graciella had loaned her and walked out to that platform not too far out to brush her hair. She walked out on to the platform and sat down and started brushing she didn't realize she had an audience. Down below people watched as the moonlight glowed around her and her hair and the snake statue was above her head. She could feel where Balik had cut out a chunk of her hair and she still wondered why but she didn't think she wanted to know.

When she was through she just sat there for a while longer and looked at the sky until she was sleepy and then she stood and went back inside. She didn't look down if she had she would have noticed people still watching her at the bottom of the pyramid. Several men trying to sneak up the side to capture her, they were the Shamans men. He was determined to get her one way or another.

CHAPTER 12

Clayton and the entire household was keeping an eye out for what Melanee was doing all the time because she had already snuck out twice to go find Samantha. She was sure they were all lying to her about the river being too high to cross and she was going to find out for herself. She had saddled Moon and she was halfway to the river before they caught her the first time. They caught her before she got out of the corral the second time but she still wouldn't listen to them. Clayton was ready to lock her in her room but he was afraid she would try to climb down the side of the house and kill herself in the fall. He finally made her sleep with him so he could keep an eye on her and the night it quit raining she climbed out of bed and went to the balcony and he just followed her.

"Do you think she is still alive?" he hadn't told her what Balik's men had told him, but he figured he better now or she wouldn't stay here when he went after Samantha. He sat her in one of the chairs on the balcony and then he sat down across from her and started talking.

"You remember when the drums stopped and the jungle got so quiet?

Melanee just nodded her head she was expecting the worst.

"Balik found Samantha and the man that had taken the two of you and he freed Sam and he killed the man." Melanee looked at her father and she got a smile on her face that he would remember for the rest of his life. She knew Balik had made Nathan pay like none of them ever could and she was glad.

"Now can you go after Samantha?"

"I will be going as soon as the water goes down enough for us to get a boat on it but you will not be coming with us it is too dangerous out there.

"You have to go as soon as you can, if you wait too long he won't let her go he will keep her." So simple but even she knew Balik wanted her.

"The men are already packed and I have two men watching the river we will leave as soon as we can get on the water and I will bring her home I promise." Melanee got down off her chair and went over and climbed on his lap and they watched the moon, it was full and they both remembered what it looked like shining through her hair at night. She just snuggled up in his lap and was going to sleep when she said.

"You have to go soon and get her that Shaman wants to kill her." He looked down at her and then he asked her.

"What are you talking about Melanee?"She looked up at him and answered.

"He wants her dead I keep dreaming she is drowning. You have to go and get her." She didn't say anymore she went to sleep in his lap and he just held her for a long while as he watched the moon but he had the awful felling she was right. He put her to bed and then he went downstairs and out to the barn. He checked with the men to see if all of the horses and supplies were ready and they were. They were going to leave in the morning even if they had to sit on the bank of the river until they could get on a boat, he had a feeling he was running out of time. He went back upstairs and lay down next to Melanee and went to sleep he was going to need it; the next few days were going to be long and hard.

When the sun came up the next morning the whole house was up and moving. The men Clayton was leaving behind were waiting to be given orders about what to do in his absence. It seemed that Russell was coming with him and Gabriel and the women were staying behind to watch the house and the children. Melanee and Steven were watching from the balcony so they didn't get in the way as they ate their breakfast. Clayton kept glancing up at them and smiling just to reassure them everything was alright. Alright he didn't know if anything was ever going to be alright again. After talking to Melanee last all he could think about was what she had said about her dreams and that Shaman. He knew Balik would protect Sam as long as he could but if it came to Sam or their religion he wasn't sure Samantha would win out and that terrified him. That blond hair of hers was both a blessing and a curse and that Shaman hated her.

When everything was ready he told the men to wait a minute and he went up to the balcony. The children were waiting for him. He got down on one knee and both children came to him and put their arms around his neck and they just stayed that way for a minute as their father started to talk.

"Now you two have got to look out for each other and listen to the grownups around here while I am gone. Gabriel and Camille are in charge until I get back. Melanee you promised me you would stay here and not follow me I don't want to have to worry about you while I am looking for Samantha so you promise me again." The little girl just looked out from under her eyelids and kind of smiled but she shook her head up and down and said.

"I promise daddy if you don't take too long." Clayton sighed well that was as good as he was going to get.

"That is not the deal young lady you stay here I don't want you to be Jaguar food do you understand me?" he hugged them again then stood up went downstairs mounted his horse and they were off. He turned and waved to the children as he passed the balcony, Gabriel and Camille were standing in the courtyard he had made provisions with him to take care of the children if he didn't come back. Patricia was standing there as well and Russell waved at her and Clayton asked him.

"What about Pat if we don't come back?" this could go sideways if Balik didn't see things his way or that Shaman was in control or god forbid that message had been wrong and Nathan was alive.

"It is taken care of she will go to my hacienda and stay there I have left orders." Clayton just looked at him. Well this was a side off him he had never seen he was really in love.

"Now let's go find Samantha and get back to our lives." They rode to the river and it was still high but it was getting lower and the men were making arrangements for a boat. By the time they had a boat ready and loaded it was dark and they didn't want to start out on that river in the dark especially as high as it was. They needed to be able to see the banks at least to have a chance of surviving. They made camp there higher up on the bank and waited for morning as they waited they could hear a jaguar screaming in the jungle. All of the men stopped and listened but one of the men said it was far away and on the other side of the river. The men ate and went to sleep with a guard standing watch and hoped in morning they could start the journey down river.

When they got up in the morning the river was a little lower and a little slower so they got on the boat and started downriver, they weren't really sure where they were going but they were looking for signs. Almost a day of traveling and the signs found them. The men who brought Melanee to them were on the bank looking out at the river. The boat they had come down on had been caught in the river current and been damaged and they were trying to repair it. When Clayton showed up they didn't need to repair it anymore. The men pulled over and the Mayan men helped them unload. Clayton was anxious to hear about Samantha but you couldn't hear over the water. After they unloaded they went to a long house not far away and set up for the night and then Clayton could get his answers.

"Alright where is she and is she OK?" it was quiet in the room everybody wanted to know the answer.

"She is with Balik and his family she is safe but he fears for her because of the Shaman." Clayton and Russell looked at each other and then asked him.

"What is the problem with the Shaman?"

"He wants to sacrifice her to the Cenote and Balik won't let him." "Russell what is a Cenote?"

"It is a big hole in the ground filled with water and the priests around here think if you sacrifice people in them you will have a good crop or rain or whatever you are praying for." Clayton looked stunned.

"Melanee has been having dreams about the Shaman drowning Samantha now I know why."

"We need to get there fast it sounds like Balik needs our help." He looked at the two Mayan men and asked them.

"He sent you to come find us didn't he?" the men nodded yes.

"Did he kill the man that took Samantha." The men nodded and pointed.

"He is not far from here we will show you tomorrow he will never leave the jungle. And the man smiled and both men got a chill down their backs it was just creepy. The men bedded down in the house that was falling down and Clayton asked.

"Did you stay here with Sam?"

"She stayed here with the dead man, Balik found them the next day and the man had hit her and threatened her in front of Balik he was trying to use her to get away Balik didn't like that." Clayton and Russell looked at each other and Clayton said.

"I bet he didn't, what did he do to him?" the man seemed reluctant to continue but he did.

"After he took the knife away from her throat and pushed her to Balik he pinned the man to a tree with a spear." Clayton was getting mad.

"Did he cut her?" the man was getting really nervous he thought Clayton was mad at him.

"Just a little but Balik got her away and protected her and then sent her away when she wouldn't kill the man herself. She told Balik to finish him and then she left and Balik killed the man."

"What did he do to the man?"

"That you will have to see for yourself, will you be mad that he killed a white man?"

"No he killed a man I was going to kill if he hadn't; he just got to him first." The Mayan was obviously relieved he was about ready to run when everybody went to sleep. After everyone was settled down for the night Clayton turned to Russell and said.

"Nathan threatened Sam in front of Balik and then hurt her; you know it is going to be bad don't you?" Russell looked at him and answered.

"Do we care? The bastard is dead and she never has to watch her back again at least not for him. Now we have to see what we can do about that Shaman or she will be looking over her shoulder for him because he is as bad as Nathan." Clayton just looked at him and nodded and they lay down and went to sleep they would deal with that tomorrow.

In the morning the men all got up and prepared to leave but they weren't in such a hurry a yesterday they all knew where they were going and none of them were looking forward to it. When they got close to the little glen where his body was they didn't have to guess they could hear a clicking noise. There were a million ants all over the body or what was left of the body probably in no more than a day you wouldn't even be able to call it that. Clayton could see where Balik had pinned him to the tree the spear it was still in him and his heart was in a bowl at his feet even he hoped he hadn't lived long.

There were several other things left behind to tell others to stay away from Samantha and now he just had to protect her from his own Shaman. There was a long lock of her hair tied to one of the trees beside Nathan if anybody had any doubts as to the reason why this man had been killed there was the reason. Clayton ran his fingers through it and wondered why the ants weren't touching it. One of the men came up and told him that Balik rubbed oil on it that the ants didn't like so they would leave it alone and it would be the only thing left in here even when most of his body is gone. When the men were gone and it was just Russell and Clayton still looking at what was left. Russell looked at Clayton and asked him.

"He asked her if she wanted to kill him why wouldn't she do it."

"I don't think she could have done it unless she was protecting Melanee and if he had hurt her she probably would have said yes. I have a feeling she doesn't even know what he did to him I think she just let him take care of it and then they moved on." "Why?"

"If Samantha had killed him it would have been quick and it would have been done, this is Balik and he wanted him to hurt so he must have hurt Sam. You know that man is not forgiving especially when it comes to people he cares for. I am surprised it is not worse he must have been furious when he got here. Nathan got off easier than that priest did from the village. Let's get out of here it is still a long way to his village.

They left the clearing but they both turned back for one finale look Balik was a man you didn't cross. They caught up with the men and just kept walking until they came to the Cenote, Russell had seen smaller ones than this one but this one was beautiful. The men were upset about something and anxious to be going and finally Russell found out what was going on. He grabbed Claytons arm and they proceeded to go down the trail even though it was getting dark. Clayton assumed they would be trying to find someplace to rest for the night but they kept going until Clayton finally stopped Russell.

"Alright what had got you so spooked all of the sudden?" Russell turned around and looked at him.

"The men told me that Shaman wants Samantha for a reason, to sacrifice her to that Cenote and he has done it before with another blond haired woman. Balik has been protecting her from him all this time. He couldn't get her home the river was to high so he had to take her to his home and now she is in danger from that Shaman we have to hurry that is why they came to get us."

"He can't kill him and I can."

"I think that is the gist of things and we are running out of time." About that time they heard a jaguar scream and it wasn't very far away from them.

"Great that is all we need another damn cat." The men went to putting some supper together and watching their backs as they cooked they didn't want that cat sneaking up on them they didn't realize she wasn't interested in them she didn't want them anywhere close to her cubs so she was moving them away from them. There were too many people around here lately so she went to move her cubs further away from the Cenote to keep them safe.

She found a hollowed out log about a mile away and they could stay hidden in there while she hunted.

She went looking for her supper while she kept her distance from the people cooking by the Cenote. She walked right by them and sat down and watched them for a while and they didn't even know she was there. She stood up and walked past them but one of the men smelled familiar to her she thought she had smelled him before on the other side of the river before she came over here. She had hunted there for a while but there was a male that had that territory and she left for this side of the river she had no competition here. She could smell a monkey in the tree and that would make a meal for her and her cubs so she went about her work and left the men alone.

Russell couldn't get what was left of that man on the tree out of his mind and he was worried for Samantha even more now. Both men couldn't get rid of the feeling they had to hurry. None of them sleep too much and they left early the next morning so they could travel as far as they could go they had no idea they were being watched by the jaguar and she was glad to see them go. After a while she picked up her kill and walked away to her cubs and fed them all the while keeping her guard up for the men close by. She would need to move her cubs again and soon.

The family had settled into the pyramid as much as they could with the Shamans men standing guard at the bottom. Balik was trying to get his men in place to take on the Shamans men but they weren't ready yet so for now everybody was staying close to the pyramid. Samantha was trying to stay out of the way she felt responsible for this whole mess and she didn't know what to do. Finally Two Turtles asked her if she would like to explore the inside of the pyramid it would take her mind of what was going on outside. She asked Balik if that was alright and he said it was but she wondered if he really heard what she asked him. Well she would be out of the way anyway so she followed Two Turtles down the hallway.

Two Turtles and his two guards started down some halls and he was explaining what the pictures were saying about the gods and their lives and how the people interwove with them. He touched the walls with reverence theses people gave to their gods all the time. He explained about the wars they fought and how they captured each other's kings and kept them as hostages and sacrificed them to the gods or traded them for more land or for brides it was an ongoing affair. They had been going down deeper into the pyramid for a long time when he seemed to be looking for something in particular he wasn't even noticing that he was drawing attention from Balik's guards so Samantha sent them back to get them some lunch. She sat down on a step on the staircase and just watched what he was doing. She noticed one of his guards had pulled out a knife and she figured she had just become a threat and she didn't even know why yet.

"Have you found what you are looking for Two Turtles or whatever you name is because if you haven't you better look fast the other guards will be back soon and you will have run out of time." He turned around smiling and saw the other guard with his knife out and motioned for him to put it away.

"He seems to think I am a threat to you am I?" Sam sat right there on that step and looked at him.

"NO you have never been a threat to me, I was supposed to be a threat to you maybe I was in the beginning. I was going to kidnap you and take you to my father as a gift to irritate Balik.

"Why is it the stupid blond hair?"

"No it is because if that picture on the wall, it is a picture of my grandfather, Balik's grandfather killed him after they had a war over some land but we never knew for sure what happened to him until today. I was at a church school my grandmother wanted me to learn English so I could talk to your people. When I heard about you and Balik I started home to take you away from him but that plan didn't work out."

"Why not your men still don't like me much?"

"I watched you dance with the little girl one afternoon in the plaza and overheard some of your conversations and decided you were worth saving so you see you have friends all over." Samantha just smiled at him.

"The guards are coming we need to get out of here before someone figures this out, you are going to have to leave this place soon. Perhaps it is time we both leave this place. By the way what is your real name?"

"I will tell you when we are both free of this place. Let's get out of here we have some plans to make." They made their way back up the stairs to the top chambers where Gabriella was waiting for them.

"Balik has had men looking for you for some time where have you been?"

"Two turtles has been showing me the inside of the pyramid all the glyphs and the pictures and what they mean. We were trying to stay out of the way I seem to be causing problems around here for both of you." She looked at Samantha and shook her head and pointed at two turtles.

"Balik is beginning to suspect he isn't who he says he is but he hasn't figured it out yet. Whatever you are going to do you better do it quickly. He is coming, make yourselves scarce we will talk later." Samantha and Two turtle turned and went to her room and started to pack some things in a bag very carefully so one would notice she was putting things aside.

"When it gets dark we will try going down the steps carefully in the shadows of the sculptures on the side, they will give us some protection from the eyes below, until then we wait. You had better eat something we won't have time to stop and have a fire so eat what you can and I will see if I can get some fruits to put in a bag to take with us." He started to get up and leave and she put her hand on his arm and looked up at him and said.

"Don't you think it is about time you told me your name just in case I come across you father first, he might think it funny if I don't know your name?" he turned around and smiled at her.

"I am called Anuka and if we ever do get out of here I would like you to meet my father." He left her and was gone for a while and then he returned with Balik by his side and they went and had supper with Gabriella. Everyone enjoyed the meal and when it was over Samantha wanted to linger but she knew it was time to leave. Anuka was waiting for her outside her room and they quickly gathered everything up and were down the hall when two of Gabriella's men met them and Sam thought they were going to stop them from going.

"Quickly follow us we will get you out of here with no one seeing you leave." Alright maybe they had a better plan than theirs. They followed them to a set of stairs Sam hadn't seen today and they began to descend and they kept going down. Maybe she had been wrong and these men were taking them somewhere that they could kill them and no one would hear them do it and they would just disappear. Anuka was beginning to be as concerned as she was because he was slowing down and the men in front of them finally stopped and talked to him and then he turned to her and said.

"They say we are going to a hidden door at the bottom of the pyramid that is for the family to escape from in case of invasion and we have to be quiet because we are getting close. When we get there they will tell us more. They continued to walk for probably twenty more minutes and the air was getting harder to breathe. Finally they stopped and they were looking at a stone wall. The men were whispering and then the torches were put out and a blacker dark she had never known. Anuka suddenly was beside her and held her arm as the other men carefully pushed the wall and it pivoted to the side just a little. Moonlight was coming in and she could see one of the men and then another slip outside and then she heard some quiet noise and then the men were back and leading them out. The door was shut and then branches and shrubs put back to hide the door when she looked back she could see nothing but jungle. Two of the men were dragging off bodies of the men they had killed into the jungle.

Anuka took her hand and he had her hold on to the strap around his back that was holding the bag of food and they were off into the jungle. She couldn't see anything there was very little light, the moon was just coming up but the men keep moving. She stumbled once and almost fell but arms from behind her kept her upright and she didn't dare make a sound so they kept on going. When she didn't think she could go anymore they stopped in a small opening of the jungle just a space in the trees but there was some light coming down from the moon and she could see the men a little and they got her over to a log and she sat down. The men were talking and Anuka handed her a mango and the water jug and got down on one knee so he could talk to her.

"I would like the pendant that you wear to send to my father as proof that you are the snake lady even though I don't know how you came to possess this piece, it is reserved for a priest." As she started to take off the necklace she told him how she came to get the necklace.

"I got the piece when I killed a Fer-De-Lance with a machete in   a bedroom one night while I was dressed in a bath sheet. The moon backlit my hair and I picked up the head of the snake and put it on the table so I could look at it. The next morning the pendant was on my plate at breakfast." He turned and looked at the men and they were telling him something.

"That is not all of it they say you stroke anacondas and one saved you from a Caiman." The men behind him were just standing there waiting for her to say something.

"I don't think she meant to save me I think I was just there. I was hung up in a bunch of branches and couldn't get loose and this Caiman was getting closer to me and then this huge snake dropped down and broke up the branches and got the Caiman and Balik got me out of there. When we were on the canoe I just reached down in the water and put my hand on one of the big snakes as she was going under the boat and felt her slid through the water it was wonderful she felt like velvet. I did the same thing with a boa constrictor. It really wasn't that big of a deal." Not one of the men was saying a word they were dumbstruck she really didn't see that she did anything different. She finished taking off the necklace and handed it to Anuka and he didn't hardly register it was in his hand as he stared at her.

"Well now what do we do?" Anuka snapped out of it and turned to his man and told him what he wanted him to do and he left and the rest of them sat down as she ate her mango but they were still just looking at her.

"Are you good we need to keep going they will be looking for us?" they started moving again Anuka was hoping his father was already looking for him and not far off so his man could find him soon. The men were moving as fast as they could the jungle was thick and they couldn't use the machetes the way they normally would because they would be heard so they were pushing the plants aside with their hands and they weren't making as much time as they wanted to that way.

She kept going but she was slowing them down and she knew it and she was running out of steam she didn't know how much longer she could keep this up. It wasn't much further until one of the men stopped and Anuka said they were going to have to hide there were too many men all around them and they were going to be discovered.

"Where, there is nowhere to go?" then one of the men pointed up into one of the trees and she blinked and then looked at him.

"You have got to be kidding I can't climb that tree." But one of the men was already getting vines and as she watched he was climbing up while she watched he had to be part monkey. When he got to the top he disappeared and then he threw a vine rope back down to the men below. Quietly they tied it around her waist and started to pull her up as she kind of cat walked up the side of the tree. Everybody was real quiet because they could hear people getting closer. When she was up the tree Anuka was not far behind and then they got further into the branches so they couldn't be seen and the men below disappeared quickly into the jungle.

"Just find somewhere to lean against and rest we may be here a while and be quiet. Anuka had hardy finished talking when men were below the tree. She could see them and they were looking all around and up but they obviously couldn't see them and they went on down the path. Anuka patted her hand and she started to relax a little. She lay back and there were purple orchids all around her it was the first good sign she had seen all day. She laid her head on her arm and drifted off to sleep.

She had been asleep for awhile when she felt something brush her leg and she didn't know what it was. She stayed still and it was coming up her leg and all she could think was 'Please don't be a snake.' Whatever it was is still coming up her side and now she was seeing little eyes and now she was really scared "Oh please be a snake.' There was a little white jaguar cuddling up beside her. Anuka had turned over to see what the problem was and couldn't believe his eyes. He looked at her and she shook her head at him he whispered.

"We picked the wrong side of the tree."

"What do you mean we this was your idea and now we are stuck with it. What do you want me to do?" before he could answer they were joined by another cub this time it was a black one. They just snuggled up to her chest and went to sleep Sam didn't know what to do so she put her arm over them and rolled over enough to talk to Anuka.

"We don't dare hurt them that will bring their mother running for sure. We will stay for a while longer and then we will leave. We will leave them up here for her to find but we will be long gone." She said it so simply like it was nothing to be laying up here with two jaguar cubs, and one of them was a ghost a white cub. If their mother came back to soon she would rip them apart. The fact that they smelled like them now didn't exactly thrill him. We can't go anywhere for a while there are too many men around. They settled back down and Sam went back to sleep with Anuka watching her and her little charges she didn't think what she did was anything special maybe that is why that medicine man hated her so much. His father was going to want her as much as Balik did and that was going to be a problem well just one problem at a time. He was too busy keeping her alive right now.

Sometime later they awoke to Anuka's men below calling to them and now she could hear a jaguar screaming in the distance.

"They have caught her and it is our fault." He knew she was going to do something stupid and he was going to help her.

Anuka got her down the vine as quickly as he could then followed her down the tree. They had put the cubs up in a nest where they would be safe until this was over and their mother could get back. When they got to the ground they explained to the men what was going on up in the tree and told them if the mother returned just get out of her way and leave. If no one returned including them they would have to kill the cubs they wouldn't be able to survive on their own, but that was only as a last resort.

"Well come on we have to save her and the only way I know how to do that is by giving that Shaman something he really wants, ME." They started to run towards the sound of the jaguar until they were right on top of the sound. They had caught her in a snare trap and she was caught by the back leg and around her neck. The back leg was pretty skinned up but it would heal but she was choking. It looked like they were going to use her for target practice. They were in a clearing and when Sam walked up and one of the men was going to put and arrow into jaguar she said.

"STOP you are not going harm that jaguar she is mine" even Anuka looked sideways at that one but everyone stopped and looked at her. The Shaman was having a hissy fit as usual as he walked up on the other side.

"What gives you the right to issue orders around here these are my men and they don't have to listen to you."He was strutting around in that jaguar cape and she had an idea.

"You let that jaguar live or I will tell all these men where that cape actually came from and who really killed It." well that shut him up as he looked around at his men. Some of his men had heard the rumors about the cape and he couldn't afford for Samantha to open her mouth maybe if she didn't have a mouth. He wanted her for a sacrifice but maybe this was better and quicker.

"Alright you want that jaguar so bad you can have her." he turned and ordered his men to cut her loose and two machete strikes later and that cat was running straight for her. Sam just stood there frozen then she closed her eyes and waited for that jaguar to knock her down. Anuka said.

"Open your eyes and get on your knees." Sam looked up; the jaguar had slowed and was coming towards her. She got close and just smelled her shirt Sam looked at Anuka and he nodded his head so she just bowed to the big cat and after a few seconds she was so close she could see there was still a rope around her neck and a man ready to kill her. Sam turned and got between the man and the cat.

"I need a knife Anuka." and she reached her hand out while still standing in front of the man that was supposed to kill that cat. He handed her a knife that he got from one of the guards who was just looking dumfounded and handed it to her even the Shaman wasn't talking. She reached down and cut the rope and quietly said.

"Go they are waiting for you." Then the jaguar ran off in the direction of the cubs. It wasn't but a few seconds and she was gone. She turned towards the Shaman and said.

"Well that is another hide you can't have." There were a few of his men around who knew what she was talking about and they were smiling. The Shaman was furious and he came after her again but now he wanted Anuka for helping her. He ordered some of his men to grab him and put him on his knees and he was to be executed. Sam turned to Anuka and said.

"You tell all these men who you are right now and he won't touch you after that, do it now." He looked at her and then turned to the men holding him and said.

"I am Anuka of the Jaguar tribe and she is now our totem and my father is our Shaman, so if you think you can kill his son go right ahead and by the way he is on his way here." It got very quiet in that clearing after that and the Shaman was very still and he was looking around to see how many men were still loyal to him and it seemed the numbers were shrinking. He wasn't aware that one of Anuka father's men had seen that whole little scene and was already running back to get his father and he wasn't that far away. The men holding him dropped him like he was contaminated and looked at Sam. The Shaman grabbed her and just started heading to the Cenote with the men while he still had some support because he could see it was dwindling fast and he could feel Balik fast on his heels.

CHAPTER 14

They were walking faster but she wasn't tied neither was Anuka the men around her just kept looking at her sideways ever once and a while she would stumble and they would break their necks to help her and her men were watching this. She got close to Anuka and whispered to him.

"Can you swim really swim?" he nodded yes to her.

"What are you planning?" she didn't say anything till they were farther from the Shaman and then.

"You know I told you I dived off the edge of the Cenote well this time I want to take the Shaman with me and take him all the way to the bottom." he looked at her stunned.

"He could kill you."

"He is going to try that either way at least this way I will have a chance and with that all costume and all that jewelry he has on it puts him at a disadvantage." He thought about it for a few minutes and then he started to talk again.

"You have to be careful of his hands if he starts to blow something in your face turn your head don't breath close your eyes, it is the power they use on prisoners before they kill them. If he uses it you Samantha you won't care what he does to you." They kept walking but now more men were coming out of the jungle on the opposite side of the Cenote and the man in the front of them was dressed like the Shaman in front of her. He had on a large horseshoe headdress and a jaguar cape and he looked like Anuka. This man could be no other than Anuka's father they looked too much alike. Sam turned to Anuka and he nodded yes.

It was indeed his father and he was furious he could tell what was about to happen and he was screaming something. Another large force was coming out of the jungle on the other side as well and it was Balik. He was not far off to the side and he was trying to get to them as well. Neither force was going to get to them in time they were on their own.

Some of The Shaman's loyal men started to push her forward as well as Anuka. The Shaman was digging into a pouch for something. Sam was at the edge of the Cenote and the Shaman was leering at her and he did indeed have something in his hand. He grabbed the back of her head and was trying to turn her around and she was struggling and then Anuka grabbed his back and said.

"GO SAM NOW." She looked at the Shaman grabbed the front of his cape twisted and pulled them both over the edge and then he was screaming and he screamed all the way down until they hit the water. He was struggling for air but she had dragged in a good breath before she hit the water. She had twisted him so he hit the water on his back and she hit the water on her side so it knocked all the air out of him. He was too busy screaming like the victims he had dropped in here before no doubt. She wouldn't let him go no matter how much he struggled and with all the stuff he had on weighing him down it wasn't that hard.

They just kept sinking and all the time she watched his face he was terrified. They were finally at the bottom and he was making little struggling breaths and then nothing and suddenly she realized she needed to breathe. Her hands wouldn't let go of the cape she was gripping it so tight. Hands from behind her pried her hands loose and put an arm around her waist then she turned around and there was Clayton. He had his arm around her and he pulled her up to the light and the air. Oh lord air and light she didn't realize how dark it was down there it was a perfect place for the Shaman to stay. Then she realized Clayton was holding her. She just stayed there for a few seconds and looked at him and then she said.

"Where did you come from and what took you so long?" and then she just put her arms around his neck and let him hold her up in the water as she kept dragging in air.

"Please tell me Melanee is alright and the rest of the family."

"Everybody is good and awaiting your return so can we go home now?

By the way that was the bravest and the stupidest thing I have seen you do yet."

"Which one the Shaman thing or the jaguar thing you need to be more specific?"

"What jaguar thing I must have missed that one what did you do there?" about that time they were joined by Balik and Anuka's father and they were arguing about something and it seemed it was about her. She could only understand about half of what they were saying and she was tired of treading water so she slipped under the water and headed to the cave. She knew Balik would know where she was going and they would have to shut up if they were swimming.

She climbed into the cave it was smaller now the water was higher but she could still stand further back and then in came three men. Balik was first because he knew where he was going then Clayton and then Anuka's father and they were screaming at each other, she just let them scream for a bit while she sat down and rested. Finally Clayton turned around and asked her.

"You got down in front of a jaguar and bowed then turned it loose are you losing it?" she looked up at him and smiled.

"Seemed like a good idea at the time." When she thought he was going to explode she explained.

"I had spent the night with her cubs their smell was all over me, she could smell them. We were hoping she wouldn't kill me so I let her loose if they had killed her, her cubs would have died." He just looked at her like she was out of her mind and then Anuka's father started to laugh he spoke English and he understood what she had said. He told Balik what she said and they both were laughing. Clayton was still furious.

"They are arguing over who gets to take you back with them for their totem." She stopped him right there.

"You can tell them I am going nowhere but with you to your home if you will still have me. I think now is a good time to get married and settle down and have a baby and if they don't like that I will personally see to it that they have a snake or a jaguar in bed with them each and every night to make my point." Anuka's father was talking to Balik while he took something off of his neck and handed it to Sam. It was a small black pendant like the jade one only this one was of a jaguar she just smiled. Now she had two pendents.

"You ever need me or Anuka just send someone I will be close." Great now she had two of them. Clayton was glaring at her and then he noticed her ankle and was going to ask her about that and she shook her head no.

"We will talk about it later."

"Tell them to go away so we can talk. I am tired we will be up in a little while then we will straighten this all out." Balik was asking Clayton something and then he turned and asked Sam.

"He wants to know when the last time you ate was?" she looked up at him and shakes her head.

"I don't remember." Balik turned and swam away as Clayton sat down beside her and she just leaned on his shoulder.

"I seem to cause you a lot of grief. Is Melanee alright?" Clayton laid her down in his lap and just looked at her there were times he was afraid he would never find her alive and now she was here.

"Melanee is fine we had to all but hogtie her to keep her from coming after you and it wouldn't surprise me if she isn't waiting at the river for us when we get back. My wife may have given birth to that child but she is yours now. When she came riding back home on Sundance she was sure she had betrayed you by leaving. She was ready to go out looking for you the next morning." They could hear Balik yelling something outside but Sam was too tired to care she just closed her eyes and lay in Clayton's lap until Balik came back with some fruit in a bag. The men up above them must have gathered it and thrown it down to him and then he brought it back to her.

"Clayton shook her and told Samantha we could go back with them and you could rest until you feel better." She got up slowly and just smiled.

"NO. If I go back I will never leave this jungle they will keep me I am becoming big medicine. Balik will try to protect me but he will get killed trying we need to leave and never come back here. Do you understand?" Clayton looked around at the men watching her and he was beginning to see the look in the eyes of the men around here. He hadn't been told yet of what had happened with the jaguar cubs or the big snake when he did he would understand she needed to be out of here and far away.

"Alright honey, eat something and get to feeling better and we will be on our way. My men are up top and we will be getting home as quickly as we can. There were mangos in the bag and Clay split them and sectioned them and she ate them and she quietly said.

"I think I would sell my soul for some of that roast pig that was cooking when I left for the Christmas pageant. Lord that seems like a century ago."

"I bet Juanita will cook whatever you want when we get you back. When I left everybody was at the house until I got you back except Russell and he came with me to find you."

"I am feeling better let's get out of here and get started home I am so tired but I want to get moving." He got her up and they got to the entrance of the cave and Clayton got in the water first and then she followed. As she swam across she saw there were some of the men pulling the Shaman out of the Cenote and she wished they had left him there. She was getting so tired and by the time they got to the side of the Cenote she could barely swim. Clay tied a rope around her and they pulled her up to the top and she sat down on the edge. She watched as they took the Shaman away she guessed to bury him. One of her men brought her a blanket an laid it out so she could rest while they got things in order and got things sorted out between the two tribes.

She guessed she fell asleep because when she awoke it was late afternoon. Anuka's father's men were leaving but apparently he was staying to see her to the river. Clayton came over and helped her up gathered up the blanket and they were ready when Anuka came over to her.

"This is for you." It was the Jaguar hide and it had something inside. There were several pieces of jewelry as well as a large crucifix. She looked at it as it slipped from her hand. I was a beautiful silver crucifix and it was inscribed SOFIA MONTOYA it was Graciella sisters and he had carried it all this time.

"They should have left him at the bottom of that Cenote." She gently curled around her hand and let the cross lay in her palm and when Balik came back over to her she showed it to him and then she put it in his hand. He didn't understand at first until she turned it over and read the name to him and smiled but he didn't want to touch it and he handed it back to her.

"What is wrong I don't understand?" Anuka looked at her and was trying to explain.

"He thinks it is cursed and he doesn't want to touch it. He is afraid the Shaman cursed it and you are the only one that can touch it now." She looked at them and wondered how she was going to fix this? The men started walking and they headed towards the river they intended to stop at that rundown house tonight. They would have to pass by the spot where Balik had killed Nathan but she was preparing for that it had to be done. Everyone walked in silence until they were getting close to the clearing where his body should have been hanging and Clayton expected to hear the ants again but this time no sound was coming from the clearing. As they got closer it was deadly quiet and when they looked in this time there was nothing no body no bones nothing it was all gone except that strand of her hair.

Samantha looked around and saw the spear in the tree and not a sigh of Nathan anywhere. It was like the whole scene had been swept clean. She looked at Clayton and he said.

"There were ants really big ants all over him when we were here and there weren't much left then. I guess they finished the job and they are gone." Everyone looked at Balik as he just kept walking like nothing had happened and they were supposed to act that way to. Another hour and they were at the house and she could finally rest. Her jaguar was talking in the night but she wasn't scared of her she would stay away from these men and protect her cubs.

The men started cooking and Sam had Anuka come over to where she and Clayton were so she could talk to him.

"That jaguar hide is mine to do with as I please right?" he nodded yes. She laid it out and started to cut off a leg and Anuka started to protest and then she leaned down and whispered something in his ear. He looked at her a minute and then he nodded as he straightened out the hide and helped her cut off the leg. They laid it out straight and then she laid out the crucifix on the jaguar leg and rolled it up in it and then she took the hat she had been wearing all this time and took the hatband of the FER-DE-LANCE off of it and wrapped it around the jaguar pelt. Then she had Anuka go and get Balik. While she had all the men's attention she presented it to Balik.

"You take it back to Graciella at least she will have that much of her sister he didn't take away from her. Maybe this will take any curse off of her necklace. Both the snake and the jaguar are guarding her." Anuka told him what she had done. It helped that about that time her jaguar started screaming. He nodded and put the wrapped necklace in a bag he carried with him but he told Clayton he was going with them to the river as well to make sure they got across. She rolled the rest of the hide up and packed it with the rest of her things the men thought since she shot it in the first place it was rightfully hers. She didn't know what she was going to do with it but she wasn't going to dishonor it either.

She ate supper and then she sat down and was looking at the rest of the jewelry in the bag the Shaman was wearing or carrying and she found a bag wrapped up inside of another bag of jewels when she dumped them out she could see rough emeralds and large and small turquoise and several small rubies. She was showing them to Clayton when Anuka came over and she opened the bag or it kind of disassembled and another necklace fell out of it. She did recognize one of the symbols on it was a turtle. She held it a second and she knew she wasn't supposed to be touching it so she just put it down. When Anuka saw it he picked it up and held it to the light and he was almost crying then he looked at Sam.

"It is my grandfathers. It is his symbol of leadership and the little pieces of turquoise probably came out of his teeth. He was one of the captured kings and now I know for sure he was sacrificed but these things should have been buried with him."No wonder he wouldn't eat the soup he was a member of one of the turtle tribe or his grandfather was. Sam just looked at him she didn't know what to do.

"This should go back to your family or do I need to wrap it up in a jaguar leg as well?" Anuka smiled at her.

I would like to take the necklace back to my grandmother but I have no use for the jewels."

"What I don't need to do my voodoo on it?" As she waves her hands over the top of the jewelry quietly so no one else could see. Clayton was laughing at least he thought this was funny Anuka wasn't.

"You want me to do something with the hide don't you and I am being flippant about it?" she looked up at him and he couldn't look into her eyes. She couldn't see that they thought of her as something magical even if she didn't. She pointed to the hide.

"Bring it over here and bring me my bag as well. Please we need to do some work on the old boy he looks a little shabby." She took out of her bag a comb and after she cut off the other leg she laid it out smooth and she combed it until it looked good again and then laid that necklace on it and rolled it up inside it. When she got to the end she finished by sinking the claws into the hide to hold it together.

"Do you think that will please your grandmother and take the bad voodoo off that thing? I will do whatever else you want but it is yours. I am tired and sunup comes early around here." Anuka took the necklace and put it in a bag he carried and tucked it away in his pack.

She went back to the corner where she always seemed to wind up and someone had laid out some blankets and she was ready to call it a day. It was the first time she remembers that she could go to sleep and not have to worry about someone coming after her. Clayton lay down next to her and pulled her next to him and asked her.

"Are we finally going home and will you marry me when we get there?" "I was hoping that was still the plan unless you have changed your mind?"

"My daughter will have my hide if I don't bring you back and Russell is in a hurry to get back as well he has plans for Pat. How do you feel about a double wedding? She rolled over and snuggled up in his arms as he covered them up and she replied.

"Works for me darlin'."

The next morning she felt like she had been beat and when no one was looking she pulled up her shirt and it looked like she had been. The Shaman had got in a couple of good hits before he finally went down. Well there was nothing to do about it now. Russell had everyone ready to go and they started the trek home the jungle had not got and thinner since she had come this way a week earlier. The men were hacking their way through the best way they could but it was hot hard work. They finally got to the river and she wasn't surprised to see it was still raging. The men were off to the side talking and she had a pretty good idea what they were talking about. Russell and Clay came walking back and they look on their faces said it all.

"We can't take a boat upriver can we? We are going to have to go downriver to a safer exit point." Clayton just looked at her.

"We have no other choice it is just too dangerous here if we fall in that river we don't stand a chance." Sam looked at Balik and said.

"It is only safe if you have a certain Mayan chieftain and a big snake looking out for you." Clayton turned around and looked at Balik and knew he was missing something.

"I will tell you later how are we going to manage this?"

"Balik is letting us use his men and the smaller boat and we are taking it to a landing downriver and they will drop us off. It is close to the church where father Michel and the village are then they will see that Anuka gets home further down the river. They will stay until they can come back upriver. We have no other choice it is now or never the rain is still falling up river." She nodded her head and headed to the boat but this time there were several men on the bank and they were taking no chances that she would fall into the river. Once she was in and the supplies were loaded the rest of the men got in. They were drifting down the river and they passed the tangle she had been caught in it was still there or at least part of it. It had no creatures on it today. Sam just looked at it as they went by. Clayton watched all the men in the boat as they watched her he didn't know what they were expecting but something. He finally cornered Anuka later and asked him.

"So what happened why are they so enthralled with her?" Anuka told him the story and then just watched his face as he took it in. He sat in silence for a minute.

"That isn't all is it what about the jaguar you said she came up to her and she didn't kill her because ya'll had been sleeping with her cubs."

"I told her to do that thinking it might save her while the other guard killed the jaguar but she got in front of the guard and wouldn't let him kill her. I hadn't counted on that. Then she kneeled down and said that cat was hers and she cut the jaguar loose and that cat ran off without touching her and I do not know why."

"Maybe she is special and we are the one who aren't getting it. Maybe the animals are the smart ones and we just haven't caught up yet?" Anuka held his hand over the bag that held his grandfather's necklace and just shook his head.

"You need to rest in the morning we should be getting close to the landing and you still have a long trek to the village. You will watch out for her won't you I think there is still something she has to conquer ahead." Somehow Clayton didn't like the sound of that. They slept through the night until they were almost to the landing. Then they were attacked by bugs from all around on the banks. There were dead animals on the banks and the flies were everywhere. All the men started paddling as fast as they could to get them past the dead animals and the flies, Sam got out her headscarf and wrapped her head up to try and keep them out of her hair. After about an hour they were again in clear running water and they weren't far from the landing.

When they finally got there it was beginning to get dark but they figured they had time to get to the village. They said quick farewells and started into the jungle again. A couple of hours and they were at the village and the same little house and out came her same little woman who had helped her before. They started to get settled in when another batch of visitors came into the village and they were loud and demanding.

"We were told we could stay the night here tell these other people to get out and give us these rooms do they not know who I am." Sam looked around the door at the man making the ruckus and he took her breath away. She went back inside and backed into Russell.

"What's wrong you look like you have seen a ghost?"

"That man is Don Eduardo Castillo."Russell just looked at her. "Patricia's father that Don Castillo?" Sam nodded as he shook her. "Oh my god what is he doing here. He can't be here. Does he know what you look like?" Sam hadn't thought about that she didn't really know if he knew what she looked like or not.

"I am not sure he ever saw me he was in another part of the castle that night playing cards and losing, or so I was told. I don't think he knows who I am. You have got to watch what you say because he is probable looking for her."

"What could he want with her after all this time?" Sam just looked at him.

"Same thing he wanted her for in Spain to sell her to the highest bidder."

"I could kill him."

"NO you couldn't, even here a Spanish nobleman would be noticed if he came up missing, I am sorry to say."

"Not if the caimans' ate him."

"Not even then, I am afraid the Queen would have to look into it. He is after all a Don a bad one but still. We need to get you out of here and get you home to Pat and stall him. If you want to marry her do it as soon as possible and he can't touch her if she is married? We can see to stalling him for a day or two and let you get home in front of us." Clayton was walking towards them and he didn't look happy.

"That man thinks because he is a Don in Spain he can run all over us here. I told him we were here first and he and his men would have to bunk elsewhere and he went nuts. So they are leaving in the morning. Why is she looking at me that way?"

"Go back and tell him he can have the other room. Russell is leaving early and won't need it and then get the men gathered that you will need to go with you. I will fill Clayton in on what is going on now go before Don Eduardo gets his men together." she grabbed Claytons arm and they went to the balcony and she let her hair down and shook it out and with it came a few flies.

"Alright what is going on Samantha?"

"That man it Patricia's father and I assume he has come to get her back. Russell is leaving in the morning early as he can and he going to the hacienda and collecting her. I suspect they will marry before we get there and then he can' touch her. We need to stall as long as we can to give them some time to do all of this. I hope you haven't given him too much information on where you were going."

"No my dear I was to mad to tell him too much. Now I need to go make peace with him and let Russell get ahead of us. There is never a dull moment with you."

"Tell Russell not to leave without seeing me first I will have a letter for him to take with him for Pat." She went into her room and started writing a letter she didn't think she had much time there was a full moon tonight and she thought Russell would make use of it. She could hear the Don next door settling in and not much latter Clayton and Russell were back at her room. They all went outside to the horses and she was right he was leaving as soon as the men could get some food packed. They were being very discreet they didn't want the Don's men to discover that they were leaving in the dead of night.

"We will rest down the road later tonight so those men don't get to suspicious of us and we will have a pretty good start. Some of the Mayan men seem to think it might rain again tomorrow and that could slow you all down again. Either way I will be ahead of you and I will take care of Pat. You just watch out for yourselves some of the Don's men were at the castle that night and they watched a blonde Texas girl dance and they might recognize you. You do stand out in a crowd." He smiled at that, climbed into the saddle joined his men and they were off.

Clayton and Sam watched for a few minutes and then they walked back in past a couple of the Don's men. They went to their room and Clay went to get them some food and he brought it back to the room. The woman from before brought more and some drinks she would help them and no one else. They found out her name was Lupe and Sam had her stay and they visited for a while. Clayton took care of the animals with the Mayan men that stayed behind she didn't know she was being listened to in the next room. Her children were well and no more snakes had appeared since she was here. She was getting ready for bed and she walked out on the balcony and was brushing her hair when she heard him behind her.

"So you are the one who stole my children?" she turned around slowly and her hair was glowing in the moonlight.

"Stole your children you have got to be kidding me, they were ready to crawl out of that castle to get away from you I just helped them do it."

"You lie you had to talk them into leaving with you."

"Really, Natasha was in a box with holes punched in it and as claustrophobic as she is I don't know how she wasn't screaming the whole way out. We got her out as fast as we could I was so proud of her and Patricia walked out of that castle dressed as a guard. Everybody was watching me in that beautiful cape and no one noticed that we went on board with six guards and five guards came off not even you. We laughed about it for days."

"My daughters love me they wouldn't do that to me."

"They may have to love you because you are there father after all. I spent months on a ship coming over here with them and I can tell you they don't like you or respect you."

"When I find Patricia I will make this up to her and we will go back to Spain and everything will be alright again. I have found a husband for her and we will be a family again."

"What if she doesn't want to go back with you what then? What happened when you saw Natasha and don't tell me you didn't because I can already tell you did?"

"I haven't seen either one of them Natasha is with her sister at some Hacienda further up the road. She married that fool Antonio Baca but maybe I can see to having that annulled."

"I don't think so she loves him they were married at the first port we came to with a priest and you have a grandson now. I don't think she would ever leave Antonio and I will see to it she is protected from you."

"We will see when we get to this Hacienda maybe the owners will have more sense than you do and they will give me back my children." Clayton was walking in about this time and was going to say something but Sam stopped him so he stayed at the doorway.

"I don't think either one of your daughters will want to go back with you. You can't make them they will have protection out here and there is nothing you can do about It." she was facing him and he came closer to her and he was almost snarling he was so mad.

"I have hired men with me and maybe I can convince the man that owns the Hacienda to think the way I do and give me my children back or maybe I will just take them. Either way I am told you are not married to the man you are sleeping with I wonder what he would take to buy you. Since you are neither a mistress or less than that you shouldn't cost too much. I would love to present you to the bishop back in Spain I think I would win a lot of favor with him if I brought you back with me. I don't usually enjoy watching women burn but I think I would make an exception in your case so you better start getting on my side or else little girl." Sam was so mad she was clinching the post she had her hand on the day Balik shot that arrow into it. Clayton was fuming but he stood just inside the door when the Don turned around and left. When he did come out Sam was shaking so bad he didn't know how she was standing up. He just picked her up and carried her into the room.

"We can't let him get to the girls we have got to stall him." Clayton had his arm around her as Lupe came into the room with some food and some juice she had heard it all and seen what had happened. Clayton just kept on talking because he figured he was going to need her help.

"Tomorrow we are going to Father Michel and we are going to be married and this time I am not taking no for an answer. That man is not going to be able to use that against you ever again." She nodded.

"I was hoping for something a little nicer than jeans for a wedding dress but I guess this will have to do." Lupe held up her hand and said she would be right back. Clayton didn't know where she went but they decided they needed to eat so they went about eating some food and it wasn't long before she was back. She was laying a lovely dress on the bed a long white skirt with hummingbird's embroider across the bottom and a lovely top with the birds across the neckline. It had been lovingly made for someone and Samantha wondered who. She held it up and just looked at Lupe.

"My daughter the one the snake killed it was for her Quinceanera." Sam just held it for a minute and started to refuse it and then changed her mind, for this woman to have offered her dead daughters dress was a great honor and she wasn't going to turn it down.

"Thank you I will wear it with honor. We are going to need a witness will you stand up for us and Anuka can be the other one." Clayton was smiling.

"We need to eat and get some sleep tomorrow is going to be a long day." The rain was already lightly starting she hoped Russell was well on his way.

They sleep for a few hours and then they were up and dressed. Lupe was there with breakfast and they ate. Clayton made sure she ate enough because he wasn't sure when they would eat again. The horses were ready and they were off before the others were even up it was still dark but father Michel was waiting for them at the front of the church. He ushered them in and the timing was good because it started to pour as soon as they entered the church. It was perfect timing because the men they left behind couldn't leave now, especially since the Mayan men had come with them. The women were led to room at the back so Samantha could dress and Lupe could help her. The dress had ties so fitting wasn't a problem and when she was dressed Lupe pulled out another bag with a mantia in it. She put it on Samantha's head and it covered her face; well it was as close to a veil as she was going to get. "It is beautiful Lupe shall we go in." as she turned she saw Lupe was crying and she understood that this was as close as she was going to get to seeing her daughter grow up. This was not a place for her to raise her children and she suspected she was alone she was going to talk to Clayton later but one thing at a time. She walked out holding Lupe's arm as if she was her mother and they walked down the center of the church to a waiting Clayton and the other men and there were quite a few of them. The Mayan men who didn't understand what was going on Anuka was explaining as quietly as he could as Father Michel watched. This church had never seen it's like before and probably never would again.

Clayton took her hand and they took their vows and Clayton put that ring he had offered her at the hacienda months ago the emerald one on her ring finger.

"Where did that come from?"

"I have carried it with me ever since that day hoping you would say yes and I would have it with me when you did. Melanee reminded me to take it with me before I left just in case I had forgotten it." She smiled at him.

"That child is persistent."

"That little girl is yours and she intends for me to bring you back. When we have some more time I will tell you just how much." They turned and there was a meal prepared for all and a small cake so everyone sat down except the Mayan men they went outside they wanted to explore the pyramid while the bride and groom did whatever they were going to do. It was still raining a little but as Sam knew that didn't bother them. Everyone had a nice time and as the afternoon wore on the rain stopped and they got ready to leave. Sam changed back into riding clothes and Clayton came into the room to help her gather up her things and she asked him.

"Clay I would like to ask Lupe if she would like to come back to the hacienda with us with her children if that is alright with you. I am thinking we could use the extra help with the baby coming and the extra guests we have.

If that is not alright I will keep my mouth shut and leave her some extra money." he just smiled.

"You do whatever you want I watch the two of you together and you two have a connection and if you want her there we will make it happen. Talk to her when we go back and see if she can get her family ready to go with us or if I need to send someone back for her?" now Sam was smiling. They loaded up and the good father had several bottles of honey for them to take with them. They were wrapped and packed in the saddle bags. He came over to Samantha and looked up at her.

"Do you remember the name of the Bishop that threatened you in Spain?"

"All I remember is Bishop Rodriguez." The father grinned up at her.

"I don't think you have to worry about him anymore a Bishop Thomas Rodriguez was killed in the countryside while he was traveling to a monastery."

"How was he killed was it an accident?"

"No one knows exactly he was just brought back to the monastery after he was found dead. His body had been burned the villagers said they didn't know how his body was burned they just found him that way but two women from that countryside had been taken as witches and never seen again." Samantha just looked at Father Michel and said.

"Sometimes karma takes care of itself. Did you tell Clayton about this before the wedding?"

"Yes, but he said not to tell you until after the wedding he didn't want you to run away again." She smiled again.

"I am not running anymore. I am going home." They started back to the house they were staying at and she got in between the men and the Mayan guards so she could talk to Lupe.

"Lupe how many children do you have?"

"I have two daughters and a young son why do you ask?"

"I want you and your children to come with me and the Patron to our hacienda when we leave to live with us. I will make a place for you and your children and you can work in the house like you do at the house now if you are interested. We will be leaving soon and I would like for you to come with us but if you can't I will have someone come back for you. Are you interested in my idea?" she thought Lupe was going to cry.

"I was going to ask if maybe I could get a position with your family I will do anything to get my children out of here, my daughters are getting old enough the owners expect them to service the travelers when they come of age."

"Do you think you can be ready when we leave in a day or so I know it is quick?"

"We don't have a whole lot I will be ready but we don't have any horses or pack animals and my little boy can't walk that far."

"I will take care of that maybe I can find a small wagon to put everything in and horses or he can ride with me, but we will figure it out. Where do you live I will help you get ready to leave and you can introduce your children to me." Lupe looked at her kind of funny but when they arrived they kept on going back behind the house into the jungle. Back to some huts and that was being kind. Lupe looked at her again and stopped her before they went into one hut.

"You need to stay here I will go and get the children." But Sam just kept right on following her inside and there was not much to see. It was one not very large room Balik's house was a mansion compared to this. There were beds or straw mattresses on the dirt floor one small alcove with a clay cooking oven, a window and not much else. No wonder that Fer-De-Lance had got one of her children and she had died, it probably bit her somewhere in the neck or face she didn't stand a chance neither did these children she had to get them out of here. Lupe was frantic about something and turned to Samantha.

"She is gone Lucinda is gone, the children say they took her to the house because I was not here to work this morning."

"Tell the children to start packing and we will be back with Lucinda. Come on lets go get her." She didn't think it would take much time to pack they didn't have anything. The women got to the kitchen and the women told them the little girl had been sent to the Don's bedroom with his food and she hadn't come back out. They had heard screaming but his men wouldn't let them go to the room. Samantha grabbed a knife off the counter and headed to the bedrooms but she told Lupe.

"You go find Clayton and tell him what is going on and come find me." She turned and started down the balcony towards the bedrooms and one of the Don's men started to stop her.

"What do you think you are doing the Don said he was not to be disturbed and we were to stop anyone from trying and that means you Punta." He then put his hand up across the doorway and on the doorjamb to block her access and started smiling. She flipped that knife over in her hand balanced it and threw it and put right in the center of his hand.

"Thinking I wouldn't do something about that hand was your first mistake. Calling me a whore was your second. My name is Mrs. Clayton Hayes and if you ever call me anything else I will use that knife and carve out your heart." She pulled out the knife and walked past him to the room the Don was using and she heard a little girl begging and she pounded on the door. Don Eduardo just said to go away and Sam backed up and kicked the door open to see a very pretty little girl maybe twelve years old with a torn shirt crouched in the corner and the Don hovering over her with a belt.

"Get out of here you are not wanted she is mine for the day." He had a belt in his hand and she could see he had been using it on the little girl. Sam got closer to the girl and got in front of her and Lupe was at the door.

"Lupe get her out of here now. You are done for the day." Sam started to leave and he swung that belt at her and hit her on the back. She turned around and slashed at him and cut him on the arm and said.

"You better stop now while you are ahead because I can do a lot more damage to you and after the marks I saw Patricia's back I would love to do some damage to you." He stopped dead in his tracks and just looked at her.

"You didn't think anyone would ever know? What was a husband suppose to think or were they of a like mind?" when he didn't answer she knew he was selling them off to people who would keep his secrets.

"Your daughters and I spent a great deal of time on a ship coming over here and the girls and I know a lot of each other's secrets. Now you are going to know one of mine. The Hacienda we are going to is owned by Clayton Hayes and your daughters are there and that man that left early the other day left to get to Patricia so he could marry her before you got there. So now both girls are safe and you can't touch them."

"Maybe this Clayton Hays will negotiate with me?"

"Will you negotiate with this man my love has he got anything you want?"

"Not a single thing. Have you meet my wife Don Eduardo, Mrs. Samantha Hayes and if I hear you or any of your men call her anything else you will regret it. Am I understood?" the Don looked down at her hand and saw her wedding ring and was amazed at the size of the stone. She saw his face when he saw the ring and she smiled.

"My husband's father was a geologist and he helped find some of the biggest gold and emerald mines down here but he kept some of the stones to make a ring for my husband's mother. So you see you don't have anything to offer that he needs as for the Mayan men out there you had better stay away from them as well, you won't do well asking them to hurt me." She didn't give him an explanation she just left with Clayton and the little girl. Don Eduardo was seething in the bedroom and he was calling for one of his men and it happened to be the one she put the knife in his hand. When he showed up to talk to him he wondered what happened. When he told him he just got madder and told the man to leave he had to think. He still thought if he offered the Mayan men enough money he could at least have her hurt or killed but not here they needed to be away from here where he had more maneuvering room. He would get out into the jungle and then they would be more vulnerable. He smiled at that he would be able to get at her easier that way. She was right the man he had picked out for his daughter wouldn't have cared if she was marked up it would not have been a problem while she lived.

They stayed for one more day to get Lupe and her children gathered up. Clayton borrowed a wagon from the church and they put everything in it and they were off. Sam rode up front with Clayton and her Mayan men stayed close in the jungle hunting and Anuka rode close to her and the group. They had been out for two days when they started to hear the jaguar at night. The first night it wasn't that close and Samantha was listening.

"That is my jaguar she has followed us she must not feel safe on the other side." It was all she said and then she lay down and went to sleep as Anuka and Clayton looked at her.

"You don't suppose she is right?" Clayton was looking at Anuka.

"I can't tell one from another but maybe she can and that cat did get up in her face maybe she did follow her."

"What do you mean got up in her face?"

"It was coming for her and the Shaman wanted it to kill her and I told her to bow, instead she got on her knees in front of it and it stopped dead in its tracks in front of her and she cut the ropes around its neck. It just looked at her and she said go they are waiting and it ran away. I don't know why it did not kill her except her cubs had been crawling and sleeping on her all night and I guess she smelled them. That is why my father gave her that jaguar pendant my people think she is a jaguar spirit now maybe she is." Clayton was stunned now he knew why she had two tribes looking out for her.

"Tell your men to watch out for the Don and his men he still wants to hurt her. Come to me with any problems." He just smiled.

The Don had already had some discussions with his men and they were not happy but he would see how far this man would push it.

The next day at lunch was as far as they got before the little pack train exploded. Clayton heard fighting and he started back to see what was going on and he told Anuka to watch Samantha. It was a trick. Out of the jungle came two of the Don's men and they tried to unhorse Samantha and Anuka. It was a mistake they would never make again. The Mayan men were there and the two men were dead before they could get her on the ground. One man each stood beside her as men started back to join them. It seemed they were going to try to capture her and use her to get the Don's girls back from Clayton. She stayed where she was as she heard fighting further back. It wasn't long before the Don and his remaining men were brought up to where she was. There were only two men left the rest were dead. The men were tied and brought before her and the Mayan men were talking to Clayton and he finally asked her.

"What do you want to do with them Samantha because they want to kill them like they killed Nathan." Sam got off of her horse and walked over to Don Eduardo and asked him.

"I told you not to try something like this are you really this stupid. I am something special to these people and I can have your life snuffed out in an instant. I am going to take you to the Hacienda and let the girls see you for one last time and then you are leaving and you are never coming back or I will see to it you are croc bait. You will be bound until we get there and if you give these men any more trouble they will kill you." She turned and started back to her horse.

"I will tell the Bishop where you are when I get back home and I hope he sends men after you." She stopped in her tracks and turned around and went back to him. She leaned into his shoulder so no one else could hear what she was saying to him.

"He is dead he was found burned in the countryside nobody knows how he died but you and I can guess can't we, someone caught up with him and someone will caught up with you I will see to that personally. I will send the Queen a letter and tell her all about your little quirks and how you treat people especially your family and she will love hearing from me." She stood back and watched his face he was almost white he didn't like other people knowing his secrets. They put the men back on horses and continued on down the trail they weren't that far from the hacienda and she was getting tired and she wanted to be home.

When they got to the jaguar statue she was really surprised it was covered with purple orchids and it had obviously been cleaned.

"Looks like somebody has been waiting for you to get home, I wonder who that could be. I bet they have been letting the children come out here and do this so they could keep Melanee from running off to find you. We are going to stay and eat you need to rest and I am going to send a man to the house to tell them we are here, want to bet someone comes a running."

"Oh you are mean." But she was tired so she sat down and they did eat and she rested while they waited but not for long Sundance was running and came charging up to her with Gabriel and Melanee on his back. She jumped off and Sam caught her midair and just sat down as that little girl just about squeezed her to death.

"You came back to me." As Sam kissed that pretty little girl face.

"I told you I would just as soon as I could I had to wait for your daddy to come and help me."

I knew you were coming when I heard the Jaguar the other night she was bringing you home. She brought her babies too." Sam looked up at Clayton and just shrugged her shoulders. His wife and his little girl were tied together in more ways than one.

Gabriel reached down and pulled her up to give her a hug.

"We were so worried about you I thought you were never coming back and that little girl was beside herself to find you."

"Well the river has not been cooperating with us to get home it took longer than we thought it would. Now Melanee would you like to eat lunch with us and then we will go home?" She shook her head yes and they sat down as they lay out the food and started to eat. Another horse was coming and she couldn't see who was on it so she asked Melanee who was coming.

"Russell is bringing Pat they weren't as fast as we were I was in a bigger hurry." Well this is the confrontation she was hoping to have at the hacienda but she guessed it was going to be here.

"I want to talk to Pat for a minute before she gets into the camp and sees her father. You stay here with your father." Sam walked out into the road and stopped them before she could be seen by her father Don Eduardo and Pat got off of her horse and she hugged her.

"Natasha didn't come with you?" Pat shook her head no and then hugged her again.

"Natasha is very pregnant she shouldn't even have come here but when she heard father was looking for her she and Antonio just ran and she only knew to come here she thought here was safe. Russell came to get me and we were to be married but the priest was gone to a neighboring village and we couldn't even get married so now I don't know what to do."

"He is not going to take you or her we will see to that he has already tried to go after me and it didn't work we were going to get to the Hacienda and you are going to tell him you are not going back. We will give him some money to go back to Spain and we will be rid of him. Now no more tears it is done." They walked into the camp and her father stood up and looked at his daughter and ordered her.

"It is about time you got here get these ropes off of me and let's be gone from this place. I want to head to a boat landing as soon as possible and get on the way back to Spain quickly. Hurry up girl I am tired of waiting on you." Samantha just turned and looked at Pat and waited to hear what she was going to say.

"I am not going anywhere with you ever again I am staying right here with my husband." That got her a sideways look from Sam and Russell but both of them backed her up. She walked over to her father not getting to close and started to talk again.

"I worked myself to the bone trying to please you and never could until your new wife wanted more and then you wanted to sell me to the highest bidder. Well I am not for sale and my new husband is giving me more than you ever could he loves me. Natasha is having another baby soon and she is very happy with the way her life turned out with Antonio so you see we did very well on our own. If it hadn't been for Samantha sneaking us out of the castle with the Queens help that night I would probably be dead by now. The man you wanted me to marry had already killed one wife and was thought to have killed the other one. Is that what you wanted for me or did you care at all?" her father had this weird smile on his face and when he answered her they all cringed.

"I didn't care one way or the other he was paying a hefty price for you and is still willing to pay it if I can get you back. His wife the one you think he killed he did kill one of them he beat her to death that is what he likes but he got carried away he never knows when to stop. The other wife I am afraid I am responsible for her she back talked me one night and I slapped her and she fell down the stairs and she broke her neck. He and I know too much about each other little flaws."

"Am I the price for his silence?" there was that creepy smile again. "That and a lot of money to keep his secrets you owe me girl."

"I owe you nothing I am paid in full, pay your own depts."

Everybody kind of backed away from him including the man he had hired. He sat back down on the log and continued to eat his lunch like nothing had happened and the others went to the other side of the clearing and sat down. Patricia was stunned she didn't know this man and now they had to decide what to do with him.

"Sam I don't know what to do. I don't want my sister to ever know what he said she thinks he is still a descent man so where do we go from here?" they weren't paying attention to what Melanee was doing. She had walked down to the wagon to see Lupe's children and she had introduced herself and they were talking when Sam called her. It was going to be nice to have some children her age at the house. They were getting ready to head to the Hacienda and she wanted her to ride with her home. Melanee wasn't paying attention and she went running right in front of the man Sam had been talking to a while ago and he grabbed her. No one was watching and the Don had got his hands loose and now he had Melanee then she screamed. Sam turned around and her heart froze not again he would not take her child.

"Stand back if you rush me I will throw her in the brush back there and there is a snake in there and I think it is poisonous it has a triangle head." His companion got up and moved aside quickly he wanted no part of this man he was crazy.

"You can leave but you are not taking that child with you I will hunt you down and kill you, take anything you want but not her. I have a small bag of gems you can have they will be easy to trade and some money in there as well." He walked up to Sundance and saw the saddle and looked at her.

"This saddle and horse will fetch a handsome price I will take them as well as the bags of gems get them now." Patricia was looking at her and she whispered to her.

"You can't let him take your horse."

"He won't get far but you have to know Sundance will throw him when I call and he could kill him in the process it is your call?" she shook her head yes.

"Get Melanee back and the get rid of him." Sam went over to her things and pulled out the bag with the gems in it and the coins and brought it to him and he wanted to see what was in the bag. She poured it out in her hand and he could see emeralds and rubies and the coins.

"There is a small fortune here and you have been carrying it around in a saddle bag where did you get it?"

"It was a gift from a Shaman for killing another Shaman." And she looked straight in the face when she said it.

"Now give me my daughter and be gone from here." "Don't you want to tell me to never come back?"

"I thought that was implied you are not wanted here." She turned and asked the man that he had hired to come with him if he wanted to go with him and he shook his head no. The man knew something was going to happen and it wasn't going to be good. She reached out to get Melanee and instead of handing her to Sam he turned and almost threw Melanee into the brush. Then he mounted Sundance while they were distracted so he could get away. Sam turned and grabbed Anuka's machete and went after Melanee she picked her up found the snake in the brush and sliced the head off the Fer-De-Lance in one motion. She walked over to Clayton and handed Melanee to her father. She grabbed the snake's tail and laid it over the tree and asked Anuka to have one of the men to skin it as she climbed over the tree trunk. Sam looked down the road and then looked at Patricia and said.

"Are you sure about this I am probably going to get him killed?" Pat looked at her and shook her head yes.

"This needs to end and he will never leave us alone as long as he thinks he can get something from us."

She turned and started to whistle and she watched as Sundance came to a dead stop and started to buck. It didn't take long and the Don was on the ground and Sundance was on top of him if he wasn't dead when he hit the ground he was now. Pat started to walk towards him and Samantha stopped her.

"Let the men take care of this you are done. I don't know how you want to tell your sister this happened that is up to you but I will back up whatever you decide to tell her." As they walked back Melanee was watching the men skin the snake. As they walked past the men she spoke quietly to Clayton and then they walked on towards Melanee and the men went down the road to take care of what needed to be taken care of down there. Sundance walked up the road to her and stood beside her.

"They are skinning this snake are you going to have it put around a hat for daddy and Steven because I have his?" she just looked at her this child was hers maybe not born to her but hers anyway she hoped Alice would approve.

"That is the plan but we need to get going now, get your things together and we will be home before sunset."

"Is Pats father coming with us?" about that time the men were bringing him in draped across horse at the end of the pack train. Sam looked at her and said.

"Yes he is coming but we will be burying him at the Hacienda he fell off of Sundance and died. If you are afraid to ride Sundance with me you can ride with someone else"

"Why, Sundance would never hurt me only someone who shouldn't have been on him and that man shouldn't have been on him." She just smiled at her and they walked to her horse and she put her up in the saddle and then she mounted and off they went home. The people around them just watched as they rode away on that horse that could stomp someone to death and then just rode away like nothing happened. Clayton mounted and followed with Pat beside him and Russell and Gabriel following.

"We better hurry or they will beat us home." Russell rode up beside her and told her.

"I am going to ride ahead and tell the household about what has happened before you get there so Natasha will stop worrying and then you can take your time coming in." Sam just nodded and he was off.

CHAPTER 15

Several hours later Russell came ridding back and he was in a hurry. He stopped in front of the women and said.

"You need to come with me now it looks like Natasha is in labor and she wants the two of you there." Sam turned and looked at Clayton and told him.

"You take Melanee and we will go on ahead and take care of this and you can come in with the rest of the people later." But that wasn't happening Melanee grabbed her around her neck and wouldn't let her go.

"You are not leaving me again. Where you go I go you are my Mama now and you don't leave me behind."

"You can stay with you daddy and he will take care of you and you will be right behind us." But no she would not let go so they finally just turned her around in the saddle and they headed to the hacienda.

"Hold on to the saddle horn we are going to be riding fast." And that is exactly what they did they put some miles between them and the pack train and they got there quickly. When they rode into the patio and they were finally home she was so grateful it seemed like a hundred years since she had left that day. Juanita came out to meet them and she could see Camille on the balcony. The house was bussing and she figured that Patricia needed to talk to her sister before anybody else or anything else went on. The women dismounted and Pat went upstairs and Sam got Melanee down and they went inside. She told Juanita she had some more help coming and some of what had been going on with Lupe and her family and Juanita looked relieved.

"We need the help there are too many people and not enough help since you have been gone and he was crazy when he couldn't find you. Does this mean you will be staying?"

"Yes we are married."

"Oh Melanee will be so disappointed she wanted to be your bridesmaid." Sam laughed.

""I think we may have another wedding for her to be a bridesmaid in and that should suit her. What do we need upstairs?"

"I am not sure everything is quite stirred up and I don't really know what is going on. The lady has been on pins and needles since she got here and the house has been full of people."

"Well Lupe can help with the extra people but I don't know where we are going to put everyone until we can move some of them to town."

"There is a small house in the back that was for the overseer he was leaving behind to run the hacienda when he was gone but he didn't do a good job so he fired him. The house just holds furniture and chests of old clothes now and some baby furniture."

"I may have to go see what is there later." Melanee came running in. "Come on mama they need you upstairs now that lady wants to talk to you." So as she was pulled upstairs she went past Steven's room and he was at his table drawing with the prettiest little boy who couldn't be anybody but Anthony's son because he looked just like him.

"Sam you are home." He came out of the room and wrapped his arms around her waist and hugged her.

"Melanee called you mama did you and daddy get married and where is he?" Sam leaned down and kissed him on the top of his head and said.

"Yes we got married and he is right behind me with the rest of the people they are a little slower than we were. I am going to talk to Natasha then I will come back and talk to you." She continued on down the hall to the master bedroom and there was Natasha and Patricia waiting for her. Anthony was standing off to the side as she entered and he looked worn out so Samantha just took over.

"Well first of all Anthony you need some rest go find a bed and get some sleep." He walked up to her hugged kissed her on the cheek and went down the hall and he went to bed.

"Well that takes care of him now what can I do for you madam fresh pillows a stiff drink? I thought you would be done with this and I would be rocking a baby by now you are really slow." That got a pillow thrown at her.

"Really, Lord how I have missed you. We will see how fast you are at this when it is your turn. OH SAM I am sorry I don't know if you are still pregnant?"

"I am so don't look so stricken the baby is fine and I am fine."

"Now you can tell me what really happened to my father instead of this fairy tale my sister is spinning. Accidently fell of a horse do I look like I was born yesterday?" Samantha smiled at her and sat down on the edge of the bed.

"We were trying to spare you all the grimy details and they are pretty slimy. Let me put it this way he had not changed since you saw him last he had got worse and I put a stop to his trying to use you two for barter without Melanee seeing too much. Instead he used her for leverage and almost got her killed and I wasn't going to allow that. We can bury him tomorrow and you won't have to worry about him anymore. I am also going to send a letter to the Queen about that man who he was going marry Patricia to and tell her some interesting things about him; she can always use some information like that. I will take care of everything downstairs you just rest. Sure you don't need a stiff drink we have really good brandy?"

"I knew when I heard he was arriving, the only place we would be safe was close to you and Pat so I loaded up my family and we started this way. I don't want to go back. Pat is staying here and you are here now I want to be here to. I have missed you since the day you got on that boat and left for Texas. When my baby was born I wanted you there it was like a part of my family was missing and I won't let you go again." Sam just stood there she had felt the same way when she left and after her father died she had thought about leaving and going to Rio but she wouldn't leave her brother maybe she should have, he might have been better off without her.

"We will get this figured out just rest Clayton and all of the others are coming." she walked out of the room and Pat followed her to the top of the stairs.

"She is serious I don't think she is going back."

"They started a dance school in Rio I assume they can start one anywhere, Gabriel has that good a reputation."

"If he had a certain partner I know he could start one anywhere." Sam just smiled and started down the stairs.

"By the way what is Natasha's sons name?"

"Mateo they had thought about naming him after our father and we decided not to. After what I heard today I am glad they didn't." Sam went down the stairs and went out the back to the little house and she was amazed she hadn't noticed it before but the men had cleared a good bit of jungle just to get to it now. When she went inside there was a lot of furniture inside and she found what she was looking for quickly. A cradle but there was two of them one was quite ornate and she pulled it to the center of the room and the other was pretty but simpler. She looked around the house and then she went back to the hacienda and meets Juanita in the kitchen and talked to her for a minute and then went to meet the people outside. They were unloading and she was getting people settled when Camille called for her from over the balcony and told her to get upstairs. She turned to Clayton.

"Make sure the children are fed and everyone gets to bed this is probably going to be a long night." Clayton reached down and kissed her and smiled.

"I love you too and sometime we may actually get to be alone." But she said it very quietly so no one else heard then she walked away. When she got upstairs Natasha was in full labor and that baby was not far away and two men were bringing a cradle up the stairs and Sam had them stop at the top of the stairs and set it down.

"Just leave it there we will tend to it later. Well girl we are all ready you just have to provide the baby for the cradle." Sam sat on the side of the bed and held her hand and Pat was on the other side and she used them to pull on as she had contractions.

"Anthony go downstairs and gets Lupe the new woman I brought with me she has had several children I think we need help. Have her come up here. Quickly please." That man was practically running but he was back fast and Lupe did indeed know what to do. She had that baby there in no time and the other two women watched what she did. Two hours later Sam walked to the balcony with a baby in her arms and told Anthony.

"Hey Papa want to meet your daughter she is a beauty." The men were all sitting under the trees drinking and smoking cigars and he bolted up the stairs. He came to a stop in front of Sam and looked down at his daughter and then looked at Sam.

"Is Natasha all right?"

"Go ask her yourself she is waiting for you." Sam stood there for a minute more and then she went in and took the baby in to her mama and then left them alone. She went downstairs and grabbed a lantern and went out back to the little house and went inside. She lit another lantern and another in the bedroom and Juanita had done as she had requested and the bedroom had been cleaned and the bed made now all she had to do was go get Clayton if he hadn't got her message from Juanita. She turned to go back to the house and there he was standing in the doorway.

"I didn't know if you got my message or not?" that was as far as she got and he was holding her in his arms and kissing her.

"I was waiting for the baby to be born and everything to be alright and you to leave and come down here but I was afraid you would be too tired and if you are that is alright as long as I can just hold you tonight."

"Oh I think I can manage more than that." Sam was unbuttoning his shirt.

"Do you think we can have a few hours to ourselves?" he pulled the blouse she was wearing over her head.

"I hope so I told Juanita to put the children to bed and not tell anyone where we were. Did you lock the door?" he just nodded yes as he laid her on the bed and lay next to her.

"I had not thought about this little house till I saw them bring up the cradle and then I was getting some ideas in my head about how I might get my new wife alone for a while."

"It has been kind of a circus hasn't it? Ever since you met me, ever regret the decision to take me with you?" he leaned back from her so he could see her face and then he said to her.

"The only regret I ever had was sending you away that night and saying those things to you and saying the things I said to Alice." She reached up and kissed him and then they were lost in loving each other. Outside you could hear the jaguar screaming. Clayton looked at Sam.

"Is she watching over you?"

"I think so but I think she feels safer over here than she did on the other side. OH the baby is moving." He rolled her under him and clung to her like she was going to disappear if he didn't hold on to her.

"I am not going anywhere but I like it when it is just the two of us and I can breathe you in. I was so worried you wouldn't come after me when

Nathan took me."

"Why did you think that?"

"I was afraid you would think I was too damaged goods to come after me again. You never asked me about the time he had me if he did anything to me are you not interested or do you not care?"

"I saw what Balik did to him and I was afraid to ask, after what he did to you the first time it terrifies me to think what he might have done this time."

"Would it make a difference in how you feel about me?"

"No it made mad the first time it makes me mad now but it can't be changed. Do you know that Melanee and Steven wanted Balik to find him before I did because they knew that he would kill him in a lot worse way than any of us would? They were exactly right and he did."

"Nathan didn't rape me he pushed me around in front of the Mayan men but nothing more, every time he tried anything else they pulled a machete on him. When Balik came to the clearing he had slapped me and then he tried to barter with me because of my hair. Then he put a knife to my neck and he cut me a little and that got him pinned to a tree with a lance. The rest you know. Balik offered to let me kill him and I wouldn't so he finished him. He probably would have died easier if I had killed him but I was done with him by then and I walked away." Clay touched her neck and he could feel the wound on her neck where he had cut her and it was a not so little cut no wonder Balik had taken his time. He smiled at that Balik would have enjoyed killing Nathan. Clayton rolled her under him and then he was inside her and in a slow rocking motion he took her over the top.

"Look at me Sam watch me I want to see those beautiful eyes when you come over the top with me, my beautiful broken bird is home and she mine." He rolled to the side of her and just held her as he watched her in the moonlight. She rolled over and laid her leg on his and started to go to sleep.

"I don't know when the children will start looking for us but we have a few hours to ourselves." She snuggled down and went to sleep. Clay just watched her for a while till he fell asleep he hadn't felt this content in a long time the men and him had talked and they had some plans worked out that he wanted to talk to her about but not tonight they would wait till tomorrow. As for the children he had told Juanita to sidetrack them in the morning and let her sleep it was about time she started to rest.

Sam had been asleep for a while when she heard a noise and she awoke. She got out of the bed and pulled on her gown and walked outside. The moon was up and it was eerily quiet and she knew her jaguar was around somewhere. She could hear quiet purring in the trees and then she saw golden eyes watching her.

"There you are. You have to stay away from here and the ranches and leave the ranch animals alone or they will come after you. Stay in the jungle and they will leave you alone there is plenty of food for you and your babies now go I will protect you." she saw the tree move and the leaves fall and she heard rustling and then nothing and the jaguar was gone. Clayton had watched but said nothing he just watched. She was wearing a sleeveless light cotton gown and with the moonlight lightly breaking through the trees on her and her hair. She looked like some goddess painted on one of those pyramid walls as she walked back. Clay didn't say anything when she came back in the room he just helped her back in the bed and she went back to sleep he really didn't know what to say. He looked out the window and wondered again if she was what the Mayan believed she was.

The next morning she awoke alone and she wondered why Clayton hadn't awoken her but she sure was glad for the rest. There were clothes on the end of the bed so she got dressed and went to the house and it was already bussing. Melanee was waiting at the door.

"Daddy said we couldn't disturb you, you were to rest are you rested now because they want you in the dining room?"

"Can I grab something to eat and take it with me in there?" Melanee smiled and nodded and took her hand and they went to the kitchen. Juanita was waiting with juice and a plate of eggs and bacon left over's from the pig she had had on the first day back. She sat down and ate quickly and then somebody was calling for her and she went to the dining room and all the men were in there and they had a large piece of paper on the table and there were drawings on it. They all looked up from the table at her but no one commented and she assumed that someone would tell her if there was a problem but no one said anything.

"Well it seems you gentlemen have something in mind so who goes first?" it seems like they had been waiting for her and they had planed what they were going to say and now it was Gabriel who started to talk.

"It seems that Russell has a small lumber mill on his land and we are thinking that we need to make it into a large one."

"Alright why do we need a large lumber mill I seem to be the only on here who doesn't know what is going on so you are going to have to fill me in from the start. Let me sit down and start talking."

"Russell and Pat want to get married and I want to marry Camille and we want to do it here and soon if it is alright with you, but that has nothing to do with the mill. We have decided to all move close to the two of you Natasha was right things haven't been the same since you left us and we want you back and that means we are going to have to come here. Camille will sell her shop and I will sell the dance school and we will start another one here Russell and Pat are going to be here at their Hacienda and Antonio wants to buy the house in town for Natasha. We are trying to figure out the financing Russell and Clayton are going to help until we can get the school and the shop sold but Antonio and I would like to invest in the Lumber Mill and be partners. How does this sound to you.

"Wait here for a minute." She walked out of the room and then came back a short time later with that bag from the Shaman. Then she poured it out on the table. She had never really looked at the contents until today and when she did they were all surprised. She spread out the jewels and then separated the coins and then she sat back down.

"I don't have the foggiest what they are worth but they cost a lot of people their lives and I can't think of a better way for them to be used than to put them to use for a project like this." the men just looked at her there was a king's ransom on the table and they all knew it. They just sat down they wouldn't have to wait to sell anything.

"Does anyone know where we can sell them because I don't? Russell looked at Clayton and smiled and then he said.

"I do and we will get a good price for them we can send money with Gabriel for the parts we will need for the mill and we won't have to borrow money from anyone or take on partners besides ourselves. Are you sure it could be some time before we could pay this back to you Samantha?'

"Did I ask you to pay it back to me? Those jewels were taken from people he killed and this is the only way I can see that they can be used in a useful manner. Maybe it will make those gods I am supposed to be in league with happy with me I hope." About that time her jaguar was screaming in the jungle she had caught something and the men looked outside. Russell commented.

"I need to get some men together and hunt the cat down I guess I better get it done."

"NO you leave her alone I told her last night to stay away from your stock and to stay away from the houses don't touch her or her cubs or you will have me to deal with am I understood? She has a black cub and a ghost cub and that one is sacred to the Maya so don't touch her or them." they all nodded and then Melanee came in and asked her to come with her so she left the room. The men stood there for a second and then Russell asked Clayton.

"She was kidding wasn't she?"

"No she walked outside and that cat was in the tree just purring like a house cat and I swear she talked to it and then it left and unless it starts to attack your animals don't touch it." They all looked at him and then Gabriel said.

"She is different since she got back I don't know how to say it but she is different."

"I know when I was watching her in the moonlight last night it was like she was one of their old goddesses. They wanted her to go back with them just to rest after she killed the Shaman and she wouldn't, she said if she went back she would never come out of the jungle again and I am beginning to think she was right. She was becoming big medicine and I think if they couldn't' have her they would have killed her. She did some amazing things when she was with them I will tell you when she isn't around they scared the Hell out of me but they make her more powerful to them. Those necklaces around her neck are big magic to them and so is she. You should have seen her when she went over the side of that Cenote with that Shaman. I went in and she still had him on the bottom I had to pry her fingers loose and pull her up or I think she would have drowned before she would have turned him loose. They told me later they had never seen a woman dive like she could I don't know where she learned to do that." Anthony answered him.

"I do. When we were in Rio we weren't supposed to go ashore it wasn't really safe and the girls were bored to death and when Sam finally got to feeling better we were in a small cove and the water was crystal clear underneath us. One night when the crew was mostly gone some of them were diving off the side and they were egging her on and daring her to do it. They didn't know she had a pond at her house in Texas. Her father was asleep and she did it and she was good so she did it again. Then every night after that until they left port she got bolder and took more chances her father never knew but she was always doing something, it was like she was running out of time and she didn't want to waste it."

"Well she is not running out of time now, down here is where she was always supposed to be so she could live a long life. I intend to see to that." Sam came back into the room and sat down and started to make plans for weddings. She was making lists of things she would need for them to get in Mexico City and then she wanted to talk to Gabriel, Russell and Clayton alone for a few minutes.

"I know you are going to someone to sell those jewels might they also sell rings for your wives?" they kind of looked at each other they hadn't even thought about that. Then she pulled Clayton aside.

"I know you have a stash of jewels that you used for my ring you might offer to sell them one for a ring if that interests you or take one out of that pile in there?"

"I think I can come up with something they might like." Clayton smiled at her and then went back into the room where his safe was and asked the men to follow him to the office. They were there several minutes when she heard Russell say.

"Holy Hell look at the size of that rock." She smiled and went outside to find the children. It took another two days to get everything ready to go and then they were on their way with Camille she had to go with them so she could sell her shop. She thought she had a dress she could wear for a wedding dress already made so they wouldn't have to worry about her. Sam was working on a dress for Pat and they were busy on it when Melanee started yelling her daddy was coming back. Something had to be wrong they had only been gone a few hours. Sam went to the balcony and sure enough they were coming back and Clayton was on a horse in back of a man holding him in the saddle. She ran down the stairs and got to the horse as they got the man on the ground it was Wayne her Wayne.

"What happened to him Clayton?"

"I don't know for sure we found him on the road barley conscious and bleeding all he could say was your name so we came back and brought him to you I barley recognized him. Let's get him to a bed and see what we can do for him."

"Take him to my old room I can take of him there and have some help watching him." They got him upstairs and they undressed him and he was badly bruised, he had been drug by something and kicked and his arm was broken. Lupe came in to help and Sam was crying.

"He is a friend?" she was washing down his body as gently as she could but there wasn't much skin that wasn't scraped up. What had happened to him?

"He helped me get away from the man who hurt me in Texas and he has always tried to protect me. Why couldn't I protect him?"

"We will fix this Juanita is bringing up soup we will feed him get him cleaned up give him something for fever and if he can make it through the night he has a chance. After they had him cleaned up and fed and he was resting she was all alone with him she took off her both necklaces and put them around his neck.

"They protected me now they can watch over you tonight old man don't you even think about leaving me. I want to know who did this to you and they are going to regret it. She laid her head on his chest and closed her eyes and just listened to his heart it seemed to beat faster now. Lupe watched from the door. In the morning he was a little better at least he wasn't dead. She awoke to him caressing her hair.

"Hello little girl you look tired did you stay up all night watching me you know that is bad for you." She smiled up at him and leaned back in the chair he was the one who always watched her back.

"I wasn't leaving until I knew you were going to be alright. Who did this to you and why weren't you taken care of when this happened?"

"I was working for a rancho about halfway between here and Mexico City and one of the hands there took a dislike to me and he started to play jokes on me but they became increasing nasty until I confronted him and he told me he had been fired because of you."

"Was his name Ty a sneaky little dude?"

"Yep that's him. When I found that out I was just going to wait for my paycheck and leave and then on the last day we were separating some bulls and my saddle strap broke and dumped me in the pen with a bull and he stomped on me before I could get away. They were outside the corral laughing and the man that owned the place told me when I finally got up that I was to banged up to work so I was no good to him so he told me to leave. Sam I haven't got any money and no place to work and I am broken all to hell what am I going to do."

"Did he not give you your pay?"

"Some of it but I had to buy a saddle from him because with my broken arm I couldn't fix mine."

"You're not going anywhere ever again this is your home now it seems I am gathering everyone around me that I love and that include you and this is where we are going to live. That work for you?"

"I can't just do anything for the rest of my life I won't stay like that."

"Well the guys are building a lumberyard I bet they could find something for you to do there, when you are healed up to my satisfaction."

"Hey what are these things on my chest they look like a snake and a jaguar totem? Sam these are Mayan and they are big magic you shouldn't have these. Oh my lord you are the blond woman they have been talking about.

YOU ARE HER?"

"You don't have to say it like that I sound like some sort of witch." He was still looking at her strangely.

"Is it true, one of the Mayan Chiefs found you when Nathan kidnapped you and he killed him? It is all over the jungle about the white woman and her blond hair and big magic." she just nodded.

"I'll bet that wasn't nice, did you see?"Then Clayton answered from the door.

"No she left and let Balik do whatever he wanted to do to him, after he cut her neck that Chief was furious." Wayne looked over at Clay and said.

"You saw did he hurt him?" Clayton just nodded his head and the two men smiled at each other.

"He killed Jeremy he drowned him trying to find me. They turned my ranch back over to me and I was going to give it to Tillie and her new husband for helping us but if you would rather go back I will give it to you."

"No baby if your offer is ok with your husband I would rather stay with you with what time I have left, you are the only family I have ever had."

"Speaking of baby that Texas doctor was wrong I am going to have to write him." That was as far as she got he was off the bed and hugging her and she didn't know how.

"You are going to have a baby with him did you marry her because if you didn't." she held up her hand and showed him the ring. He hugged her again.

"It was worth the beating." Clayton chimed in about that time.

"I want the name of the rancho and the name of the owner we are going to have a talk to him on our way to Mexico City."

"Don't worry about it, it is done." Sam was putting her necklaces back on and the look in her eyes was scary.

"No it is not, not by a long shot they hurt one of my family and they are going to regret it."

"Are you sure about this I know nothing about a lumberyard?"

"Me neither we will learn together it should be interesting." Wayne looked over her shoulder at Clayton and the woman he was holding wasn't the same woman he had come down here with.

"We will be leaving tomorrow or the next day and we will get things started. We will get the parts for the sawmill and then get back here so you just rest and when we get back we will start putting things together."

"Now you lay down you are in no shape to be moving around. I am afraid you still have a fever." Wayne lay back down and they left the room and went downstairs. "Sam what do you want me to do when I get to this man's rancho how do you want me to handle this?"

"I want him to know this man is a friend of mine and this kind of treatment will not be tolerated just because he was a friend of mine. Maybe I should come with you?" Clayton put a stop to that idea in an instant.

"No ma'am you will not you are in no condition to be riding anymore and that is final you will stay here and take care of the wedding preparations and try and act like a pregnant lady."

"Oh I will are you laying down the law now?" but she said it with a smile on her face.

"Yes ma'am I am but I don't want to leave until I know your man is safely out of the woods he took a pretty bad beating and I am like you I want to know why. I will find out. Since we have one more night together do you want to sneak out to the little house later?"

"If Wayne is better Yes, Lupe has been taking very good care of him I will see if she wants to take care of him tonight." It was going to be a long night Wayne took a turn for the worse he did indeed have a fever and it got worse. Moving around caused him to start bleeding again and the women were working as hard as they could to take care of him. When Clayton came up later Sam was in a panic and all she could say was.

"We have got to get those ribs wrapped and tight and we have to get him still. I think his arm is not mending right and it is swollen so badly I can't even tell if it is set right. I want to use the powder the shaman left for you but we are going to need your help and probably Gabriel as well to hold him. We will get everything ready and you go get Gabriel." Lupe was trying to hold Wayne and she finally said. "He is easier when you hold him he knows it is you even like this." Sam took Lupe's place and sure enough Wayne calmed down even though he was barely conscious, she just hummed to him and stroked his head until the men arrived and then she went back to work.

"I am going to give him a little laudanum for pain and then I am going to blow a little dust in his face and after that he won't care what I am doing."

"That is what the Shaman was trying to blow in your face that day at the Cenote isn't it? What is it used for?"

"I am not sure you want to know." She had given Wayne the laudanum and then she turned his face and gently blew the powder into his face and it wasn't long until he quit moving.

"I am sorry my friend but you will be better tomorrow I hope." The men were looking at her as she and the women wrapped his ribs and then she was checking his arm and as she felt the bone and she was shaking her head.

"The bone is out of line and it is pinching off the blood I am going to have to reset it if it hasn't grown back together."

"And if it has?" "Just help me get it straightened out and we will go from there." She started working and had Clayton get behind Wayne and hold him as she straightened out his arm and then she started to pull and she was afraid she was going to have to break it again when she felt it give. She lined it back up straight and then she put two light boards on either side so she could watch the swelling and lightly wrapped it. They gently lay him back down and covered him up and all the while he had not made a sound.

"He is breathing alright and he should sleep for a while. Now with the arm fixed the swelling should go down."Clay was staring at her.

"Tell me what the powder is for, I think I know but I am pretty sure I don't know it all."

"I didn't know all of it Anuka told me most of it. They use it on their victims before they lay them on a stone alter and cut out their beating heart and then cut off their head. The Shaman planned to use it on me before he threw me into the Cenote so I wouldn't struggle on the way down. I had other plans. Well now you know, I am tired the ladies and I are taking turns watching him tonight so I am going to bed." She leaned over Wayne and said something to him that no one could hear and then she left the room. The men were still just staring at each other.

"She knew what he had planned for her and she still took him over the side with her no wonder she said she had to leave the jungle."Gabriel just looked at him.

"She said if stayed she would never walk out of that jungle they would keep her or kill her and Balik would die trying to protect her. I think even Anuka understood she had to leave. I am not sure the Shaman didn't get some of that powder in her face, when I got to her she was still holding on to the Shaman and I had to pry her hands free and drag her to the surface." The men left and Lupe smoothed the covers and sat down beside Wayne and then laid her head on the bed next to him and closed her eyes as she held his hand. It was nice to have someone to care for again

In the morning Wayne was much better but Clayton decided to stay one more day they had some things to do in town before they left. Anthony and Russell went to town and finalized the deal on the house for Anthony and Natasha. While they were gone Sam could start getting it ready for them to move in. The next day when they finally got back on the road again everything was ready and signed on the house and the wedding preparations were well underway.

"Everything is taken care of and there are plenty of men around you don't go to town alone. Russell has men taking care of his place so just stay here."

"Are you through? We are fine just go so you can get back we have things to do and we can't do them without the grooms and one of the brides so get a move on and don't get killed trying to deal with whoever hurt Wayne just find out who it was and I will take care of it." She backed away and Clayton realized she would have Balik go after whoever hurt Wayne he didn't like this side of her.

"I will take care of this you don't have to send Balik after these people in fact you promise me you won't. Sam promises me."

"You find out who and why and then I will promise. Now go." they rode away and Clayton looked back to see if anybody was following but he didn't see anybody but he wouldn't have. Sam went back inside and back upstairs to the sewing room to do some more work on Pat's wedding dress. Before she did she looked back to see two Mayan men following Clayton she wanted him watched to protect him from other tribes and other white men. He was carrying to many valuables and money she was not about to lose him or any of them now.

The next day Sam, Pat and Anthony went into town to look at the house and see to the renovations. They had left instruction for the outside to be trimmed and the trees and bushes cleaned up the jungle took back everything quickly. Maids had been hired to clean the house before Anthony and Natasha brought the children home and Sam wanted everything perfect. They had brought the plain cradle with them until Natasha could have her furniture shipped up here from the dancing school. That was going to take some time and they weren't sure it was worth it to even ship most of it. It might just be easier to have it made here or bought in Mexico City.

Gabriel had already contacted people in Rio and they had told him they were interested in buying him out if he thought the man running the school now was capable of continuing to run it. Gabriel did, the man running the school was from France and had come to them about a year ago when he left Europe for a better life. He was very capable and Gabriel was mulling over the offers, if this worked out he could just have their personal belonging packed and sent to them and he wouldn't even have to go back. That would be safer than traveling all the way to the coast and then coming back it was a long trip. They could meet halfway and sign papers and it would be a lot safer.

"There is still something bothering you, why don't you tell me what it is?"

"Natasha has wanted to come to you ever since Gabriel found you. She has been lost without you. You are like family OH I don't know how to explain it to you. She and Pat have just been lost since the day you sailed away." Sam just smiled at him and then looked ahead as she said.

"It was the same with me I cried all that day and the next it was like someone died and I couldn't explain it to my father. When he passed away I thought about coming down to Brazil but the war broke out about then and I couldn't leave my brother. I was so lonely and my world was shrinking the girls had to know how I was felling? When Nathan came in that night and told me my brother had lost it all I was relieved I could leave and find ya'll and my brother could do whatever he wanted. It didn't work out that way but that was the plan. You can build something here just like you did in Rio I know you can. The people will come here just like they came to you in Rio it may take a little longer but they will come. So smile this is all going to work out you will see." Anthony still didn't smile and the girls were wondering what was going on till he said kind of under his breath.

"I guess we will have to start over again it would have been easier if we could have stayed in Spain." Both women stopped in their tracks and just looked at each other.

"Is that what you have been telling Natasha is that why she has been so desperate to find me, does she want to leave you or is it the other way around?" he wouldn't look them in the face finally Sam asked him.

"Is there another woman or what is exactly going on start talking?" "It took everything we had to get the school up and running the first time we were all but starving until father got there and then it was better but she didn't know that. Now she wants us to start again she doesn't know how much work it takes to make the school work." Sam thought Pat was going to take him apart.

"You are such a liar Natasha worked like a dog cleaning and getting that building fit for a school even when she was big and pregnant with you preening and showing off to each and every new client. You think she didn't see she did. You used every bit of money we brought with us and then the money Gabriel brought. There was plenty and then some for you to gamble so don't tell me you didn't have enough. If you think you will leave her here to go back to another woman you will leave her with her freedom so she can find someone else not just hanging here waiting for you. So make up your mind and soon because you have until they come back and then we will tell your father what is going on and let him handle it from there. He can't go back to Spain and neither can you. Do you really think you would be safe if you went back even with Natasha's father gone. There are people that will do you harm if you ever went back."

"You won't disappoint her we will see to that won't we Patricia?" you have some decisions to make and we better approve of them or you can go back to Rio and leave her here a free woman and never see your children again." both women walked away and went on with getting the house ready and left him standing in the dust. This conversation didn't turn out exactly like he wanted it to. He followed behind and didn't say much.

"Don't think about taking the children either because I will find you and I will leave you in the jungle for the ants to finish." She didn't even turn around but he stopped walking, how did she know what he was thinking. The women pretty much took care of things in town and they went back to the hacienda and Anthony didn't say much to anybody. He went in and saw the baby and acted like a dutiful husband and then went to bed. After everyone was down Samantha went to Natasha's room and was rocking the baby when she woke up and she was staring at her.

"What happened in town he is paying attention to me and to the baby what has changed?"

"You knew something was wrong? Is that why you came out here to find me?" she started to cry quietly as Pat came into the room and sat beside her on the bed.

"You want to tell us what is going on?"

"I don't know for sure but he has not been happy for a while and he blames me for everything and he thinks we should have stayed in Spain. I don't know how that was going to have worked out hiding from my father except he changed his mind and he just wasn't man enough to tell me."Sam looked over her head at Pat and rolled her eyes.

"Well it is a little late now to change his mind." Natasha looked up at her and said.

"You know don't you? What did he tell you? I am not sure I want to know but I don't want him alone with the children especially my son he might just get the idea to take him and run."

"Darlin' he is not taking your child anywhere I promise you that." Natasha just looked up at her.

"You threatened him didn't you?" "A little he was being such an ass."

"Thank you I knew coming here was the right thing to do. I knew my children and I would be safe with you." And she hugged her.

"Alright we will get this figured out one way or the other." She put the baby in the cradle and Pat and she walked out of the room to check on the rest of children and Wayne. He was doing a lot better they had kept him in bed and the arm was better and he was eating and Lupe was taking excellent care of him. Sam liked the way they were looking at each other this was going to work out fine.

"What are we going to do now?" "I am going to have extra guards put out to make sure your brother-in-law doesn't get any ideas about leaving at least until Gabriel gets back. After that they can talk and we will see what they decide to do but he will not take those children anywhere. Shall we go and have supper I am hungry."

CHAPTER 16

Clayton and his little band had been ridding for three days when they came upon the rancho that Wayne had told them about. He had been watching the jungle and he was pretty sure they had a Mayan guard, they weren't showing themselves but they were there. He was sure Sam had sent them for safe keeping and he wasn't going to raise too much Cain about it because they were carrying too much money and jewels it was nice to have a little extra protection.

They went inside the gates of the Rancho and were met by several men and one of them was Ty. Clayton was pretty sure he was going to see him here so it did not shock him that much but when the owner came out he did. It was the man from the auction that threatened Samantha and the little mare now the picture was beginning to fall into place. The owner came strutting out and stood in front of Clayton.

"Can I help you?" Clayton stayed on his horse to talk to the man he was afraid if he got down he would beat one of these men to death.

"You had a hand that you let get stomped by a bull and then you let ride out of here broken all to hell his name is Wayne. I would like to know who hurt him and why you would let your men do such a thing." the smaller man walked up to Clayton and kind of smirked and said.

"It is my land and I can do anything I want to on it besides he was a friend of the woman who gave me grief that day at the action and it was nice to give a little back. How is she by the way? I hear that man that was hunting her caught up with her did he find her? I told him she might be down your way he said she was his woman."

"She wasn't his woman she was running from him. He almost killed her and you sent him right to her and he kidnapped her but a Mayan chief rescued her and killed him. Now she is protected by that Mayan chief and you hurt one of her people and she sent me here to find out who you are. Her Mayan men are in the jungle watching so she knows who you are now don't you feel better since I told you who she is and how she is doing. I would like Wayne's saddle and I am sure the man who hurt him is Ty but I won't point him out because that will get him killed." A man brought out a saddle and handed it to Clayton who handed it back to one of the other men who put it in the small wagon they were pulling. He started to leave then turned back around and said to the man on the ground.

"I didn't even get down off this horse because I figured I would kill you and I told Samantha I wouldn't do that but you had better watch your back because I am sure she won't be that forgiving." Before they got out of the corral another man came up to them with a bag and said.

"These are the rest of Wayne's clothes and his belonging and anything else I could find that belonged to him." Clayton looked down at the young man and suddenly knew if he didn't take him with them he was probably dead.

"Whatever your name is I just hired you get your things and your horse and come with me now." The young man looked at him and back at the men and started to say something changed his mind and went back inside the bunkhouse. It didn't take him long and he was back with his stuff and his horse and they were on their way again. Clayton didn't look back but he knew he did the right thing taking that boy with him. They hadn't got past the corrals when Ty climbed on top of the gate and started to yell at Clayton.

"She must have been a pretty good piece I hear you married her. All that blond hair gets to you, that man Nathan said he had her first so you got taken. She was just a punta." And then he started laughing, the rancho owner was trying to pull him down and Clayton just looked back and he knew he was looking at a dead man. He just turned around in his saddle and they headed on up the road. He could hear Ty laughing as they went down the road and he was glad when he couldn't hear him anymore.

They road for almost another day and a half and it was starting to rain. When they were making camp for the night they were approached by two men who asked to share their camp. Clayton looked them over and asked them.

"You don't look like you are from around these parts, where are you from?"

"We are Texas rangers and we are looking for a man and the woman he was chasing. They tell us the man is probably dead but we need to know for sure he left several people dead in Texas. We would like to know that the woman is safe."

"Would the man's name be Nathan Miller and the woman's name is Samantha Rodgers?" Clayton was very interested now why were they looking for Sam.

"Yes that is exactly the people we are looking for but how did you know?"

"You might as well get down and spend the night with us you aren't going any further tonight it is going to rain. I will tell you about Samantha and Nathan and he is dead. How many people did you say he left dead in Texas?"

"How do you know for sure?"

"I saw what was left of his body and I am married to Samantha so she is safe and at my Hacienda getting ready to have our child." Both men looked at each other and then back at him they didn't know if this situation was of her choosing or not but they were going to find out.

"We need to talk to her and have her sign some papers so we are going to have to see her in person. He killed her brother and we found two women buried not far from her house the town people suspected him of one but not the other." These men thought she was being held against her will, boy did they have the wrong woman.

"We thought there might be one woman buried out there. Tomorrow you can be on your way and you can talk to her yourself and make sure she is alright. I would like for you to do something for me on the way if you would. There is a rancho you will pass in a couple of days I would like you to check in on the people there and see if they are alright." The rangers thought that was an easy enough request so they agreed.

"Is there a problem at the Rancho?"

"Maybe one of the men has a loud mouth and spoke out against my wife and he shouldn't have done that there are too many ears in the jungle around here and my wife is well thought of." That got a cough form several men in the group behind him.

"What are we missing?"

"I guess you have heard the rumors about the white woman who was kidnapped and then her kidnapper was killed by a Mayan chieftain?"

"Yes it is a good story."

"Not a story it is about Nathan taking Samantha again and a Mayan chieftain who was protecting her found her before I could and he took care of Nathan so you will find no body the ants and the jungle took care of him. My blond haired wife is something special to these people and you don't insult her even out here so please check on that rancho for me."

"We will but surly nothing....."

"Like I said just check on them for me. I am sorry I don't catch your names."

"I am Cory Sutton and he is Davis Moore nice to meet you."The men stayed the night and when they left in the morning they did indeed feel eyes on them.

"Is it just me or do you feel like we have company?"

"I have since we went into that camp and I still do. I know you don't think anything strange about this woman but I would appreciate it if you wouldn't badmouth her out loud around here." Davis turned around in his saddle and laughed at the older man and said.

"This has got you spooked hasn't it? It is all a bunch of hocus pocus." "Fine whatever gets you through the day just keep your mouth shut." "This is going to be a long ride." Cory said under his breath 'It already has been.' They camped for the night and kept a watch they didn't even know what for but they kept one anyway. They got up early eager to be on the way. When they were getting ready to start a fire Cory noticed their packs had been moved not a lot but they had been moved.

"Did you move the packs last night?" Davis looked at him and shook his head NO. He walked over to the packs and Cory was carefully pulling back one of the flaps and inside was a small figurine of a jaguar. Both men looked at each other.

"Didn't Clayton say she was revered by one of the jaguar clans?" Davis just nodded and looked down at the small statue. Someone was in their camp last night and had put that there without them knowing or seeing them. The hair on the back of their neck was standing up.

"I didn't really want any breakfast did you? We can eat something on the trail and I think we need to get to that Rancho as soon as we can." They were dressed and were gone quickly and now they felt eyes even more keenly. Cory didn't have to worry about Davis talking too much they were both to terrified and more so for the men at the Rancho they were going to. They barley stopped for lunch just to water and rest the horses they were on a mission to get to those men and see if they were alright. They had convinced themselves they had to be, that this was all just hysteria or joke they had fallen for. When they got to the Rancho they changed their mind the whole place was deserted. They got to the gate and called out and finally someone answered.

"What do you want you are in danger here you should go away." Still no one would come out of the buildings.

"Clayton Hayes sent us to check on you people to see if you were alright." Suddenly from the side of the building a man came and carefully opened the gate and whispered.

"Come inside if you dare, into the main building and my boss will talk to you." Then he slipped away into the darkness around the side of the building. Cory and Davis got to the front of the building and tied up their horses and went inside to find a couple of men sitting in front of a fireplace and the house boarded up from the inside. They were making a stand inside this house. The man they were looking at wasn't well, he was bandaged up everywhere and white as a sheet. Another man had his arm in a sling.

"Well why has Clayton sent you to see if we were all dead because that is what they are trying to do one at a time. What do I need to do to protect my men I will do it just tell me?"

"You really think she is responsible?" the two injured men looked at each other and then started talking.

"They captured me and my man Ty and took us out in the jungle and tied me to a tree and made a dozen little cuts all over me and just let the ants work on me all night. I wish they had killed me and we haven't seen or heard from Ty since they took him. Larry was just feeding the horses and they shot him with an arrow two nights ago so we can't even feed the animals now so we hide like bats until she calls them off or we all die, are you going to the Hacienda?" "We have to take her some papers to sign so we are on the way to see her." "Please if I write her a letter will you deliver it to her for me it is the only chance we have left and Clayton may not be back for a month and we won't last that long?" the two men weren't sure they wanted to get into the middle of this but looking around they were the only hope these men had.

"Write your letter and we will take it to her but do it quickly I don't want to stay here tonight we will camp further down the road."

"That is probably a good idea. I will be back in a few minutes my men fixed you a meal you might as well eat while I write this note." While they were eating the man that had let them in the gate came in the door with a piece of cloth in his hand and took it back to the owner and then they went behind closed doors.

"Wonder what that is about." Davis looked at the older man." Don't know don't care just want to get out of here and get down the road. The owner was coming back as he wiped off his hands with a towel and he handed the men a letter.

"Please get there as quickly as you can our lives depend on it."

"Even when we get there I don't know how she is going to turn this around and keep your people alive. How is she going to get word to this Mayan guy?"

"Oh I think she can stop this if she wants to just give her the letter." They left the Rancho and rode just as hard and fast as they could until they couldn't see anymore and they had to stop.

"We have got to stop I can't see in front of my face anymore and we are going to walk our horses into something that will get us all killed." They got off their horses and laid out their camp but they didn't spread it to far they were afraid now. They lay close to the horses they thought they would warn them if anything got to close. And one of them tried to stay awake and on guard but they were just too tired. When they did wake up the sun was up and they were starving and there was a fire started Cory said.

"I thought we would just eat on the road like we did yesterday and get an early start." Davis turned around and he was white as a sheet.

"Didn't you start the fire because I didn't?" they both looked at each other and then looked into the jungle and then they both sat down at the fire and pulled out some cans and made breakfast.

"I guess we are being told we should eat before we go on." They both looked at each other and ate and then got on their horses and went on down the road as if nothing had happened.

"Do you suppose that was for our benefit or for the horses we have been pushing them hard maybe they thought they needed a rest. Maybe we should take better care of them. I don't know if you noticed but they had fresh grass off to the side this morning and I didn't put it there did you?" Davis shook his head No after that they slowed down their pace some and took better care of their horses. It took another day to get to the hacienda and when they rode up into the courtyard it was almost sundown. Anthony came down to see who was in the courtyard.

"I need to talk to Samantha Rodgers is she here?" a woman came to the balcony and leaned over and the sun was shining through her hair and it looked like it was on fire and it took his breath away.

"I am Samantha what can I do for you." We are Texas Rangers and we need to talk to you and we have a letter you need to read from a man up the road at a Rancho that is under siege because of you." She came down the stairs and she was wearing a white dress and all that blond hair he could see why the Mayans thought she was something special. Davis began to open his mouth and he was getting to sassy." Listen lady you need to read this letter those people up there think you can do something to help them I for one don't, I think they need the Federales. They think just because they said something against you or were mean to you or one of your people they have brought your wraith down on them, well I for one think that is stupid."

"Would you like to stop your man before he winds up in that jungle tied to a tree or shall we just let him rant some more? Let me see the letter and my last name is Hayes now." She sat down opened and read the letter put it on the table called Juanita and when she came out to the table she told her.

"Please feed these men and fix them a bed upstairs for the night. I will be gone for a while I have to take care of something. Before he says anything else you should have him read the rest of that letter. You will have to stay here tonight it will be too dangerous to go to town they have heard too much. You won't be safe but please tell him to keep his opinions of me to himself at least for the rest of the night." She got up from the table and walked out to the edge of the jungle and waited there and as the men watched Mayan men walked out to her first one then another till there were four then she walked into the jungle with them and she was gone. Both men started to get up and Juanita said.

"Where do you think you are going?"

"To help her." "She doesn't need any help sit your butts down and eat and I think she said read the rest of the letter. She will be back when she has taken care of what needs to be taken care of." The men started to eat and Cory picked up the letter and was reading it and he wished he had waited until he had finished his meal because he no longer had much of an appetite. He just pushed his chair back and waited for his partner to finish is meal and when he asked him what was in the letter he told him.

"He begs her pardon for what he did in Mexico City and for calling her a Punta and everything else and would she please forgive him. Ty wouldn't be a problem anymore they brought his shirt to the gate before we left with his tongue inside it so he won't be coming back. His other men didn't' take part in the hurting of Wayne so please forgive them and call off the Mayan men." The two men just sat and looked at each other so they had insulted her and badly, about that time drums started in the jungle. It wasn't long till she walked out and she was walking back and the night was coming alive with drums.

"The Rancho will be safe in a couple of hours are you satisfied now?" "He said you could take care of it and you did."

"He is not a very nice man but he doesn't deserve to be tortured anymore the other man must not have taken my husband's warning to heart and kept his mouth shut, these people take insults to me seriously. I think you men need to stay a couple of days and show these men you are a friend to me. What papers do I need to sign?"

"Your ranch was signed back to you and I need to know for sure that Nathan is truly dead because he has several outstanding warrants for his arrest for murder and assault."

"Who did he kill and how many and who did he assault?" the ranger looked at her she already knew one but she had to hear from him" He killed your brother and we found the bodies of two women not far from your pond a woman named Tillie told someone in town that there might be a body out there how did she know."

"Nathan's big mouth, she overheard him but what about the assault he hurt that doctor didn't he?"

"Yes but not too bad the people in his town protected him and he filed charges as soon as he could so he could keep him off of your back as long as he could. When we talked to that man he told us what he had done to you and he wanted him hung. We kept chasing him I don't know why a man just keeps coming after a woman who doesn't want him and you really didn't want him. We will take you back if that is what you want to do?" Cory half hoped she would say yes but he already knew she wasn't staying here by force. About that time Melanee came running down the stairs and wrapped herself around Sam.

"Mama the baby is crying again it is always crying."

"Well my dear in a few months your brother or sister will be here and they will be doing the same thing so you better get used to it. The drums are making it cry it will be better in a little while so go find the boys and play. Stay in the house these drums are going to make the jaguars unhappy so stay close. Now gentlemen about the ranch I would like to sign it over to Tillie and her new husband and I assume you can take those papers back or do I need to mail them?" the drums were getting quieter as they went further up the jungle and it was getting quieter around the hacienda.

"We can take them as far as we need to go back into Texas and then we will mail them. About that Jaguar we can take care of that as well we have heard him several times the last several days and that would make a wonderful pelt to take back with us." If looks could kill they would be dead on the patio.

"Gentleman the jaguar is off limits she belongs to me as well as her cubs you leave her alone." As they walked into the house Davis said quietly.

"She doesn't own all the land when we are away from here she won't know." Samantha turned around and looked at them and said.

"Next time you think about hurting MY JUAGUARS my people will leave more than a figurine in your pack I am a snake spirit as well and you have been warned." How did she know about the figurine they hadn't told her the only way was someone out there told her. Let's go inside I need to get my other children to bed and I need to see to getting you set up for the night and yes you will be safe in here no one would dare touch you in my home." she led them to the back bedrooms and got them settled and went upstairs and got the children down and then went back outside and listened to the drums until she was satisfied that everything was taken care of. One of the men came back out of the trees and talked to her and said it was done and no one else would be hurt. He also asked about the men in the house and she assured him they were alright. She was right to keep them here tonight they weren't safe on the road. She went back inside and closed the house and Wayne was waiting for her someone had given him the letter.

"Your people don't take an insult lightly I didn't know what had been done to you as well. It wasn't that much but these people don't take things lightly."

"I stopped it but not before they killed the other man. I am keeping the Rangers here for a couple of days they have been keeping to close an eye on them and I don't want any more lessons." Wayne just nodded and then he went back to bed there wasn't anything else to do the drums were getting quieter so the other jungle noises were coming alive. She walked out on the balcony and the moonlight hit her hair and gave it that eerie effect. She didn't know it but Cory was down below just watching it was the strangest thing he had ever seen. He had wondered why Nathan had followed her all this way and taken all those chances trying to find her now he knew. The man was a fool he damn near killed her trying to keep her. She was gone before her ever had her. Then he took her again and led her into the arms of the people who would guard her with their lives something Nathan would never do. What a fool he was he drove her into the world she belonged in all the time. Samantha turned and went back to her bedroom and went to bed just as her jaguar was calling.

When they got up in the morning Sam asked them to help her move Anthony and Natasha into town and their new house. Sam and Pat had made a deal with Anthony they would keep their mouths shut until Gabriel came back and he could talk to him if he would keep up the dutiful husband routine. When Gabriel was back they would decide what to do after that. Both women would take turns coming to town and helping with the baby and keeping him in line and if he strayed the deal was off and he was on his own. Anthony was deciding he better decide what he wanted or these two women were going to kill him. They got everything moved and Natasha liked how everything looked and they were settled in and Sam had arranged for a woman to come in and cook and clean every day.

The evening was coming on and they were getting ready to leave and the Rangers asked if there was any place in town to stay and Sam told them about the small hotel across the from the patio.

'We brought our things so we will stay there tonight and we will start out tomorrow we have everything signed and we see that your papers get sent as soon as we are in Texas. We wanted to thank you for your help with the Rancho but we need to be heading back now and unless you say we aren't safe, we plan to go tomorrow."

"I will see that you have safe conduct back home and if you pass by my husband tell him to hurry home I miss him."

"Yes ma'am I will do that. It was nice meeting you there is only one thing that I wish I could have gotten to have seen you do." "And what is that?"

"They said in Mexico City they never saw anyone dance like you do." She just smiled. "Not exactly the place for the Flamenco."

"No ma'am but I hear a guitar player and my mom taught me to two step can you do that?"

"Yes I can do that I am from Texas after all." They walked to the patio where she had performed in front of the crowd before Nathan had taken her and Cory asked the man to play a song and he came back to her.

"Can I have this dance?" he bowed and took her hand and led her out on the patio. She was drawing a crowd as they danced she was better than he was but it didn't matter they just danced then another pair of arms took hold of her and the music quickened and they were off. Anthony had her and they were gone and he could barely keep up the crowd was getting bigger and the guitarist was good. The Pasa Doble was intoxicating and they went round and round until she was breathless. He finally stopped and leaned her over his bent knee like his father did and the crowd went crazy as did Cory this was what they had told him about in Mexico City and he got to see her perform. If nothing else he had this to remember. They came walking back to him and Anthony was apologizing.

"I am sorry it was just too good to pass up to dance with her again please forgive me."

"Are you kidding me it was wonderful to watch the two of you dance I have never seen anything like it before."

"I am sorry no Flamenco wrong shoes."

"They are telling me you are going to have a dancing school here is that right?"

"That is the plan."

"Well if I don't get shot I will come back and build me a house and live here just so I can watch you two dances."

"We are also building a lumberyard so this might be a good place to move for other reasons so don't get shot and come back we need good people and I know a number of pretty women." Couldn't be prettier than the one he was looking at but he would get shot for going after her.

"Have a good trip and be careful we are leaving now. You will be watched over till you get close to Mexico and then they will leave you, so be good." She mounted her horse and they were gone but he watched until he couldn't see her anymore.

"Do you really think we will have an escort?" Cory just looked at him and shook his head yes.

"Don't even think about going after that jaguar or you will get us killed and I am serious about coming back here, don't screw it up for me. Let's get a room for the night I want to leave in the morning." Anthony watched as they went to the hotel and then went home he was changing his mind about a lot of things lately. The way other men were looking at his wife infuriated him and the way Sam and Pat were planning the new school without asking him what he wanted was galling. It was his own fault he had told them he wasn't going to be here and now what was he going to do. He could hear his baby crying in the house what had he done. If he was going to make this right he had better hurry before Natasha found out what was really going on or he was going to lose it all and right now he didn't want that. He walked into the house and Natasha smiled at him and once again he was lost in that smile.

CHAPTER 17

Samantha had been waiting for days and she was sure that today was the day, when a runner came into the yard and talked to her. When he left she went inside and Juanita and the girls started cooking. Soon people were coming to the kitchen and Melanee asked.

"Daddy is coming home today isn't he?" Sam turned around and just shook her head yes. Melanee squealed and went running as she informed the rest of the house. Soon the kitchen was full of people asking questions and she was trying to cook and answer them at the same time.

"He is on his way they should be here by nightfall so help us get the house ready and the beds made and we will get the pig cooking. We will be ready for them when they get here. Melanee came over and wrapped her arms around Sam's legs till she picked her up.

"He is coming home to all of us?"

"Yes love to all of us." She hugged her neck again and then slid down her and off she went.

"He is coming home to a different little girl." Pat looked at Sam and then they went back to getting things in order. It took all day of cooking and rearranging to get ready but they had everything ready when they finally arrived just at sunset. Sam was waiting in the courtyard with everybody else when they finally got in. The stable men were taking pack animals and wagons and the men were trying to get down without being mauled by the women on the ground. Sam just stood back an d waited for Clayton until he came to her. Melanee got to him first as she lunged at him and he caught her.

"Daddy I thought you would never get home but the men in the jungle told mama you were coming today and now you are here." She was hugging his neck to tight he could hardly breathe but he was looking at Samantha and she was looking at him strangely.

"Well the man in the jungle was right and now I am home so can we go talk to your mama? Is something wrong mama you are looking at me strangely?"

"Just didn't know if you would be mad at me about your escort or not so I thought I would feel you out first. They took care of you I didn't want to lose you to the jungle it took me too long to find you to lose you to something stupid like a snake or bandit." He smiled.

"As if any snake would bite me and as for bandits my escort was formidable I would not have gone up against them. In the morning we had fresh firewood and sometimes at little totem a snake or a jaguar just so we knew who it was that was there. We stopped posting a guard because I was afraid somebody might accidentally shoot one of them by mistake. They never made a sound. I assume it was you that took care of the problem at the Rancho, by the way they are well and he sends his deepest apologies to you. So are we done, I am starving and you can tell your guards we are home and they can go eat as well."

"I will be in momentarily I need to talk to Gabriel for a minute and then I will join you. Gabriel may I talk to you before you go inside? You need to go to town in the morning or tomorrow sometime and talk to Anthony about going to Rio there are some things he needs to tell you about the school and staying here."

"You mean he wants to talk about that woman he was seeing back in Rio?"

"You knew about her."

"I thought he had ended it when Natasha got pregnant and then when she came out here I thought maybe she knew."

"I don't know if she knows for sure but she knows something is wrong, so she ran to come find me and Pat and she won't go back with him. She has vowed to stay here with or without him and we will take care of her but if he leaves he leaves with her a free woman. Then she can do whatever she wants with her life without him, we will see how he likes that." Gabriel just nodded his son had made a mess of this now they would see if he was man enough to fix it. Sam took his arm and they went inside to eat.

They ate dinner and he could hardly pry his daughter off of him and Sam was most amused at her husband's reaction to her this was a different child than the one he had left behind. She wouldn't shut up she was telling him everything and some things Sam was not so sure she wanted him to know quite yet. Clayton just looked up at her a couple of times and smiled and she figured she was going to get an ear full later but she just kept on listening to the conversation until she finally wore out. By the time she was done she was falling asleep in her father's arms. They got up from the table and went upstairs and put her to bed. Steven followed and told them goodnight and went to his room. Then he called down and said.

"I am glad you are home Dad I just couldn't get a word in to tell you, she has stored all that up for weeks and she was about to explode. See you in the morning." Clayton followed Sam into the bedroom and she was out on the balcony and she was looking at the moon and it always took his breath away when he saw her like this it was like the first time. He went to her and put his arms around her and just held her.

"I understand from my daughter the Rangers were smitten with you?" "One of them wanted to kill my jaguars and he had to be corrected for his insolence." Clayton turned her around in his arms and looked at her this woman was different she was more commanding.

"Insolence who am I talking to?" and the woman he was looking wasn't Sam.

"Someone who won't let it get out of hand like I did with the Rancho it won't go that far ever again. If I feel slighted I will handle it, nobody else, there will be no loss of life no recriminations on my behalf again. If I want something done I will ask for it to be done."

"How are you going to make them understand that?"

"I am not sure but enough is enough. I am tired of people being scared to even talk to me and that is going to stop. They will respect me though and they will listen to what I have to say and respect my family, and my children all of them."

"You are scary sometimes but can I take my wife to bed now and leave the scary woman out here to watch over the Hacienda and all the other creatures of the night?" she just smiled at him as the jaguar screamed in the distance.

They went inside and he snuggled down with her and they made love in the moonlight like they had never been apart and he got a resounding kick from his child. When they were done he was rubbing her belly and he asked her.

"Do you know what the baby is you seem to know everything else?" "Maybe but I am not telling you so you will be surprised. Do you have a preference one way or the other like you can change your mind once it is here."

"I do not care one way or the other as long as you and that baby are fine in the end. Why are you going to town in the morning I heard you talking to Gabriel before supper what is going on?"

"Anthony is trying to pull a fast one on Natasha and we aren't going to let him get away with it and we want his father there tomorrow when we confront him."

"Who is we just you Natasha and Gabriel do you want me to come with you?" she just shook her head.

"It is going to be a big enough mess without you there, if it gets to bad I will send a man for you but I would rather you stay here and spend the day with the children.

"Alright but you take the wagon you don't need to be riding anymore you are to pregnant. Then if things get bad and you need to bring her back you can."

"Alright so can we go to sleep now it is going to be a long day tomorrow?" he just pulled up the covers and they drifted off to sleep at least he did she was still awake and when he was good and asleep she went back to the balcony and there were two men waiting for instructions and she made some signals. She held up four fingers and the she pointed two fingers in each direction and the swished her hands away and the men dissolved into the jungle and the guard was set for the night. Then she went to bed and Clayton never knew she had placed her guards around the house he wouldn't know for some time yet."

The next morning she had left before the house awoke and she and Gabriel talked on the way to town. They met up with Patricia just as they were getting to town and she was already mad, she was just learning what all was going on. They continued on and when they got close to the house they figured they would have to tell Natasha what was happening but that wasn't going to be a problem. When they got close to the house they could hear screaming and breaking crockery and the nanny was outside with the children and she was looking around wondering what to do. Gabriel got down first and then got Sam down while Pat was running into the house. Anthony was backing out of the house while Natasha was hot on his heels throwing things.

"Natasha what is going on here stop for a minute and tell me."

"He wants me to file for divorce so he can go back and marry that whore of his and he wants to take my children with him. He wants me to leave the house because he is the man and he has all the rights." They all kind of stood there stunned until he opened his mouth and then it got worse.

"She is worthless and I can take care of the children so they need to be with me and that means that the house should be mine too." He stood there so smug with these people looking at him all the time not knowing they wanted to kill him until Sam started to talk.

"First of all Natasha is not worthless and if you open your mouth again I will kill you. Second of all the house is hers and the children are hers. If you want a divorce you can have one but you will never leave this jungle without signing those papers so she is free of you. She left her home in Spain to come with you and you have betrayed her from the start but no more, we will pack your belongings and you can leave but with nothing."

"I don't have to take orders from you Samantha you are nothing to me and I will do what I want with my wife." And the evil grin on his face said it all. Clayton was coming up about this time.

"You will do what my wife says or I will shot you where you stand. My men will pack your belongings and they escort you to the boat landings. Gabriel gets the papers ready for him to sign for your dance studio and the divorce papers and I will make sure they are taken care of today. Ladies take the men inside and take care of what needs to be taken care of and I will stand guard out here." Sam came over and put her hand on his leg.

"Perfect timing my love." By now Russell was arriving and the two men were talking and he wasn't any happier about the situation than Clayton was. The women went inside and the first thing Sam did was turn Natasha around and ask her.

"Talk to me is he hurting you I saw the look he gave you and it was one of pure evil." She couldn't look her in the face. Both women knew right then he was and Sam was furious she turned around and went back outside and she went to Anthony and she slapped him.

"I can't call you a bastard or a son of a bitch because I know your parents and they are good people so where did you go wrong?" he just grinned at her so she punched him and she put him on the ground.

You are worthless and you don't ever come back here do you understand me ever or they will find your bones hung up in a tree with the ants feasting on them." That finally got his attention and he was scared because he knew she could do that. They couldn't get everything ready that day so he had to stay at the little hotel for the night with a guard but the next day the paper work was ready and signed and he was ready to go. Natasha let him see his children one more time to say goodbye and then he was escorted to the boats and he was gone. Gabriel had given him some money for passage on a boat to Rio and then he was to be part owner of the dance studio but he was going to have to work to make a living and that was something he had never really had to do before. Once he was gone Natasha went to pieces and Pat said she would stay with her to make sure she was alright. There wasn't much else to do she just had to make the best of it and start over.

Sam went back to the house and they continued to make the dresses for the wedding, they were to be in a week on the patio out back or that was the plan. While they were working on the dresses one of the men came to the back door and asked to speak to the blond lady if she would see him. Juanita came up and told her he was very nervous but he wanted to talk to her. Sam came down the stairs and recognized the man he was one of the men that had escorted Anthony to the boats and her skin started to crawl. She walked out to the patio and motioned the man to sit down in one of the chairs because he looked like he was about to take flight. After she sat down she said.

"Well what is wrong there is something on your mind?" she could hear Clayton walking up behind her.

"Madam it may be nothing but when we were taking the man to the river I overheard that man talking about his wife and it wasn't good. He said awful things about her and then he asked the other men if they would kidnap the small boy for money. He didn't care about the baby or the woman or if they hurt them just the getting the boy. I don't know if they would really do it or not but those men, they scared me. Should I have kept silent?" Clayton was already going to the stable to round up some men. When he came back he was going to take the man that was talking to Sam with them. He had a wagon and was ready to go.

"I will go get them and bring them all back here and put a guard on them he is just stupid enough to try and take that little boy and he wouldn't care who got hurt in the process. I am leaving some men here just in case he had other ideas on getting back at you as well." Sam wasn't saying anything to him and he was sure if he came this way he would be sorry and it would be the last mistake he made. Gabriel was inside the house with Camille and he had heard most of it and he was going with Clayton to town and the men were leaving he just looked back at her and didn't even say a word.

Camille came outside as men came out of the jungle and came towards Sam and Camille grabbed her arm and finally said.

"Please don't have him killed until we at least know for sure what is going on, it would kill his father if this isn't true." Sam told the men something and then turned around and told her.

"I am just having the house guarded more closely until I know what is going on and then I will decide what to do now we need to finish the dresses for next week." She walked back inside like nothing else was going on but she could see men placing themselves around the house in the jungle. Clayton made his way to town as fast as he could in the wagon on that narrow trail and that wasn't easy the jungle took back what belonged to it very quickly. Clay and Gabriel didn't talk much going to town but they were both worried. When they got close to the house they knew he had done what the man had said he was going to do because the heard a woman screaming. They approached quietly and went to the back of the house and one of the men had Natasha with a knife to her throat and the other man had Mateo and they were ready to leave with him.

"This is a bad mistake gentlemen you don't know who you are angering by taking that little boy or hurting his mother especially you." And he pointed to the man who had the knife at Natasha's throat.

"My wife is her best friend and that child's godmother and she will kill you for this or her guardian will and Balik takes no prisoners and you can't run far enough to escape him." The other man looked at him and asked.

"What has Balik got to do with this?"

"They are under my wife's protection and she is under his, she is his snake goddess the blond one." The man almost threw Natasha on the floor as he backed away.

"She is La Luna the one they talk about the blond one he protects the one that wears the jade pendant of the snake?"

"Yes, she wears a Jaguar pendant as well from Anuka he protects her too. I think this was a bad idea so you had better let the child go now as well." The other man didn't understand what was going on and he started to yell at the first man until the other man told him something and the man got white as a sheet and then the man put down Mateo and looked at Clayton and started talking.

"Please we didn't know he didn't tell us who the boy was we were just supposed to bring him to the boat. Please tell her to have them kill us quickly." The look on their face said it all they were terrified "Maybe we can make a deal to save your lives, that would be even better, you will have to come with me and meet La Luna don't worry you will be under my protection." They neither one looked convinced. They pretty much figured they didn't have any other choice so they followed him to the wagon like a couple of doomed men.

They loaded up and started to the ranch and every so often out of the jungle came one of the Mayan men and just looked at the men in the wagon and they knew they were dead men. Clayton looked back at them and told them.

"As long as you are with me they will not touch you, so stay in this wagon don't you even think about running you won't get far." As soon as they got to the Hacienda she was waiting on them and she went to meet them at the wagon.

"Good this will make it easier you brought them to me they won't have to chase them." And she turned away from Clayton.

"I offered them protection if they would do something for me in return."

"You had no right to do that and I don't have to honor anything you said to them." He grabbed her arm and turned her around.

"Is that right, so anything I have to say is nothing La Luna?" He pointed to the man standing under the tree.

"I am still your husband or is there another husband I don't know about? Balik was always looking at you like you belonged to him did you? Did he call you La Luna as well, start talking I think this conversation is long overdue and tell those men to back off." There were Mayan men coming out of the jungle as they spoke.

"Yes, he called me that sometimes what of it and yes he asked me to marry him when he thought his wife was dying but she didn't. I figured out the Shaman was poisoning her and I stopped him that is why I was on the run and had to get out of the jungle so fast the Shaman was going to kill me. Balik never made love to me it has always been you."

"That is why you said we needed to leave, Balik would have kept you?" she nodded her head and her drew her to him and hugged her.

"That is why all the guards he wants to know you are safe?"

"My love I am big magic to the tribes now and he is afraid somebody will try to take me so I am guarded it is just a fact of life now so get used to it. If you told these men they are safe you better tell me why and what you want from me."

"I want them to take a message to Anthony from me and his father and deliver it personally and then never come back any of them will you allow that?" she nodded her head yes and they headed to the house. After Gabriel wrote a letter to his son they made sure the men were escorted to where Anthony was waiting and he was given the letter and the men told him what had happened and what would happen if he returned. He didn't believe them until several Mayan men came out of the jungle then he boarded the boat and they left. As he went downstream he saw Mayan men come to the water's edge several times and once they even shot an arrow into the boat with a snake charm on the arrow it was a sign to stay away. The captain finally came up to him and asked him.

"Who did you anger and whoever it was they are playing nice because you are not dead." He was being a smart mouth.

And he answered back.

"I anger La Luna." The man looked at him strangely and then said. "Samantha is mad at you? If we were anywhere but the middle of this river you would be off of my boat but at the next landing you are gone. I want no trouble with the Mayans and you are Trouble. I should have known when I saw the snake totem on that arrow."

"She wants me out of this country and fast, please get me out of here you will be doing her a favor."

"We will see about that I will ask the men with you if they tell me the same story I will get you to the coast if not I will leave you in the jungle to rot." He came back a little later after talking to the other men.

"They said she wanted you gone that is why you have an escort. I will get you to the coast but until then stay away from me and my men Samantha is special to us and you are not." He made himself scarce after that and when he got to the coast he boarded a ship and he was gone. The other two men disappeared and were never seen again but Sam let them go they did what they were supposed to do.

The wedding was this weekend and everything was ready they had decided to move it to the patio in town where there was more room. There was going to be a big arch of flowers by the fountain and they were going to do the ceremonies together with Father Michel officiating and he was due here any day now. Sam was sitting on the balcony early when she heard someone coming down the road and she figured it was the good Father but she was surprised when the Texas Ranger Cory Sutton shows up.

"Well good morning I was not expecting you so soon." He looked up at her and smiled she was still the most beautiful woman he had ever seen.

"What do you mean so soon?"

"I figured you to show up sooner or later but you showed up sooner what happed?"

"I got shot."

"That would do it you want some breakfast?" he just shook his head. Clayton was walking up about that time to help with his horse. They walked to the table and she was putting down some eggs and ham and juice.

"Well, start talking."

"We got back to Texas I mailed your letters went to the nearest Ranger station got sent out the next day after some bandits and we were held up in a canyon with no water for two days and then I got shot in the arm. I thought about nothing but the green down here and when I got back to the station I turned in my badge got my pay and headed back down here. I even had a few escorts as well along the way."

"I figured you would be back I told them to watch for you." Clayton just smiled at her.

"You are just in time for the wedding and there are a lot of pretty girls around here if you are looking."

"I need to be looking for a job but I still have a little money." Then Clayton said.

"We don't have any law around here and we have got a thriving sawmill any interest in either think about it."

"Eat boys I need to check the children." Mateo was running down the stairs and Natasha wasn't far behind him.

"I thought she lived in town with her husband and children?" Clayton saw the look in his eyes that man was smitten.

"She is out here for a while Sam ran off her husband he was hurting her. She is getting a divorce then her husband tried to steal her son away from her so they are staying out here so we can protect them." He heard Cory say under his breath 'I could protect them.' Clayton motioned for Natasha to come over to the table so he could introduce Cory to her.

"Natasha this is Cory Sutton he is a Texas Ranger that was helping Sam with some papers back in her home and he has come back to live here after he was shot."

"Oh are you alright do you still need care?"

"NO NO I am fine now will you join me for breakfast?" Mateo was climbing into his lap and that seemed to be perfectly fine with him it seemed he had five younger brothers so they sat and had breakfast and just talked while Clayton watched and then Sam joined him.

"They make a good couple don't you think?" he looked at her funny. "You had this planned didn't you?" she looked up at him and smiled.

"Oh my dear that would make me a witch." She started to walk away and Clay grabbed her arm and they walked around to the side of the house and he stopped where he could talk to her and no one else could hear what he was saying to her. "That comment is not funny but you haven't been the same since the Cenote and think it is about time we talked about it don't you?"

"You are right but I don't know exactly what to tell you. I knew Cory was coming a week ago, I know they will marry in about six mounts from now, I know that Antonio is going to have problems in Rio and want to come back and I know the child I carry is a girl. I know all this and I don't know how but when that Shaman and I were in the Cenote and he was dying maybe I was drowning too and maybe some of his magic got passed to me in that dark water. I don't know how but Balik knew something was different with me that is why he keeps such a close watch to keep the others away from me."

"What do we do will they come after you?"

"I don't think so; it seems to be just between Balik and me so I need to keep it that way. That is why the jaguars followed me and stay so close they know they are safe here. That little white cub is big magic too." He didn't know what to say or do what he had been feeling about her was true and there was nothing he could do about it except keep her close. He pulled her close and hugged her.

"Are you afraid of me now?" she wouldn't even look up at him. He just leaned down and kissed her hair.

"No now I am more scared than afraid this child is going to look like you, she is isn't she, that is what is scaring you isn't it?"

"Yes if she does they will think she is big medicine to and I don't know what they will want to do about that." that scared the hell out of both of them and there was nothing they could do about it.

"Maybe she will have dark hair like mine and it won't be a problem." She smiled up at him and he already knew that wasn't going to happen she already knew.

"Do you already have a name?"

"I was thinking about Luna but after today maybe not."

"I guess we wait and see." They walked around the side of the house and sat down at the table with Cory and Natasha and he watched as she worried.

The wedding was that weekend and it was going as planned the dresses were ready as were the brides. Gabriel and Russell were worse than the brides Clayton had them down at the patio drinking his best brandy because they were nervous wrecks. The brides were dressing at Natasha's house and Cory was on guard he was not very far away from Natasha and he was always armed. This was already a done deal Sam said.

"I am going to check on the grooms and make sure they are still standing you ladies take your time just not too much time." As she walked to the patio she noticed she was watched from the jungle she had more and more eyes on her lately it was making her paranoid. She kept far away from the trees anyway she was too pregnant to run she felt better when she could see Clayton she wouldn't walk alone anymore. When she got up to Clayton she seemed frightened and she was never scared so he wrapped his arm around her and just looked down at her and she smiled.

"We will talk later." But she stayed by his side the rest of the day she was scared.

"Alright gentlemen are you ready for this because the ladies will be here any minute straighten up your jackets and get yourselves together it is time." The good father came over to talk for a minute and then she went to the end of the patio and signaled the guitar players and everyone got quiet. Clayton took both women's arms as he walked between them and walked down the patio to the grooms. Both men were all but crying it was perfect it was just what Sam had imagined for her friends and soon Natasha would be happy again as well she just didn't know it yet or did she.

The ceremony was perfect petals fell from the trees like snow even the baby slept. When it was over the town was ready to party and it was a party everybody had been invited and there was food and wine and dancing and Gabriel put on a show. Sam danced some but she was just too big to perform this time but she did have a waltz with her husband it seems Gabriel had been teaching him just for this occasion at Clayton's instance. It was the perfect cap for a perfect day. When everything was done and they were headed home he finally asked her what was wrong.

"Maybe it is nothing but this afternoon when I was coming to the patio alone there were too many eyes on me from the jungle and I was scared for the first time in a long time I don't think these were Balik's men."

"What you were worried about is coming true what do we do Sam?"

"I am going to send a message to Balik tonight and find out if something is going on I need to know about, until then I want some of your men around the hacienda and the children inside." He just nodded his head.

"I am tired but I enjoyed our dance." Then she fell asleep on his shoulder. Later that evening she walked out to the jungle but she didn't walk in this time she had the men come out to her to talk she then sent a message to Balik and came back to the house. Things went on as usual for a couple of weeks the new sawmill was doing well and Cory was hired as Sheriff and rented a small house in town. Gabriel and Camille were renting while they built a new house Russell and Pat were at their ranch and they didn't see much of them. Then word came from Balik, there was a war going on another chief was trying to take his place and had almost succeeded. Balik and his men had been successful and killed the other man but he had been watching her he thought if he had her he might have a bargaining chip. Instead it got him killed for even threatening her. Balik and his tribe were safe now as was Sam and Balik had a new Grandson.

"Tell Balik La Luna wishes him and his family the best and I wish could see his new grandson, wait." She went inside the house for a minute and then came back out with something in her hand and handed it to the man.

"Give it to Balik he will understand it is for his grandson from me." Clayton had watched from behind her and hadn't said a word until they left and then he asked her.

"What did you give him?"

"A little jaguar pendent made of jade wrapped in a piece of Fer-De- Lance skin it will be a good totem for the baby especially coming from me. Supper is ready." Clayton watched as the men left he wanted to make sure they were gone.

"Where did you get the little jade pendant?"

"People give me things all the time." The weeks passed and life went on sure enough Cory asked Natasha to marry him sooner than Sam had expected. The divorce wasn't quite finalized but it was almost done when the letter Sam had been expecting showed up from Antonio and he was in fine form.

NATASHA

I have been a fool and I want to come back to you and our children I hope you can forgive me and let me have another chance. I know I was a fool and I hurt you but it will never happen again.

ANTONIO

When Natasha showed it to her sister and Sam she was in tears she didn't know what to do but Gabriel showed up a short time later with a letter of his own and the true story came out and the tears stopped.

"This is from the man that bought half of my dance studio and I am getting the real story from him about what is going on in Rio. He says Antonio got back there and he expected everybody to wait on him and make a living for him. He didn't want to work that was somebody else's job. It was Natasha job before and now he wanted somebody else to do it, he managed to gamble most of the money I sent with him away on the trip down there. The woman he was going back to had found someone else and had already married and didn't want him anymore. The man that had bought half of my studio bought him out and he gambled away that money too so now he has nothing so he wants to come back here. I can't tell you what to do but you are a fool if you let my son back in your life you have a better man and a better father for your children in Cory let Antonio go." Natasha looked around the room and then looked at her children and nodded yes and said.

"NO MORE he stays away from me and my children I will post a letter in the morning he is on his own." Everyone smiled it was about time she had put up with enough it was time for her to go one with her life. The letter got to Rio but it seemed Antonio disappeared he had lost a lot of money and was drinking a lot and they couldn't find him to give him the letter when it arrived a few weeks later. Patricia looked at Sam and quietly asked her.

"Did you do something to him?"

"I didn't touch the man I said I would leave him alone unless he came back here I don't know what happened to him he seemed to make enough enemies of his own without my help." That was the last time they talked about him and he was never heard from again. Sam smiled though she would have loved to have staked him to a tree full of ants for a day or more.

Cory and Natasha were going to be married as soon as the divorce was finalized and now that Antonio couldn't be found it seemed that wasn't going to be a problem so they were planning for a month from now.

Things were going smoothly with her pregnancy and her sugar problem seemed to be under control everybody watched her and made sure she had sugar around. The only problem seemed to be a lot of extra people in the jungle lately they seemed to be awaiting the birth of her baby as well. Even the jaguars weren't very far she heard them every night lately. Tonight she just couldn't find a spot to get comfortable and she was on the balcony when she saw a purple orchid on the steps and she knew Balik was here. She looked for him but she couldn't see him so she went to get up and go to the rail when the first labor pains hit. She grabbed the rail and called for Clayton and he was there in a few seconds he was never far away.

"What is it honey?"

"I think it is time and we have company." and she pointed down at the orchid.

"Well you figured they would show up I just figured they would show up after the baby got here guess I was wrong. Let's get you inside." He called down to the men in the bunkhouse and told them to go get the Doctor and they were off. Clay got Sam in bed and they waited as Juanita and Lupe were helping her it looked like the baby was going to beat the doctor getting to the hacienda. It took a few hours but the baby arrived before the doctor did. When the doctor did show up there was a beautiful little girl just like Samantha said. Pale blond hair and blue eyes Samantha took her and then she told Clayton.

"You might as well take her out there and show them they are waiting to see her and they are not going away until they do."

"Are you sure that is what you want Sam you know what we talked about."

"If they don't see her they will think something is wrong with her or with me and they will panic and they will come in with or without your permission." He took the baby and wrapped her up and walked to the door and walked to the balcony and then down the stairs to the courtyard and there was Balik standing there waiting. Then out of the jungle came more men. Balik wouldn't let them to close he was the only one that got close and he just looked at the tiny girl and touched her hair and smiled. He asked about Sam and Clayton nodded.

"Your grandson well?" Balik lit up like any grandfather would and then he presented him with a small bundle and said it was for La Luna. He put it in Claytons hand and then he turned and he and the others were gone but before he left he looked up and Sam was at the balcony and she smiled at him and in the moonlight she was glowing again. Clayton just turned around and looked at his wife with his tiny daughter in his arms and listened to the jaguars scream. Steven and Melanee came to stand close beside her. Samantha had done what she had set out to do she made his family whole and complete finally.

www.ingramcontent.com/pod-product-compliance
Lightning Source LLC
Chambersburg PA
CBHW020055310726
48970CB00002B/332